C0053 93095

LAST
LULLABY

D1492877

ALSO BY CAROL WYER

LAST LULLABY

CAROL WYER

Bookouture

Published by Bookouture in 2018

An imprint of StoryFire Ltd.

Carmelite House
50 Victoria Embankment
London EC4Y 0DZ

www.bookouture.com

Copyright © Carol Wyer, 2018

Carol Wyer has asserted her right to be identified
as the author of this work.

All rights reserved. No part of this publication may be reproduced,
stored in any retrieval system, or transmitted, in any form or by
any means, electronic, mechanical, photocopying, recording or
otherwise, without the prior written permission of the publishers.

ISBN: 978-1-78681-697-9
eBook ISBN: 978-1-78681-696-2

This book is a work of fiction. Names, characters, businesses,
organizations, places and events other than those clearly in the
public domain, are either the product of the author's imagination
or are used fictitiously. Any resemblance to actual persons, living or
dead, events or locales is entirely coincidental.

CHAPTER ONE

FRIDAY, 2 MARCH – LATE EVENING

Adam Brannon looked like he was going to explode. He slapped the steering wheel with the palm of his hand and, taking his eyes off the road, stared at his wife in the passenger seat, arms folded tightly across her chest. 'Oh, for fuck's sake! Give it a rest, Charlotte.'

Charlotte's bottom lip, crimson from the Chanel lipstick she'd put on in the restaurant toilet, jutted out. 'Don't tell me to shut up. I'm not the one who behaved like a complete prick tonight.'

Adam's nostrils flared. 'If I were you, I'd shut it before you say anything else you might regret. You should have laid off that fucking red wine. It's gone to your head. You're coming out with all sorts of crap.'

Charlotte twisted her upper body towards him, the seat belt pulling tight against her ample chest, revealing milk-white flesh that spilled over the low neckline of her cashmere sweater. 'Pull over, you dick. I'll walk home!'

'You most certainly won't. You'll sit there and shut the fuck up.' His last words were hissed slowly, voice dripping with menace. A car drew up close behind the Bentley Bentayga, its headlights on full beam, dazzling him and making him squint. 'Twat!' he muttered as he dipped his mirror to lessen the glare.

'Who are you calling a twat?' She was off again. That was the trouble with Charlotte. She was a lightweight when it came to drinking, and her parents – who could politely be called sociable – were hardened to it. They'd all spent the last three hours at a pretentious restaurant, chosen by Kevin Hill, his father-in-law, supposedly celebrating her parents' thirtieth wedding anniversary. They'd started with champagne and swiftly moved on to a full-bodied Shiraz. Kevin favoured red wine, especially with the venison he and his wife had chosen as a main course. As designated driver for the night, Adam had stuck to water and Coca-Cola.

'I wasn't talking to you. There's some tosser right on our tail and he's blinding me with his headlights.'

A silence ensued, during which Adam glowered darkly into the rear-view mirror. The bloody car hadn't dropped back. If he'd been alone he'd have come to a screeching halt, forced the vehicle to pull over and then taken the driver to task, probably with the heavy spanner he kept in the side pocket in case of such incidents. Charlotte was staring at him, her eyes two narrowed slits. Between her and the numbskull behind him, he could hardly concentrate on his driving.

'Look, I know it didn't go well tonight…' he began.

She let out a snort and adopted the folded arms position again. 'You were in a huff from the off. It was their *wedding anniversary*, you know?'

'I know.'

'Then you should have made more effort.'

'For crying out loud, I did make an effort. Your mother kept freezing me out of the conversation. You know she doesn't like me.'

She threw back her head, chin high, and sighed dramatically. 'She does like you. You make it so difficult. Every time she asks you something, you behave like a sulky schoolboy who doesn't know the answer to a question.'

'That's ridiculous and you know it. You should try sticking up for me now and again. Your upbringing was worlds apart from mine, and I don't know the first thing about fucking point-to-point, or sodding golf, or which glass to drink port out of. You know that and so do your parents. They deliberately try to make me feel like an outsider. And tonight it was all, "What *was* the name of that delightful young man we bumped into at the casino in Monte Carlo, Charlotte? The one who invited us for cocktails on his yacht," and, "Shares in Tarquin Dunn-Hamilton's company soared on the stock market last week, darling."' He adopted the same plummy voice his mother-in-law, Sheila, had used to drive home his argument.

Charlotte stared ahead into the darkness.

'Like I give a shit about people I've never heard of. Your folks were bang out of order. They deliberately excluded me and you encouraged them. You didn't once change the subject to something that included me. Know how that makes me feel?'

'You're being ridiculous.'

'Am I? I'm not the one picking this fight. You are. Look at you sitting there all hostile, arms crossed and a fucking great sneer on your mouth. There was a time when you'd have supported me, not given up and let them walk all over me.'

She released a humourless laugh. 'Yeah, cos loads of people walk over you, big man, don't they?'

The car behind them had edged closer still. Adam cricked his thick neck left and right. It emitted a loud crack.

'Do you have to do that?'

'The jerk behind me is getting on my nerves.'

'Pull over and let him overtake, then.'

'Hell, no. He's in the wrong. He should drop back.'

'Adam. Pull over.' Her eyes flashed.

'Whatever,' he said, and, slowing the car, he manoeuvred closer to the roadside to allow the guy behind to pass. The car pulled out and accelerated away at speed, exhaust popping. Adam stuck up his middle finger as it overtook but didn't glance at the driver or the vehicle, his attention on Charlotte, who was giving him the evil eye again.

'Feel better now? You're pathetic sometimes,' she said.

Adam lapsed into silence. Charlotte reclined her seat. The alcohol was having an effect on her. Her father always made sure her glass was topped up, and tonight, thanks to Adam, she'd kept knocking it back. All she knew was she was really, really pissed off with Adam. He'd been so rude to her folks on their anniversary. It was always awkward when they all got together but tonight had been harder than all the other times put together because, for once, Charlotte hadn't stood up for her man. She'd let him flounder. He'd deserved to. She was sick of his swaggering macho performances. She was tired of the chip that was permanently on his shoulder and the arguments they had day after day. It didn't matter that he didn't earn a fortune. She'd never cared about the money. She had stacks of bloody money in her trust fund. Adam was a hypocrite. He moaned about her folks being wealthy and making him feel undervalued, and yet he lived in a house her parents had financed, and he loved driving *her* Bentley that *her* father had bought, so what was his problem? The answer was he was jealous of his wife's financial independence, and the support she got from her family.

They pulled onto the driveway of their home, built in the style of a modern log cabin but with two enormous downstairs windows, both the size of garage double doors. Adam looked at her, eyebrows high on his forehead, dark eyes fringed with lengthy eyelashes, full of remorse, and let out a sigh. 'I'm sorry, babe,' he said.

'Fuck you,' came the reply. 'I'm going to bed. You'd better run Inge home. I'll send her out.'

She fumbled for the seat belt but couldn't release it. He leant across and unclipped it for her. Without a word of thanks, Charlotte threw open the car door and clattered out, skyscraper heels kicking the scuff plate. She weaved towards the house. Adam remained in the car.

'Inge,' Charlotte called, kicking off her shoes in the entrance and lurching towards the sitting room. The television was on low volume. On the screen, several well-wrapped-up figures in coats and hats were huddled beside an open lake. Judging by the subtitles that flashed up on the bottom half of the set, Inge was watching some foreign drama. The flat-screen set was one of the largest available and had been bought for Adam so he could watch sport in high definition on a wide screen. Charlotte didn't care for many of the programmes on television unless it was reality TV. She'd rather check her social media any day, or her blog.

Inge, in jeans and a baggy sweater, looked up and smiled. The girl was quite plain but had a wide, sweet smile. 'Did you have a good time?' she asked, picking up the remote and flicking the off button.

'It was fine, thanks. How was Alfie?'

'No trouble. He slept the whole time you were out. I thought he was going to wake up earlier. There were a few mumbles and I checked on him but he was fast asleep on his back. I left Ewan the Dream Sheep turned on.'

The sheep was six-month-old Alfie's favourite toy. He couldn't sleep without it and preferred the heartbeat out of all the sound options that could be set. Charlotte had tried putting Alfie down without it but he wouldn't settle. In the end, she'd decided to let him have his way. He'd grow out of it one day. The baby monitor crackled slightly. The noise of a steady heartbeat from Ewan, replicating what Alfie would have heard when he was growing inside Charlotte, was audible.

Inge picked up a notebook and biology book lying open on the wide, coffee-coloured leather settee.

'You get much studying done?' Charlotte tried to appear normal although the room was now beginning to sway slightly.

A nod was the response. Inge was very studious: she wanted to be a midwife or maybe even a doctor like her mother, Sabine, who was one of Charlotte's friends. She may have only been seventeen but she acted far more like an adult than many girls her age, and Charlotte had been glad to have her watch over Alfie on the occasional nights she and Adam went out. Inge only lived a couple of miles away in the village of Brompton and was, thanks to her bookish nature, nearly always available at a moment's notice.

'Adam's outside. He'll run you home as usual. Thanks again.' Charlotte slurred the last words and held onto the door frame for support. She needed to get to bed.

Inge eased out of the door, books in hand, and disappeared from view.

Charlotte headed straight to the kitchen end of the open-plan lounge – contemporary and sleek in white – with an unusual, curved worktop under which sat white stools, designed and built by a top firm in London. The silver range cooker had been her idea, but given she wasn't much of a cook, it was more to create an impression than for preparing meals. She opened the steel-grey American fridge-freezer, inset into the units, and pulled out a water filter jug, then zigzagged towards the cupboards opposite to fetch a glass. She chugged cold water that barely touched the sides of her throat then poured another to take upstairs with her. That was the solution to a hangover – drink as much water as possible before going to sleep.

She collected the baby monitor and with a glass in hand, bounced off the walls and somehow managed to propel herself up the wooden staircase to the bedroom. She set the monitor down beside the bed, alongside the glass, and tiptoed into the adjacent room.

Bo-boom, bo-boom, bo-boom. The noise was calming and the purple glow from the sheep instantly relaxing, like the sounds and dim lighting used in spas. She wondered if her own heart had beat that quickly and if Alfie really believed he was still cocooned inside his mother. She bent over the cot and took in the little figure, flat on his back, arms wide open, his face the picture of perfection with pale downy hair sticking up, a slightly upturned nose and chubby cheeks. His fists were tightly clenched. Charlotte wanted to uncurl them and hold them in her own hands but she knew she was too drunk. Sense had finally kicked in.

'Night, my handsome little prince,' she whispered and tiptoed out of the nursery she had so carefully prepared for the birth of her baby, with soft toys all lined up at the head of the cot and a large white toy box in the corner, Alfie's name spelt out in large letters on it. The heartbeat continued, strong and comforting – a protective force like a mother's love.

On the landing, her stomach lurched. The wine soured in her throat and she hastened to the bathroom. She'd drunk way more than she ought to have. *You know why.* She hadn't been celebrating her parents' wedding anniversary at all. She'd been building up courage. *Too much wine.* She turned on the shower, and while the water ran warm, she peeled off her clothes, leaving them in an untidy heap on top of the laundry basket. She rested her head against the cool tiles for a moment before stepping into the wide cubicle and allowing the hot spray to sprinkle onto her back and head. She soaped her hands with the gift her mother had given her for Christmas, an opulent oil that ran smoothly over her flat stomach and thighs as she tried to rub herself sober, further massaging the oil into her shoulders and arms and over her chest as the water cascaded onto her, cleansing her.

She twisted the perfectly shined chrome tap to the off position and, allowing the fat drips to tumble from her body into the shower tray, rested her open palms against the screen. She stared out at the double his and hers oyster-shaped sinks with their waterfall taps: neat rows of perfume bottles above hers and aftershaves over Adam's. *The perfect couple.* She grimaced at the irony of this. She clambered out onto the bath mat to dry herself off with one of the towels and then, naked, moved into the bedroom where she threw back the heavy duvet and slid under it. She sank into the fluffy, white pillow and began to drift effortlessly away from reality – far away from Adam.

Charlotte couldn't work out what had woken her. Was it Adam shifting about in bed or had Alfie come to? All she knew was her tongue had glued itself to the roof of her mouth and she had the mother of all headaches. Reaching her hand out tentatively to the left, she established the sheet was cool. Adam had not yet come to bed. She opened an eye, her lids heavy with sleep, and rolled onto her side. The digital display on the bedside clock read 23.03. She blinked hard.

A crackling from the baby monitor caused her senses to kick in. Alfie was awake. That must have been what had disturbed her. Even in the deepest slumber, one cry from her baby would rouse her in an instant. She listened hard but there was nothing. Alfie wasn't grumbling or crying. *Where's Adam?* She recalled the row they'd had in the car. That wouldn't have been enough to cause him to spend the night away. That wasn't how he played it. He was bullish and argumentative. He wouldn't back off or disappear with his tail between his legs because Charlotte had suddenly verbally attacked him. *So where is he? Is he in Alfie's room?* The monitor crackled again, making her jump. She strained her ears and held her breath. Then it hit her. The toy sheep's regular heartbeat had ceased.

She pushed herself up onto her elbows and pressed her ear closer the monitor, listening for Adam's voice. Alfie stirred and gurgled. The sound lifted her spirits momentarily. Her baby was a smiler. He never woke up in a bad mood.

A cough. And not Adam's.

Hairs rose the length of her bare arms. Somebody, who was not Adam, was in her baby's room.

The urge to scream was great. She fought it back. Thoughts bounced and collided and veered in all directions like beads falling from a broken necklace onto a tiled floor.

She had to get help. She had to save her baby. With the flat of her hand she searched for her mobile in vain, patting the bedside table in desperation, before the horrific recollection that her phone was downstairs in her handbag.

A gentle whimper came from the monitor: a helpless cry that froze her blood, and paralysed with fear, her mind whirred. There was somebody in the house and her baby was in danger.

A new thought spurred her into action. Adam kept a baseball bat under his side of the bed in case of intruders. She'd grab it, rescue Alfie then run like crazy and scream and yell outside until she'd woken all the neighbours in the street.

Every cell of her body vibrated with fear but she placed her bare feet onto the carpet and shuffled around the bed in the darkness, spurred on by the knowledge someone wished her child harm. One step. *I'm coming, Alfie.* Two steps. *Mummy's coming, baby.* Three steps. She dropped down on all fours, knees grazing the carpet, and fumbled for the bat, fingers fully outstretched, locating nothing. It wasn't there. She patted the area. It had to be there. Adam was paranoid about somebody breaking in or trying to steal one of the cars from the drive. It was what he called his insurance. He wouldn't have removed it. Finally, her fingers alighted on the object, and as she withdrew it a sound halted her – a click. She lifted her head. The bedroom door was opening inch by inch. A scream stuck in her throat. Rooted to the spot, she stared with ever-widening eyes as the door flew wide open and a figure burst into the room.

CHAPTER TWO

SATURDAY, 3 MARCH – EARLY MORNING

Natalie Ward shifted onto her side, flicked on her mobile and let out a soft groan. It was just after 1 a.m. She let out a heavy sigh that didn't disturb her husband, David, who was fast asleep on his back, loud snores filling the room. She gave him a shove for the third time and was relieved when he finally shifted onto his side and the noise desisted.

The alcohol was to blame. Every time he had too much to drink, she had to go through this same process. With him now quiet, she relaxed her shoulders and reflected on the evening. It had passed off much better than she'd expected. She wasn't the greatest dinner party hostess and certainly wouldn't win any awards for her culinary skills, but the meal had been passable and David's father, Eric, and his new girlfriend, Pam, had both been good company. The children had been on form too, and sixteen-year-old Josh had managed to smile politely at Eric's terrible jokes, while fourteen-year-old Leigh hadn't grumbled once about the slightly overcooked macaroni cheese her mother had offered her as an alternative to the roast lamb and salsa verde.

She stared up at the ceiling and attempted to still her thoughts that rose like champagne bubbles and fizzed and popped in her mind. She wasn't like David, who usually crashed out as soon as his head hit the pillow. She'd suffered from insomnia for many years and learnt that when her mind was unwilling to allow her to sleep, she had to let it play out its thoughts. She couldn't even blame the alcohol. Last night she'd only drunk soft drinks. It wasn't that she hadn't wanted to join in with the others and get merry – she certainly had – but she hadn't wanted to ruin the meal. It was the first time Pam had been invited to their house, and Natalie had wanted it to be successful for Eric's sake. He'd been nervous about introducing his new girlfriend to his family, especially to David, who in spite of his smiles had found it difficult to see his father with somebody other than his mother.

Eric had been a widower for ten years. It was long enough in her book. She was pleased he'd found somebody else to share his life with. It was a pity David didn't feel quite the same way about it…

'You don't get it, do you?' David pulls at his right sock as he speaks. 'It's not your father.'

Natalie bites her tongue even though she wants to tell David to stop behaving like a petulant child. His mother has been dead for ten years. If either of her own parents had survived the other, she'd have wanted them to have found happiness again. David seems to have forgotten she's lost both her mother and father and is rambling.

'She's way too young for him. She's only fifty-six. He's almost seventy. What does he think he's trying to prove?'

'That he's alive,' she says, carefully. 'He's a youthful seventy-year-old. He wants to enjoy himself while he still can.'

David emits a noise like a flat raspberry but doesn't pursue the conversation. He tugs at the other sock and throws it onto the floor beside the bed, on top of his other clothes. 'I've had too much to drink,' he declares as he draws back the cover and gets into bed.

'I know. Get some sleep.'

'Sorry.'

'It's okay.'

She picks up his clothes and drops them onto the chair in the corner of the room in case he gets up in the night and falls over them, then gets ready for bed. By the time she's cleaned her teeth, David is asleep.

Natalie understood his concerns. His father was a constant in their lives. Eric was the person they rang if they needed anything fixing in the house – he was a dab hand at DIY – and he popped around most weeks to help out in the garden, or just for a pot of tea and a chat, and he'd been their go-to babysitter for many years before the children were old enough to be left alone. David was frightened of him drifting out of their lives. Natalie didn't see it the same way. Eric needed to live out what time he had left, doing what he wanted to do, not to be at their beck and call. Besides, people often grew apart. It happened all the time. Look at her and Frances. She'd had no contact with her estranged sister for several years and she didn't miss her. *Really? Not a little?* She ignored the small voice in her head that had piped up. Instead of getting sleepy, she was becoming more agitated, as was often the case once she started thinking about Frances.

They'd decided to take the kids into Manchester for a shopping trip today. If she didn't get some sleep soon, she'd find the hour-and-a-half journey to town and subsequent drag about the shops too gruelling. She tried the relaxation techniques she'd been taught by a psychiatrist. She scrunched her toes and released them, then moved onto her calf muscles, which she tensed then released. Little by little she tightened and released the muscles in her thighs, her stomach, her diaphragm, her chest, her shoulders, arms, hands and fingers until every ounce of tension evaporated. Her breathing slowed and she began to spiral down a long, dark passageway into oblivion.

She didn't sink into sleep. The soft burr coming from her mobile dragged her back to the here and now, hauling her inch by inch from the warm pit where she'd finally found comfort and peace to reality. It was work. She lifted the phone to her ear. Superintendent Aileen Melody sounded alert and anxious.

'Natalie, there's been a murder.'

Natalie snapped to in an instant and, throwing back the covers, swung her legs out of bed and drew up into a seated position. 'Where?'

'Eastborough. I'll text you the address. It's a young woman by the name of Charlotte Brannon. Her husband found her dead in their bedroom. I know you're on leave but I want you to head the investigation. You okay with that?'

Natalie stood up. 'On my way.'

There was a short pause. 'Thank you. And Natalie, I ought to warn you… there's a baby too.'

Natalie stopped mid-track. 'A baby?'

'Their son. He's unharmed but he was at home during the attack on his mother. I've sent Mike across.'

Mike Sullivan, who was in charge of Forensics, also happened to be David's best friend. 'Okay. I'll be there in fifteen minutes tops.'

David stirred. His voice was thick with sleep. 'You okay?'

'Yeah. Go back to sleep.'

'What's happening?'

'Work.'

He mumbled a response and pulled the duvet high around his neck. Before she'd finished dressing, he'd dozed off again. He was familiar with the routine. She slipped out of the bedroom and downstairs into the kitchen still harbouring the warm aroma of cooked spices and wine and a hint of conviviality. She searched for her car keys in the dish by the kettle and, grabbing a coat from the hook by the back door, went out into the cool morning.

Maddison Court in Eastborough, a smart suburb of Samford, was a prestigious estate of thirty architect-designed houses. Each property boasted a sweeping driveway and about half an acre of garden, and was worth upwards of three quarters of a million pounds.

The blue flashing lights from the emergency vehicles already present – an ambulance and three police cars – strobed across the dark sky. As Natalie donned the protective clothing she kept in her car, she glanced around and spotted a plump woman with bright-red hair squatting beside the open passenger door of a squad car and talking to an individual sitting inside, head in hands. It was Tanya Granger, the family liaison officer. Natalie took a moment and allowed her gaze to run up and down the road. The neighbouring houses were lit up, with most of the residents either peering out of their windows or standing by the open front doors, with dazed looks of total disbelief on their faces, observing her as she suited up. The estate was alive even though it was 2 a.m., and as she strode purposefully up the sloped driveway, past the new Bentley 4x4 parked next to a black BMW Coupé, she was mindful of the neighbours gathered in small groups, mobiles in hands to snap photographs or film the comings and goings outside the Brannons' home. No doubt they'd be uploading them to social media with shocked comments and speculations about what had happened.

She showed her ID to the policeman on the door, who added her name to the crime scene log. She caught sight of Murray Anderson, one of her sergeants, and PC Ian Jarvis as they pulled up behind her car. She signalled to them to join her.

'Canvass the area, would you? And make sure everyone goes back inside. They're not helping by filming events. Politely suggest they desist and find out if anyone saw anything suspicious.'

She didn't wait to ensure they'd followed orders. She knew they would and that the streets would be clear of voyeurs when she next came out. She crossed the threshold into a large entrance with grey slate tiles and found herself looking into a downstairs cloakroom with toilet and scalloped sink.

She moved through the door on the left and took in the enormous room with floor-to-ceiling windows to one side and gossamer-thin curtains draped artistically beside each, but not pulled to. Natalie found the place charmless – little more than a sparkling show home, or dressed for a *Homes & Gardens* magazine feature, and lacking in any homely touches. Tall white lamps with pleated white shades stood on the floor adjacent to a grey seven-seater settee. Sculptures of cartoon-like birds filled up spaces on grey shelves above a fake inset fireplace, while others of angel-like figures were dotted about the room on grey modern tables. Black-and-white paintings by the same artist were grouped on white walls: one of people clutching umbrellas against the wind, another of a man and boy on a tree branch, both holding fishing rods, and a third of a child riding a bicycle and towing a barrow of red hearts.

It was stylish, but Natalie couldn't get a feel for the couple who lived here. There were no normal indicators of family life other than the very large flat-screen television on the sitting-room wall. A staircase broke the open-plan room into two, the far end opening up into the kitchen, equally trendy and lacking in the sort of chaos and clutter she linked to family life. There was no evidence of a baby in this house: no highchair or toys, no paraphernalia she would ordinarily associate with a baby, and no photographs. *Who doesn't proudly display photographs of their children?* she thought to herself. Her own house was filled with memories of her children: framed pictures of Josh and Leigh as babies, as toddlers, and more recently as teenagers on most of the downstairs walls and even stuck to the side of her fridge.

The room was palatial. Even with several officers scattered throughout, there was space for many more. *A party house.* Ordinarily, crime scenes appeared cramped with forensic units and police rammed into the same area, but not in this house. Natalie didn't have to squeeze past anyone to look for Mike. He was standing in front of a steel-grey American fridge-freezer the size of her pine kitchen dresser, his head bowed as if in thought. She crossed the length of the room, passing a sweeping staircase, and joined him.

'Hey.'

'Hi,' he replied. 'I always fancied a fridge this size. I could fit in stacks of beer. Look: you can make ice cubes too.' He pointed at the dispenser. The smile didn't reach his bloodshot eyes.

Natalie understood he was trying to make a difficult situation easier. She'd been with him in similar circumstances and knew how he worked. Judging by his ashen pallor, he'd already been upstairs and seen the victim. His words confirmed it. 'It's the worst I've ever seen. I needed a moment.'

She gave him a brief smile. 'I'm about to go up.'

'Want me to come with you? It's really bad.'

'I'll be okay. You stay here for a while.'

He glanced about at his team hard at work, heads down, and nodded. 'Adam Brannon, the husband, is outside with Tanya. The baby's been checked over by the paramedics and seems fine. He's with a social worker at the moment. As far as we can tell, there's no obvious sign of a break-in. They might have managed to pick the lock but that would take skill and the right sort of equipment. There are no surveillance cameras fitted, inside or out, so nothing there to help us. There *is* a sophisticated burglar alarm, but it doesn't seem to have been set.'

Natalie considered his words. 'Charlotte might have let her attacker in?'

'Or they had a key.' He let his words hang. She thought briefly of the man outside in the squad car.

'What's through there?' She indicated the door at the back of the room.

'Games room. Got a full-sized pool table in there and a desk. No evidence of any unusual activity but we'll go through it.' He paused momentarily, his wide shoulders dropping slightly, before speaking again. 'Pinkney's on his way.'

'Good.' Natalie liked the pathologist whose no-nonsense approach would be welcome. He managed to balance empathy and practicality perfectly and would keep her mind off the horror of the situation through facts and information, which he'd readily divulge. Sometimes, it was best to bury yourself in the facts.

She couldn't put it off any longer. She retraced her steps and climbed the staircase that rose and then twisted gently to the right to a cream-carpeted landing, where she halted. The smell of death was strongest here. Sickly sweet, it would coat the back of her mouth and fill her nostrils with its cloying aroma. Some officers used menthol vapour rub under their noses to hide the smell, or chewed gum, but she'd come to realise it didn't matter what she used to disguise it, it always permeated her skin and entered her airways regardless. It was best to deal with it full on.

Several rooms ran the length of the landing. Doors to all were open and soft murmurings indicated the presence of officers inside. She mused on how strange it was that in these situations everyone whispered or spoke softly as if the dead could hear them commenting as they rummaged through personal effects. She inhaled deeply, regulating her breathing as best she could. *In. Out. In.* A soft rustling behind her caused her to turn her head, and she smiled slightly at the sight: Detective Sergeant Lucy Carmichael.

'This is pretty sick shit,' Lucy said. 'You seen her yet?' As she cocked her head, the ceiling lights illuminated her heavy blue-black fringe, making it glisten like crow feathers.

'Just about to.' Natalie didn't need to say any more. A glimpse of a white protective suit and a flash of a camera bulb signposted where they needed to head. The official photographer was working in the first bedroom.

'DI Ward and DS Carmichael,' called Natalie as she approached. 'We're coming in.'

The photographer moved to one side. Natalie stepped through the doorway and took in the sight in front of her: grey wallpaper with a silver thread running through it; a Georgian, white-painted, king-sized bed, bearing a crisp white duvet and a yellow patterned throw that had tumbled partly onto the floor; four yoke-yellow and four dove-grey cushions, tossed in the corner of the room; bedside tables in white and an open door leading to a dressing area; sketches of stag's heads in matching yellow above the bed next to yellow shelves, large enough for only a white pillar candle each. Between the pictures was one word: '*why?*'

Natalie studied it for a few moments. The letters were about eight inches high, written in lowercase and slightly sloped.

'Is that what I think it is?' she asked.

The photographer spoke quietly. 'Yes. It's been written in blood.'

She tore her eyes away from the wall and over the bed. A pair of silver embroidered slippers at one side of the bed, and at the other, the battered body of Charlotte Brannon, naked in a pool of blood.

Natalie swallowed and kept her cool. It was important to look at the whole scene, not just the body, and get a feel for what had happened. Her eyes flitted across an oval-shaped digital clock, now showing 2.15 a.m., and an empty glass, resting upon a baby monitor at an odd angle, as if it had been knocked accidentally. She moved towards it. The flashing light indicated it was function-ing. Cocking an ear to it, she picked up muffled commands from forensic officers in the nursery. A pillow bearing an indentation was half-on, half-off the bed. Charlotte must have dragged it with her as she tried to look at the clock or pick up the monitor. The silver slippers had been kicked away and one lay upside down. Charlotte had not put them on. She'd walked to the opposite side of the bed – the side she didn't use. The pillow there had not been slept on. It was fluffed up in readiness. There was nothing on that nightstand other than some loose change.

Natalie forced her eyes to Charlotte's pale body. She was on her back, chestnut hair sticky with blood, nose crushed and flattened, chin and cheeks a crimson mess. One brown eye stared at the ceiling; the other was swollen and closed with crusted blood. One arm was thrown out above her head, a slim hand the only part of her body unharmed. The other arm was bent back at the elbow at an unnatural angle. Her knees were together and her entire lower body twisted to the right. Natalie's eyes lit upon the tattoo of three butterflies on Charlotte's left shoulder, then travelled the length of her shattered body to the carefully painted crimson toenails as red as the blood that she lay in. Charlotte resembled little more than a broken doll.

'Make sure you photograph that,' she said, indicating the bedside table that contained the baby monitor. The photographer lifted his camera and began clicking once more.

'We think we've found the weapon,' said Mike from behind her, making her jump. She quickly regained her composure and, following his outstretched arm, spotted the handle of a wooden baseball bat in the large, plastic evidence bag. She stepped closer and identified brownish-red stains that could only be blood. 'It was hidden in the bin outside, under some rubbish. It's a thirty-four-inch, wooden, heavy-duty baseball bat.'

'The bin isn't the greatest hiding place,' said Natalie. 'The killer was either in a rush to get away and dumped it without much thought, or they weren't too worried if it was found.'

'Or they simply might not be very bright,' said Mike.

Next to her, Lucy spoke, her wide eyes seeming even larger. 'The fucker smashed her to death with that bat?'

'Looks that way. There's significant blood pooled around the body along with impact spatter on the bedlinen that side of the bed. Luminol will reveal if there's any other bloodstain spatter or microscopic droplets, but I reckon it was a frenzied attack, confined to that area of the bedroom.'

Natalie tried to envisage the scene: an angry attacker with a baseball bat, a defenceless woman. Had Charlotte been trying to escape her assailant by hiding under the bed? Could this possibly have been a burglary that went wrong or a domestic dispute that got out of hand? Charlotte was still wearing her wedding and engagement rings. Natalie crossed to the dressing table and hunted through it for valuables. The top drawer contained a large Ted Baker make-up bag and pouches of colourful beaded necklaces and jewellery, none of which looked to be very expensive. The other drawers held silk and lace lingerie, most of which had been purchased from Agent Provocateur, La Perla and Eres. They'd been neatly folded and appeared to be untouched. To Natalie's trained eye, there was nothing obvious missing.

'We need to know if she owned any expensive jewellery and if it – or anything else – was stolen. Maybe there's a safe. Her husband's outside. He'll be able to confirm if there is.'

Lucy answered her. 'Yes. He gave a statement earlier. You want to talk to him?'

'In a minute. I want to see the nursery first.' Natalie retreated from the room back onto the landing, where she steeled herself before going through the second door. The room shocked her into a heavy silence. There may not have been any evidence of a child downstairs but this room bore every trace of one and was filled with love. The theme was once again white and grey, but this time the room held a warm charm: light grey wallpaper covered in white clouds; a white-framed picture of a group of friendly blue rabbits; a grey-blue toy rabbit propped against a star-shaped white cushion on a large white chair; a blue beanbag in soft leather sat on a fluffy white rug; a blue wooden train on the floor next to two more toy rabbits, larger than Alfie; more toys and children's books on shelves alongside photographs of mother and child; a white toy box with the name Alfie spelt out in blue lettering in one corner of the room, and in the other, the most beautiful white cot Natalie had ever seen. Charlotte would never again hold her baby in her arms in this gorgeous room and comfort him or love him. Natalie felt something constrict inside her chest like a tourniquet and she struggled for breath. She discovered Lucy by her side, clearly experiencing similar emotions.

'At least he's alive,' was all she said, then blinking heavily, marched out of the room. Natalie followed her and was relieved to see the pathologist, Pinkney Watson, approaching. He and Lucy got on extremely well and usually enjoyed lengthy verbal sparring matches, but today he said nothing and, halting her on the staircase, rested a hand on her arm.

'You okay?' he asked.

She sniffed a response and shook her head.

'Go outside and get some air,' he said, kindly.

She gave a brief nod and hastened downstairs.

Catching Natalie's eye, he spoke again. 'I assume it's not easy for her, not with Bethany expecting.'

Bethany Green was Lucy's partner, a serious-faced accountant who was eleven years older than Lucy. They'd pooled all their savings for fertility treatment and, using sperm donation, Bethany had fallen pregnant immediately. While it was no secret the couple had wanted some biological connection to their child, it was not common knowledge that Lucy's best friend, Sergeant Murray Anderson, had donated the sperm.

'She'll be fine,' Pinkney continued. 'She's a tough cookie, that one.'

His warm smile reached his intensely blue eyes, deepening the wrinkles around them. Pinkney wasn't a handsome man, his nose a fraction too long for his face and his eyes set slightly too far apart, but he was, even at fifty-five, as enthusiastic and energetic as a toddler and, in Natalie's opinion, one of the best pathologists in his profession. His dedication to his job was one of the reasons he'd remained unmarried and lived in a Victorian three-storey house in Samford with two Aegean cats. Although his name suggested eccentricity, his only foible was a bright-green 1960s VW campervan called Mabel that he drove to the ends of the UK at every opportunity. Given he spent so much of his time staring death in the face, Natalie reasoned he was right to head off to remote locations in Scotland or Cornwall, where he'd go walking and 'remind himself of the greatness of nature'.

'I'll be outside if you want me,' said Natalie. 'I'm going to talk to Mr Brannon.'

'Sure. I think I can cover it all here. If you wish to remain outside, I'll come and talk to you once I've checked the victim over.'

'Thanks, Pinkney.'

She descended the stairs, mind on what could have possibly happened to Charlotte. Mike caught her up at the foot of the stairs. 'Bastard.' Anger cracked his voice. 'How could someone do that to her?'

Natalie had no answers. At this stage, all she knew was some deranged individual had murdered a young woman, and a child had lost his mother.

'Natalie, whatever you need, you just say.' A deep furrow had appeared between his eyebrows, dragging them together. 'Whatever.'

She acknowledged his words and moved towards the door. There'd been no sign of a break-in. The killer had gained access either through an unlocked door, by invitation, or had a key. One such person was waiting outside to be interviewed by her. It was time to talk to Adam Brannon. She spoke to Tanya Granger who was close to the house.

'How is he?'

'I had a long chat to him before you got here. He seemed remarkably composed for a man who'd witnessed the results of a brutal attack on his wife. I assume it's shock. He acted oddly when we talked about the baby. He kept repeating it would be better if Charlotte's parents looked after Alfie for the moment.'

Natalie nodded. 'You don't think he might suddenly blow and go storming off on some vigilante exercise?'

'I didn't get that vibe. If anything, he seemed to want to retreat. Kept asking if he could get away from the house. It was freaking him out being here.'

Natalie nodded. 'Can we have another quick word after I've spoken to him?'

'Sure. I'll be here.'

Natalie moved towards the police car and the figure inside. Was it shock that was making Adam nervous about staying around, or guilt?

CHAPTER THREE

Adam stepped out of the police car, his six-foot frame towering high over the Jaguar F-Pace. He rested both hands on the roof of the car and looked at his splayed fingers, focusing on the wedding band on his left hand. His dark eyes were filled with a sadness that Natalie had seen on many faces in her career. She extended her condolences and waited for the man to be able to tell her what had happened. He refused her offer to talk inside her car or head to the station.

'Have you anyone you can stay with tonight – a friend or relative?'

'No. I'll sleep at my boxing club. There's a sofa bed in the back office and a changing area with showers and toilets. I can stay there for now. I can't… go back inside. I'm not sure I'll ever be able to,' he said. 'Where's Alfie?'

'He's with social services for now.'

He nodded. 'That's probably for the best. I can't deal with all of this at the moment. I can't even think straight let alone look after him. Maybe he could go to Charlotte's parents for a day or two until I get my head sorted.'

His reaction puzzled her. Why wouldn't he want to be with his boy? He hadn't even kicked up a fuss about Alfie being taken away from him. It was odd, to say the least.

'We'll have to let social services handle that side of things. My job is to find out who did this to your wife. Tell me what happened this evening.'

He spun lightly on his feet to face her, forcing her to tilt her head upwards, and she was struck by the power he exuded. It was no surprise to have learnt he was a semi-pro boxer. Apart from his eyes, his face showed little emotion: his eyebrows were neatly groomed and rested on a wide, unblemished forehead, and his chin and cheeks, covered in dark stubble, still revealed strong bone structure. When he spoke his voice was deep and low.

'We'd been out and returned at about ten. Charlotte went straight inside to go to bed. She said she was tired. I drove the babysitter, Inge, back to her place before heading to the White Horse in Samford for a drink. I met up with an old mate, Lee Webster. We had one there and then went back to his place for a couple more. In case you're wondering, I only drank orange juice at his house. I got home at about twelve. I didn't go upstairs at first. I watched *GLOW* on Netflix. At some point Alfie started crying. I figured she'd deal with him, feed him, change him or whatever, like he normally does, but she didn't. She always goes to him, almost as soon as he wakes up. I stayed where I was but he got louder and louder. I don't know what I thought: she'd crashed out because of the booze she'd drunk at the restaurant and hadn't heard him, or was waiting for me to take a turn – I really can't say, but I went straight to the nursery, where he was bawling his eyes out, his face all red, waiting for his mum to come. I picked him up, tried to calm him down, walked about making the right noises but he kept crying and wouldn't be comforted, so I carried him to the bedroom to ask her to try and quieten him while I got his feed… and she was on the floor. I didn't need to check her. It was obvious she was dead. I took Alfie back to the nursery, put him back in his cot and rang the police immediately. He kept crying, waiting for his mum to come and pick him up…' He swallowed hard but couldn't continue.

'He's okay. He's safe.'

He calmed again and nodded.

'Was the bedroom door shut?'

'Yes.'

'You didn't spot anything odd before you went upstairs? Nothing out of place? Front door unlocked?'

'Nothing. You think I'd have sat downstairs watching telly if I'd thought something had happened to either of them?'

'I'm not suggesting that, sir. It's important I establish all the facts before I begin the investigation. Something might come to mind; something you didn't think important at the time but is relevant now.'

His nostrils flared momentarily. 'Yeah. I guess so.'

'The burglar alarm wasn't activated.'

'No. She must have decided to leave it off until I got back. We usually set it when we go to bed.'

'Do you keep any valuables in the house, maybe hidden in a safe?'

He snorted. 'Just cos we live in a big house doesn't mean we're rich. The cars – they're the most valuable things we own. There are some paintings and sculptures that cost a bit but probably aren't worth what we paid for them, and there's Charlotte's jewellery – especially her engagement and wedding rings – but she was wearing those when I… I've got some boxing memorabilia – gloves from fights, posters, that sort of stuff – and a couple of watches. One of them's worth a couple of grand.'

'Which room are they in?'

'My den. It's behind the kitchen. They're in the bottom drawer of my desk. There are a couple of necklaces belonging to Charlotte there too, and a diamond ring. She didn't like wearing expensive jewellery. Was always scared she'd lose it so stuck to cheap stuff – lookalike gear. It's locked. Key's taped under the top drawer.'

Natalie recalled Mike mentioning the games room. He must have meant that.

'The room with the pool table?'

'Yeah.'

She made a mental note to tell Mike and check the drawer. 'Has anyone, other than you and Charlotte, got a key to the house?'

'Only Charlotte's parents.'

'You're certain the door was locked when you got in?'

'Yes. It locks automatically when you push it to. I used my key to open it.'

'Could your wife have left it open when she went in?'

'Maybe she did but Inge came out soon afterwards and I'm fairly certain she shut the door behind her.'

That narrowed it down to three remaining possible scenarios: the killer was able to pick locks, they had a key or Charlotte had let them in. Natalie continued.

'You took Inge home and then went to the White Horse to meet up with Lee?'

'That's right.'

'Was there any particular reason you went off to the pub straight after a night out with your wife?'

'I didn't have a "night out" with my wife, as you put it. I went to dinner with my in-laws and I needed a stiff drink after that. I told Charlotte I was going out for a while afterwards. She was fine about it. She knew I didn't especially enjoy socialising with her folks.'

'You don't see eye to eye with them?'

'They're not the easiest to get on with. I feel really bad, you know? I have literally no idea what to say to them or what to do next.'

'You've already spoken to PC Granger. She'll help you through this. You could do with some support from family too.'

'There was only Charlotte. And Alfie. There's no one else. Her parents aren't my biggest fans. They'll blame me for this. I know they will.'

His eyes clouded again as fresh pain reached him. Natalie was at a loss as to how to console him.

'Is there anybody you could stay with, friends maybe? You shouldn't be alone.'

His words were deflated. 'Yeah, right. You don't exactly make lots of friends in my profession; more the opposite, in fact. You don't tend to make friends on the boxing circuit or running a boxing club for youngsters from run-down housing estates.'

'What about Mr Webster, the man you went to meet at the pub?'

He shook his head.

'You say you have no friends and, in your words, "more the opposite". Do you know anyone who you think capable of harming your wife?'

'I meant the guys I know would like to lay me out and take me on in the ring. Not hurt my family. I can't think of anyone who'd harm Charlotte. It makes no sense at all.'

'I'm going to need the names of those men.' She took note, even of those he claimed not to have had dealings with for a few years.

He rubbed his close-shaven head with the flat of his hand. 'One of those white-suited blokes took my phone. Can I get it back soon?'

'They'll return your phone once they've finished checking it. It's procedure.'

'They took Charlotte's mobile too and the computer.' He looked back at the house, twisted his neck left then right and caused it to crack. His face screwed up as if in pain. 'Fuck this. I can't stay here any more. I need some time out, alone. I can't think here. I'd like to head off to the club now if I can. I'm going mad sitting here watching police coming and going and all the while my beautiful Charlotte is upstairs.' He stopped once more, fought for control. 'I'm going to need some clothes and shaving kit for the next few days. And Alfie will need his stuff. Can someone fetch them for me?'

'I'm afraid the forensic team might want to leave everything in situ for the moment.'

'Does that mean my car too?'

'Yes. We need to examine everything.'

Adam rubbed his head again. 'Sure, fuck it then. I'll manage without. Get someone to drive me to the boxing club. I'll crash out there. I have to get my head around what I saw in there. It was like some fucking horror film.'

'Of course you do. Would you like the liaison officer to accompany you and stay with you?'

'No. I want to be left alone. I can't take all of this shit in. I need space. You saw what that fucking bastard did to my wife.' He clenched his fists.

'I'll talk to the officer and arrange for you to leave. Before you go, can I ask you one question? Do you own a baseball bat?'

'No, I don't. I want to go now. I need to go. I can't stay here with Charlotte…' He exhaled noisily. 'I just can't, okay?'

'I understand. I'll arrange for you to leave. I truly am most sorry for your loss.'

Natalie left him standing by the car and returned to Tanya Granger.

'Anything?'

'No. He said pretty much the same thing to me about leaving though. He can't wait to get away and he doesn't seem unduly concerned about Alfie. I'll station an officer to keep an eye on him.'

'The parents have been informed and we've tried to contact the sister, Phoebe, but her phone's off. From what we can gather, she's on a long-haul flight back to the UK. She's cabin crew. I thought I'd head over to the Hills' as soon as possible. Adam wants Alfie to stay with them.'

'He told me that too. Said he couldn't look after him for now. I'd have thought he'd want to keep the baby as close to him as possible after such a traumatic experience.'

'Shock can affect people in all sorts of ways. I'll let social services know and they can decide if Alfie ought to go to his grandparents' house for now.'

'I'd like to talk to Charlotte's parents too.'

'I'll meet you at their home if you like.'

'Yes, that'd be best. I just need to sort things out with my team and I'll join you there.'

Natalie's team were huddled outside the Brannons' house. Lucy had recovered her composure and was talking to Ian in a hushed tone. Neighbours had returned inside their own homes and the street was given over to the police. A lengthy black-and-yellow cordon had been placed across the driveway and light spilled out of the front doorway onto the tarmac.

'Adam's going to spend the night at his boxing club. Will one of you drive him there and keep an eye on him until I can arrange for an officer to take over from you? Just in case he suddenly decides to bolt for whatever reason. He's bottling up his anger and is upset. If he has any idea who's behind this, he might go after them himself. He's admitted to knowing a few people who'd like to take him on. Here's a list of names to be checked out. He didn't call them enemies, as such, but that's the impression I got.'

'I'll do that,' said Murray.

Ian tapped his notebook with his pen. 'One of the neighbours, Mrs Margaret Callaghan, reckons she saw two figures running down the road around eleven fifteen. She's an elderly lady in her late seventies. She thinks they were in their twenties or thirties and wearing dark clothing. She said she'd stay up for while if you want to talk to her.'

Natalie checked the time. It was almost three o'clock. 'I'll have a word with her now. We'll need to run checks on Adam. He went out with his wife, took her home, dropped off the babysitter then claims he went to the pub to meet up with his friend Lee Webster. Find out everything you can about the pair of them, Ian. Talk to Lee too.'

'Sure. I'll get on it immediately. We're done here for now.'

'Better go with him,' said Lucy. 'Two heads and all that.'

Natalie thanked them and agreed they'd catch up later.

Margaret Callaghan had a blue-rinsed perm that looked like soft candyfloss on the top of her head. For a woman in her seventies she was sprightly, and her button-like eyes were unusually clear. She cradled a small, white shih tzu in her arms as she spoke to Natalie, her voice a clipped received pronunciation like that of a BBC announcer back in the 1950s.

'I don't sleep much these days so I'm often up at night. I'd gone to bed early, around nine, and dozed off. I woke at quarter past eleven and came downstairs to warm up some milk. Casper,' she said, bouncing the dog slightly to indicate who she was referring to, 'sat by the front door, so I opened it to let him out and as I did so, I caught a glimpse of two people who seemed to come from the Brannons' driveway. They sprinted towards the main street. At first, I thought they were friends of the Brannons, and given there was no burglar alarm going off anywhere, my suspicions weren't raised. My milk was on the stove and I didn't want it to boil over and, to be honest, I didn't spare the pair any more thought. I don't generally nosy at what my neighbours are up to. We're quite a private bunch and although I know a few of the people here, I keep myself to myself. Nobody likes a busybody, do they? Especially an *old* busybody. Anyway, I sat for a while with my drink, probably twenty minutes or so. I read an article in my magazine and waited for Casper to finish his business. When I let him back in, I noticed the Brannons' car pulling onto their drive. I returned to bed but I still wasn't tired, so I stayed awake reading, and when all the police cars began to arrive, I realised I might have been frightfully remiss and maybe the two people I saw had committed a crime.'

'You think you saw them running from the Brannons' house at about eleven fifteen or just after?'

'It must have been about that time. I can't be certain, of course.'

'Can you describe the pair at all?'

'Oh my, now you're asking me. They were a fair distance away and there isn't a great deal of illumination around here. Judging by their movements, I'd say they were young – anything between twenty and thirty – and dressed in dark clothing.'

'Thin, fat, tall, male, female?'

'Male, I think. They were both of slim build but as for height…' She gave an apologetic shrug.

'How well do you know the Brannons?'

'I've exchanged a few words with Mrs Brannon on the odd occasion I've seen her, maybe when I've been walking Casper, or when I'm gardening in the front. She sometimes wheeled the baby out in his buggy. I've only waved at Mr Brannon. I'm afraid to say I know almost nothing about them. You wouldn't think anything like this could happen in such a nice neighbourhood as this one. I've always felt safe and happy here. If you'd told me such a wicked crime could have been committed on this estate, I'd have laughed at you.' She shook her head sadly. 'It's a real shock.'

'Do you live alone, Mrs Callaghan?'

'No, dear. I live with my husband, Peter, but he's visiting his brother this weekend, in Edinburgh. I shall be very glad when he returns home. As soon as you leave, I shall put the chain across and keep Casper nearby.'

'I'm sure you have nothing to fear, but it is always wise to keep the house secure.'

Natalie thanked the lady for her time and wandered back outside. The road was a little emptier with some vehicles having departed. Two paramedics were transporting a gurney containing the body of Charlotte Brannon, now concealed in a body bag, into the ambulance. Mike and Pinkney emerged from the house together and she strode towards them.

'Adam claims he doesn't own a baseball bat.'

'We'll check it out for prints and so on. The writing on the wall is in Charlotte's blood. Can't find any implement the killer used to write those letters though,' said Mike.

'He also told me there's a key taped to the upper drawer of his desk in the games room. It opens the bottom drawer where he keeps his valuables. Might be worth ensuring they're there.'

'There's no obvious sign of robbery. I think whoever came into the house had one thing on their mind and one thing only: to murder Charlotte.'

Pinkney nodded. 'I agree with Mike. The attack was vicious and intentional. She was bludgeoned to death. The killer wrote a message in her blood on the wall.'

Pinkney placed a warm hand on her shoulder for a moment.

'I'm heading to her parents' house. I'll talk to you both later.' Natalie's shoulders suddenly seemed too heavy for her, like a weight was pressing on them.

Mike followed her eyes. 'That poor woman, and all the while, her baby was in the room next to hers.'

'Find me something, Mike,' Natalie replied. With a farewell nod, she returned to her car.

CHAPTER FOUR

SATURDAY, 3 MARCH – EARLY MORNING

Tanya Granger met Natalie at the Hills' front door. She looked pale. 'Mrs Hill was in such a terrible state, the doctor sedated her. You won't be able to talk to her until it's worn off.'

'I'd like to have a quick word with Mr Hill.'

A shadow fell across the entrance. The drawn face of Kevin Hill appeared behind the liaison officer's shoulder.

'Mr Hill, I'm so sorry for your loss.'

He shook his head as if it weighed too much. 'You have any news?'

'Not yet, sir. We're doing everything we can.'

'We heard Alfie was with social services. He won't be put into care, will he? We don't want that to happen.'

'I'm sure social services will be in contact with you tomorrow to talk through possible arrangements.'

He nodded weakly. 'Who would do this terrible thing? Who could kill…? I can't take it in. No. I'm sorry… I can't do this.' His eyes filled and he lurched in the direction of the door.

'He crumbled soon after I got here. It's all too much for him. I don't think he'll be of any help at the moment,' said Tanya.

'I'll come back in a few hours. Any news from their other daughter, Phoebe, yet?'

'Her phone's still off. She's on the Doha flight but that doesn't land until six a.m.'

'Okay. I'll catch you later. You staying here?'

'Yes, for now.'

Natalie plodded back to her car. Time was ticking. She shivered, not from the cold morning air that caressed her face but from the thought Alfie would wake again soon and need his mother.

The state-of-the-art station in Samford was lit up as if it were seven in the morning rather than four. The front doors opened with a quiet swish onto a wide reception. A night-duty officer looked up at her arrival. She glanced left and right. Several of the interview rooms appeared occupied.

'What's going on?' Natalie asked.

'Night exercise,' came the reply from the officer behind the desk.

Samford Police headquarters was home to local officers, CID, public protection and forensic staff, and as Natalie marched towards her own office on the first floor, she passed one of the glass-fronted briefing rooms filled with plain-clothed officers around a large oval table, deep in discussion.

Upstairs, Ian and Lucy were logged onto the larger computers at the far desks, empty plastic cups beside them. Lucy looked over as soon as Natalie arrived.

'You want a coffee? I was about to fetch us both one.'

'I'll stick to water, thanks. Found anything?'

'Lee Webster didn't answer the door and his mobile was switched off so we haven't been able to speak to him yet. However, we've found some information.' Lucy picked up her notes. 'Adam Brannon, born in 1986, was known to police in his youth as one of the Samford North gang notorious in that area of Samford between 1999 and 2002, and along with other members was accused of gang-related crime including shoplifting, graffiti, vandalism, fare-dodging and assault. However, nothing was pinned on him, although some of his fellow gang members were convicted of those crimes and possession of knives. He began training as a boxer in 2003 at what used to be a free gym on the outskirts of Samford, near where he lived at the time. It's no longer there. Closed in 2007 and became part of a housing development.

'Adam cleaned up his act, dumped his gang friends and was taken on by a manager by the name of Bobby Manchego. He applied for his boxing licence in May 2005 and then membership to the semi-professional boxing federation. Won quite a few bouts and was beginning to gain quite a reputation on the circuit but then he was sent down. He was convicted back in January 2014 for GBH on a twenty-year-old Asian guy, Sandeep Khan. He claimed Sandeep and his friends had been threatening him, saying they were going to skin him, and when Sandeep followed him into an alleyway behind an off-licence, he thought he was going to be attacked so he acted. Adam served nine months in prison in 2014, nine months on licence, all of which was before he met Charlotte.'

Natalie sat on the edge of the nearest table and folded her arms.

'How did he assault Sandeep Khan? Did he use a weapon?' Natalie thought momentarily about the baseball bat found in the outside bin.

'Punched him in the face with his fist and broke his jaw. It was deemed to have been an intentional attack, given Adam was a boxer, and he was sentenced accordingly. He served his time at Sudford Prison. When he came out, he set up his own free boxing club and gym just off the Ashmore Estate, using the winnings from his previous fights.'

The Ashmore Estate was one of the more run-down areas on the edge of Samford, consisting of twenty blocks of flats that ought to have been demolished long ago, and was notorious for gang crime.

Lucy took over. 'Charlotte and Adam had only known each other very briefly before marrying in August 2016. Interestingly, the house is in her name only, not joint names. According to the website Zoopla, it was purchased for £745,000 in January 2017. I checked out the land registry and solicitor details and it appears it was bought by Mr and Mrs Kevin Hill, Charlotte's parents.'

'Really? And how does Adam fund the running of this free boxing club of his? Through holding matches or sponsors?'

'He still boxes but he doesn't have a manager any more. Bobby Manchego died of a heart attack while Adam was serving his sentence. I assume his winnings go towards running the place,' said Ian. 'I've yet to find any sponsors.'

'Did Charlotte work?' Natalie asked Lucy.

She shook her head. 'She didn't seem to have ever been in any full-time employment. She ran a blog about affordable fashion and was a massive Instagrammer. She had ninety thousand followers and posted regularly.' She pulled up the images of Charlotte, dressed in a white sheer lace top with enormous bell sleeves over a gold bralette, low-slung black skinny jeans that exposed a flat brown stomach, and a soft black-felt fedora hat tilted at a jaunty angle. Natalie skimmed through more outfits and poses. Although Charlotte didn't have supermodel looks, the woman had style and looked good in all the photographs. She also had what Natalie would have deemed a friendly face with wide, brown eyes and plump lips made fuller thanks to the expert application of a shiny lip gloss.

Lucy continued with her summary. 'Born in Samford in 1995, so she was nine years younger than Adam. Father is Kevin Hill of Hill's Farm Feeds, an animal feed supplier that sold out to an overseas company in 2012. It was started up by Kevin's father, who died in 2014, two years after the sale. They have another daughter, Phoebe, two years older than Charlotte, who's senior cabin crew for Emirates. She's unmarried, no children and owns a flat in London, purchased by Mr and Mrs Hill.'

Natalie cocked her head to one side. 'Let's back up… Charlotte's father bought their house?'

'And one of the cars. Kevin Hill purchased the Bentley Bentayga outright, no finance, and made Charlotte the registered keeper. I managed to draw down her financial details. She also has a trust fund that pays £55K per annum into her bank account.'

'Let me guess. The trust was set up by her parents.'

'You got it. They set it up in May 2014 after the death of her grandfather. They also set one up for Phoebe.'

Ian released a lengthy sigh. 'I wish my folks could afford to pay me to stay at home.'

Natalie butted in. 'Check if Charlotte had taken out a life insurance policy or if one had been taken out on her.'

'You think Adam might have attacked her for money?' Ian asked.

'He wouldn't be the first person to kill over it,' Lucy replied.

Natalie considered the possibility that Adam was behind the murder. It had to be considered even if it didn't feel right to her. She could understand why a fight over money might ensue, but to kill Charlotte? She pushed it to the back of her mind for the moment. Stranger things had happened and she had to keep an open mind.

The communications unit crackled into life. Murray was calling in.

'Adam seems to have turned in for the night. I've checked around the back of the building and the only exit leads to the alleyway at the side, so I'll have eyes on him if he emerges.'

'Cheers. I'll have another officer sent across to relieve you as soon as possible.'

'Roger that.'

The comms unit fell silent once more.

Ian was keen to continue. He read from his notebook. 'You asked about the guy Adam met in the pub. Lee Webster, aged forty, currently employed by Samford Council as a waste operative at the Samford recycling depot. Lives in rented accommodation in Lower St Johns Street, Samford. He was convicted of robbery and actual bodily harm in 2011. He served his time in Sudford Prison, the same prison as Adam. He was released in March 2015, five months after Adam's release.'

'Then they probably knew each other from doing time together. We'll talk to them both later today,' Natalie said, looking at her wristwatch. 'We've got sufficient information to get this investigation under way. It's almost four thirty. Let's wrap this up for now, grab a coffee, breakfast, a nap – whatever. We'll meet up again at eight a.m. sharp. I'll see if I can find someone to take over from Murray.'

With an officer dispatched to relieve Murray, Natalie finally left the station sometime after her officers. The sky was dark but striated with faint strips of soft pink and orange that in ordinary circumstances would have filled her with a wonder for the magic of the universe. This morning, nothing nature had to offer, not even the early-morning call of a blackbird from somewhere in her front garden, could warm her soul. Somebody had murdered a young woman in a barbaric manner in her own home.

The house was silent but friendly, still harbouring the faint aroma of the meal from the night before. It felt welcoming and safe. She wondered if Charlotte had felt the same way about her place. She padded quietly upstairs to the main bathroom she shared with her children for a quick wash and to undress, then, taking her clothes, she slipped into the bedroom. David was fast asleep, cocooned in the duvet like a giant caterpillar, with only his hair showing. Natalie slid in beside him, snuggled close in search of comfort and put an arm around his waist. He gave a contented grunt and slept on. She hung onto him, sharing the warmth from his body, appreciating him being there. Thoughts turned to baby Alfie, in his cot while his mother was being attacked.

She had to sleep. Even if only for an hour. Her mind would function better if she did. She listened to David's steady breathing, trying to emulate it until she was inhaling and exhaling in tandem with him. Outside, a new day was dawning. As she drifted out of consciousness, her last thoughts were of dark-eyed, calm Adam, who didn't want to look after his son and whose face revealed little emotion. Could he have killed his own wife?

CHAPTER FIVE

'Sorry about last night. Think I might have spouted a load of nonsense about my dad and Pam.' David winced as he drank the glass of cold water.

'Headache?'

'No. I've got an oversensitive tooth. Plays up when I eat or drink anything hot or cold. I think the enamel is wearing thin.' He rubbed his jaw.

'Old age must be setting in,' she joked.

'I certainly feel bloody ancient at the moment.' He opened the dishwasher and grimaced at the contents. 'I thought I'd switched this on last night. See: I'm getting forgetful too.'

'You and your dad polished off the best part of a bottle of malt whisky. I don't think you were in any state to remember much at all. It's a wonder you found your way upstairs to bed.'

He grinned at her, reminding her momentarily why she'd fallen for him. He'd retained a fair amount of the same boyish charm he'd had when they'd first met, even if he was now pushing fifty. 'Dad had a good night though, didn't he?'

'Yeah. I think he was relieved Pam fitted in with us all.'

David nodded in agreement and set about rinsing a dish, scraping at the dried-on leftover food with his thumbnail. 'What time did you get in? I vaguely remember you leaving.'

'About two hours ago. I have to return to the station. Murder enquiry.' She downed her cup of black coffee.

'So much for a few days' leave.'

She shrugged. 'You know how it is.'

'And so much for a shopping trip to Manchester.' The dish squeaked as he ran his fingers backwards and forwards in rapid movements over it, clearing off the last of the debris.

She pulled a face. 'Sorry. You still want to take the kids?'

'Not really. Leigh takes forever to choose anything whether it's a pen or a pair of jeans. I'll pull out what's left of my hair. It'd be better if you were there too. I'll offer to drop them off in Castergate to meet their mates. They'll enjoy that more than hanging out with me.'

'You're the best,' she said and pecked him on the cheek.

'What's that for?'

'Because I felt like it. Don't get too used to displays of affection though. Normal service will be resumed later.'

He threw out his chin and gave a low chuckle then winced.

'Headache?' she asked again.

'Okay. Yes. You're right. I've got a slight hangover.'

'Drink plenty of water and go for a run. It'll help you sweat out the toxins.'

'Yes, Doctor. Any other instructions?' The smile on his face didn't quite reach his eyes. A warning note had crept into his voice. Natalie recognised the sign that she'd overstepped some invisible line. David could swing from good to bad mood in a flash and had become more sensitive since losing his full-time job at a law firm and taking up freelance translating. He didn't like being ordered about and Natalie had just touched a nerve. She shook her head and smiled at him to defuse the situation that threatened to brew. He returned his attention to the dishwasher.

'I'll see you when I see you, then,' he said, head in the cupboard as he searched for dishwasher tablets.

She pulled on her ankle boots, yanked the side zips up and left him to it. She stood for a second in the hallway, filled with cast-off trainers and coats slung on hooks, and was momentarily grateful for her cluttered home and the chaos that was her life. It was a far cry from the Brannons' almost sterile home.

'Don't wait up. It could be a long day,' she said before slipping out into the cool air.

Ian stared outside the glass-fronted office at the multicoloured leather seven-seater settee on the landing. He spun around at Natalie's voice.

'You seem lost in thought, Ian.'

'Just thinking about last night and Scarlett…' He left his words hanging.

Natalie understood what he was trying to say. His ex-girlfriend Scarlett had given birth to their baby girl, Ruby, in October of the year before, and the child was almost the same age as Alfie Brannon. It was inevitable he would be drawing parallels. Ian spoke very little about his private life so Natalie only knew a few scant details: that twenty-year-old Scarlett had moved out of their flat and returned home to her parents and Ian now had little involvement with his child.

'It's only natural,' she said. 'You're bound to be affected. After all, you're human.'

His eyes crinkled for a moment, then he caught sight of Murray stalking towards the office and he shook his shoulders as if squaring up for a fight. Ian and Murray didn't always see eye to eye. Football rivalry, and something else Natalie couldn't put her finger on, had them circling each other from time to time like two animals sizing each other up.

Murray shoved open the door and stomped in. 'Fucking shower's broken down at home. Going to have to call a plumber.'

'Why didn't you take one here?' said Ian.

'Now why didn't I think of that?' He scowled at Ian and then sighed dramatically. 'I'm not brain-dead, am I? I used the showers downstairs. Look, I've got damp hair.'

His grumbles were interrupted by the arrival of Lucy, who sprinted into the office in fitted black trousers and a white blouse. Even dressed in the plain clothes she wore for work, Lucy had presence. 'Sorry, got stuck in traffic,' she said. She dropped onto a chair furthest away from the door as she waited for Natalie to begin the briefing.

Natalie spoke, 'There've been no further developments at the scene and I've no news yet from Forensics or Pinkney, although I expect word from them soon. We gathered a fair bit of information last night and there are a few people we must interview first thing. I want to start with Charlotte's parents, Kevin and Sheila Hill. The FLO on this investigation is Tanya Granger and she's currently at the couple's home, just outside Samford. Neither was in a fit state to talk to me earlier and the other daughter, Phoebe, was on a flight back to London. Tanya's since messaged me to say the daughter's now been contacted and is on her way to her parents' house. I've arranged to meet Tanya and the parents at their house after this meeting. Murray, I'd like you to accompany me.'

Murray nodded his assent.

'Onto Adam. The officer stationed outside the boxing club has been instructed to alert us if Adam leaves the premises. Adam was extremely composed last night, and although he could be perfectly innocent, I'd like to keep an eye on him. As you know, in these cases, a spouse or a loved one is often the perpetrator of the crime. Did you establish if Charlotte had a life insurance policy?'

'Nothing in her name,' said Ian.

'We can rule out an attack on her for that reason, then. What about a prenup? If she was that wealthy and her parents were so disapproving of Adam, they might have insisted she had one drawn up?'

'Doesn't look like it. There's none registered.'

She paced to the far end of the room and peered out of the blind-free windows that overlooked the road below. Traffic was beginning to build up, people making their way into town for the day. She blinked away thoughts of her own children, who she ought to have taken shopping.

'Obviously, we need to work out who might have had a problem with Charlotte. Given her huge social network, that might appear an onerous task, but nevertheless, we have to check out anyone who might have a serious grievance or motive.

'Adam says he was with Lee Webster, a friend who served a sentence at Sudford Prison around the same time as Adam was inside for assault. Lee didn't answer the door or phone earlier, and it's important we not only hear his version of events last night but we rule out any possible involvement in Charlotte's death.'

Lucy spoke. 'I tried his phone just before the meeting but it was still switched off.'

'Try his workplace. Track him down. We need to confirm Adam's alibi. Next up is Inge Redfern, their seventeen-year-old babysitter, who Adam drove home. She might have been the last person to speak to Charlotte. She knew the family. Could she have a grudge against Charlotte? We can't rule that possibility out at this stage. If not her, we need to establish if she shut the front door behind her when she left the house. From what we can gather, there's no evidence of a break-in and the burglar alarm wasn't activated, so whoever is responsible had access to the door keys or entered an open house, or there's also the possibility that Charlotte might have let her attacker in. The only other set of house keys is with Charlotte's parents.'

She glanced at the faces in front of her. 'With regards to other potential suspects, there were two unknown individuals spotted fleeing down the street between quarter past eleven and eleven thirty-five. The witness, Margaret Callaghan, who lives in the next house along from the Brannons, is unsure if they actually were at the Brannons' place, but given we have no persons of interest other than Adam, we have to find out who they were. If nothing else, they might have spotted something untoward. Check out CCTV footage in the area in case these two individuals appear again.

'Finally, we have the word "why?" written in eight-inch-high letters in Charlotte's blood on the wall above her bed. The killer has left a message. At this stage, I don't know if that message is intended for us, the police.'

Lucy piped up. 'The killer could be taunting us with this message. They might also have intentionally left the murder weapon in an easy place for us to find.'

Natalie nodded. 'Could indeed be their intention or the message might have been left for Adam or Charlotte's parents.'

'Or for Charlotte,' offered Ian. 'Maybe she did something to upset somebody.'

Natalie continued, 'We must consider all possibilities. That's it for the moment. Anyone got anything to add?'

'Nothing new from me,' said Murray.

The others shook their heads.

'Right then, Lucy, you and Ian start with Lee Webster.'

Walnut Cottage was anything but a cottage. Set on a hillside about six miles from Samford, it might have once been a modest dwelling but had since been modernised and extended to make the most of the views that stretched over miles of countryside. The sitting room to the rear of the property was more like a giant conservatory, with its floor-to-ceiling glass panels, than a room for watching television and chilling out, and as Natalie sat in the vast space on a fat round chair and looked up at the sky above, she understood why Charlotte's house had been so minimal and sterile inside. She'd developed the same taste in furnishing as her parents.

Murray had already made a comment coming up the drive. As they'd pulled up in front of the house, he'd declared the place would make a cattle ranch in Texas appear minuscule.

Tanya Granger was standing next to a life-sized sculpture of a horse painted in various hues of purples, blues and pinks. Natalie and Murray had already come across another such sculpture, covered in vibrant yellow and orange blooms that grew from its fetlocks to cover its flanks. This one appeared to be a random collection of colours but when examined closely revealed tiny painted jigsaw pieces over the entire body. Tanya, clearly exhausted, shifted from one foot to the other then, straightening her spine, drew herself back up to her five foot four inches before speaking.

'Can I get you anything, Kevin? A cup of tea, maybe?'

'No, thank you. Thank you all the same.' The voice was quiet. Kevin Hill, still wearing a dressing gown, pyjamas and a pair of leather slippers, stared at the palms of his hands. Although in his early sixties, he'd retained thick hair, now silver in colour, and a handsome face, currently lined with grief. A solitary tear rolled down his cheek, losing itself in the greying stubble of his chin. Still he studied his hands as if he could change the fortune now embedded in their lines.

Natalie wanted to say more, to offer some words of comfort, but she had nothing that could make him feel better.

His wife, Sheila, awake but even now a little dopey from the drugs, sat next to him, face slack and eyes misted over, a housecoat covering her ample frame. Tanya glanced at Natalie who cleared her throat.

'Last night, you met up with Adam and Charlotte at Valentino's restaurant just outside Derby. How did Charlotte seem?'

Kevin lifted red-rimmed eyes towards Natalie. 'We haven't heard from social services yet. We want to know how Alfie is. Is he with his father?'

'You'll hear very soon, I promise,' Natalie replied.

'Alfie needs to be with his family,' Kevin said.

Natalie nodded. 'You'll be contacted shortly. For now, I really need to ask you a few questions to help me with my investigation. How was Charlotte last night?'

'Chirpy. Bright. Beautiful. What do you want me say?'

'I wondered how she'd behaved throughout dinner.'

'Same as always. We chatted, had a few drinks, enjoyed ourselves.' His voice became flatter.

'No, Kevin. She wasn't chirpy,' Sheila said slowly. She shook her head and tugged at the sleeve of her housecoat. 'She tried to be. You were making jokes and she laughed at them but she wasn't her usual self. I noticed that. She drank more than she usually does, for one thing, and she ignored Adam a lot of the time.'

'Ignored him in what way?'

Sheila tucked her knees up under her coat and blinked into space. 'Adam's not an easy son-in-law. He hasn't had the same opportunities in life that Charlotte had, and he can be prickly sometimes. We've had a few run-ins with him. Nothing major but when it happens, Charlotte sides with him. Last night she didn't. She was more like our old Charlotte: less submissive, less clingy.'

'You think her personality altered after marrying Adam?' Natalie asked.

'For certain it did. You see, Adam doesn't really like us or understand us. He's wary of us. He didn't have any parental assistance of his own and he didn't want Charlotte to have the emotional and financial support we gave her.

'His father ran out on his mother when he was an infant. By all accounts, she was a heroin addict. We don't know the full story but he was taken into care in his teens and she passed away soon after. He didn't like the fact Charlotte had so much and he had so little. He wanted to be the only person in Charlotte's life. He suffocated her, transformed her and stopped her from being who she really was.'

'You're reading too much into it all, Sheila.' Kevin shook his head. 'Now isn't the time for that.'

'No, I'm not reading too much into anything,' she replied, sadly. 'You didn't see what I saw. You never noticed the looks that passed between them, or how Charlotte was changing, pushing us both away. You saw what you wanted to see.'

Kevin shook his head, sprinkling tears onto his lap.

Sheila continued talking in a monotone voice. 'Charlotte used to say Adam was trying to escape his past, put it behind him and start afresh, but I didn't believe her. While I never approved of my daughter's choice of husband, I certainly tried to accept him and make him feel welcome; however, he made it abundantly clear he didn't want to be part of our family. He was almost impossible to get along with: petulant, brooding, unsociable and there was a darkness behind his looks and actions. He is the polar opposite of Charlotte, and for the life of me, I can't think why she married him.' She shifted her legs and stared off into the distance then spoke again. 'Charlotte was overcompensating for him last night. She wanted us to have a good evening but there was something else, a hidden agenda that I sensed. Call it mother's intuition or whatever, but I'm convinced there was something going on between them. He spent a lot of last evening texting on his phone rather than joining in the conversation, and when Charlotte reprimanded him, he gave her such a look.' She shivered at the memory.

'Did he ever threaten Charlotte?' Natalie looked directly at Sheila, who returned the gaze and nodded. 'Charlotte let it slip he'd been becoming more aggressive towards her. He hadn't hurt her physically, but there'd been some terrible arguments and she feared he might. She tried to tell me something else last night in the ladies', but she stopped midway and clammed up.'

'What did she say?'

'She began by asking me if I thought she'd made a mistake marrying Adam. I told her she was a grown woman and whatever she decided I'd always support her actions. Then she looked away and chewed her lip. I recognised the sign. She always used to do that when she was concerned. She said she was worried. She had to tell Adam something and she wasn't sure how he'd take it. I asked her what she meant but she shook her head and laughed it off. Said she'd drunk too much and was letting everything get out of proportion because she and Adam had rowed. Told me to forget it and let the subject drop.'

'Did you pursue the subject?'

'We returned to the table and started talking about something else, and then time raced by and Adam announced it was time to leave. It was coming up to ten and they'd promised the babysitter they wouldn't be late. I hugged her goodbye and whispered if ever she wanted to talk to me, she could. She didn't answer. I could tell whatever was troubling her was still there. I could see it in her eyes.'

'You didn't say anything to me about that last night,' Kevin said, his gaze fixed on his wife.

'I wanted to find out what it was first. I was going to ring her today and ask her to bring Alfie around, then mention it again.' She spoke directly to Natalie. 'We're worried sick about Alfie. He should be with us until Adam is able to look after him. It'd be much better than a stranger looking after him. We'd like to have him. We *want* to have him. He's our grandson.'

Natalie nodded. Tanya would sort that out with social services. She wanted to steer the conversation back to the night before. Kevin was clearly still focused on the events.

'I didn't notice anything going on between them,' Kevin said, more to himself as a reprimand.

Sheila didn't respond.

'Adam didn't join in the celebrations last night?' Natalie asked.

'No. It was a mistake to have invited him. I thought it would help bring us closer. We've seen so little of either of them, what with us travelling so much recently and them busy with the baby.'

Sheila stopped suddenly, eyes filling. Her final words came out as a choked sob. 'I thought there'd always be more time for seeing them.'

'I understand this is a very distressing time for you both, but I'd really appreciate your help by answering a few more questions. Charlotte had a trust fund, didn't she?' Natalie prompted.

Sheila blew her nose on a tissue and rested her forehead against her knuckles. Natalie glanced at Murray who leant forward and spoke to Kevin.

'Can you tell us about the trust fund?'

Kevin appeared to come out of his reverie at the sound of Murray's voice. 'My father sold the family animal feed business in 2012. When he passed away two years later, we decided to give both the girls some money to help them through their lives. We set up funds for them both.'

'What about the house? I understand you purchased it in January 2017,' Murray asked.

Sheila glanced briefly at Kevin, who swallowed before continuing. 'Phoebe, our other daughter, had been promoted to senior cabin crew for Emirates and was flying out of London a great deal. Rather than have her commute and stay in digs as she was, Sheila and I thought it would be an idea to buy her a flat in London so she could travel more easily. Charlotte was living with Adam by then. They'd bought a house in a… How can I put it? In a less than salubrious area of Samford. She wanted to move away but they couldn't afford a property in the area where she wanted to live. She'd seen a house in Eastborough on a prestigious estate and wanted it. Having just bought a property for Phoebe, we couldn't really refuse her request. The money was there. No point in waiting for us to die to inherit it, we thought.' He turned his head for a moment to regain his composure, giving a small shake as he did so.

Natalie spoke up. 'Did you talk to Adam about buying the house?'

'No. I wanted to provide for my daughters. I chose not to have the properties put in joint names. Although Phoebe was single at the time, I knew she'd find herself in a serious relationship at some stage, and Charlotte was married to Adam. I didn't want a situation to arise where either of my girls found themselves fighting over half of a property if their relationships broke down. The house was Charlotte's. If she and Adam had split up, she'd have always had a roof over her head and money to fall back on. Not everyone sticks at marriage these days. I thought I was protecting her.'

At the moment, Kevin looked like he'd give up all his wealth to have his daughter back.

Natalie would have to get Adam's thoughts on the matter later. At present she was more concerned with potential suspects. She continued with her questions.

'Apart from the incident in the toilets at the restaurant when she spoke briefly about Adam, has Charlotte mentioned being concerned about anyone else?'

Kevin looked across at his wife, who shook her head.

'She didn't have any run-ins?'

'No.'

'And she wasn't seeing anybody else?'

Sheila drew a quick breath and released it crossly. 'Absolutely not. Alfie was the apple of her eye and she loved Adam despite his shortcomings. She wouldn't be having an affair. I'm certain of that.'

'Were Phoebe and Charlotte close?'

'They used to be when they were younger but less so these days. They chose very different career paths. Charlotte was always into fashion and design and wrote a fashion blog. Phoebe loves travelling. They shared a flat together in London while Charlotte was studying there. After she married Adam, they saw little of each other and then Phoebe got engaged and is always jetting off to one location or another.'

'I'd like to talk to her when she arrives. Would that be okay?'

'Of course. She's coming up with Jed, her fiancé. We'll ask her to call by the station unless you want to talk to her here.'

'It would be more convenient if she could come to the station. I understand you have a key to Charlotte and Adam's house.'

'We have one in case of emergencies, or if they needed us to let in a workman, that sort of thing. We've never needed to use it. It's on a hook in our key cupboard,' said Kevin.

'Does anybody other than you have access to that cupboard?' Murray asked.

'No. Only us.' He left the room and returned quickly with the key which he handed over to Murray. 'I'd like it back in time.'

'Is Adam under suspicion?' Sheila's voice was hesitant.

'We're talking to everyone who knew Charlotte,' said Natalie, sidestepping the question.

With little more to be gained by questioning the distressed parents, Natalie and Murray thanked them and departed. Murray put the car into gear and hesitated, foot on the brake, before drawing away.

He glanced across. 'Can you believe them? Buying a property for each of their daughters without consulting the partners. And what was Charlotte thinking of? If Yolande and her parents pulled a stunt like that on me, I'd be livid. I'd probably tell Yolande where she could shove her fancy house and trust fund, even though I'm batshit crazy about her. Adam can't have been happy about that. Would you go behind your daughter's husband's back and offer her money and a house if you could afford it?'

'That's hypothetical because I can barely afford the mortgage on the house we own, let alone shore up either of my kids.'

'You wouldn't though, would you?'

Natalie considered his point. It was a fair one. The Hills had overstepped the mark. They probably had good intentions but they hadn't considered Adam's feelings. And neither had Charlotte. Had it driven a wedge between them? Their marriage maybe wasn't what it appeared to be.

'It's a weird one, I'll grant you that.'

Murray pulled off the drive. 'I reckon there's a lot of tension in that household – Adam and Charlotte, Adam and his in-laws – and I wouldn't be surprised if he hadn't blown his top last night.'

'There's a huge difference between blowing your top and bludgeoning your loved one to death and then scrawling a message in her blood on the wall,' Natalie replied. She looked at her phone screen. There was a message from Leigh, her daughter.

Murray picked up on her tone and concentrated on the road, leaving Natalie to chew over what they'd learnt. She opened the message.

Dad says we can't go to Manchester today. I really wanted to buy some new boots. When can we go?

Natalie hated letting down her children, and Leigh had been especially excited about going to the city, where there was a far greater choice of shops than where they lived. She thumbed a response, knowing it wouldn't be what her daughter wanted to hear.

Got called into work. Bad timing, I know. We'll definitely go as soon as I get a free day. Love you. X

She sighed. It was always difficult when she had to neglect those she loved most. She wasn't alone. Work had ruined her colleague and husband's good friend, Mike Sullivan's marriage. Finding the balance between it and family life was a constant juggling act that relied on everyone's comprehension and patience. Leigh would understand, Natalie reasoned. She was merely disappointed at the moment. She'd bounce back quickly.

She turned her attention to the investigation. Adam didn't get along with Kevin and Sheila, and Charlotte had told her mother she needed to speak to Adam about something important that would anger him. If Sheila Hill was telling the truth, then the marriage wasn't all it appeared to be. At this stage, however, Natalie couldn't rely on any of her witnesses. People lied and she could trust no one. What she needed was some solid evidence.

CHAPTER SIX

Lucy and Ian found Lee Webster at the recycling depot on the outskirts of Samford. Wearing a high-vis orange jacket, he guided their vehicle around the route towards a bay in front of some skips marked for general waste.

At five foot six, he barely reached Lucy's chin, but what he lacked in height he made up for in breadth. Lee's neck was as thick as a bull's and covered in tattoos. Behind his ears were inked designs of dragons with open mouths, shooting flames over his temples and scalp.

'Fuck me! Poor sod. Charlotte was killed?'

'I'm afraid so. Were you a friend of the family?'

He barked a laugh. 'Nah, I wouldn't have been welcome round his house, let alone his neighbourhood. Charlotte was definitely not keen on anyone from his past turning up, love.'

Lucy tried not to bristle at the comment.

'We were at your flat and tried to rouse you early this morning at about three but you didn't answer the doorbell.'

'Didn't hear you. Sorry. I sleep like the proverbial log. I always do. It comes from having a clear conscience.'

'And your phone was switched off.'

'I always turn it off at night.'

'You don't use it to set your alarm?'

'I have a proper alarm – a clock. I like old-fashioned stuff.' He smirked.

'You didn't respond to the message we left for you to get in touch.'

'Sorry. I didn't pick it up. I was in a hurry to get to work. I was running late. I would have contacted you once I'd listened to it.'

Lucy couldn't prove otherwise for the moment, so she decided to continue interviewing him. It was important to establish Adam's alibi. 'You knew Charlotte?'

'Not especially. I used to see her out and about when they lived at their old place, which was closer to Adam's boxing club, but not much since they moved, only on the odd occasion around town. I've spotted her driving around.'

'How would you describe your relationship with Adam?'

'He and I have history. We shared accommodation for a while, shall we say?'

'You mean you were at the same prison at the same time?'

'No, I mean we shared a cell in the same prison.' His jaw moved up and down as he chewed some gum. His eyes never left her face. 'He was my cellmate. We stayed in touch. When I came out we hooked up again.'

'We're trying to establish Adam's movements last night.'

'I *can* help you with that. He was with me. We were both at the White Horse. He came in for last orders and then we went back to my flat in Samford. Had a couple of cans and he left before midnight.'

'Did he walk to the flat?'

'Nah. He drove. We both drove. I took my car. He took his.'

'Which car was he driving?'

'The Bentley.'

'Any idea of the exact time he left you?'

'Eleven forty.'

'You seem very certain of that fact.'

'I checked the time after he went. I had to set my alarm clock for work.' The corners of his mouth pulled into a half-smile. 'So that's how I know.'

'He was with you the entire time?'

'That's right.'

'Did anyone else see either of you together?'

'The barman at the White Horse. Name's Vitor. He's from Portugal. He'll remember Adam – we go there often. There wasn't anyone else in at the time.'

'I imagine, from what you said earlier, that you've never been to Adam's house?'

'I didn't even go round to their old house. We might be mates but I wasn't welcome there. Charlotte wouldn't have liked that much.'

'And do you know that for certain? Did Adam tell you Charlotte didn't want you around?'

His eyes narrowed and a sly smile crept across his face. 'You're suggesting I had a problem with Charlotte, aren't you? I know how you lot work. Well, love, as it happens, I didn't want to drop in for cosy chats with Adam and his missus. I'm a loner. I don't like folk knowing about my past. Adam knows more about me than anyone else and I like to keep it like that. It suited us both to meet up at his gym or at the pub. Anyway, from what little I know about his wife, Charlotte was a fucking basket case.'

'In what way?'

He released a puff of irritation. 'In the same way many women are. She blew hot and cold all the time; threw tantrums when she didn't get her own way. He didn't discuss their relationship, only let off steam when he was pissed off because she was giving him a hard time, or her parents were.'

'When did you arrange last night's meeting?'

'Yesterday afternoon.'

'Did he tell you he was going out for dinner first?'

'Mentioned something about it. Said he'd be in the pub before last orders.' He glared at her. 'Listen, love, this isn't working. You're leading me to talk about Adam and then try and pick holes in his alibi. Give up now. The poor fucker's lost his wife. Adam and I meet up a couple of times a month, usually after he's finished work. I like the guy. We have a shared history together. In a place like Sudford Prison, you soon find out who to trust and who to avoid. Look at me. I look a right hard bastard, don't I? I haven't always looked this way. When I first went inside, I was ordinary-looking and I found it really fucking difficult, if you get my drift. I quickly made enemies. When Adam was sent down, he became my cellmate, and he looked out for me. Nobody dared mess with him, and consequently they left me alone too. He helped me get into better physical shape. He trained me up in the cell. Put me through a daily routine. Taught me moves so when he was released, I was able to handle myself and manage without him. We formed a proper friendship, the sort that stands the test of time. Nobody in the real world wants to know an ex-con. Adam did. He let me sleep in the back office at the boxing club until I could find a job. He helped me get back on my feet. He even loaned me money. Nowadays, I train at his club, help out with the youngsters there when I can, and we go out for a drink now and again.'

'Did he ever talk about his son?'

'I'm an unmarried ex-con who works at a shitty recycling unit. I rent a crappy flat and spend my free time wanking off to porn or trying to get laid. Why would I want to listen to some bloke banging on about his wife and kid? I'm not fucking interested in that sort of thing.'

Lucy wasn't going to be sidelined by his aggression. 'Did he mention his in-laws last night?'

'Only to say they were being total wankers as usual.'

'He doesn't like them?'

'Adam's like me; he doesn't like many people. Can't blame us, can you? We have to be extra cautious. First sign of trouble and the police come straight for us. Adam's a decent guy. He does a lot of good for the community. He runs a free boxing club for youngsters who haven't had a promising start in life – boys and girls like him – and he lets blokes like me, who can't afford membership fees at other places, use it too. I bet crime's gone down with him giving those kids a place to go to on an evening. You should thank him for making your lives easier. He was with me last night. I can promise you that. You ought to give him a break, love, not be trying to hound him.'

'I can assure you we're not hounding him, as you put it. We have to check the whereabouts of everyone who knew the victims.'

'Yeah, right. Course you do.' He chewed again then spat on the ground. 'We done here?'

'What did you do after Adam left last night?'

'Went to bed.'

'You didn't go out?'

'Why would I do that, *officer*?' He smiled as he hissed the last word. 'If you think I did, then prove it. I was in my place until eight a.m. when I came to work. Check my mobile or whatever it is you do to find out my movements. It's a fucking nanny state in this country these days. Everyone's being watched all the time. I'm sure you can figure out where I was and find out I'm telling you the truth.'

'Did Adam contact you overnight? Did he ring you to tell you about his wife being killed?'

'How could he? My phone was switched off. I didn't know about it until you told me. Why are you asking these ridiculous questions?'

'Just checking.'

'Now you've checked, I have to get back to work,' he said, looking up and spotting a red Volvo estate car pulling in behind

Lucy and Ian's car. 'Have to help folk dump their stuff in the correct skip.'

He sauntered off, whistling tunelessly, leaving Lucy frustrated. She'd have a quick chat with Vitor, the barman at the White Horse, and then she'd have to call it in. If he was telling the truth, Adam was not guilty of murdering his wife. That left them with the problem of finding out just who did.

'Tough nut,' said Ian.

'Bit cocky but unless we find a hole in his alibi, we're stuffed. Look, let's go to Inge's and then I'll drop you back at the station to attend the meeting, and I'll talk to Vitor.'

'Fine by me.'

After half an hour of fast driving, Lucy and Ian found themselves in the kitchen of 29 Pebble Avenue, Brompton. Two kittens were hurtling around the room, tumbling over each other as they scooted between chair legs and onto shelves, then dived onto the floor again.

Inge Redfern blew her nose loudly on a tissue. Her mother, Sabine, a pleasant-faced woman with light-grey eyes, stroked the girl's hair, her face screwed up in confusion.

'I don't understand,' Sabine said. 'I only saw Charlotte yesterday morning. We had coffee together.'

Inge let out another sob that warranted soothing sounds from her mother. 'Shh, sweetheart,' she murmured.

'I understand it's a terrible shock for you both,' said Lucy. 'We really are most dreadfully sorry for your loss. Were you very close to Charlotte?'

The kittens knocked over a vase, sending it clattering to the floor. Sabine pounced on them, scooping them into her arms and putting them outside the back door. 'Sorry, I can't be doing with them.' She let out a heartfelt sigh. 'I've only known Charlotte for about a year but we were close enough. We met when she first came to the hospital where I work, for check-ups. I'm an obstetrician. I actually delivered Alfie.' She stopped to brush away a tear that spilled over her eyelashes. Outside, one of the kittens jumped onto the window ledge and miaowed plaintively. Lucy had to wait until Sabine could speak again. She moved towards her daughter and stood close to her.

'We hit it off and I liked her hugely. She was such a vibrant, fun person. She and I used to go out regularly for coffee or a drink when I wasn't on shift. It was me who suggested Inge as a babysitter. She needed someone reliable and I thought of my own daughter.'

Lucy smiled at the stricken girl, whose hands now clung to her mother's. She kept her tone light. 'Did you babysit Alfie often?'

'Once or twice a week. I only started working for them a few weeks ago. If I wasn't at college, I looked after Alfie so Charlotte could go to salon appointments and some evenings she and Adam went out together.' She sniffed back sobs. Her mother smoothed back a stray strand of hair.

Inge spoke again. 'Alfie usually sleeps. He sleeps such a lot. Now and then, he wakes up and I put him on his activity mat or play with him, or cuddle him. He's started smiling, you know? He recognises my face and he smiles at me when I pick him up. He kicks his feet like he's excited to see me.' Her eyes filled.

Her mother hugged her tightly. 'It's okay, Inge. It's okay,' she whispered.

'What happened to Charlotte?' Sabine asked Lucy.

Lucy was ready for the question. 'We're trying to piece together the events of last night to work that out, Mrs Redfern. I understand it's extremely distressing for your daughter, yet we really need to know what happened after Charlotte and Adam came home. Can you tell us, Inge?'

Inge snivelled some more then managed to speak. 'Charlotte came in alone. I was watching TV. The programme had only just begun, so it must have been soon after ten. She seemed pretty drunk, to be honest. She was slurring her words and kept swaying. She had to hold on to the door frame at one point. I've not seen her like that before. She didn't think I'd noticed and was trying to play it cool. She told me Adam was waiting to take me home so I collected my books, said goodnight and went straight outside to the car. Adam was searching through some music on his iPhone. He put on Rita Ora – we both like her – and drove me straight home.'

'Did he discuss or mention his plans for after he'd dropped you off?'

'No.'

'Did you see him turn the car around and head back in the direction of Eastborough?'

'No. I didn't watch him leave. I came straight inside.'

'Were you at home when Inge got in, Mrs Redfern?'

'No. I was on shift at the hospital.'

'And your husband?'

'He's in Bratislava this weekend on business. He'll be back on Sunday evening.'

'Can you remember shutting the door behind you when you left the Brannons' house, Inge?'

The girl looked up at her mother, a moment of confusion on her face. 'I think so.'

'Charlotte didn't shut the door after you, then?'

Her eyebrows furrowed. 'No. She wandered off into the kitchen, I think. She definitely didn't follow me to the front door, and I'm certain I shut it behind me. I tugged at the doorknob to make sure it was closed. I always do that. I do the same with our door handle.'

Lucy gave another smile. Ian continued writing notes in his notepad, head lowered as he did so.

'How did Adam seem?'

'What do you mean?'

'Was he in a good mood?'

Inge shrugged. 'He was, I dunno, just Adam.'

'And how was that?'

'He drove me home and paid me.'

'He didn't discuss the evening, or Charlotte, or ask you about your studies?'

'He asked how I was getting on with my revision. He knows I have exams coming up.'

'Did he seem anxious or angry?'

Inge shook her head, eyebrows lowered further. 'If he was, I didn't notice.'

'Did you ever hear Adam and Charlotte arguing?'

'Mu-um, I don't want to talk about them any more.' Inge looked up at her mother, tears once more in her eyes. Her face crumpled.

'You have to, sweetheart. Tell them.'

Inge sniffed before speaking, face contorted as if each word were painful to utter. 'I heard them arguing once or twice. Adam was cross with her last night when I arrived because she took too long to get ready. Nothing serious. Charlotte likes clothes and make-up. She likes to look good. She looked beautiful last night.'

'You never heard Adam threaten her?'

'No. Never. He didn't hurt Charlotte. I know he didn't. He wouldn't.' She was becoming hysterical again.

'We won't trouble you any further, Inge. When you feel more able to, I might like to ask you some further questions.' Lucy stood up. Inge was resting her head in her mother's lap.

'I'm truly sorry to bring you such bad news.'

Sabine acknowledged her with a small nod. 'There's something. It's probably nothing...' she started to say then changed her mind.

'Go on? It might be useful,' Lucy said.

'No, it's nothing. Charlotte mentioned one day – about a month ago – that Adam didn't want anything to do with the child: wouldn't change him, push him in his buggy or anything. Some new fathers need time to adjust. They resent a newborn taking up the mother's time and love. They feel left out. I advised her to encourage him to spend time with Alfie alone and to include him more in everyday activities. I think she was partly to blame. She was so protective of Alfie.'

'That's not true,' said Inge. 'Adam loved Alfie. He told me so.'

Sabine ignored the fresh outburst. 'Charlotte told me he left everything to her. He told her it wasn't his place to deal with the baby. I'm not saying he didn't love Alfie but he kept his distance. I think it caused problems between them. Charlotte said they argued a lot about it. She was at the end of her tether with him. You asked Inge if Adam and Charlotte rowed, and from what Charlotte told me, they did, usually over Alfie.'

'You're making Adam out to be some sort of monster. I saw how he looked at Alfie. He'd go into the nursery and just stand and look at him. He cared about Alfie, Mum. He cared.' Inge's face was red and blotchy and her voice had risen. She was close to hysteria.

Lucy decided it was time to depart. They had some information. How useful it would be, Lucy didn't know, but it was at least a starting point.

As they walked to the car, Ian let out a sigh. Lucy had an idea what was troubling him. He was thinking of Ruby, his baby daughter. He'd mentioned her a few times in the office when Natalie and Murray weren't about. 'You want to talk about it?' she said.

'You reckon that's possible?'

'What?'

'That a man can father a child and not want to be involved in his or her life?'

'Human nature always confounds me,' she answered, unlocking the car and standing beside the driver's door. 'We're very complex and our emotions often lead us to behave in ways others may find peculiar. You're talking to somebody whose mother gave her away when she was a baby. The answer is yes, I think it's quite possible.'

Ian climbed into the passenger seat. 'I can't imagine it. I'm finding it hard not being able to see my daughter every day. I want to be part of her life, even if her mother doesn't want me to be part of hers.'

Lucy turned the key in the ignition and threw the car into gear. She offered him a genuine smile that transformed her looks. 'Then your daughter is a very lucky girl,' she said.

CHAPTER SEVEN

Back at Samford Police headquarters, there was more news awaiting Natalie, in the shape of Mike. Natalie took in his wide shoulders, intense bright gaze and unshaven face that enhanced his good looks and was reminded of their fling. It had taken place over a year ago but some days she found it hard to look at him without thinking about that night.

This morning, Mike was completely focused on his presentation. He set out transparencies neatly, ready to share his knowledge. Natalie greeted him and threw herself onto the nearest seat. Murray slumped against the wall.

'You got anywhere?' Mike asked.

'Just spoken to Charlotte's parents. They're not on best of terms with Adam. Mother thinks there was something strange going on between him and Charlotte.'

'You'll be interested in our findings then,' Mike began. He halted at the arrival of Ian. 'Just in time.'

'Lucy's interviewing a barman to confirm Adam's alibi. She'll be here afterwards. We've spoken to Lee and Inge.'

'Okay. Grab a seat, Ian. Mike's about to bring us up to speed. Mike?' Natalie said.

'We found the key to the valuables drawer. It was where you said it would be, stuck to the underside of the top drawer. Watches and jewellery were in the locked drawer. To our knowledge, nothing was stolen from the house.' Mike flicked on the overhead projector. A photograph of the wall above Charlotte's bed, bearing the word '*why?*', flashed up. Mike cleared his throat.

'We've identified the blood to be Charlotte's. We took the dimensions of each letter and looked at the depth of each smear on them. From that we concluded the letters were written using a forefinger, although we think our perp was wearing gloves so no prints.

'We believe the killer took the blood from beside her body. There are repetitive dabs in this area.' Once more, Mike took a transparency and, removing the first, placed it onto the projector. Charlotte's head swam into vision. Above the crown was a pool of blood. Mike pointed out the area he'd referred to.

'Could you lift no prints at all from it, Mike?' Murray asked.

Mike shook his head. 'If indeed the killer used their finger to write the word, they made sure it was covered up. However, talking of prints, I have something significant for you.'

A third picture replaced the one of Charlotte. It was of the baseball bat.

'The bloodstains on this bat have been identified as Charlotte's. We pulled fingerprints from the handle too and several of them are Charlotte's.'

'She was holding the bat in self-defence.' Ian's brows had knitted together.

'That might have been the case,' said Mike, pointing towards the top of the handle. 'The prints suggest she took hold of it here. There's a thumbprint belonging to her towards the top of the handle. It's facing in the opposite direction to what I'd expect from somebody picking up the bat as normal, and there are also several partials all belonging to her, here, here and here.'

'They're further down the handle,' said Murray.

'Correct. This pattern of prints suggests she was trying to grasp hold of the bat. Here are two prints: forefinger and middle finger. Here, three prints in a row, commensurate with somebody feeling for and pulling it towards them.'

'She was trying to wrestle it from her assailant.' Natalie's words were more a statement than a question.

'Possibly so. We also found another partial print on the handle but it wasn't Charlotte's. It belongs to Adam, her husband.'

Natalie's eyes widened. 'The lying son of a bitch. He touched the bat. He told me he didn't have a baseball bat.'

'It's definitely his fingerprint. The bat itself is a heavy-duty, wooden, varnished one. The logo on the barrel indicates its brand – Wollowo – sporting merchandise readily purchased in stores and online.'

'Then if she purchased it, she bought it for the same reason many others do – protection,' said Murray.

Mike rummaged in his bag once more for some notes before speaking again. 'Blood spatter indicates she was struck with force beside the bed. There are blood droplets ascending in a pattern against the bedside table and micro droplets above it that support that theory.' He put up a photograph of the crime scene and shook his shoulders free of tension.

'This is where we believe Charlotte was attacked.' He pointed to the far side of the bed. 'We discovered microscopic carpet fibres in the folds of the skin on her knees and again on her right elbow. From those, we surmised she was on all fours. There are also fibres under the nails of her right hand.'

'Carpet fibres?' Murray asked.

'Again, that is possibly the case. We've yet to identify them. If they are, it might suggest she was trying to hide under the bed. We think the attacker surprised her there, struck her on the side of the head and knocked her to one side, then hit her repeatedly with the bat. Our initial thoughts are that she was rendered unconscious from the initial blow and Pinkney's report might confirm that.' He drew a deep breath and turned off the projector. 'That's it for the moment.'

Natalie cocked her head. 'If Charlotte was indeed trying to hide under the bed, why didn't she drop down under it from where she was sleeping? Instead, she got out of her side of the bed, walked or crawled around to the other side, and hid there. That's not logical.'

'Maybe she was on all fours, searching for the bat hidden there?' Murray offered.

'If it was hers, wouldn't she have kept it under her side of the bed? She could reach it more easily if it were there,' Ian said.

Natalie added her thoughts. 'Based on what Mike's just told us, it'd be logical to assume Adam Brannon owned that bat and he – or somebody else – killed Charlotte with it. We'll bring him in for questioning.'

'I'll be upstairs if you need me. We're examining the fibres we found to ensure they all match.' Mike packed away the transparencies then lifted a hand in a farewell gesture and slipped out of the office.

Natalie took his place at the front of the room to set them off. 'Just a quick update on Alfie Brannon. He's still with social services but there's every chance he'll be staying with his grandparents soon. Obviously, where he ends up or what will eventually happen to him depends on where this investigation takes us, although I've been given to understand Charlotte's parents are keen to take custody of him should Adam not want to, for whatever reason, or if indeed he is charged for Charlotte's murder. Okay, over to you.'

Ian was the first to speak. 'Inge, the babysitter, confirmed Adam drove her home around ten p.m. but she doesn't know where he went afterwards. He didn't say. Her mother, Sabine, told us Adam had little to do with his son and that caused tension and arguments between the pair.'

Murray scratched at the back of his neck. 'Sheila, Charlotte's mother, thought Adam and Charlotte had been arguing. Charlotte had wanted to talk to her about it but then changed her mind at the last moment. She told her mother she had something to tell Adam and he wouldn't like it.'

'Tension between them, arguments, a secret and a baseball bat. All of which leads us in one direction; we need to speak to Adam. Bring him in, Murray,' said Natalie.

As she waited for Adam to come to the station, she scrutinised the photographs of the crime scene once more. If Mike was right and the person had used their forefinger to write the word above the bed in blood, the letters were surely too narrow for Adam to have done so. He had large hands and big fingers. She rang upstairs and asked Mike to send down exact dimensions of the letters.

'He needn't have used all his finger, Natalie,' he said. 'Only the tip of it. The marks aren't the exact size of his finger.'

'Can you tell how big his fingers are from the writing?'

'Not with any degree of accuracy,' came the reply.

'Cheers. It was just a thought.'

She hung up again and flicked through the statement the neighbour, Margaret Callaghan, had given her. Even though they would question Adam, there were other avenues she ought to pursue. Her phone lit up. It was Leigh.

Can I look for boots online?

She repressed a sigh. She had more important things to handle than her daughter's desire to get new boots, yet she couldn't ignore the text.

Search if you like but no buying. Wait until you can try on in a shop and make sure they fit comfortably. Love you. X

She hoped it was enough to satisfy her daughter. She picked up the brief notes she'd made on the two individuals Margaret had spotted. 'Ian, run through local surveillance cameras in the area, will you? See if anyone matching this description turns up.'

'There are no cameras near Maddison Court but I'll try the streets closest to it. Eastborough only has a few cameras in place.'

'You'd think there'd be loads of cameras on an estate like that,' said Natalie. 'There are some very expensive places there. Surely the houses have surveillance equipment to protect against burglary.'

'I'll check with the neighbours. See if any of them have cameras on their properties. We know Adam didn't own any. He only had a burglar alarm.'

Natalie pulled out the photograph of Alfie's nursery one more time. She studied the fairy-tale cot with a canopy, curtain drapes with bows, and soft toys laid out to greet him when he awoke. His life would probably be changed forever now. He might even live with his grandparents and never return to this room that had been lovingly put together. She examined the framed photos set up on the shelves and noted there wasn't a single one of Adam with Alfie. Why were there only pictures of Charlotte with her baby? Adam hadn't been keen to look after his son when Charlotte was alive, and he was equally reluctant now, after her death. It didn't add up. She absent-mindedly chewed on a hangnail. Adam might be a semi-pro boxer but he was no match for her. She wasn't going to release him until she was satisfied he had nothing to do with Charlotte's death.

CHAPTER EIGHT

SATURDAY, 3 MARCH – LATE MORNING

Adam Brannon filled the chair in the interview room, his long legs barely fitting under the table. Murray handed him the coffee he'd requested, which he took, heavy lids half-closed on his eyes. Everything about him appeared lazy and calculated, yet Natalie recalled the way he'd spun to face her the night before when he'd been by the squad car. Appearances were deceiving. Adam had sharp reflexes and a quick reaction time.

He sipped the coffee. 'You got any suspects yet?'

Natalie answered him. 'We're pursuing a couple of lines of enquiry.'

'You better find the bastard before I do,' he said.

'I don't suggest for one minute you go looking for the person responsible. That's our job.'

'You don't seem to have any idea yet of who's behind her murder. What do you suggest I do? Sit quietly and wait it out? My wife was murdered. I saw Charlotte. She was a mess. Some fucking bastard beat her to a pulp and you tell me to back off. I know people who can help me track this motherfucker down.' The words were coming faster now. This wasn't the same reaction Natalie had met with a few hours earlier. Adam was far more emotive. He clenched the mug in his wide hand so tightly Natalie expected it to shatter in his grasp.

'Mr Brannon, last night I asked you about a baseball bat and you denied owning one. I'm going to ask you the same question now and I'd like the truth this time.'

He rested his forearms on the table and stared at her, then his eyes flicked to one side and he slumped forward, his outburst forgotten. 'Okay. Okay.'

'Do you own a baseball bat?'

'Yes. I have one.'

'Why did you deny it last night?'

'I don't know. It was stupid of me.'

'You must have realised it was important to my enquiries.'

'I didn't think of anything. Alfie had been taken away. I was messed up big time. You were asking all sorts of questions and I couldn't think straight. I was trying to get my head around everything: finding her dead, the writing on the wall, Alfie being there when it happened, and imagining what if the fucker had killed him too? There was so much happening and none of it felt real. I spoke to you, and all the time I could only see Charlotte's body on the bedroom floor. I was in a living hell. Besides, the police have interviewed me before in the past and not done me any favours, if you get my drift. When you're like me, you kind of get used to saying nothing to anybody. After my time in prison, I learnt to keep schtum if I got pulled, until I worked out what the police actually wanted from me. I get a lot of hassle from the cops. It's no surprise because I run a place in a rough part of town where tearaways and hoodlums hang out. Whenever something kicks off in the hood, the police come straight to my club and question me.

'Last night I couldn't think quickly enough. You fired off a whole bunch of questions and I couldn't answer them because I couldn't work out what to say in case something incriminated me. I'd already admitted I didn't find Charlotte until after Alfie started crying. That must have looked bad. I wasn't prepared to say anything else until I'd had a chance to figure out how to handle this, and now

I've decided I'm going to play it the only way I can – I'm going to be completely upfront with you. I didn't kill Charlotte. I swear I didn't. I spent all fucking night thinking about it and I know how it must look to you.'

'And how might that be?'

'Big bastard of a husband who's been in the nick before and is handy with his fists, bashes up his wife cos he can't control his temper – that's what it looks like. But I didn't. I didn't kill Charlotte.' He cricked his neck, bottom lip out defiantly, and bit back tears.

'Why do you own a baseball bat, then?'

His dark eyes bored into hers and he snorted. 'Why d'ya think? Insurance. If some fucker decided to break into our house, I'd be ready for him. I'm not the only one, you know? Check out the reviews for baseball bats on Amazon. Reckon you'll find they've all been bought for protection.'

'You're admitting you bought the bat for protection?'

'Yes, that's exactly what I'm saying.'

'Why not have security cameras and alarms? They're far less dangerous.'

'We have got alarms but if somebody decided to break in, I needed to be able to take charge of the situation. Alarms and cameras don't protect you if some motherfucker gets in and attacks you. They're deterrents. That's all. I've done time. I've hung out with guys who've broken into houses to steal stuff to sell for drug money. They're desperate. They don't care about cameras or alarms, and if someone gets in their way, they won't think twice about using the knife or the gun or whatever weapon they're carrying. They threaten people. The bat was there in case I needed it.'

'We found your fingerprints on it,' said Natalie, keeping her voice smooth.

'Yeah, and so what? They would be there, wouldn't they?'

'We also found Charlotte's prints on it.'

'Maybe she picked it up when she was cleaning.'

'Where did you keep the bat?'

'Under the bed. Oh, holy shit, I get it! She was hit with the fucking bat, wasn't she?' He smacked the palm of his hand down on the table with tremendous force, causing the table to shudder, and then pushed himself upright onto his feet. He backed away, waving a finger at Natalie. 'No, you don't! You do not fucking pin her death on me. I did *not* kill my wife. You check that bat out again and you discover some more prints on it and then you find who they belong to, cos I did not hit her with it.'

'Mr Brannon, please sit down. We have to ask you these questions. We believe the bat you own was used as a weapon and it's important we try to establish exactly what happened. Could anyone else other than you and Charlotte have known about it being there?'

He emitted a sound akin to a horse blowing air through its nostrils and dropped onto his seat. 'I don't think so. Look, I'm levelling with you. I know it looks bad but I've met some seriously warped blokes who get off on not just stealing your gear but cutting you or anyone in your family to get it. I don't trust alarm systems and surveillance equipment. There are all kinds of crazy people out there who can get through all that shit and I wanted to protect my wife and son. That's all I wanted to do. Fucking mental, isn't it? I bring in something to look after my family and somebody uses it against Charlotte. This is a complete fuck-up.' He stood again and turned his back to Natalie and Murray. It took a moment for him to be coaxed back onto his seat.

'Can I ask you about the financial arrangements in your house? We understand the house was in Charlotte's name and she had a substantial income from a trust fund.'

'That's right. Her folks bought the house and put it in her name.'

'How did you feel about that?'

'This is complete bullshit. Why are you asking me this? It doesn't matter about the house or how much money Charlotte had. It was hers. Her parents were rich. If you think I murdered her cos she owned the house, then you're off your fucking head.'

'Please calm down, Mr Brannon. We're trying to understand Charlotte and find out why she might have been killed. She was obviously wealthy.'

'So what? I don't give a shit about money. I never had any when I was growing up. Besides, I earn enough through boxing. I could have looked after Charlotte and Alfie without *their* help. We didn't need Kevin and Sheila's charity, but Charlotte, she was used to the nicer things in life. I couldn't argue with that, could I?'

'But you weren't happy about the arrangement?'

'Happy? To be honest, I wasn't that bothered. I was cool about it. It didn't matter whose name the house was in. We lived there. Together. I tell you what I really wasn't happy about. I wasn't happy that her parents kept muscling in on our relationship, treating her like she was still some precious teenager who'd never flown the nest, buying her expensive gifts, arranging for designers to come in and alter our home, transform it into some palace, and making out like I wasn't good enough for her. Stuck-up sods. They had no idea. Some tournaments, I can earn big money. Charlotte knew the score. Sometimes I bring in the bucks, other times I don't. She was quite happy about the arrangement. If I had plenty of spare cash, I'd hand it over so she could treat herself. I paid for all sorts of things and household expenses. I bought her things. She took her parents' money but not to put me down. She took it cos she liked having money. She loved spending money. We never rowed about money. She even encouraged me to keep the lion's share of my winnings to reinvest in the club, make it even bigger and better, and continue to do good for the community. She spent money on whatever she fancied – clothes were her big thing. She was mad about fashion and she looked great in everything she wore, so I didn't care about that either. We were actually really good together. I didn't kill her. I'd never hurt her,' he said, his voice now not much more than a whisper.

'How did you feel about becoming a father?'

'What sort of question is that?'

'Could you answer it?'

'I was over the moon. Alfie is my fucking universe. He's the cutest little dude.'

'But you don't change him, play with him, take him out or get involved in any way with him.' Natalie watched his eyebrows knit together.

'Who the fuck told you that? I do my bit.'

'That's not what I heard.'

'You heard wrong. I try to help out. I offered all the time, but she pushed me away. Charlotte was overprotective of him at times and wouldn't let me get involved.'

'Yet she allowed a friend's seventeen-year-old daughter to look after him while she went to the salon, or out with friends. That doesn't sound like an overprotective mother.' Natalie kept her voice level.

Adam's eyes narrowed further. 'What are you suggesting?'

'I'm trying to understand what sort of relationship you have with your son and work out why your wife didn't want you to be involved with him. You haven't once asked how he is. You haven't demanded to see him. He's your son, yet you seem happy he's out of the way.'

'That's more bullshit. Alfie's six months old. He isn't exactly waiting for me to play football with him or have a game on the Xbox with him when I get in after work. He spends most of the time asleep. What the fuck are you supposed to do with a sleeping baby? I haven't asked how he is cos he'll be fine. He's in care, isn't he? He doesn't need me at the moment. He just needs somebody to feed and change him.'

'He's *your* son. He's lost his mother. You're his world now.'

Adam shook his head. 'I'm not ready. I need more time. He looks too much like Charlotte. Every time I look at him, I'll think of her on the floor…'

Natalie noted the lines on his forehead and clenched fists. For whatever reason, Adam couldn't face his son at the moment. His reaction was strange. Natalie would have assumed he'd want to be reminded of the woman he loved, not push away his flesh and blood.

'Would you say you and Charlotte had a happy relationship, then?'

'Here we go with the "happy" thing again. What's the definition of "happy"? Is anyone happy? Are you happy, detective?'

Natalie sidestepped the questions. 'What sort of relationship did you have? Did you get along well?'

'I loved Charlotte. I love Alfie. What more do I have to say?'

'You didn't argue or you didn't ever hit her?'

He paused for a second, chin jutting forward. 'I never laid a finger on either of them.'

'But you argued?'

'All couples have fall-outs or rows. It's part of being a couple. We always made up afterwards.'

'What did you argue about?'

He heaved a lengthy sigh. 'Look, detective, I know what your game is. I never once hit my wife. We had the odd difference of opinions. She was quite single-minded. We'd disagree on a number of matters: the usual stuff that couples argue about. There was nothing wrong with our relationship.'

'How did you feel about her online presence, her blog?'

'It was what she enjoyed. She couldn't live without all that Instagram and blogging shit. I've got social media accounts too. It's quite normal to promote businesses online. She was far more into it than me.'

'Did you ever monitor her online social media sites to see who was contacting her, or who was following her blog?'

His mouth turned downwards. 'No. Why would I?'

'To keep an eye on her and make sure she wasn't flirting or having any online relationships with other men.'

He let out a deep laugh. 'She wouldn't do that. I told you, we were sound.'

'You didn't feel even a little jealous about her parading herself online in outfits that might be considered revealing?'

'Do you think Kanye West worries about Kim Kardashian being online? She looked great in those outfits. She had the figure for them. It was her vocation. She was working her audience to become a serious online blogger and earn money from what she enjoyed doing. She wasn't putting up pictures of herself to show off or attract male attention. You got Charlotte all wrong. And me. You got me all wrong too.'

'Then clarify it for me.'

'She and I were opposites. We bickered now and then but we loved each other. She wanted me to follow my dream and I wanted her to follow hers. We both loved Alfie. He wasn't planned or expected but he completed us. She was nuts about him. Used to sing him to sleep every single night. She had a lovely voice. I tried once but I only made him cry. I can't sing for love nor money. She sang him to sleep before we went out. Some lullaby she knew from her childhood. I could hear her as I got dressed. The last lullaby, eh?' He shrugged and swallowed hard. 'Yes, she was reluctant to let me muscle in, play too big a role in the little man's life, but she didn't exclude me. She was overcautious, that's all. She didn't want me dropping him, or putting his fucking nappy on upside down. I'm that boy's father and I love him. End of.'

'Did she talk to you about anyone who might have been stalking her online or hassling her?'

'No. And she would have if there had been. She knew I'd have sorted out anybody that gave her grief. She'd have told me if she'd been scared or worried about some weirdo. You think that's what happened? Somebody decided to stalk her and found out where she lived?'

'I don't have any answers for you at the moment, but rest assured we'll do everything we can to bring the guilty person to justice.'

He pointed his finger at her. 'Make sure you do, because I'm not going to let whoever did this to her get away with it.'

CHAPTER NINE

SATURDAY, 3 MARCH – AFTERNOON

Vitor Lopes, the barman at the White Horse, placed the rattling crate of soft drink bottles onto the bar, wiped his hands on his jeans and smiled at Lucy.

'Can I help you?' If there had been a Portuguese accent, it had been almost erased by a strong Brummie one.

'I'm investigating a murder and wonder if you can assist me.' Lucy lifted her ID card.

Vitor revealed startling white teeth made all the brighter by his Mediterranean complexion. 'And how can I help?' The smile was still in place, like a Cheshire cat's. Only the icy-blue eyes gave away his true reaction to her presence.

'Do you know Lee Webster?'

The answer was quick. 'Yes.'

'Was he here last night?'

'Yes.'

'Was he with anybody?'

'For a while he was alone. Adam Brannon came at ten fifteen and joined him for one drink.'

Once again, the answer was quick; too quick. 'How can you be so certain on the timings?'

'It went very quiet in here after nine thirty last night, which was most unusual for a Friday night. Lee came in at the same time as a large group was leaving, and we talked for a while because there was no one else to serve. Adam arrived later, ordered a pint and they moved across to sit over there.' He nodded at a table in the corner.

'And you're positive Adam arrived at ten fifteen?'

Vitor flashed an even wider smile and pointed a finger to his left. She glanced that way. A clock showing the correct time was hanging above a strip of peanuts.

'Are you friendly with Adam?'

He shook his head. 'I only pass the time of day with him when he comes in with Lee. I've watched him fight though. He's fast on his feet and has a good left hook. He runs the boxing club just off Ashmore Estate, although you probably know that already, officer. Heard good things about him. People are glad he's given the youngsters there a place to hang out and work off some of their frustrations. He comes in here about once a fortnight or so. He's not much of a talker. He and Lee are mates. I know Lee better.'

'How did Adam seem last night?'

'Normal.'

'Did he say anything to you?'

'Only remarked that it was dead in here and asked what I'd done to frighten away all the customers. Laugh a minute is Adam.' The smile didn't falter.

'And he said nothing else?'

'Not to me. He nudged Lee and suggested they sat down. I got on with collecting glasses and cleaning up. They talked.'

'I'm sorry to inform you, Mr Brannon's wife was murdered last night.'

The smile froze.

'So, it's imperative you give me correct information regarding Mr Brannon. You understand?'

'You saying I'm lying?'

'I'm not suggesting that. I'm asking you to think carefully and confirm that the information you've given me is accurate.'

He nodded. 'Yeah. It's accurate.'

'Thank you.'

'I didn't know his wife.' The words seemed out of place. Vitor grabbed the crate again, his biceps bulging as he raised it from the bar. 'You think he killed her?'

'We're currently eliminating people from our enquiry.'

Vitor nodded thoughtfully.

'If you think of anything that might help us, here's my number.' Lucy pushed a business card across the counter. She received a curt nod. He moved away, the bottles chinking in the crate as it bounced against his skinny hips. Lucy watched as he disappeared into the back room then took her leave.

Outside, standing in front of the shabby entrance, she pressed her mobile to her ear.

'Natalie, his whereabouts have been confirmed. He was with Lee Webster from ten fifteen until he left Lee's to go home, close to midnight. Barman also remembers them both being here at the White Horse pub beforehand.'

'Shit. We'll release Adam for now but I'll ask Ian to check out CCTV and ANPR cameras to try and locate Adam's car at around those times. We need concrete proof he was where he said he was.'

Lucy hung up, satisfied Natalie wasn't going to accept the word of two witnesses to Adam's whereabouts. That was one of the things she admired about her boss. She examined all the evidence and didn't merely rely on what people told her. She strode to her car and drove away.

Vitor was watching her movements from a window in an upstairs stockroom. He watched her car drive off and then dialled a number and spoke. 'Police were here. Yeah, I told them. You better bring that money in later today like you promised or I might have to change my story. You didn't mention murder, you fucker.'

Natalie paced the floor of the office once more. They'd had no grounds to hold Adam and he'd returned to his club. Ian and Murray were searching for any evidence of the two figures spotted running away from the Brannons' house around 11.15 p.m. and for any sign of the Bentley Bentayga which would confirm Adam's alibi. She checked her watch. Phoebe, Charlotte's sister, ought to have arrived at her parents' house by now. She considered driving over there to speak to the woman and then try to talk to more of her contacts. 'Ian, do we have a list of Charlotte's friends?'

'I'll print one out. I've nothing so far on the two figures running away from the house. I can't spot anything on the cameras.'

'Keep looking. We're going to nail whoever's behind this, and soon.

Her mobile buzzed and interrupted her thoughts. It was Pinkney, the pathologist.

'Courtesy call to let you know I'm almost finished with Charlotte. Time of death was between eleven and twelve last night. Charlotte died of blunt force trauma to the temple and fractures to the cranium, resulting in haemorrhaging of the brain. I'll email my full report over shortly.'

'Was she sexually assaulted?'

'Nothing to suggest that was the case.'

She thanked him and ended the call. She thought about Charlotte singing her baby to sleep. Natalie had never been musical, but she'd sung lullabies to both her children when they were babies too. Nowadays they only cringed if they heard her singing along to the radio. The printer whirred into life and churned out a sheet of A4 that Natalie grabbed. She read through the names and was circling the first few when Lucy stomped in.

'That Lee Webster is a complete wanker,' she said, eyes flashing. 'Repeatedly called me "love". I don't know if I trusted his answers. He could be covering up for his mate Adam. What's going on?' She directed her question at Ian.

'Still trying to get info on the pair seen near the house at around the time of the murder. The techies are searching Charlotte's phone and computer in case she met up with somebody from an online dating site or on social media, and we're about to talk to friends and see if they know anything that can shed some light on this investigation,' he replied.

Natalie looked up from the list and spoke. 'We've got a list of Charlotte's contacts. I've circled some of the names I'm going to contact, but I want to speak to Charlotte's sister, Phoebe, before I begin. Make a start on the others, will you?'

She rang the Hills' home phone to talk to Phoebe. She got Kevin Hill.

'Phoebe and Jed got held up in traffic. They've only just arrived at the house. I'll ask her to come to the station as soon as they've had a cup of tea. Sheila needs some time with her.'

'I understand that but I need to talk to her as well. Would you prefer me to come around?'

'No. We've got somebody from social services here too. We want Alfie to come home to us and, well, it's all a bit much. I'll make sure Phoebe visits you shortly.'

'Please do. Time is of the essence.'

'Yes,' he said wearily. 'I understand. I have to go now.'

Natalie stared at the black mobile screen. He'd hung up. As irritated as she felt by that, she'd give it an hour. If Phoebe hadn't shown by then, she'd head to Walnut Cottage and demand to see the woman, regardless of what was happening at their house. She'd use the time meanwhile to work through the list of friends. The first name on Natalie's list was beauty salon owner, Candice Westfield.

'I can guess why you're ringing,' she said as soon as she heard who was calling. 'One of my clients told me the police are still outside her house. It's so horrible. None of us can believe it.'

'I'm very sorry about Charlotte. I understand you were friends.'

'When I started up my beauty salon in Eastborough, she was one of my first clients. Used to come in once a week for a massage, treatment and manicure, regular as clockwork.'

'Candice, I need your help so try to answer my questions as fully as possible. Did Charlotte confide in you at all?'

'We talked a lot. You do when you're dealing with clients. You talk about all sorts of stuff: travel, television, boyfriends, everything really. She wasn't like my bestie or anything but she was really nice and I liked her a lot. She was always so glamorous. I follow her on Instagram and her blog. She featured my salon on it one time. She didn't tell me all her secrets if that's what you mean. We chatted – girly stuff.'

'Do you know her husband, Adam?'

'I don't know him, as such. I've spoken to him a few times when he's been in the salon. At first, he never came in. He used to wait outside like some sort of bodyguard, lurking by the window until she was ready to leave. He'd wait for ages. He's a scary-looking bloke but he's all right really – quite shy and romantic. He always put an arm around her and kissed her.'

'Did she talk much about him?'

'All the time to start with. She'd always be going on about him, his fights and his club. She was totally loved up.'

'You said "to start with". Did she stop talking about him?'

'That was when they first started going out together and got engaged. After they married and moved out of their old place in Samford to their fabulous new home in Eastborough, she mostly talked about the house. There was so much going on: her folks had hired a professional designer to furnish it for them, so we'd discuss what they'd chosen for the place… and clothes, of course.

Then, in February last year, she found out she was expecting. Her life was so exciting. She had everything.' Her voice trailed away. 'Poor Charlotte.'

'Candice, did she ever mention another man or suggest she was seeing somebody other than Adam?'

'Not to me. I can't imagine she would. She was mad about Adam and he was pretty much always by her side. I think she might even have felt a bit suffocated by him. There was one time when she was about to leave the salon after I'd done her nails, and he was waiting in reception for her. I heard her telling him to give her some space.'

'Did she seem different to you after Alfie was born?'

'Difficult to say because once she had the baby, she stopped coming to the salon regularly, apart from Thursday when she came to get her nails done.'

At the other end of the phone, Natalie's eyebrows rose. This seemed at odds with what they already knew. Inge had told Lucy and Ian that Charlotte often left her babysitting Alfie so she could go to the salon. She made a note to follow it up. Had Charlotte been making excuses so she could see somebody else?

'What time was that?'

'She had a ten a.m. appointment.'

'How did she seem that day?'

'Very quiet. Not at all like she used to be when we used to joke about. She brought Alfie into the salon with her. He didn't make a peep. Such a sweet baby. He gave me a lovely smile. She said she'd not had much time for herself since he was born. I figured she was like lots of mums I know – worn out.'

'She didn't mention Adam?'

'No, but I think he called her while she was here. Her phone rang and she made a tutting noise and then answered. I didn't deliberately listen in but she wasn't happy. She was very short with him. Responded in one-word answers, you know like you do when you're angry with somebody? Something along the lines of, "No…

I will… Tomorrow." I didn't pry. She rolled her eyes afterwards and said, "Men!" and we both laughed, then I told her about my recent holiday in Bali.'

The conversation with Candice had been enlightening. It seemed Charlotte had spoken to somebody while at the salon Thursday morning. They'd check to see if it was Adam. Natalie joined Lucy and, together, using the information from Charlotte's phone provider, pinpointed the call made to her mobile on Thursday between 10 and 11 a.m. There had only been one and it came from a local fixed-line number. Natalie rang it and found herself talking to an estate agent called Suzie Connolly. She introduced herself and asked about Charlotte. There was hushed whispering as Suzie spoke to another person in the office. She returned, her voice full of professionalism, and answered smoothly.

'I'm sorry, but we don't know anyone called Charlotte Brannon. You might try our colleague, Rob Cooke. He works here too, but he's out of the office this weekend. He's at a conference.'

'Do you have a mobile number for him?'

'I'm not supposed to give out personal details.'

Natalie was firm in her response. 'I'm heading an investigation into her murder and I'd very much appreciate your assistance. I need to speak to Mr Cooke and find out if he knows Charlotte Brannon. So, could you please give me a contact number for him, or do I have to waste valuable time and come to your office for it?'

The woman became flustered. 'One moment. I have to find it. I'll pop you on hold if you don't mind.'

Natalie was left listening to irritating Peruvian pan flute music. The woman returned after two verses of some song Natalie couldn't identify. She wrote down the contact details and hung up.

Rob Cooke didn't pick up so Natalie left a message for him and hunted through the police general database in case his name cropped up. It didn't. Her stomach growled, reminding her she'd missed lunch. She searched through her handbag and pulled out one of the bars of chocolate she kept for such situations; she almost unconsciously unwrapped it and ate while she tried to make sense of what they'd learnt so far. A report pinged into her inbox. It was from the technical team. They'd not found any dating apps or dating website activity on Charlotte's phone or laptop. They were currently searching her social media for any possible boyfriends or useful information.

Lucy was on the phone talking to another of Charlotte's friends. She put a hand over the receiver and mouthed, 'Nothing yet.'

Natalie swallowed the last of the chocolate and absent-mindedly brushed crumbs from her lap. She dialled the second name she'd circled. Madeleine Downley had attended the same school as Charlotte and her sister, Phoebe. She'd also learnt about Charlotte's death from friends on social media.

'It's all over Facebook,' Madeleine said. 'One of our old class-mates posted about it. He said the police were outside her house last night and her body was taken away in the early hours of the morning. Was it an accident or was she killed?'

'We can't release any details yet but we are treating her death as suspicious.'

There was the sound of breath being sucked in. 'Oh my gosh! That's so awful.'

'We're trying to build a picture of Charlotte. What can you tell us about her?'

'I haven't seen her since she and Adam got married. I got an invite to the wedding but I was on holiday at the time, so I couldn't go. I wasn't that fussed about it. We'd drifted apart. After school, I went to college in Leeds and she went to London. We met up a few times during holidays and after we'd finished our courses, but it wasn't the same as when we were younger.'

'What was she like?'

'At school she was, like, a right rebel. All the teachers thought butter wouldn't melt in her mouth, but Charlotte would be behind the bike sheds with the rest of us, smoking and showing her tits to whoever was there. We had some fun times after we left school too. Charlotte was always up for a good night out, or a party. She had a thing about bad boys too. I think that's why she ended up with Adam. She found out he'd been in prison and she was, like, fascinated by it. She went to his boxing club to watch him fight. Made me go along with her. She was all over him afterwards, making big eyes at him. It was around that time I stopped hanging out with her. She only ever wanted to go where she thought Adam would be but I wasn't comfortable with that. We fell out about it. She wanted me to double date with one of his creepy friends and I wouldn't.'

'She chased after Adam?'

'That was Charlotte all over. She always went after what she shouldn't have. She was spoilt rotten, you know? Her parents gave her and her sister everything they wanted. She only had to ask her dad and she'd get it. She used to joke about it. Sometimes she'd ask for stuff she didn't really want for a dare. We'd say, "Ask for a new phone," and so she would and come back with one the next day. She also used to try to piss them off. There was the time her mum told her she couldn't get a tattoo, so Charlotte did anyway, and a belly piercing. She was, like, mega-confident. You know those girls who don't look amazing, but they know how to put together really edgy outfits and suddenly they're like, wow? That was so Charlotte. She could make anybody stare at her just by what she was wearing. You seen her online photos?'

Natalie replied she had.

'Then you know what I mean. She had something really powerful about her. An attraction, that's the word. She drew people to her, like a magnet.'

'Did you know her sister Phoebe too?' Natalie was tiring of the upward inflection at the end of every sentence Madeleine uttered, making each sound like a question.

'Phoebe was too old and posh to hang out with us. She's nothing like Charlotte.'

'You haven't spoken to Charlotte in over a year?'

'No. I tried to get back in contact, for old time's sake. I messaged her on Snapchat and she sent a photo of her baby.'

'Then you have been in contact over the last six months?'

'Only that one time. She didn't keep up the conversation. No biggie. I have other friends and a life.'

Natalie tapped her pen against the notepad on her desk. Charlotte didn't appear to be the person everyone imagined she was. To some she seemed uber-confident and happy; to others, she was trapped in a love-lost relationship, feeling suffocated. Both Inge's mother, Sabine Redfern, and Charlotte's own mother, Sheila, believed Charlotte was having marital problems. She'd told Sheila her husband was becoming increasingly aggressive; Sabine, that Adam was having trouble bonding with his son; and Candice, the salon owner, thought she felt suffocated by him. Adam had vehemently denied the accusations. To his mind, he and Charlotte were in a sound relationship. Was he bluffing? Had Charlotte been telling the truth to these people?

Her parents believed her to be a loyal daughter who required their assistance and yet both Adam and Madeleine had affirmed Charlotte was playing them purely for money. Was Charlotte a manipulative, selfish individual who would happily say whatever she felt necessary to get what she wanted? Somebody was definitely lying. Maybe Phoebe could help Natalie get a better understanding. The room smelt of sweat and cheese-and-onion crisps. Natalie decided to get out for some air. As she rose to her feet, her mobile rang. The voice at the other end was concerned and breathless.

'I'm Rob Cooke of Cartwright and Butler estate agency. I got a message to phone this number and speak to DI Ward. What's happened? Is it Charlotte? Has he hurt her?'

CHAPTER TEN

SATURDAY, 3 MARCH – LATE AFTERNOON

'Rob Cooke, Charlotte's secret boyfriend, is on his way to the station,' said Natalie. 'Let me know as soon as he arrives.'

'You've got another visitor,' said Murray. 'Phoebe Hill, Charlotte's sister, and her fiancé, Jed, are here. He's gone to the drinks machine and said he'll wait outside in the corridor for her. She's in interview room C.'

'Cheers, Murray. I'll talk to her.'

Phoebe was immaculate, from her dark, groomed eyebrows to her perfect French pleat and her painted nails. As slim as Charlotte but with russet-brown hair, lighter brown eyes and sharper features, it was still obvious she was Charlotte's sister. Both could carry off any outfit but while Charlotte had an edgier, more flamboyant sense of fashion, Phoebe was more conservative. She tucked one neat ankle behind the other and sat, hands folded in her lap.

'I'm so sorry for your loss,' said Natalie.

Phoebe bowed her head in acknowledgement. 'Thank you. It's my parents I truly feel sorry for. That's why I'm here talking to you. They need to know what happened to Charlotte and for her killer to be found. They're in bits at the moment and all I can do is be there for them. I can't bring my sister back.'

'Have you any thoughts on who might have killed her?'

'Nobody springs to mind.'

'Have you been in touch with her recently?'

'No. She and I haven't been close for some time. We see each other at family get-togethers but that's all.'

'Have you fallen out?'

'Not fallen out, just not on each other's wavelength. I found her difficult to get along with.'

'Can you elaborate?'

Phoebe shrugged her slender shoulders. 'She was more adventurous… less cautious than me. She was by far more of a risk-taker. I wasn't her biggest fan. In fact, I was glad to live miles away from her.'

'You didn't like her?'

'Not really. Just because we're related doesn't mean we have to like or love each other.'

Ice formed around Natalie's heart. Her own sister, Frances, had said similar words before she'd left for good. She pushed the memory away.

Phoebe continued, 'Charlotte liked to push the boundaries.'

'In what way did she push boundaries?'

'In many ways: relationships, life. She tested us all. My parents stood by her but I found it better to distance myself. She was toxic. I couldn't put up with her wheedling or treating our parents the way she did. It was heartbreaking to watch her manipulate them and give so little in return.' She pulled herself into an even straighter sitting position and regarded Natalie once more. 'Charlotte was never satisfied. We had loving parents, money, opportunities and she wasted all of them.'

'Can you elaborate?'

'I can tell you she was a devious, heartless bitch. Does that make it clearer for you? She didn't care whose feelings she trampled over to get what she wanted.'

'I take it she hurt you?'

'Many times, with her lies and her stupid antics that caused my father and mother pain. She was accomplished at playing the innocent. Let me give you some examples: when I was twelve years old, I desperately wanted a pet rabbit. Finally, my parents bought me one and I loved it. I looked after it, cleaned it, played with it and fed it. I thought the world of it. Charlotte then decided she didn't want to be left out and demanded a rabbit too, even though she'd never wanted one before. She pestered and pestered my father until he gave in. She came home one afternoon from school triumphantly clutching a beautiful black rabbit, which she put in the same hutch as mine. Within two days, she got bored of looking after it, and instead of admitting it, or asking me to help her with it, she deliberately unlocked the hutch, opened the door and let both rabbits escape. I was genuinely heartbroken my pet had gone. Charlotte, however, blamed me for the open door and made an enormous fuss of her loss, cried endless crocodile tears and eventually, to calm her down, Dad bought us a kitten to replace the rabbit.

'It sounds like a silly, petty story but the point I'm making is when Charlotte wanted something, she got it and then she tired of it. You can't behave like that as an adult, and yet she did.' Phoebe was not paying attention to Natalie. She was lost in a world of memories and continued with more stories about her sister's selfishness.

'She decided to work in fashion but she had insufficient qualifications for such an ambition, so she cajoled our parents into paying for an online course in fashion design, which she gave up after a year. Then she persuaded them to pay for a course at a local college so she could learn journalism, and when she flunked that course, she convinced them to pay for her to study for a fashion diploma at the London College of Style. She managed to pass that qualification, and what did she do with it afterwards? Nothing. She messed about on Instagram and with a so-called fashion blog.'

'This sounds more like sibling rivalry.'

Phoebe pursed her lips. 'Yes, I suppose it might sound that way to you. I'm trying to create an image of her for you. You see, she bored easily and when that happened, she'd become reckless. When she was in London, studying at the fashion college, we shared a flat. She went out partying most nights and I never knew who she'd bring home with her: drug-taking dropouts, scary men with foreign accents, tattoo-covered louts with body piercings and attitudes. Charlotte was experimental. She slept with whomever she felt like sleeping with. She took drugs and she did other crazy stuff. Sometimes she was wild, uncontrollable. She'd take off with a stranger in the middle of the night on the back of his motorbike purely for the excitement of it. She'd jump naked into a freezing cold river for the simple reason somebody had dared her to. She got into some tricky situations too: out of her head on drugs and locked in a toilet because she was scared rigid of aliens, slumped in the back alley of a nightclub with some junkie mates, with no money to get home. I'd usually get a phone call from one of her so-called friends and have to get her. She did whatever took her fancy and never considered the consequences.'

'Why didn't you tell your parents about her behaviour if you were concerned about it?'

'She begged me not to. Promised she'd sort herself out. Claimed she didn't want to upset Mum and Dad. She was so contrite and convincing that I believed her. I *wanted* to believe her because she was my sister and I cared about her at the time. However, she didn't change. She caused all sorts of trouble, and on each occasion I sorted her out, fixed the problem and promised I wouldn't tell our parents. I was relieved when her course ended and she returned to live with them. By then, I'd got my position with Emirates and was travelling abroad a lot. I had the perfect excuse to have as little as possible to do with her. It was far better that way. I was tired of her games, lies and antics. She was untrustworthy and so were many of the people she hung out with. It comes as little surprise to me she has met her end in such a horrible way. She didn't only test me. She tested others too.'

Phoebe lifted her eyes and waited for Natalie to speak.

'Who do you think would have wanted to kill her?'

'If she was up to her old ways, then she will have annoyed those closest to her. I don't need to spell it out, do I, DI Ward?'

'You're suggesting her husband murdered her?'

Her shoulders lifted slightly. 'Maybe. Especially if she wound him up enough. She wasn't just a handful, she had a darker side. She killed the kitten I told you about. Yes, there was another, more sinister point to my story. She tired of the cat that replaced the rabbit and put a plastic bag over its head until it couldn't breathe any more, then cried her heart out when it was found dead outside in the garden. I didn't tell my parents. Charlotte always wanted to be the centre of attention. She is now, and for all the wrong reasons. I hope you find her killer because I want my parents to be able to put this horror behind them. It's going to be a long, painful journey for them and I blame Charlotte for that.'

'I understand your fiancé is with you?'

'Yes, Jed Malloney. He came with me. We only got engaged a few weeks ago, although we've been going out together since 2016. He's a drummer in a band – The Darkest Knights.'

'Where's he from?'

'He's American, from Connecticut, but he's lived in London for about ten years. Why, is that important?'

'Did he know Charlotte?'

She shook her head. 'He's barely spoken to her, only at a couple of family events. Like I said, I didn't have much to do with her so we never visited her and Adam.'

'But you saw your parents frequently?'

'From time to time. We invariably met up with them in London. They'd come down to see us. It's difficult to do stuff together when one partner is in the recording studio or touring and the other is on long-haul flights. Whatever free time we have we prefer to keep for ourselves. We certainly didn't want to waste any by hanging out with Charlotte and Adam.'

'Do you like Adam?'

'I don't have any feelings about him. He's always seemed okay. But, as I said, I haven't spent much time with him or Charlotte.'

'One last question, Phoebe. Do you know anyone called Rob Cooke?'

Phoebe looked directly at her and shook her head. 'I've never heard of him. My parents haven't mentioned him.'

Natalie thanked her for her cooperation and ended the conversation. Phoebe stood in one fluid movement and picked up a red cardigan that had been placed on the back of her chair. 'If you have any further questions for me, I'll be staying with my parents for the next few days.'

Natalie accompanied her to the corridor, where a young man with striking features, long blond hair and dressed in a leather jacket and ripped black jeans put an arm around her and walked her towards the exit.

She departed, leaving Natalie feeling discombobulated. It wasn't so much the icy tone Phoebe had used throughout the conversation that had taken her aback, or the thought that two sisters who, like her and her own sister, Frances, had once been close had come to hate each other, but the fresh knowledge that Charlotte had calmly killed a small, helpless animal. What sort of person was she?

Rob Cooke was hunched over in the seat, his silver-grey eyes now puffy and red-veined from crying. He held the plastic cup of water in long, pale fingers and stared at the contents, salty tears rolling down his cheeks, staining them, unable to control them. Natalie had called in Lucy to help her talk to the man who could barely string together a sentence at the moment.

He'd seemed composed when he'd first appeared, escorted by an officer into the interview room where Natalie was waiting for him, but his demeanour had altered as soon as he'd grabbed hold of her hand to introduce himself. He'd crumbled instantly.

'Mr Cooke, would you like us to call anybody to be here with you?' Lucy's voice was gentle.

He shook his head and snivelled. 'Sorry… be okay…' He heaved in gulps of air.

It took another full five minutes before he was able to speak again. He put the cup on the table and blew his nose with one of the tissues from the box Lucy had placed before him.

'I'm sorry,' he said once more.

'It's fine,' said Natalie. 'You've had some very bad news.'

He raked his fingers through his dark hair, a fashionable buzz cut at the sides leaving enough length on top to style with product. A dapper man with neat fingernails and eyebrows, slim and slight-built, he was a contrast to the masculine Adam. He dropped his hands onto skinny jeans and shook his head.

'I should have insisted on us leaving sooner.'

'Can you go into more detail, Rob? What were you intending to do?'

He lifted his reddened eyes. 'We were planning to get away from this area, go somewhere new where he couldn't harm her or Alfie – Scotland.'

'Are you suggesting Charlotte was concerned about her husband?' Natalie asked.

His eyebrows rose high on his forehead. 'Of course. You must know how violent he is? Haven't you looked into his past?'

'I think it might be best if you explain exactly what was going on. You and Charlotte Brannon were lovers. Is that correct?'

'We were in love.' He held up a hand, palm forward, and sniffed back tears then continued, his eyes never leaving Natalie's face.

'I met Charlotte at a coffee shop in Samford. There were very few seats available but there was space at her table. She let me take the remaining seat. We got chatting. There was a spark between us from that first moment. It became our regular haunt, a place where we'd sit and talk when I had a lunch break or time between appointments. We'd spend ages lost in conversation. Then one day, I noticed a bruise on her wrist. She laughed it off but I knew it was more serious than she was willing to let on. The next occasion we met up, I spotted she had a mark on her cheek, even though it was partly camouflaged with make-up. She insisted she'd knocked herself on a cupboard door, but her eyes told a different story and I extracted the truth, that her husband was beating her. He's a really jealous guy – a boxer by profession – and thought nothing of giving her a thump now and again. She was concerned about her son, Alfie. Adam was showing little interest in him and she worried for his future, living with a hostile, violent man.'

He stopped to take a sip of water. He shook his head sadly. 'Our affair began shortly after that revelation. She was too scared to leave him and terrified of what he'd do to either of us if he found out we were sleeping together. I wanted her to report him to the police, but she refused point-blank, saying he had friends who would cause us both serious harm if he got wind she'd told the authorities about the abuse. We were trapped. She couldn't leave Adam.

'We played the dangerous game of seeing each other whenever we could. It became more and more serious between us. Then, last month, we made the big decision to uproot our lives, head north and live as a family – me, her and Alfie. We were going to a little place on the outskirts of Edinburgh so I could get work in the city. We found a couple of cottages to rent until we found somewhere to buy. She decided it would be best to make our escape when Adam was occupied. He has a fight coming up in a couple of weeks and would have been busy training instead of checking up on Charlotte all the time. I guess he got wind about the whole thing.'

He released a pained, shuddering sigh.

Natalie spoke up. 'When did you last see Charlotte?'

'A week ago. We snatched a few minutes in the park.'

'And you talked about running away together?'

'You make it sound like love-struck teenagers who don't know their own mind.'

'I didn't mean it to come across that way.'

'No, of course you didn't. Sorry. I'm… well, you know. Yes, we talked about getting her and Alfie away from her abusive husband.'

'And did you contact her during the week?'

'Twice. I rang her on Thursday morning, before I left the office.'

'What did you ring her about?'

'She was going out to dinner with her parents at the weekend to celebrate their wedding anniversary. I told her to have a good time and to give what we'd been discussing some deep thought. It was time to leave Adam.'

'I was given to believe Charlotte's response was, "No… I will… Tomorrow." Can you explain that?'

'"No" was in reply to my question, "Can you talk?" I always started a conversation that way, so I knew if we could chat freely. '"I will" was in answer to me telling her to have a good time. "Tomorrow" was when she intended making preparations to leave Adam.'

'You said you contacted her twice.'

'The second time was Friday afternoon. I sent her a photo on Snapchat of the view from my hotel room as soon as I got there. I had a good view of the sea.'

'Where were you?'

'Isle of Wight. I was at an estate agents' business event about selling property abroad. It was held at the Fairfield Hotel. There were various seminars followed by a dinner and it went on until quite late, and then there was a final breakfast meeting at nine this morning. I left immediately after that meeting ended. Took me almost five hours to drive back. I have details here, somewhere.' He stood up and pulled out a wallet from his trouser pocket, thumbed through it and, sitting once again, passed a business card to Natalie. 'That's the organisation who set up the event. They'll be able to confirm I attended.'

'Did you usually contact Charlotte using Snapchat?'

'Yes. She discovered Adam was monitoring her other social media sites to see who she was talking to, so she stopped using them. He also used to regularly check her phone log and messages. That's why I rang from the office phone on Thursday. It was better to ring from a local landline number and less likely to cause suspicion than a call from a mobile he didn't recognise. Snapchat is the safest way to communicate. As you are no doubt aware, conversations are deleted immediately, so Adam couldn't find out what had been said between us.'

'Did you confront or talk to Adam?'

He shook his head. 'Never. Charlotte didn't want him to know about me at all. That was for protection. With him having no idea who I was, Charlotte and Alfie would have been safe living with me.'

'How long were you and Charlotte in a relationship?'

'Since the beginning of December. It'd be three months tomorrow.'

Lucy left the room to check the details of the convention. Rob sipped his water and stared into space.

'I should have intervened,' he said eventually. 'I ought to have reported the violence and got her and Alfie away from him. I'll never forgive myself for this. I could have saved her.'

'We haven't charged Adam Brannon. This remains an ongoing investigation.'

'But surely he's your prime suspect?' he persisted, eyebrows knitted together.

'I'm afraid I'm not at liberty to discuss the case.' She understood his confusion. It seemed logical that a man with a history of violence might attack his wife but Adam had told her he'd never laid a hand on Charlotte and Phoebe had assured her Charlotte was an accomplished liar. If this were true, perhaps Rob had been duped by her lies.

Lucy returned. 'Thank you, sir,' she said. 'I've spoken to Serena Holloway, the organiser, who remembers you checking in on Friday the second. She also confirmed you attended the seminars and the evening event. She handed out the name badges. She was there when you checked out this morning too.'

'I remember Serena. She had a nice smile. Told me to have a good day.' His hand shook as he sipped the drink again. 'Ironic, eh? There's nothing good at all about today. What do I do now? What do I do?' He lifted damp eyes to her.

Natalie shook her head slightly. 'I'm afraid there's nothing you can do other than maybe talk it through with friends or family.'

He dropped his head into his hands and sobbed. 'I wish I'd convinced her to leave him.'

CHAPTER ELEVEN

Natalie leant against the door and attempted to straighten her spine. Having sat for the last hour, she needed to release the tension in her neck and shoulders. Mike tapped against the glass. She sidestepped to allow him entry.

'Hi.' The voice was cheery but his eyes looked even redder than they had that morning. He tucked his shirt into his trousers. Natalie noticed the band had loosened on them. Mike had probably missed out on lunch too and was surviving on his usual diet of cigarettes and packets of crisps from the machine.

He waved a file. 'I have information regarding both Charlotte's and Adam's phones and their computer. There's plenty for you to sort through – Adam's contacts, messages we managed to retrieve, web browsing history and so on. Unsurprisingly, Charlotte was the main Internet user and appears to have spent at least three hours a day online, more if you add in all the time spent on apps. Technicians are still working through all the websites she landed on. So far, they're mostly fashion-related, research sites, celebrity fashion, popular culture and so on. She's not been on any dating sites and her phone has no dating apps on it. She has the usual social media applications with little to almost no activity on Twitter and Facebook since 2016. She's a big Instagram user, which no doubt you already know, and uses WhatsApp and Snapchat. She's got Uber and numerous shopping apps – even one for choosing the right OPI nail varnish colour – all the usual applications you'd expect to see on a twenty-three-year-old woman's phone. Adam, however, doesn't seem to have used the computer much at all. He has an email account he rarely uses. As for applications, he mostly uses a wide range of online games and fitness apps and WhatsApp. Most of the conversations are with his wife.'

'His mother-in-law said he was texting during the night out at the restaurant.'

'Techies didn't find anything for that night. Phone's as clean as a whistle. There are a few texts to Lee Webster, confirming meet-ups, some to event organisers and other boxing club managers to arrange fixtures, and messages to a couple of men, Daniel Kirkdale and Fahad Baqri, who we believe are sponsors for some of the kids who train at the club. Most messages are to and from Charlotte. Maybe Sheila was mistaken and he was scrolling through some apps or even playing a game that night.'

'Did you get any impression things were tense between him and Charlotte?'

'You'll see from the text message transcripts we printed and the chats we pulled up from WhatsApp, everything appeared to be fine. There seems to be plenty of affection between them.' He passed the file to Natalie, who opened it and thumbed through the first few sheets, scanning the conversations.

'They chatted a lot.'

'No more than a lot of young couples. That's right, isn't it, Ian?'

Ian looked across and smiled. He didn't mention he and Scarlett had split up and neither did Natalie.

'What about Charlotte?'

'She sent surprisingly few text messages. Her more recent conversations on WhatsApp, over the last six months, are pretty much limited to Adam, her mother and a friend, Frankie Miller.'

Natalie recognised Frankie as one of Charlotte's friends. Lucy had tried ringing her but she hadn't answered. Natalie would try her again as soon as she left Mike.

He continued to speak. 'Charlotte responds to all comments on her Instagram account and her blog, but she doesn't appear to be friends with any of her followers, and that is all I have for now. I'll let you get on.'

'Cheers. Talk to you later.'

'Francesca Miller, known as Frankie, twenty-five years old, works on *She Devil* fashion magazine. She's single and lives with her parents in Samford,' said Lucy. 'I managed to get hold of her at last and she's just arrived at the station.'

'Good. That's timely. I wanted to speak to her about recent conversations with Charlotte.'

Both Lucy and Natalie went downstairs to interview the woman who was dressed in exercise gear and a hooded top bearing a sporting logo. She wiped away tears on seeing the officers and hearing Natalie express her condolences.

'I'm sorry. It's being here at the station. It makes it seem so real. It was all over social media earlier. I rang her parents but I spoke to a woman who said she was a liaison officer and they couldn't speak to me. I went to the gym but I wasn't in the mood for any exercise routine so I sat in the changing rooms and cried. I'm going to miss her so much.'

Although Natalie was sympathetic to the girl's grief, she needed to crack on with the interview. 'When did you become friends with Charlotte?'

'We met at a nightclub in Samford soon after she'd completed a diploma in fashion, so that'd have been in 2014. She found out I was also in the business and we got chatting. She was setting up a fashion blog and wanted some pointers for it. I helped her out.

We became good friends after that. Before she married Adam, we hung about regularly then afterwards, we'd hook up at least once a month for a girls' night or even a weekend together.'

'What can you tell us about Charlotte that would help us better understand her?'

'Umm, she had a great sense of style? She wanted to try to break into the fashion industry but wasn't having any luck, so I suggested she took selfies wearing affordable fashion outfits and put them on Instagram, to get a following and help make a name for herself.

'I write for a fashion magazine and she gave me some inspirational ideas, and in return, I helped promote her from time to time in the magazine, maybe make mention of her blog, that sort of thing. She was desperate to work for the magazine itself, and she used to pester me to put in a good word for her. She was bored rigid at home and couldn't find anything to keep her stimulated. That was before Alfie, of course. To be honest, I wondered for a long time if she only hung about with me in the hope I'd get her a position at the magazine.'

'What sort of person was she?'

'Crazy, fun, wild, mad as a box of frogs at times.'

'In what ways?'

'One time, she decided we should buy the worst clothes we could from a charity shop and wear the outfits out clubbing, so she ended up in a pink velour tracksuit with army boots. On another occasion, she suggested we throw a dart at a map of the UK and we'd visit wherever it landed. It was two in the morning and we hitchhiked to Inverness. Got a lift in a Transit van with a guy from Hungary. And there was the time she insisted we went to watch an up-and-coming rock band performing in Stoke. After the gig, she and I sneaked around the back and blagged our way into their dressing room with fake press passes she'd made. She swanned right up to the bouncer on their door, waving her laminated pass at him, and got us both in. The guys in the band were totally taken in by us and they invited us to stay for drinks with them until their manager showed up and booted us out. Charlotte wasn't going to be put off. She headed to the hotel after them but I backed out. She rang me the next day to tell me I'd missed out on a great night. That was Charlotte – a party girl.'

'Didn't she worry that Adam would find out about this behaviour?'

'No. He was wrapped up with his boxing club and Charlotte did whatever she fancied. She wasn't in the least bit worried about him. He knew what she was like. He married her because she wasn't boring and predictable. He was even a bit turned on by it,' she explained, seeing the look of confusion on Lucy's face.

Frankie paused and gave a small sigh. 'She calmed down once she fell pregnant. She stopped coming out on an evening. We still met up in the daytime and went shopping together. Charlotte loved shopping. It was a drug for her. Even when she was expecting, she'd shop every day. She lost interest in her blog about then. It was a shame because I'd spoken to my editor about her putting together an article on stylish yet affordable outfits for pregnant women. Charlotte was perfect for it and my editor loved the idea. I couldn't wait to tell her, and when I did, she just shrugged and said she didn't feel like doing it. Said she was thinking of giving up her blog and her Instagram account. I couldn't understand why. It was nuts given she'd spent all that time building an online presence to get into the fashion industry and I'd just offered her the break she wanted. I was annoyed about that. I'd stuck my neck out and then had to tell my editor it was a no-go. I hated losing face like that. I challenged her about it and she said something about Adam not being keen on the idea.'

'Do you know her husband, Adam?'

'I certainly do. I was at their wedding. I was surprised at how quiet he was. He looks so macho and yet he was like a pussycat around Charlotte.'

'Did Charlotte discuss him with you?'

'Before they tied the knot, he was almost her sole topic of conversation. She was obsessed with him. After they married, not so much. That's normal, right? I have many other married friends who barely mention their other half other than to complain about them and lament the fact they're not single like me.'

'Would you say they came across as a happy couple?'

'Sure. They were okay.' There was a touch of hesitancy as she spoke.

'Did Charlotte share any personal secrets with you? Something that might be significant in light of her death? Was she having an affair? Was she worried about anything?'

'You never knew with Charlotte. She'd come out with an outrageous claim that was almost believable, and then crease up with laughter at my reaction. I nearly always fell for it. Then sometimes, she'd say it was true. For example, she told me she'd been in a porn movie, pre-Adam, but I didn't believe her on that occasion, so she found a clip of the film online and showed it to me. It was only a cameo appearance, but she'd been telling the truth. Another time she told me she'd murdered her kitten by holding a plastic bag over its head. I was absolutely horrified and then she burst out laughing at my shocked reaction and told me she was only kidding.

'We met up for lunchtime cocktails about a month ago. She really wasn't herself. I thought she was tired, what with having a young baby, but it was more than that. She downed her first cocktail very quickly and ordered another immediately. I asked if she was okay and she looked me in the eye and told me she'd been having terrible thoughts about killing her son. He'd been crying all day and night and by the second day, she'd got so annoyed and was so tired of his screaming she'd nearly smothered him. She was completely shaken up. Said she'd terrified herself for even thinking such a thing and that she wasn't fit to be a mother. She began crying, really crying. I hugged her and told her she needed some rest and to let Adam or her mum look after the baby. She agreed, drank the second cocktail and seemed to get over it. She told me I was a good friend and she hadn't got many of those. Then she asked if I could keep a major secret. When I asked her what it was, she said Adam wasn't Alfie's father then she caught sight of the look on my face and doubled over laughing. She was winding me up again. But now, I'm not so sure. For a minute, she looked really serious and worried. I think she really might have been telling the truth.'

Natalie got off the phone to Mike, who'd helped confirm what they'd just learnt from Frankie. She rested her palms against the desk and spoke out. 'Forensics have found Alfie's personal health guide record, or red book, in the nursery.' Natalie explained what it was. She'd had one for both of her children and had recorded their development as they'd grown. 'Alfie's blood type is B-positive while Charlotte's is A-positive. Mike also checked Adam's blood, which is O-positive. He says while blood groups can be complicated to understand, and children *can* have a different blood group to their parents, it's extremely unlikely that two parents in these two blood groups would produce a child whose blood group was not either A- or O-positive. Bearing that in mind, he's running a paternity DNA test on Adam, who he's pretty certain is not Alfie's father.'

Murray let out a low whistle. 'I wonder if Adam knew he wasn't the baby's father. Maybe that's what Charlotte wanted to speak to Adam about. Her mother said she was drinking too much and had something to tell him.'

'Would she have waited this amount of time before telling him?' Natalie asked. 'Surely, she'd have told him before now, or not at all? Why now?'

'She was being pressured into telling him,' Murray offered.

'Possibly so, or she'd decided she'd had enough of hiding the truth from him,' Lucy said.

Natalie gave a light shrug. 'We'll have to ask him. Sheila was certain her daughter wouldn't cheat on her husband, but it appears she was wrong because not only was Charlotte involved with Rob Cooke, she might have had an affair before that. Frankie couldn't give us any further details on who might be Alfie's father, but maybe Charlotte's other friends can. If Adam isn't Alfie's father, we need to establish who is.'

Ian rubbed his eyes and shifted uncomfortably in his chair. The team had been at it solidly since first thing and with hardly any sleep the night before.

'Right, that's it. Time to call it a day.' Natalie stood up. 'Get some rest and we'll reconvene at nine a.m. tomorrow.'

'I can hang back a while and check through more CCTV footage,' said Ian.

Natalie shook her head. 'It's easy to make mistakes when you're too tired. Give it a break and go home.'

Ian lifted his jacket from his chair and put in on. As he did so, Murray ambled over to him and whispered, 'Arse-licker.' Ian flipped him a middle finger.

Natalie, occupied with putting away the files, missed the exchange between the men. By the time she was ready to leave, only Lucy was in the office.

'What did you make of Frankie's revelation?' asked Lucy.

'That Adam isn't Alfie's father?'

'No. That she thought about killing her child.'

'She was just frazzled. I wouldn't read anything more into it than that. When Josh was two years old, he contracted a virus and cried non-stop. He wouldn't sleep; he wouldn't eat. He just screamed. There were moments when I wished he'd just pack it in. For about a week, I was completely sleep-deprived. It was bloody torture.'

'Yes, but you didn't think about *killing* your son, did you?'

'She probably only said that in the heat of the moment or she wanted to shock her friend. You heard what Frankie said. Charlotte liked to get a rise out of people. Don't focus on it. Adam said Charlotte was an attentive mother. She rushed off to Alfie whenever he woke up and cried. She sang him lullabies every night, for goodness' sake. It's unlikely she'd have harmed him.' Natalie didn't want to discuss it any more. Alfie was alive. Charlotte wasn't. This bore little relevance to the case.

Lucy buttoned up her jacket and marched out, bag slung over her shoulder. Natalie stood by the door and watched her retreating form. Lucy was overly anxious because of Bethany's pregnancy. The baby would be here in a few months and she was clearly worried about how she'd feel or react once it arrived. Tomorrow she'd be in a different frame of mind. Natalie thought about her own children. No, she'd never once wished them ill. Charlotte probably hadn't either. She must have been terrified somebody was going to harm her baby. She pulled on her coat and turned out the light, all the while thinking about what she'd unearthed. If it transpired Adam wasn't Alfie's father, then who was, and had they murdered Charlotte?

CHAPTER TWELVE

SUNDAY, 4 MARCH – MORNING

When Natalie woke she found David's side of the bed empty. She turned onto her side and squinted at her mobile. It was almost eight and she'd slept like a log. She languished for a moment in the warmth of the covers, easing herself into the morning. Outside, a car door banged and an engine spluttered into life. A dog yapped for a couple of minutes. The street was waking up. These were familiar sounds. The detached house in the small community of Castergate had been their home for many years. She and David had bought it when they were expecting Josh, and although they were in danger of outgrowing it with their children now both needing more space, it was still their home; a special place.

Natalie stretched and threw back the covers. A rush of cool air circled her bare ankles as she slipped them into the furry animal-face slippers Leigh had bought her for her last birthday. *Forty-five next December.* She needed little reminder that time was passing quickly. David was troubled by ageing more than she was. That was due to having lost a vocation he loved and plunging into an abyss of despair. He'd not managed to get any further full-time employment and his work as an online translator wasn't as fulfilling as his job with a law firm. He'd begun to turn the focus of his attention onto himself too often.

Her thoughts flicked to Charlotte. She'd had too much time on her hands.

She ambled downstairs in her pyjamas and dressing gown.

David greeted her with a smile and a mug of tea. 'Toast will be ready in a jiffy.'

'What's this? Sunday morning and you're up and about and making me breakfast. Where are the kids?'

'Still asleep. You looked done in last night. Thought you needed some TLC.'

She took the mug in both hands and sipped. It was exactly as she liked it. 'I got a text from Leigh. She was upset about not going shopping.'

'Yes. She had a meltdown. She wanted to buy some boots and some clothes from Superdry to wear bowling in two weeks' time. Said there was a group of them from her class going and, from what she said, I think some of them are boys.' He threw her a meaningful look.

'Ah, that's why it was so urgent. She wanted to know when we could next go and I can't commit. If I can't get time off, maybe I ought to let her get something online. What do you reckon? She needs some new boots.'

'Up to you.'

'I'm not too keen for her to shop online. I'd rather she tried clothes on in a shop. No chance then of having to return it or it not fitting properly.'

'I suppose I could take her if it's so important to her. Hasn't she got other clothes she can wear?'

'Probably but she obviously wants to get something special for the bowling. She's been saving her pocket money.'

David nodded. 'Okay. If you're tied up next weekend, I'll take them both to Manchester.'

'Thanks.' It was one problem she could put aside, allowing the case to have her full attention.

'My dad and Pam have invited us over for Sunday lunch.'

She suddenly understood the reason for his unusually thoughtful actions and behaviour. He'd agreed to the shopping trip without complaint. She braced herself for a spat.

'It's okay,' he said, holding up a hand. 'I know you're heading a murder investigation. I don't expect you to come along.'

She waited. There was more. She could tell. He was rubbing the back of his neck, a nervous tell that he was going to say something else.

'I understand you're busy but if you could drop by for half an hour, maybe. Just to show face. Her son's going to be there. Give me some moral support.'

There it was: David didn't want to go alone. He was unsure about how to deal with the new woman and family in his father's life. David was still a little boy at heart.

'What time are you due there?'

'Twelve thirty.'

'I'll see if I can get away.'

'Great. Oh shit! The toast.' He leapt towards the toaster, cursing as the bread emerged slightly burnt.

'It's okay. I'll have it like that. Slap some extra jam on it to hide the taste,' she said. There was no point in starting the day badly. She'd try and slip away for a short while. Her being there would obviously mean a lot to David. That's what relationships were about, giving and taking.

Lucy was online, scrolling through Charlotte Brannon's Instagram photos.

'Nice,' said Bethany, leaning over her shoulder and pointing to a picture of Charlotte in a 1980s stretchy black minidress with a lace neckline adorned with teardrops and rhinestones. She'd posed with her wide mouth slightly open, coral lips shining, and glossy hair scraped back in a casual fashion. 'That'd suit you.'

'Please tell me you're joking,' said Lucy. 'I don't do lacy and I certainly don't do bling.'

'You should try something like that. You'd be surprised how good it'd look on you. Make a change from your usual rock-chick style. Not that I don't love that look.' Bethany dropped onto the settee near Lucy and, balancing the bowl on her belly, spooned cereal from it. Lucy continued searching through the pictures. Charlotte's style was like her personality – it wasn't consistent. In one photo she'd be in gypsy-sleeved outfits with flowing skirts, and in another, a tight black leather skirt and crop top that exposed most of her flesh.

'Any idea what time you'll be home tonight?' Bethany asked, letting the spoon fall into the bowl.

'Sorry. You know what it's like when we're on a murder investigation, even on Sundays.'

'No problem. Spud and I will veg out and watch something on Netflix.' The baby had acquired its nickname only recently. Over a meal of baked potatoes, Bethany had mentioned it would probably have grown to about three to four inches in size at this stage of the pregnancy, more or less the size of the potato on her plate. Lucy had immediately named it Spud.

'You not seeing your folks today?' Bethany and Lucy often went around on a Sunday for a catch-up with Bethany's parents.

'They've gone to Devon for a weekend break.'

'We should do that too. Get you some fresh air.'

'I get plenty of air here.'

'I mean sea air. It'll be good for you and the baby.'

Bethany smiled. 'Why not? I'll find out where they're staying and we'll go down when you get your next weekend off. Best do it soon. We'll be full on when this little one is born.'

Lucy spun around and studied her partner. Bethany had large, serious brown eyes, long mousy hair and a nose she hated because it was hooked, but Lucy loved everything about her. Bethany was the gentlest, kindest soul she knew. Whatever her own concerns about raising a child, she had every confidence in Bethany. She'd be the perfect mother.

'Who is she?' Bethany asked. She rarely enquired about police work. 'She looks beautiful. Beautiful yet sad.'

Lucy hadn't noticed the sorrow in Charlotte's face before, but Bethany was right. Charlotte's smile never reached her eyes, and in some photographs she appeared wistful. 'Charlotte Brannon.' Lucy didn't want to give too much away. She didn't want to upset Bethany with any of the details and certainly didn't want to mention Alfie. 'She was murdered on Friday night. It's a tricky case. Can't seem to get any leverage.'

Bethany pushed herself up, empty bowl in hand. 'You will,' she said, dropping a kiss onto Lucy's head. She moved off into the kitchen. Lucy clicked onto Charlotte's fashion blog once more and read through a few of the articles going back to the start of the year. She noticed there was a gap around the time she'd have been three months pregnant, when Charlotte had lost interest in her blog before deciding to pick it up again. It married up with what her friend Frankie had told them.

She picked up the list of websites Charlotte had visited in the last month and glanced down it. Mike hadn't been kidding when he said there was plenty of fodder. Charlotte spent hours looking at almost anything and everything to do with fashion and make-up, along with searches for celebrities, fashionistas and top brands, amongst a host of other sites. She flicked through the list, hoping for something to catch her eye, but spotted nothing.

'If you need to be at work for nine, you'd better get going,' called Bethany from the other room.

'Shit, is it that time already? I lost track.' She switched off the computer and grabbed her black jacket. 'I'll see you later.'

'We'll be here,' said Bethany, who'd emerged from the kitchen, a hand on her belly.

'Bye, Spud!' Lucy blew a kiss to Bethany's stomach and raced off.

*

Natalie was surprised to find Ian already in the office waiting for her.

'I've spoken to all the residents at Maddison Court about security cameras. Only one family on the entire estate uses them; that's Mr Henry Knowles at number 14. I asked him to check his footage for us.'

'Where is his house in relation to the Brannons'?'

'Four doors down. It's closer to the main road than the other houses.'

'Okay. Good work.'

'Morning!'

Natalie spun around. Mike was leaning against the door frame, dressed casually in jeans and a light-blue shirt that brought out the colour of his eyes.

'Hi.'

'Hi. How's it going?'

Natalie gave a small smile. 'Piecing it together but not getting the full picture yet.'

'I have some information for you that might help or hinder your investigation. Hope it's the former. I had Adam's DNA sample expedited. I pulled some strings and it was examined overnight. According to the results of the paternity test, Adam is definitely not Alfie's father.'

'Thanks for that, Mike.'

'Not a problem. I knew it was top priority. I'm heading off now. It's my day to have Thea.' A smile tugged at the corners of his lips. Mike's wife, Nicole, had recently left him, taking their four-year-old daughter, Thea, with her. Although on the surface he appeared to be coping without them, Natalie knew from their chats he was missing them, especially his daughter.

'Then go and enjoy your day off.'

'I shall. If you need anything, Naomi is in.' Naomi Singh was one of the most dedicated forensic scientists on Mike's team. He patted the door frame lightly and then, with a farewell gesture, disappeared.

Ian looked up. 'You want me to carry on searching for Adam's car?'

'Please. We only have Lee Webster's word at the moment that Adam was with him on Friday night.' There would be some footage – a surveillance camera or ANPR point – that would confirm Adam went to the pub when he said he did, or that he left Lee's house at eleven forty and drove home.

She picked up the notes she'd made on Phoebe Hill. Something had been bothering her. Phoebe had talked about Charlotte releasing her rabbit and killing a kitten and behaving outrageously when she shared a flat with Phoebe in London. She'd complained about Charlotte spending their parents' money and these were valid reasons for her disliking or even hating Charlotte. However, in Natalie's experience, something majorly important needed to have happened for sisters to fall out to such an extent they avoided each other. After all, Charlotte and Phoebe had been housemates together in London long after Charlotte killed the kitten and let the rabbit escape. Phoebe had looked after her when they shared the flat and had kept her sister's secrets. What had happened to change their relationship? She and Frances had crossed swords on numerous occasions, but what had driven them apart had been serious – truly serious. Phoebe hadn't told Natalie everything. The more Natalie thought about it, the more she was convinced of that fact.

She entered Phoebe's name into a general search engine, not really expecting to learn much more about the woman. There were a few photographs of her with Jed Malloney. She recognised the blond-haired drummer to be the same young man she'd seen in the corridor the day before, arm around his fiancée's shoulder.

'You know anything about a band called The Darkest Knights?' she asked Ian.

'They're a rock group. Scarlett's a massive fan. Lead singer is Seth Thorndike. They were on one of those television shows where they battled it out with other bands to become famous. I didn't watch it but Scarlett did. I'm not into rock.'

'Am I missing something?' asked Lucy, sidling into her seat.

'Just discussing The Darkest Knights. Mike prioritised Adam's DNA for us and has confirmed Adam isn't Alfie's father.'

'Wow! That was super fast. He only got the sample yesterday evening.'

'Yes, he surprised me too. We really need to find out who is Alfie's father now. It might well be relevant.'

'Whoa!' Ian's voice rose.

Natalie's head snapped up.

'Got him,' said Ian.

Natalie raced across.

'The Bentley Bentayga,' said Ian, his neck flushing. 'That's Adam at the wheel.'

Natalie craned her neck. 'That's definitely him. When and where was this taken?'

'An ANPR camera close to the White Horse pub in Samford picked him up. Oh! That's not right. What time did he say he met up with Lee Webster?'

'Just after ten,' said Lucy.

Ian shook his head. 'Not possible. This photo was taken at ten fifty-five, almost an hour later. The car's headed in the direction of the pub, not away from it.'

Natalie let out a hiss. 'Bastards. They've been lying to us. Haul their arses back in here. Now!'

CHAPTER THIRTEEN

SUNDAY, 4 MARCH – LATE MORNING

Vitor Lopes, the barman at the White Horse, wore a look of distress on his angular face as Murray marched him down the corridor and into the interview room. Lucy was waiting there for him and motioned for him to be seated. Murray took up position by the door, thick legs splayed, arms folded, face impassive, like a bouncer on a nightclub door.

'Vitor, when I last asked you about Adam Brannon, you told me he had come into the pub at ten fifteen. Is that correct?'

'Yes. I think so.'

'You think so? Yesterday, you were quite adamant about the time of his arrival, pointing out the clock above the bar, as I recall.'

'Then it was ten fifteen.'

Lucy maintained an icy gaze. 'I have a problem, Vitor. We now know that Adam couldn't have arrived at the White Horse at ten fifteen. If he turned up at all, it was around eleven o'clock, and I believe at eleven you were shut. Now, how can you explain this mystery?'

He flashed a nervous smile. 'I can't. Adam was there at ten fifteen. I saw him.'

Lucy didn't respond. Instead she continued to stare at Vitor in silence.

Vitor glanced in Murray's direction. 'I can't explain it,' he said eventually.

Lucy eased back into her seat, spun a pen between her fingers and spoke casually. 'I can only come up with one or two explanations. Either you didn't see Adam at all that night and were covering for him, or you served him as you said you did, but it was after eleven. If it was the latter, then I'm afraid you were serving drinks after time and that's against the law. I'm sure your employers wouldn't look very kindly on that.'

Vitor's mouth twitched and he tried to smile. 'Maybe I was a little out with my timings.'

'Let's not play games, Vitor. You and I both know you didn't see Adam Brannon on Friday night. What I want to know is why did you lie for him? Who put you up to this? Was it Adam?'

'I don't know what you mean.'

'Oh yes, you fucking do. We can play this one of two ways. You tell me the truth or I have Detective Sergeant Anderson here march you down to the cells.'

'This is crazy…' Vitor began.

'Up to you. I'll count to five and then I'm out of here.'

'You don't understand. I can't tell you.'

'One.'

'He's not somebody you mess with.'

'Two.'

'He'll kill me.'

'Three.'

Vitor chewed on his knuckle for a moment.

'Four… and five. Goodbye, Mr Lopes.' Lucy stood up and walked towards the door.

'It was Lee Webster. He paid me five hundred pounds.'

Lucy turned towards him. 'I'm listening.'

'Lee said Adam needed an alibi. Lee came in like I told you about nine thirty on Friday night and asked me to say Adam was in the bar if anyone asked. I didn't know I was going to be giving him an alibi for murder. I swear I didn't know that.'

'Why did you think he'd need an alibi then?'

'I don't know. I guessed he might be cheating on his wife. Lots of guys do. Figured he needed me to stick up for him. Look, I needed the money. I don't earn a lot and it was an easy five hundred quid.'

'Oh, please!' Lucy's voice was full of exasperation. 'You expect me to believe your shit? He was hardly going to give you that amount of money to tell a few lies so Adam's wife would be put off the scent. You reckon I'm stupid or something? I think you had a bloody good idea of why he was asking for your help.'

Vitor held up his hands. 'On my life. Okay, maybe I thought it was because Adam was doing a job – a robbery – or smacking somebody up, like one of those little hoodlums he lets use his gym, but I never, for one moment, thought I would be protecting him from a murder rap. I didn't think it through. When you quizzed me, I had to stick to the story. You don't double-cross Lee. I rang him after you visited me. Told him I didn't want the money and didn't want anything more to do with this whole alibi thing. He told me if I said anything, he'd cut off my balls. And he probably will. You can't let him know I told you.' Vitor had begun snivelling, eyes wide with fear.

'You realise you could have jeopardised a murder investigation? A woman was murdered and you think it's okay to tell lies to protect somebody who might be responsible? Now you stay in that seat and give your statement to an officer who'll be here in a minute. Then, you're going to the cells until we decide what to charge you with. Got that?'

'Please don't say anything to Lee.'

Lucy turned smartly on her heel and walked out, leaving behind Vitor's pleas. Murray followed her into the corridor.

'Ouch! I'd hate to see you really angry,' he said.

'Oh, I'm fucking fuming,' she replied. 'That piece of shit has lost us time on this case and has been covering for a potential murderer. I'll find somebody to take his statement. You coming to interview Lee?'

'You bet I am.'

While Lucy was interviewing Vitor, Natalie, in the room next door, was facing Adam. He'd refused a lawyer and now avoided her gaze, preferring instead to look at a spot on the wall and remain silent.

'You're not making this easy for yourself, Adam. Come on. You're not stupid and you can see how it looks to us. You weren't at the White Horse at ten fifteen. I don't know where you were, but you sure as hell weren't there.' She nodded at Ian, who pushed across the photograph taken by the ANPR camera.

'For the recording, PC Jarvis is showing the suspect a photograph of his car, with him at the wheel, snapped at ten fifty-five on Friday the second of March. What do you have to say about this, Adam?'

Adam cricked his neck and stared ahead. 'I haven't got anything to say.'

'Do you deny this is you?'

He shook his head.

'Could you answer the question please, for the recorder?'

'It's me.'

'I don't need to spell this out, do I? Your wife was murdered. You have no alibi for the time it happened. Unless you level with me, you're in one enormous pile of shit. If you're as innocent as you keep saying, we need to account for your movements from the time you dropped off Inge until the moment this picture was taken. Where were you?' She spoke the last three words deliberately slowly.

He shrugged a response.

'Were you aware she was having an affair?'

Adam's eyelids fluttered briefly. 'No.'

'She was seeing another man and was going to leave you, Adam.'

'No. She wouldn't have done that. That's utter fucking shit. You're trying to wind me up.'

'It's true. We've spoken to her lover. They'd been seeing each other for several months.'

Adam's face darkened. 'I'd have known if she was.'

'Obviously not.'

'Who is he?'

'Didn't she tell you? Is that what happened, Adam? Did she taunt you? Did she tell you she was going to take Alfie and leave you, and you hit her out of rage?'

His voice was quiet. 'No. She said nothing to me. If she was seeing anybody, I didn't know about it, but I have no reason to believe she'd ever leave me. We understood each other. We were made for each other. I didn't hurt her. I would never, ever have harmed her no matter what she did or said. She was my universe.'

'For crying out loud, Adam. I'm not going to be able to help you if you don't open up. I want to believe you had nothing to do with Charlotte's murder but you're making it impossible. I'm at the end of my patience. This is your last chance to tell me where you were between ten and ten fifty-five.'

'I didn't kill her.' His voice was quiet. 'I swear blind I didn't touch her.'

'You can protest your innocence all you like, but I work on evidence, and at the moment not only are you doing yourself no favours by refusing to cooperate, you're putting yourself in the frame. You're leaving me with no other choice than to charge you with her murder.'

'But it wasn't me,' he insisted.

'There's only one way to prove that. Where did you go after you dropped off Inge?'

*

Lucy was still seething when she entered the interview room further down the corridor. Lee, with one leg casually draped over the other, cackled at the look on her face. 'You look stewed up, sweetheart.'

Lucy dumped the files on the desk with a clatter. 'Firstly, let's get one thing straight. I'm not called "sweetheart". I'm Detective Sergeant Carmichael. Got it? Right. Let's get down to business, Mr Webster. I'm going to charge you with perverting the course of justice and bribery, for starters. After that, I'll throw in accessory to murder. Any questions before I go ahead?'

'I think I might need a lawyer if you intend on throwing the book at me.'

'Then get one and make it quick.'

The cocky expression disappeared. Lee looked across at Murray. 'She's serious, isn't she?'

'Deadly,' Murray replied. 'Vitor's confessed, so you haven't really got a leg to stand on.'

'Fucking wanker. I thought he had more balls than that.'

'It appears not. So, in light of that, would you like to make a statement?' Lucy glared at the man.

'No, I wouldn't. Best get that lawyer, sweetheart.'

Natalie and Ian had been in with Adam for over an hour. He still refused to tell them anything. Natalie glanced at her watch. It was past twelve. She'd have to ring David and explain she wouldn't be able to go to lunch at his father's house.

'This is your final chance. I'm going to give you a few minutes to mull over what I've said, and if you still refuse to talk to me when I return, I'm going to charge you with murder. No more pissing about, Adam. I'm sick of playing this game with you. PC Jarvis will remain here if you decide you want to talk to me.'

She marched into the corridor and thumped the opposite wall with her bunched fist. She'd backed herself into a corner. If Adam didn't open up and she charged him, they'd be reliant on the scant evidence they had against him, which in turn meant it would be difficult to get the charges to stick. She might have just cocked up the investigation. She headed to the office to retrieve her mobile. Murray was going through paperwork.

'Any joy?' Natalie asked.

'Fucker won't talk,' said Murray. 'He wants a lawyer. Lucy's gone outside for a cigarette. She's pretty irate.'

'I'll speak to her. I know how she feels. Adam's saying nothing either.'

She collected her phone and took the stairs to the top floor, an open roof terrace where staff could grab some air or a cigarette. Lucy was leaning over the low wall, staring at the traffic below. Grey smoke curled around her ears.

'Some days I wish I hadn't quit,' said Natalie, nodding at the cigarette. 'Can't get a sodding word out of Adam other than he's innocent. I haven't told him Alfie isn't his baby. I was hoping he'd say something about it, but maybe he genuinely doesn't know. It's my last card and I'll have to play it soon. I'm really hoping it'll provoke a response and we can move on or I'm screwed.'

'That bastard Lee Webster won't speak either.'

'He's got to you, hasn't he? Let it go. He's a nobody. We'll break him. He's a bit tougher than some because he knows the drill, and he also knows how to push your buttons. Don't give him the satisfaction, Lucy. It isn't like you to get so wound up.'

Lucy dragged on her cigarette then stared at it. 'I promised Bethany I wouldn't smoke around her or the baby. I was going to give up altogether. Bought one of those electronic cigarettes but it was like sucking a pen.' She flicked the cigarette over the wall and watched it spiral to the ground. 'Lee reminds me of one of my foster parents. He was a bastard too. I'm having trouble separating the two of them. I look at Lee and I see my foster father's sneering, domineering face.'

'You want to let Murray take over? It might be better for you to disassociate with him. You can come in with me and try to crack Adam.'

'No. I'm going to break this fucker. He's made it personal by trying to wind me up.'

'That's not the right approach, Lucy.'

'It might not be but we need answers and I'm going to fucking get them.'

Natalie put a hand on Lucy's shoulder. 'Fair enough, but don't let your personal life or issues interfere with this. I don't want mistakes made because of temper tantrums. It's about Charlotte not you, okay?'

Lucy nodded. 'I know. I needed to blow off steam. I feel better now I've told you. I haven't thought about my foster parents in a long while. Brought back some memories I'd rather forget. I had a blip. I'm back in control now. I'll help Murray while we wait for Lee's lawyer to arrive.'

Natalie waited for Lucy to disappear before she rang David. She could hear Josh laughing in the background.

'Hey, you're cutting it fine,' David said. 'You going to be long? Pam's gone overboard here. There's enough food for an entire village. Smells great. I'm already on my third gin and tonic, so you'll probably need to drive me home.' He laughed. The levity was false. She knew David. He was only drinking because he was nervous.

'I'm in with a suspect. I don't know how long I'll be.'

'Is that Mum?' Natalie heard her daughter's excited voice in the background. 'Is she coming?'

David shushed her away and lowered his tone. 'Natalie, I thought we agreed?'

'I promise if I can get rid of him, I'll come over.'

'You won't manage it. I know you won't.'

'Look, I'm really sorry.'

'You always do this to me and the kids. It was only for half an hour.'

'That's totally unfair and don't bring the kids into this. You sprung this on me this morning just as I was leaving. Don't make out you're so hard done by. I always try to be there for you.'

'Well, obviously not on this occasion.' It was difficult to ignore the hurt in his words; however, it couldn't be helped. The murder investigation took priority and he shouldn't need her to hold his hand.

Irritated by his sulkiness, she let rip. 'Sometimes, David, it's bloody impossible! Today is one of those days. It's Sunday lunch at your father's house not a life or death situation. Cut me some slack. I said I'd try and come over if I get through this interview.'

There was a pause before he spoke again. The petulance was still there. 'I'll tell Dad you can't make it. We'll have to get a taxi home. I've been drinking so I can't get behind the wheel.'

'I'll try to come over and pick you up later, then. Stay there for a while longer. Get to know Pam and her son more.'

'No. Don't bother. I'll sort it.' He ended the call, leaving Natalie feeling annoyed and at the same time shitty about letting him and the kids down. She shoved the phone in her jacket pocket and stared at the cars trundling past on the road below her. A voice made her turn around. It was Murray.

'Just had a call from a bloke called Henry Knowles. He lives near the Brannons. He's been through the footage on his security camera and says it's picked up two youths running past his house at eleven twenty-one on Friday night. One of them's carrying what looks like a piece of metal pipe.'

CHAPTER FOURTEEN

The video footage was playing on Lucy's monitor when Natalie rushed into the office. Two individuals in dark clothing as the neighbour, Margaret Callaghan, had described, ran past the camera, which was directly aimed at the entrance to the property's drive. One turned his head and shouted something to his companion, allowing a brief glimpse of his face. He was wielding a length of steel pipe in his left hand. Natalie checked the time on the digital display at the top left of the screen. The pair had passed the house in the direction of the road at 11.21 p.m.

'Can we make that image clearer?' asked Natalie.

'I'll see if I can enhance it,' Lucy replied. She fiddled with the control buttons, clicking on various sliding tools. Natalie watched as the face darkened, lightened and grew slightly. The suspect appeared to have dark eyes, razor-sharp cheekbones and an aquiline nose. 'This is the best I can do. I can't get it any clearer.'

'It's not much to go on, is it? Print it off all the same. We'll see if Adam can identify him.'

'Can't get vision on his mate at all. Could be anyone. Just shots of his back.' Lucy zoomed in and out of various stills to no avail.

'We'll work with the slightly sharper image. It's not great but somebody might recognise them.'

'I'll get some copies of it run off,' said Lucy.

'I was also thinking about how to handle Adam and Lee. Adam isn't cooperating. He's definitely covering up something from Friday night, even if it isn't his wife's murder. The technicians were positive his phone was clean. It all seems a bit too tidy, too organised. Sheila Hill claimed he was texting throughout the meal and Charlotte reprimanded him for it, yet there was nothing on his phone. I suspect he might own a second phone – a burner phone.'

Lucy looked up, her head cocked to one side. Natalie continued.

'He was really keen to get away from his house and spend the night at his office rather than at a hotel or with his so-called friend Lee. He might have wanted to use the time to arrange an alibi and the only way he could have done that was by using a phone. Or a computer,' she added.

'He might have sorted out his alibi with Lee and Vitor beforehand and actually killed Charlotte.'

Natalie nodded. 'That's true but he keeps denying murdering her and saying he's innocent. If that's the case, he can only have organised it after he discovered Charlotte. There was nothing on his phone to indicate he'd got in touch with anyone and it was confiscated as soon as the forensic team arrived, leaving him with no way of contacting anyone. My gut says he rang Lee or Vitor from his office. I'm requesting a search warrant for the premises. See if we can flush something out there. He and Lee can stew for a while longer.'

The boxing club was simply called 'Adam's'. Set on a run-down, disused, small industrial park, at first sight it appeared to be no more than a warehouse, but once inside, it proved to be a vast space containing a full-sized boxing ring and, behind that, workout stations: free-standing weights stacked on racks, a multigym machine for working groups of muscles, punch bags hanging from hooks fitted into wooden crossbeams, three huge plastic boxes containing skipping ropes, boxing gloves and pads, and next to them a pile of worn floor mats. It was a basic gym, lacking in sophisticated equipment. A pungent smell of sweat hung in the stuffy atmosphere. Natalie wrinkled her nose at it.

'Reckon Adam or somebody's been training recently. He could do with some air con,' said Murray, waving a hand in front of his nose. 'I've trained in some affordable gyms in my time, but this is pretty crude by comparison. A spit and sawdust gym.' He examined one of the faded, ripped padded seats on the multigym. 'He didn't invest a lot of money in this. The equipment is second-hand.'

'He's running a free gym for juveniles and adults on low income who can't afford to join a club or gym. I don't suppose he wants to make it too five-star.'

'Nah, this is tatty stuff. I don't think he has much income to support it.'

They moved through a door past a toilet and shower, tiled floor to ceiling and in need of a deep clean.

'Is grubby-white an actual tile colour?' Murray quipped. 'Christ, this is a far cry from his house, isn't it?'

Natalie agreed. The place was filthy and obviously in need of money for improvements. She left the room and tried a door which opened into a long, narrow room. The stale smell was strongest here. Several posters were stuck on the magnolia walls in an attempt to brighten them. Each advertised a boxing match, Adam's name emblazoned on them, and in two of them, a photo of the man himself, gloves up, adopting an aggressive pose, dark eyes narrowed for the camera. On the left stood an empty wooden desk and to the right, an open sofa bed, bedding left in a heap, as if somebody had just got up. There was a cupboard opposite the bed, door slightly ajar, inside which hung training kit: jogging bottoms, zip-ups and vests. A pair of trainers had been left beside it. Natalie looked around. There was nothing else. She patted the pockets of the jackets but they were empty; lifted the trainers and tipped them upside down, but again nothing was hidden inside them. Murray rifled through the bedding, a scowl on his face.

The desk caught her eye. It had only three drawers. She pulled open the top one and found it stuffed with receipts and a notebook. She rummaged through it. It was Adam's attempt to keep track of expenditure. Murray was right. There wasn't a great deal of income. The second drawer contained some fitness magazines and the bottom drawer a set of glasses and a half-drunk bottle of vodka.

'Nothing. I was sure he'd have another mobile or even some other equipment to connect to the Internet,' said Natalie, slamming the drawer shut.

As she did so, she remembered the other desk in his games room at their house. He'd hidden a key in it. Would he? She opened the top drawer again and, kneeling down, felt along its top edge. Her fingers lighted on an object stuck to the underside. Teasing the tape, she released it.

'Eureka,' she said, a smile creeping across her face.

'We'd like to talk to you again about your whereabouts on Friday evening between ten and eleven,' said Natalie, breezily. Ian sat beside her next to the recording device. 'Before we do so, I'm offering you the chance to contact a lawyer.'

'I don't want a lawyer. I haven't done anything wrong,' Adam insisted.

'Fair enough. Let's start with this.' She pushed a plastic bag containing the mobile phone towards him.

Ian explained what was happening for the recording. 'DI Ward is showing Adam Brannon an iPhone 6S in black.'

'I don't know what you expect me to say.'

'Is this your phone?'

'Could be. The forensic team took mine away so I don't know if that's it or not. They all look very similar.'

'This particular phone was not the one you handed to the police. That was, in fact, this phone.'

'DI Ward is showing Mr Brannon another iPhone 6S in black.'

'We found this one taped to the underside of a drawer in the desk in the office of your boxing club.' She tapped the relevant phone with her forefinger.

The muscles in Adam's jaw flexed.

'We've been through your records: contacts, messages and so on. It appears you've been having an affair with someone called Sugar, Mr Brannon. Would you like to make any comment?'

'No.'

'You may have thought in deleting any messages we wouldn't be able to find them. Unfortunately for you, we have a dedicated and highly trained team of technical staff who've resurrected all your recent ones.' She gave him a tight smile, which he ignored.

'I see from your texts that you were having a conversation with your lover while at dinner with your wife and in-laws. Quite a raunchy conversation at that.' Natalie selected a piece of paper from an open manila file in front of her. She cleared her throat and read, 'First message received at eight p.m. "Bored off my tits. Shall I send you a photo of them?" Your response: "If you do, I'll get a hard on and scare my MIL!" Another message received ten minutes later: "I'll send a photo of me licking an ice cream then. Yum." "Fuck. The thought of your mouth on my cock is making me squirm." Want me to continue?'

'I know what the text messages said. You have no right to read them or take my phone.'

'Mr Brannon, I have every right. Charlotte was murdered on Friday night after you dropped her off and left her at your home. I don't especially care about your affair, or relationship with this person, but the fact you were, or still are, involved in one gives rise to concern. You professed to love your wife; that you and her "were sound", yet during a family celebratory meal, while sat with her and other family members, you exchanged several suggestive messages with somebody else by the name of Sugar. Once again, it's helping to paint a picture for us: of a man who actually didn't care for his wife, or her family; who wanted to spend time with his mistress. If you add into that mix the fact your wife was wealthy and you, Mr Brannon, will undoubtedly inherit that wealth, I'm afraid we are being led inextricably to one conclusion alone, and that is that you were responsible for her murder.'

Natalie let her words sink in. Adam's eyes flitted around the room. He was becoming uncomfortable. Natalie finally had him against the ropes.

'And as you know, Mr Brannon, there were other text messages on that phone: messages to Lee Webster, sent in the early hours of Saturday morning, asking him to procure an alibi for you for Friday night. Begging him to sort out somebody else who was reliable and stating you'd pay that person five hundred pounds to say he'd seen you before eleven p.m. Lee's response was that he'd convinced the barman at the White Horse, Vitor Lopes, to testify you'd been in the pub all that time. Have you anything to say about that?'

'No.'

Natalie maintained the smile and nodded slowly. 'We have Lee Webster in the other interview room and he confessed a short while ago.'

'He wouldn't.'

'He had no choice. Not in light of what was on that phone – your phone. His own has been taken away and is currently being examined, and soon we'll have even more evidence pointing at the both of you. Now might be a good time to ask for a lawyer.'

'I don't want one.'

'I'd get one if I were you, unless you can tell me who was sending you racy messages and explain where you really were on Friday night before you went home and found your wife dead.'

Adam remained silent. Natalie only had one card left to play and she hoped her timing was right. She needed Adam to crack. She waited a few moments, all the while studying his face before speaking.

'New evidence has come to light. Evidence regarding Alfie.'

He flinched immediately. He understood what she was alluding to.

His thick fingers knotted together, knuckles whitening. 'I know,' he said quietly.

'Know what?'

'Alfie isn't mine.'

'That's a big admission and one that casts further doubts on your innocence. You understand that, don't you?'

'I knew he wasn't mine but I loved him.'

'Come, come, Mr Brannon. That's most unlikely. How could you love him when every time you looked at him, you'd be reminded your wife cheated on you?'

'It wasn't like that.'

'Charlotte slept with another man. She fell pregnant by somebody else and you just held up your hands and said it was okay? I hardly think so.'

His eyes glowed. 'You understand nothing. When Charlotte told me we were having a baby, I was stoked. Really overjoyed. I watched as her belly swelled and I grew to love him even before he was born. I was at his birth. The midwife put him in my arms first. He was so tiny, so bloody tiny, but perfect, you know? And he opened his eyes and looked straight at me, and in that instant, something exploded in me like my heart was a huge, happy firework. I'd only ever loved Charlotte and now there was this little man who was looking at me and relying on me. I was his protector. I was his world. You get that? Me. Adam. I was that boy's daddy and I made a promise to him that day I'd never let anyone hurt him like I was hurt, and I'd never let him get into any trouble, and I'd be there for him through absolutely everything, no matter what.'

Sheila Hill knew Charlotte had something to tell Adam but if he already knew Alfie wasn't his baby, what else could it have been? Natalie wondered what it might have been. The actual name of the father perhaps or that she'd been sleeping with Rob?

He paused, shaking with emotion. 'Charlotte told me the truth two months after he was born. I was complaining about her pushing me away from him and not letting me help out. She sat me down and she told me I wasn't the boy's biological father but I *was* his real daddy.'

'And you were okay about that?'

'See, you still don't get it, do you? No, I wasn't okay about it. Of course I wasn't okay about it. She'd shagged some bloke and it was his kid I was trying to rock to sleep and whose fingers I was holding. But Charlotte, she was so repentant. She didn't even know who the guy was. It had been a blur. She'd been out of her head on drugs at the time. You bet I was furious with her and all the time she kept saying she was sorry, she didn't know why she'd done it and she loved only me. It was a shit time. I was going to leave her. I was going to leave them both but when it came to it, I couldn't. I'd made a promise to Alfie. It felt like he was my son. Nothing had really changed between him and me. He still needed me to look out for him and guide him. If I left him, I'd be doing what my dad did to me. I'd be turning my back on him and I couldn't do that.'

'And Charlotte, how did you feel about her after this revelation?'

'Charlotte was full of spirit and fight and determination. She was wild when I met her. She was Charlotte and I married her for better or worse. I knew in my heart I'd always expected her to do something crazy and she had, but she loved me and I needed her. I couldn't leave her.'

'Yet you are having an affair.'

'It's sex. That's all. I figured Charlotte owed me some fun time. Plenty of men have affairs and still love their wives. I loved her and I still love Alfie. When I get my head straight, I'll look after him on my own. I'll be his father. I don't want him to have a life like I had. I'll work it out somehow. I genuinely didn't hold any of it against Charlotte.'

'That's not how it will look to a jury. They'll assume you had a blazing row with Charlotte and attacked her. There are witnesses who will testify you didn't help out with him and you weren't bonding with him. She not only had one affair and a child by that man but she was seeing another man behind your back. You really are stuck between a rock and a hard place unless you come clean. Tell us where you were the night she died.'

Adam ran his tongue across dry lips. 'Was Charlotte really seeing another bloke?'

'Someone has come forward, yes.'

'Fuck. Who is he?'

'It's not relevant.'

'It is to me. Oh, man, I can't believe this shit. I thought we were over that. She said she only loved me and would never look at anyone again. How the fuck could she do that?' He tipped his head back and sighed heavily. 'Okay. I'll tell you, but she absolutely had nothing to do with what happened to Charlotte. I want to make that clear. You mustn't go after her.'

'I'm waiting.' Natalie sat back in her seat and folded her arms.

'Inge. I've been seeing Inge Redfern, our babysitter.'

CHAPTER FIFTEEN

SUNDAY, 4 MARCH – LATE AFTERNOON

'I had to release him for now. We need to talk to Inge Redfern,' said Natalie. She faced her team. 'She can confirm his whereabouts.'

'Why couldn't he have come clean before?' asked Lucy.

Natalie lifted her hands up. 'He claims Inge's scared witless we'll think she's to blame for the attack on Charlotte and claim she carelessly left the door open that night, thus giving the person or persons responsible entry to the house. He says he was only protecting her. And she's terrified of her parents finding out about their affair. He was trying to prevent that from happening.'

'You're kidding.' Murray shook his head in disbelief.

'That's what he said. He decided to keep quiet about his relationship with her because he didn't think it was relevant to our enquiries.'

'Bloody idiot,' Murray snarled.

'I agree. The way I see it, it's not merely a question of us blaming Inge for leaving the front door open. We can't rule out the possibility she's actually responsible for Charlotte's death. She was the last person to see Charlotte *and* she was having an affair with her husband. For all we know, she could have deliberately left the door open for somebody to get in and attack Charlotte on her behalf.' Natalie rested her hands behind her head. Tension was rising in her neck.

'Did Adam recognise the men running away in the photograph?' asked Murray.

'He said it looked like half of the kids that use the club, and some others that live on the estate near it, and that it wasn't clear enough for him to identify either suspect,' said Natalie.

Ian added his thoughts. 'He could be lying given he's lied about so much already. You'd think he'd want to know who killed his wife and help us hunt them down, but all he's done is cover his own back and protect his girlfriend, which goes against what he said from the off. At first he was all for tracking down the attacker and sorting them out. I can't figure him out. What the fuck's wrong with him? If anyone harmed my girlfriend, I'd be desperate to get justice. Wouldn't you, Murray?'

'Yeah. Guy's a total wanker,' Murray said in an unusual display of solidarity.

Lucy joined in. 'Lee Webster couldn't identify that pair from the CCTV pictures, but I don't trust him either. He's sticking to his new story that Adam met him outside the White Horse at just before eleven p.m. and went home with him for a drink.'

'Any way he can prove that?' Murray asked.

'I didn't find anything on the cameras to support that,' said Ian.

'Ask the tech team if they can enhance that photo of the two suspects and we'll show it to them both again. Keep checking the camera footage too. Margaret Callaghan, the neighbour, saw Adam's car pull up on his drive. Before that, she saw the two youths running down the road, and we know that would have been at eleven twenty, so the difference in time from them leaving and Adam arriving was however long it took her to drink a mug of warm milk and read an article in a magazine,' said Natalie.

Ian offered his opinion. 'If Adam left Lee's at eleven forty as Lee says he did, then that would be about right. It would only take about five minutes from Lee's flat to the Brannons' house at that time of night. It depends on whether Lee is telling the truth this time.'

Natalie spoke once more. 'His lawyer insisted he be released, so at the moment we have no suspects and are now searching for the identities of two individuals, one of whom we can barely make out and the other we can't see at all from the picture we have.'

She drew a breath. 'We have to keep working. Grab half an hour for some food and take a few minutes out. Let our minds clear a little. After that, Murray, talk to Lee's neighbours and the residents near the street where he lives. See if anyone spotted a Bentley Bentayga parked there Friday night between eleven and eleven forty p.m. It's a noticeable car. Someone might have seen it. Lucy, you up for interviewing Inge with me?'

'Count me in.'

'Ian, I'll leave you to deal with that picture. If we can't get any names from Adam or Lee, we might have to go public on this and release the photograph to the media.'

Natalie headed off to the vending machine downstairs. As she waited for a packet of crisps to be grabbed and dropped and a black coffee to be discharged, her phoned buzzed. It was David. She sighed.

'Hi.'

'Don't bother going to my dad's. We got a taxi home.'

'I'd have come and got you.'

'No need now, is there?' His voice was slightly slurred. 'So now you can stay at the station as long as you like.'

'David, it's not about me wanting to stay here. It's a murder investigation. You're being completely unreasonable. You've had too much to drink and I don't want to discuss this now. I'm really busy and I can't waste time having a pointless argument with you. We'll talk later.'

'Whatever.' He ended the call. Natalie groaned. The bloody alcohol had made him insufferable. It was only a fucking meal with his father. She walked over to the full frontage glass windows, rested her forehead against the cool glass and shut her eyes momentarily. The dying sunrays in the low sky bounced off the buildings opposite and strobed in front of her eyelids. The day was stretching into evening and she was no closer to finding the person responsible for murdering Charlotte. She reopened her eyes and watched as lines of dark vehicles crawled past the headquarters, their occupants heading back to warm homes and television programmes and video games. She thought of Mike driving his daughter Thea back to his ex-wife's house and hoped he'd enjoyed his day off.

She lifted the plastic cup, drank the tepid liquid and braced herself for a long night.

Lucy drove the short distance to Brompton. Natalie was thoughtful as they overtook cars with bikes attached to their rears and camping cars now returning from the ever-popular Peak District, back to towns and estates where they'd be parked up for another week until the weekend trippers would go travelling again.

'You believe him?' Natalie said out loud. 'You think he was telling the truth about Adam being with him from eleven until eleven forty?'

'Lee? I think he'd say anything to muddy the waters. His type like making it difficult for the police. He's one of those sorts with a perpetual chip on his shoulder. He did wrong and got banged up for it, but thinks he was the one ill done by. He hates his life and his job and he blames society rather than himself. At least, that's my take on it.'

'He's sticking up for Adam, isn't he?'

'Honour among thieves or whatever the expression is. He seems to be standing by him. Told me Adam was good to him in jail. Kept an eye out for him.'

Natalie made a non-committal noise. 'That's what I figured. If Adam was with Inge from ten until almost eleven, there's still a chance he returned home, killed Charlotte and then went out for a while to clean himself up. Or Inge and Adam were in it together.'

'You think that's likely?'

Natalie opened her eyes. 'Honestly, I can't call it. If we could locate a witness and ensure his alibi was airtight, it would really help us. In my opinion, Lee isn't reliable enough. If we knew for certain, we could turn our attention to those two individuals running off down the street. At present, we can't do anything other than follow every lead and chase after shadows. It's so frustrating.'

They turned down a lane and past some animal sheds. Large-faced cows, chewing at hay-covered byres, watched them speed by. A sign mounted on a wooden post surrounded by yellow daffodils, announced they'd arrived at Brompton. They drew up outside the house in Pebble Avenue and rapped the door knocker. Inge opened the door.

'Inge, we'd like to talk to you again. It's concerning Adam and Friday evening.'

Her mother, Sabine called out, 'Who is it, Inge?'

Inge opened the door wide and stood to one side to let Natalie and Lucy come in. 'Police, Mum.'

'Police?' Sabine appeared, concern etched on her face.

'Hello, Mrs Redfern. I apologise for the visit on a Sunday evening, but we'd like to talk to your daughter regarding Adam Brannon.'

'Inge?'

Inge's face was a mask. 'It's okay, Mum. I can handle this.'

'You can't question my daughter without me present. She's only seventeen.' She directed her words at Natalie.

Inge put a hand on her mother's arm. 'Mum, I don't need you.'

Sabine cocked her head. 'What's going on, Inge?'

'Nothing. I want to talk to them without you there.'

'We'd rather you were present, Mrs Redfern. As a seventeen-year-old, she has the right to have an independent adult present during questioning,' said Natalie.

'Mum, I can do this alone.'

'That isn't going to happen. Okay, ask away. I want to know what this is about.'

'I'm sorry, Mrs Redfern, we need to verify Adam Brannon's whereabouts on Friday evening. Inge?'

Inge's shoulders dropped and she faced her mother. 'It wasn't planned, Mum.'

'What wasn't planned?'

'Me and Adam.'

Sabine raised her hand to her mouth. 'No! You and Adam? You were sleeping with him! How could you? You were looking after their baby. And you're only seventeen! Oh my God! Inge, what have you done?'

'We must talk to Inge, Mrs Redfern. Can I ask you to hold back with your own questions until we've spoken to her, please?'

Sabine took a step backwards, eyes narrowed. 'Inge, how could you?'

'It just happened. I didn't mean for it to.'

Natalie steered the conversation back to the night in question. 'What happened after Adam brought you home on Friday night? Did he drop you off as you told us?'

She shook her head. 'No. We came inside for a while. He wanted me to… you know?'

'Have sex with him?'

'Yes,' she whispered, her face flushing crimson.

Sabine put her face in her hands. Inge's eyes remained downcast following the revelation. 'I'm sorry, Mum.'

'How long have you been involved with Adam?'

'Two months. His club's not far from my college. I used to hang around the place in between lectures and at lunchtime and so on. I was seeing a guy called Finn, who wants to be a professional boxer. Adam was training him personally. I got to know Adam through him. It was obvious straight away Adam liked me. While Finn was doing weights or whatever, he'd let me wait in his office and do some studying or coursework. Sometimes, he'd come and talk to me, or we'd joke about and such like. Nothing serious. Then one night he saw me walking home from college and stopped to give me a lift. He asked if I fancied a drink, and Mum wasn't home, so I said yes. We went to a really nice pub the other side of Samford and we had such a laugh. We went back to his office afterwards. He told me I was beautiful – really beautiful – and he couldn't keep his hands off me. We kissed. That's all. He was a proper grown-up and treated me nicely. Gave me compliments and stuff. I was getting bored with Finn by then and dumped him. After that, Adam and I started seeing each other whenever I had any free time. It got serious. He even got a separate phone so we could stay in touch without Charlotte or anyone finding out.' She paused and looked at Natalie with huge eyes.

'You were having sex with him before you became their babysitter?'

Inge nodded miserably. 'Mum told me she'd arranged with Charlotte for me to babysit Alfie. I didn't know what to do. I texted Adam and he said it was a great opportunity for us to see even more of each other.'

'And on Friday, what time did Adam leave your house?'

'Mum was due back at eleven so he left about ten minutes before that.'

'He's not texted you since then, has he?'

Tears sprang to her eyes. She looked at her mother, whose face was ashen. 'No. The last time I saw him was that night. I can't get what happened to Charlotte out of my head. If he hadn't been with me, she might still be alive. And I don't know how anyone could have got into the house. I shut the front door. I'm certain I did. Adam didn't murder her. I know he didn't. Charlotte was bossy at times and Adam complained she was a handful, but he didn't hate her. He'd have left her but he wouldn't have killed her.'

'Did you and Adam discuss him leaving her?'

She nodded. 'We talked and talked about it. He told me only a week ago he wanted to spend the rest of his life with me. I said we should wait until I turned eighteen and finished college and he agreed with me. Reckoned if I finished college and still wanted to be a midwife, it would make it easier for my parents to accept our relationship. He loves me, you know? And I love him.'

Sabine released a low moan like a wounded animal and spoke quietly. 'He wouldn't have left Charlotte, Inge. He was stringing you along.'

Inge shook her head vehemently. 'You're wrong. I knew you wouldn't understand. He loves me. He *was* going to leave Charlotte.'

Natalie only had Inge's word that this conversation had taken place. It might have been more one-sided than she claimed, and Adam might have told her he would never leave Charlotte. Was Inge putting up a convincing performance and had, in reality, arranged for somebody to kill Charlotte? At the moment, they had no evidence to support that theory. All they had was an alibi for Adam's whereabouts, unless Inge was lying about that, and she and Adam had plotted to kill Charlotte together. The only problem with that assumption was Inge had only given Adam half an alibi. Lee had provided the other half, and the trembling girl in front of her didn't seem capable of being an accomplice to a murder. However, Natalie wasn't going to work on supposition. For the present, she'd follow procedure and see if the investigation threw up anything that would make them further suspect Inge's involvement. 'I'd like you to make a full statement at the station, confirming what you've told me. It might be used as evidence in court.'

Inge chewed her bottom lip, looked across at her mother again and nodded. Natalie's phone rang. It was Ian. She excused herself and went outside to take the call. It was fresh outside now, the cool air catching her unawares and making her draw a quick breath.

Light had faded and darkness had crept in. A car was approaching and pulled into the driveway. A gentleman with greying sideburns, a balding head and a weary expression got out of it and walked towards the door. Natalie heard sobbing as Inge threw herself into her father's arms. The sounds faded into the background as she concentrated on Ian's voice.

'Found a bloke who didn't see a Bentley Bentayga parked on the street on Friday night but did see Lee Webster climb into a white van at about ten thirty. He's positive it was him. He got into the driver's seat.'

Natalie groaned. 'Lee stated he was at the pub at that time. The sodding barman vouched for him.'

'The man's adamant it was Lee, which puts him in that van not at the pub.'

'I'll get Lucy and we'll head back to the station.'

She ended the call and grimaced. Lies and deceit were interfering with her investigation, and the trio of Adam, Lee and Vitor had given her the runaround. She stomped back towards the house to collect Lucy. Nothing annoyed her more than being lied to, even though she came against a lot of it in her profession. People would say anything to save face or their necks. The next interview with these men would produce the truth. There was no way she was letting them off lightly.

CHAPTER SIXTEEN

Dr: Tell me how you feel today.

Patient X: I don't feel much different to the last time we spoke a couple of weeks ago.

Dr: Have you been experiencing the same dreams we talked about on your last visit?

Patient X: I have – night after night. But here's the thing that's been really bugging me, Doctor. I simply can't believe they are merely dreams, or even your fancier name for them – 'episodes'. They seem far too realistic and intense for them to be labelled so simply. I suspect they're my innermost desires trying to manifest themselves into thought and they can only do that when I'm unconscious and unable to fight against them.

Dr: We've discussed this before. These dreams have originated or been born from traumas you experienced in your childhood. That's what we've been exploring over the last couple of months. We need to help you get over those traumas and then the dreams will stop. I explained during your last visit that people place too much importance on their dreams: some believe they are prophecies or signs from those who've passed on. My training has led me to only one conclusion: that dreams are exactly that – dreams. Yours seem realistic to you, but they're still only dreams.

Patient X: Then answer me this, Doctor. When I have them, why do I feel so alive? I awake, or come to, feeling refreshed and even elated. I experience a sense of euphoria that I believe comes from releasing the message hidden in those dreams.

Dr: What do you think the message is?

Patient X: I don't know. I thought you might have the answers. I dream about killing women. What's the message in that?

CHAPTER SEVENTEEN

SUNDAY, 4 MARCH – EVENING

'How do you want to play this?'

Murray's question was directed at Natalie. The entire team was gathered in the office once more, and as Natalie appraised the tired faces in front of her, she made her decision. 'We'll sit on it until morning. We're sure they're lying but we have to back them into a corner so they confess. If we press on now, we might make mistakes, and if we do that, Lee's lawyer will probably find some loophole to get him off. We can't afford for that to happen. It's imperative we don't screw this up. If Lee and Vitor are lying, then Adam probably has no alibi either. Once he left Inge's house, we don't know where he went. He might have killed Charlotte and we still can't be certain he and Inge didn't murder her together.'

Lucy commented, 'He'd really have to want to be with Inge to have no other option than to kill Charlotte. It seems excessive. He could have just left her for Inge. It seems messy: beat the wife to a pulp, leave a bloody message, make up some story about having sexual relations with the babysitter at her house before her mum got back.'

Natalie felt the same way but investigating was about examining all options not discounting some because they didn't feel right. 'But it's still possible. Inge insisted the plan was to wait until she was eighteen and then Adam would leave his wife and child for her. She made a full statement earlier to that end and I'm not under the impression it's fabricated. Still, weirder things have happened, so we'll keep an open mind. Once we can establish where Lee and Adam both actually were, we might be a little closer to working out who our perpetrator is.'

With general consensus, they cleared away for the evening, leaving Natalie alone. She wrestled with the idea that Adam and Lee were both involved in Charlotte's murder. It was plausible. Yet it wasn't. She'd interviewed many suspects over her time and there was something about the way Adam accepted he was a suspect, that his alibi was weak, yet repeatedly denied killing Charlotte that resonated with her. If he had murdered his wife, he'd have ensured he had an airtight alibi and certainly not raced off for an hour with the babysitter before arranging some half-arsed explanation with a bartender he barely knew and a friend who was also known to the police. He'd have ensured Inge vouched for him for a longer period of time or sorted out something more concrete. It was all too woolly.

She shuffled her paperwork into order. She couldn't fully con-centrate any longer. When she'd told the team they might make mistakes, she was also aware that she was exhausted; she wasn't having the investigation crumble because of a bad call she'd made. Besides, she was needed back home.

Bethany's bright-green Post-it note was stuck to the fridge door. She'd opted for an early night and gone to bed. Lucy was too wound up to head upstairs immediately. If she went directly to bed, she'd fidget and wake her partner. She peeled the note away, smiled at the cartoon potato with a smiley face Bethany had added to the message, then opened the door and grabbed the half-drunk bottle of Australian white wine that had been open a couple of days, and poured a glass. She took it and the note through to their small lounge and flopped onto the comfy, pale-blue settee. Bethany had cleaned the room and a faint aroma of almonds rose from the wooden table as she set down her glass. She tilted her head back and shut her eyes. Her thoughts turned to Charlotte and what she must have experienced. The baby monitor was beside the bed. One of the crime scene pictures showed it turned at an angle. To Lucy's mind it looked as if Charlotte had pulled the monitor towards her to listen to the sounds coming from it. Had she heard the killer in her baby's room? The thought was chilling.

She slugged the wine. It was unlikely to have the soporific effect she hoped for but it might help her relax. Her laptop, along with the list of websites Charlotte had visited, was on the small writing desk in the corner of the room. Lucy hoisted herself up and crossed over to it. She'd gone through many of the sites that morning, and if she continued now, she might even finish the list before she went to bed. The sticky note was still attached to the base of her forefinger. She removed it, stuck it on the desk then opened up her computer and started trawling through the web pages.

Leigh was on the settee, ensconced in a film, legs curled under her. She lifted her chin at her mother's greeting.

'Hey, what are you watching?' Natalie slid next to her. Leigh unfurled her legs, resting them on Natalie's lap. Natalie placed her hands on them and gave them a gentle squeeze.

'*17 Again*,' Josh mumbled from the big brown chair, where he was half watching and half playing a game on his phone, thumbs moving across the screen at a steady pace.

'You didn't make it to Grandad's.' Leigh's words were directed at her mother.

'Darling, it was a murder case. It was very tricky to get away.'

Josh looked up briefly. 'That boxer's wife?'

'Yes. You heard about it?'

'One of my friend's mates boxes at the bloke's club. Says it's shut for the moment.' He returned his attention to his game. He was used to his mother's occupation and rarely asked questions about it.

'You have a good time at Grandad's?'

'It was okay. Pam made Yorkshire puddings,' said Leigh, looking away from Zac Efron for a second. 'They were this big!' She opened her hands wide. 'Honest. Weren't they, Josh?'

'Yeah. Huge. And fluffy.'

'Is this a hint you want me to make some like them, or a criticism that mine are flat and like rubber to chew?' She grinned.

Josh laughed. 'No. I don't think you'd manage to cook them like that. Cooking's not your thing, is it? No offence.'

'None taken. Where's your dad?'

'Went to his study. Said he had an urgent translation.'

'You meet Pam's son?'

'He's really nice, isn't he, Josh?' said Leigh, again turning away from the film. 'He's called Zander and he runs his own gaming software company. He and Josh were in geeky heaven talking about computer games.'

Josh scowled at his sister. 'I'm not a geek. He was interesting. He knew how to level up on *Fortnite Battle Royale*.'

'That so sounds geeky,' said Leigh with a smirk.

Josh reached behind his back, pulled out a cushion and hurled it at his sister, who squealed at him. 'Geek!'

'That'll do, Leigh. Don't wind him up,' Natalie said.

Josh gave an amiable shrug. 'She can't wind me up. I said she could watch this crummy film. I'm a kind brother so she has to be nice to me.'

'Actually, you said you wouldn't mind watching it too.'

'Yeah, right.'

'You did.'

'As if.'

'He did,' said Leigh to her mother with a sly grin.

Natalie smiled. Being home with two normal teenagers was exactly what she needed after the day she'd had. 'How long has it got left to run?'

'Fifteen minutes,' said Josh.

'Okay. Get off to bed when it finishes. School tomorrow, remember?'

'How can I forget,' said Leigh, hunkering down, attention back on the screen.

David ambled in. He gave her a black look that neither child noticed. 'Thought I heard you come in.'

'I hear I missed a treat – gigantic, fluffy Yorkshire puddings.' Natalie kept her tone light. She wasn't going to argue in front of Josh and Leigh.

'They were, weren't they, Dad?'

'They were huge,' he replied, ignoring Natalie and ruffling Leigh's hair. 'You enjoyed them though, didn't you? All *three* of them.'

'I didn't eat three,' said Leigh, patting her flat stomach and directing her statement at her mother. 'I ate two and a half. I couldn't manage all of the third one.'

'You fancy a cup of tea or anything?' Natalie asked David. The question was a signal for them to leave the room and talk in private. They never drank tea at this time of night. A sullen nod was all the response she got. She stood up.

'I'll leave you two to your film.' As she left the room she heard the thump of the cushion as it hit Josh.

David stood near the kettle, hands flat on the worktop behind him. 'Well?'

'Well, what?'

'You got something you wanted to talk about? You asked me in here. Or do you want to point out what a busy day you've had?'

'Oh, for crying out loud! What's got into you? I'm heading a murder investigation. That's pretty fucking important. A woman was brutally murdered and I'm sorry if I didn't drop everything to come to Sunday lunch with you, but it wasn't possible. It isn't like you to be so petulant and argumentative. What's going on?'

David finally met her eyes. 'I needed you there.'

'It was only lunch with your dad. Admittedly he was with his new girlfriend and her son, but it wasn't a big deal.'

'It was to me.'

'Then I'm sorry I wasn't there for you.'

'It was one huge fucking deal for me, Natalie. My father's not just got a new woman in his life: her son is a pretentious prick and Dad couldn't stop singing the bloke's praises. I felt like shit. There I am, a washed-up nobody, and my own father was bigging up some tosspot of a bloke I don't even know or like. I thought *I* was his son.' David clenched the side of the worktop.

Natalie didn't want a full-blown row. David was taking this whole girlfriend thing badly. She chose to reason with him. 'It's probably awkward for him. He's seeking Pam's approval and probably thinks he'll get it if he butters up Pam's son.'

'You reckon?'

'Seems logical to me.'

David wiped a hand across his face. A muscle in his cheek twitched. 'I didn't handle it too well. In fact, I made a right fucking tit of myself. Zander was rabbiting on about his software company, how great it was doing, what the sodding turnover was, with this massive ear-splitting grin on his fat face, and all the while Dad was nodding and beaming like the prodigal son had just walked in. I wanted to punch the guy's lights out. He was so... arrogant.'

Having not been there, Natalie couldn't judge what had really happened. She suspected David had been slightly jealous. His career had gone from good to bad as opposed to Zander's, which seemed to be on the ascent, and worse still, Josh had liked the man. She felt a little guilty at having let David down. He'd have felt better if she'd been there.

'Look, I really am sorry I couldn't come and support you, but you must see I couldn't drop everything.'

'Yeah, I know. I was just racked off about it. I felt I had no one on my side. Even the kids liked Zander and couldn't see what an insufferable show-off he is.'

With David's eyes downcast and his face a picture of misery, Natalie gave in. He needed her to make the right move and say the right thing to pander to his dented ego. She approached him and slipped her arms around his waist. 'He was probably nervous as hell and just spouting off shit like some folk do in those situations. It's a normal defence mechanism. He was most likely worried about you too. He only had his mum there. You had two boisterous kids and your dad. It was lunch at your father's house so he was on your turf. He maybe even felt defensive.'

David brightened a little. His shoulders relaxed. She'd given him the reassurance he needed. He kissed her lightly on the lips. As he did so, the door flew open and Leigh marched in.

'Oh, yuck.'

'What do you mean, "oh, yuck"?' Natalie asked.

'That. Kissing. It's not normal for people your age. I'm going to bed. Night, Mum. Night, Dad.'

She paused, hand on the door handle. 'Mum, can we go shopping in Manchester next weekend? Please say yes. You promised we could go yesterday and then we couldn't. The shops around here are rubbish. You can't get any trendy clothes.' Leigh pulled a face. Natalie was used to her children's demands. As much as she'd liked to have agreed, the investigation took precedence, and if it was ongoing, there'd be no choice.

David intervened. 'Your mum and I were just discussing the subject before you came in. I'll take you to Manchester if she can't get time off. Now off you scoot. It's past your bedtime. I'll make sure I have a pile of Yorkshire puddings ready for you for breakfast,' said David.

'You are *so* not funny, Dad,' she replied drily, then in a show of affection, she rushed back and planted a kiss on his cheek.

They watched as she breezed out.

'Sorry. I forgot to tell her earlier. Other things on my mind.' He took her hand and she squeezed it. It had been a difficult day for both of them.

'I think I'll go up too. I might take a quick shower. Sorry you had a lousy time. You mustn't take it to heart. Zander will calm down once he gets to know us, or, more likely, he'll not be around much in our lives. It's Pam your father's seeing, not her son. I bet Zander is as concerned about his mother dating again as you are about your dad.'

'You're probably right. It's hard to get my head around it at the moment, that's all. Dad's never had anyone in his life since Mum passed away and suddenly there's Pam, and in no time at all, he seems to be head over heels for her.'

'Then we should be happy for him, shouldn't we?'

'I'll try but I don't know if I can.'

'You need time to get used to the situation. This time next year, it'll feel normal, and Pam's really nice, David.'

He returned the squeeze and dropped her hand slowly. 'Yeah, she's okay. Go on up. I might do some more work before I turn in.'

As Natalie crossed to the stairs, the door to David's office swung open with a slight creak. The latch on it was broken and it wouldn't remain closed. It was a problem David's father had promised he'd address. Natalie hoped he hadn't forgotten. Eric was quite the handyman. As she drew the door to, her eyes shifted to the illuminated computer screen. David had come out at the sound of her voice and abandoned the translation he was working on, except it wasn't a translation. The screen sparkled and twinkled and the familiar image of a brightly lit city at night made her close in on it. It wasn't a translation document she was looking at. It was Jackpot City David had been visiting – a gambling website.

He was up to his old tricks. She stole out of the room, closing the door behind her, unsure what to say to him. To tackle him on the subject would probably result in a massive argument and maybe even worse. She reasoned he might only have visited the site, not placed a bet. He knew the trouble, heartache and mountain of debt it had caused last time. He wouldn't be so stupid. She had to trust him yet she couldn't leave it. It wasn't in her nature to sit back and believe everything was rosy. That wasn't how it was in the real world.

She changed for bed and waited until the children had settled in their rooms. Leigh would be asleep soon after her head hit the pillow. Josh might be a little longer.

When the noises had ceased, she headed back downstairs. David was still in his study. She tapped and opened the door quickly, coming into the room before he got a chance to speak. A document with corrections in red was up on the screen. He removed his glasses and turned to face her. 'What's up?'

'The door swung open earlier and I saw inside. You had a gambling site up on the computer. I want to know if you've started laying bets again. Don't piss me about. It's a simple yes or no.'

He rubbed a hand across his chin, a sign of nervousness. 'Shit. No. No, I'm not. I admit the site was up. I was looking at it.'

'Why? Why would you look at it if you didn't intend playing on it?' She folded her arms and stared at him.

'I felt fucking awful after we got back from Dad's. Bloody Zander and his successful company. And what am I? I'll never have his wealth or potential. I wondered what it would be like if I won big. If I could win a great hand at poker or something similar, I'd at least feel worthy.' The creases by his eyes deepened as he screwed his face in concentration. All the while, Natalie looked for any tell that he was lying. He continued, 'I don't think you fully understand how shitty I feel some days. It's like I'm wasting time. My kids can't say they're proud of their dad cos I don't do anything impressive – not like you. I had a few minutes of pure fantasy. That's all. I pulled up a few gambling websites and dreamt of winning a ton of money. It was no more than that.'

'For fuck's sake, David. I thought you'd put all this behind you. You were addicted. An addict doesn't merely go onto a site, look at the bright colours, fantasise and then get off it again.'

His face hardened. 'Are you saying you don't believe me?'

'I find it difficult to understand how someone who struggled as much as you did to break this habit would be able to stare at a gaming website and not feel tempted to place a bet.'

'Incredible! You actually don't believe me, do you? How am I supposed to place a bet, Natalie? *You* control the household expenses. All our income goes into our joint bank account. You pay the fucking mortgage and bills out of it. Not me. You don't trust me to do it any more. Check the account. See if any money's missing. Go on if you don't believe me.' His voice rose and two flecks of red appeared in his cheeks.

'Too true I'll look at it.' Natalie wasn't going to merely back down, even if he was telling the truth. Not until she was certain he was.

'Go the fuck ahead. There's not a single penny missing from it.'

'Good. I'm glad to hear it.'

His eyes narrowed into slits. 'So, if the money is still in the account, I can't have been gambling, can I? How am I supposed to place a bet if I have no money? Answer me that. Now, I've had it up to the eyeballs today with crap from everyone. I'd have expected more support and some understanding from you, not cross-examining me like I'm one of your suspects. I'm going to bed.' David stood up, turned off the computer and pushed past her. 'And I don't expect to be interrogated again.'

He stomped up the stairs. Natalie headed into the kitchen for a glass of water. While she was there, she opened the banking app on her mobile. There'd been no activity on their account since the last transaction she'd made. She ought to believe him but still she couldn't completely understand his logic. And there was the way he'd defended himself. He wasn't usually so aggressive in his manner. She drained her glass. She'd have to trust him and hope the tiny nagging voice in her head was wrong. David wouldn't be so dumb as to put at risk everything he had. Not after the last time. Would he?

CHAPTER EIGHTEEN

MONDAY, 5 MARCH – MORNING

Natalie was the last to arrive at the office. The revelation that David might have started gambling again prevented her from falling asleep immediately. She'd stayed awake long after he'd dozed off, with memories of the damage David's addiction had caused their relationship swirling in her mind. They'd unearthed the root of it and he'd stopped, but not before he'd wiped out their savings and tested her mettle. Finally, in the early hours of the morning, she decided he wouldn't allow that to happen again. He cared about her and their children. He'd been hugely upset over the thought of his father finding new love, and put out that Zander had gained a place in his own father's affections. David couldn't live without those he loved by his side.

She tossed her bag onto the floor and greeted her team. Judging by the buzz in the room, they were busy collecting information.

Lucy bounded across to her. 'This may be something and nothing but Charlotte visited this site several times.'

'The Darkest Knights' official website.' Natalie looked at the photo of the band members.

'As we know, Jed Malloney is their drummer and also happens to be Phoebe's fiancé.'

Natalie nodded. 'Could have been checking him out for that very reason – curiosity?'

'I thought that to start with, so I delved further back into her website browsing history: eighteen months ago she ran several searches for Jed. For the next few months she landed on that page regularly, along with several others all about Jed. I then found a list of all the venues The Darkest Knights had played. One of them was at Stoke-on-Trent on Friday the second of December, 2016, around fifteen months ago, before they became really well-known. Charlotte's friend Frankie told us about a gig they went to for an up-and-coming band. I suspect it might have been this one.'

Natalie drummed the desk with her fingers, absorbing the information, then voicing thoughts of her own. 'Frankie also told us Charlotte went back with the band to their hotel. She might have slept with Jed. If so, that would account for why Phoebe hates her so much.'

'There's another possibility – Alfie. He's six months old. By my calculations he would have been conceived around the time of that gig.' The scar over the bridge of Lucy's nose became even more pronounced as her eyebrows drew together. 'I know we shouldn't make assumptions but…'

'There's one way to determine the truth. We'll get a DNA sample from Jed. And while we're at it, establish his whereabouts on Friday night when Charlotte was murdered.'

Lucy returned to her desk and set about the task. Natalie strode to the window and watched the morning traffic, chin in hand. A shuffle alerted her to Murray's presence. He handed her a file. 'I came across something that might be relevant. There was an unresolved murder of a woman, Lucia Perez, who was killed in Nottingham two years ago. She had an eighteen-month-old child, Diego, who was found unharmed in the living room, with the door shut. I requested the file and was cross-referencing it when I thought of something. The murder took place on Saturday the seventh of May, 2016. The husband, Rodrigo Perez, was believed to have been responsible and was charged but later released when there was insufficient evidence and it eventually became a cold case. Something about the date and place rang a bell and I remembered the fight posters Adam has on the wall of his office. I was sure one of those took place in May 2016, so I checked through the fight events calendars for May 2016 and he did have a fight the night before, on Friday the sixth of May, in Nottingham.'

'That's interesting. What do we know about this case?'

'The victim, Lucia Perez, aged twenty-one, was beaten to death in the hallway of their flat during the afternoon. Rodrigo Perez was already known to the police. There'd been a number of reported incidences of screaming and shouting from their flat, but on each occasion, when the police arrived, those claims were refuted. One of Lucia's friends told police that Lucia had tried on several occasions to leave Rodrigo but he wouldn't let her take their son with her. The same friend said she was considering going but leaving Diego behind with his father. Police looked into these claims and Perez was initially charged, but later his vehicle was found on CCTV footage at a warehouse in Liverpool around the time of the attack, and he was released.'

'Did the attacker leave a message?'

'No. There wasn't anything written in blood, or anything else for that matter.'

Natalie crossed the room and stood by the front door, arms folded. It was a sign she wanted to address them all.

'Okay, listen up, folks. We're getting all sorts of leads and information now, and we have to sift through it quickly. Something new has come to light and there's a possibility Jed Malloney, who is engaged to Charlotte's sister, Phoebe, is Alfie's father. We're trying to establish where he was the night of the murder. As we discussed last night before we left, there's also some ambiguity surrounding Lee's and Adam's alibis. Murry's uncovered something that might be relevant to this investigation.' She ran over what Murray had told her about Lucia Perez.

'With this latest information concerning the murder of Lucia Perez, we have Adam back in the frame. Murray, talk to the DI who was involved in the Perez case. See what else you can find out. Lee wasn't at the pub as he told us so we need to get hold of that barman and bring him back in before we grab Lee and find out why he was lying. What else have we got?'

Ian waved a sheet of paper. 'I've got a name. Finn Kennedy. He could be one of the two suspects running away from the Brannons' house.'

'Who identified him as Finn Kennedy?'

'I've got a tech-savvy mate in Birmingham who helped trial some facial recognition software for the police force back in 2014. It can identify suspects from CCTV images or smartphone photos from a database of about 100,000 mugshots. The techies managed to make the photograph more recognisable so I sent over the still to him, and it's come back a match for Finn Kennedy. He was charged for possession of a firearm in 2016 and was on the database.'

The corners of her mouth pulled upwards slightly. 'Good job.'

Lucy spoke up. 'Finn? Inge was going out with a lad called Finn before she dumped him for Adam. Where does he live?'

'Close to the boxing club in one of the tower blocks on the Crossways Estate,' Ian replied.

Natalie picked up her car keys. 'Then he's also a person of interest. Let's talk to him too. Until we've eliminated these new suspects, or found out what they know, we're not going to act on the information that Lee was seen climbing into a van at ten thirty on Friday night and was not in the pub as he claimed. If he and Adam are involved in this murder, I require cast-iron proof before they're charged. Lee's a slippery character and his lawyer is red-hot. We can't mess this up.'

Natalie and Ian were on their way downstairs when Mike called to them.

Natalie stopped in her tracks and faced him. 'Hi. How was your day off?'

Mike's face said it all. He beamed at Natalie. 'Worth the horrendous queue at the cinema with all the overexcited children.'

'We've got a few leads. Just going to follow one up.'

'Good. That key you gave me for the Brannons' house, it has several sets of fingerprints on it. Charlotte's parents and a third set, which we've identified as her sister Phoebe's prints.'

'That's a lot of prints on one key.'

'They're mostly on the key fob.'

She recalled the pink plastic oblong attached to the door key. 'Any others?'

'Nothing else. Only the family members touched the key and the fob. That's all I have. I'll let you crack on.'

He turned away, and as Natalie and Ian bounded down the stairs, Ian said, 'Phoebe isn't at home very often, is she? I wonder why her prints are on the fob.'

'Not sure. It looks suspicious. She can't have used it to get into the house that night though. She was on a flight, miles away.'

'True.'

Natalie pondered his words as they charged across the car park and into the unmarked BMW. She couldn't ignore the fact that Jed and Charlotte had possibly had an affair and Alfie was their son. If Phoebe had also found that out, could she have murdered her sister? It was mere supposition at this stage but maybe worth pursuing. 'Double-check she was on that flight. It's probably wise to confirm her whereabouts.'

He threw her a smile. 'I'll do it as soon we get back.'

They were approaching Crossways Estate, an area not as badly run-down as Ashmore but still lacking funding. An abandoned children's play area was slap bang in the centre of the small estate. It harboured a sense of decay with the graffitied walls and rubbish scattered over the tarmac-covered area. A lone seesaw had the message 'FUCK YOU' scrawled along it, a climbing frame had been decorated with rolls of toilet paper, and the swing seats and chains that attached them to the overhead struts were long gone. Natalie couldn't imagine any children wanting to play there.

'There. That's it. Red Towers.' Ian swung into a spot on the road near the grey block. It was one of three named unimaginatively after primary colours.

Natalie climbed out of the car, rested her elbows on the roof and studied the block. Thirteen storeys high and with each flat having a balcony, the blocks would have been considered modern and even smart back in the sixties when they were erected. Now, its white façade had yellowed with age and the balconies were filled with broken washing machines, endless lines of washing and bicycles, even a motorbike on one floor.

'He lives with his brother on the second floor. Their flat is at the rear of the building so there's every chance he hasn't spotted our arrival,' said Ian.

Natalie set off with a determined stride. Ian kept pace and together they passed through the side entrance. They'd seen nobody. It was extremely quiet for a Monday morning: no mothers, buggies, youngsters or any comings and goings. 'I hope he's in,' she said.

'He's unemployed so there's a fair chance he'll be in at nine thirty on a Monday morning.'

The stairwell stank and somebody had drawn crude images on the walls. Empty cans of lager had been left, along with a bottle of vodka containing dark-yellow fluid at the bottom of the stairs. Natalie wrinkled her nose at the stench of urine, stronger here; nodding towards the lift, she suggested they take the stairs.

'It's probably the lesser of two evils.'

Ian emerged first onto the landing and turned right towards the back of the block. Natalie followed him, looking over the concrete balustrade as she did so. There was still no activity below.

'It's along this corridor,' said Ian, counting off the flat numbers until he reached number eleven.

'Go on. Do the honours,' she said as he hesitated in front of the door marked with a warning sign, stating an attack dog was on the premises.

He rapped hard on the door. There was no barking. The dog either didn't exist or had gone out. There was no sound from inside.

'Try again.'

Ian knocked harder and for longer. He opened the letter box and shouted, 'Finn Kennedy, it's the police. We'd like to talk to you.'

They waited but still there was no reply. 'Looks like he's out,' she said. 'Any thoughts as to where he might be?'

Ian, unwilling to give up, thumped on the door with his balled fist. 'Finn Kennedy. Open up. It's the police!' He turned his head towards Natalie. 'I heard someone in there.' He bashed again, calling out Finn's name.

A man dressed only in boxers opened the door, yawned and took in the two officers.

'Mr Kennedy?'

'I'm Mr Kennedy but I'm not Finn,' said the man. 'I'm Patrick. Finn's brother. He's not been home for two nights. I've no idea where he is so don't even bother asking.'

'Have you any idea at all of his whereabouts?'

'I told you I don't know. If I knew where he was I'd go fetch him myself. He owes me two months' rent, the little shit.'

'What about his friends? Could he be staying with them?'

'Don't you think I've tried them? I've been looking for him myself. I put the word out but no one knows where he is. He's been a miserable little turd since he got kicked out of the boxing club and lost his sponsorship. He's been floating about the estate and getting on my nerves.'

'Which boxing club?'

'Adam's. It's the only one around these parts. Bloody shame Finn screwed up his one big chance. Ma would turn in her grave if she knew how he was behaving.'

'You look after him?'

Patrick gave a hoarse laugh. 'I don't look after him because you can't look after Finn. He's his own man. I let him live here for forty quid a month, and for that I make sure he gets fed and doesn't get into too much bother. I also try to kick his backside now and again and encourage him to get a job. Ma asked me to keep an eye on him when she got the cancer so I try to but he's a handful.' He rubbed a hand over his naked torso. 'That it?'

'We'd like to know who he hangs out with.'

'Why, what's the little fucker got up to?'

'We're investigating a suspicious death. Finn was spotted in the area at about the time the crime was committed.'

'Jeez! You think he killed somebody? Finn's lots of things but he is no murderer. I'd swear to that.'

'We need to find him to clear his name and to find out if he saw anything.'

Patrick absorbed the news with more sternal rubbing. 'So, he might have spotted the murderer. Is that what you're saying?'

'Possibly. We also need to identify who was with him at the time and just what they were doing in the vicinity of the Brannons' house.'

'Brannon. Adam Brannon?'

'Yes. And you said a minute ago Finn was thrown out of Adam's boxing club.'

Patrick's hand moved to his face and he wiped it across his chin. 'He had a fall-out with Adam. I don't know anything about it. You best talk to the man himself.'

'Have you any idea who might have been with him?'

'Could have been any one of his friends or not.'

'And Finn hasn't been back here the last two nights?'

'No.'

'When did you last see him?'

'Saturday lunchtime. I was going out when he got up. I asked him for the rent money and he told me to fuck off cos he didn't have it. I told him he'd better get it and if I didn't have it by Monday, he could find somewhere else to live.'

'Have you been concerned by his disappearance?'

'Not really. He's often out for two or three nights at a time, even a week. He hangs about with his mates and comes and goes as he pleases. I thought he was keeping out of my way until he came up with the money.'

'If he turns up, will you please call us immediately? Here's my business card.' Natalie handed it over.

Patrick stared at it blankly. 'Do you think something's happened to him?'

'I honestly can't answer that, Mr Kennedy. If you give us his mobile number and a list of names of his friends, we might be able to establish where he is and find out for you.'

'You can forget the phone. He's not answering. It goes straight to answerphone, like it's switched off. I've rung him quite a few times. He's usually with the lads from Ashmore Estate. You should start with those who use the boxing club. And try Hassan Ali. They're good mates. I spoke to him yesterday. He didn't know where Finn was but he might have been fibbing.'

Natalie changed the subject. 'Did Finn used to go out with a girl called Inge Redfern?'

'Yeah. He was mad keen on her but she dumped him. He was turning a corner too, settling down and had a chance to be a boxer, even have a career, but it fell apart after they split up. Finn took the break-up badly and became feral again. She was the only thing that kept him anchored. I doubt you'll find him with her. He'd got to the stage where he hated her. Shame they broke up. Ma would have loved her.'

'Thank you for your cooperation. We'll be in touch.'

'I bet you will.' He edged back into his flat and shut the door.

'Believe him?' asked Ian.

'For now. He could be protecting him. He is his brother, and if his mother truly asked him to look after Finn, he's unlikely to give him up to us. We'll try Hassan Ali and then Inge.'

CHAPTER NINETEEN

'Come on, sweetie-pie, let's get your coat on.' Samantha Kirkdale wiped a strand of dark hair from her little boy's forehead. He gazed at her with large brown eyes and revealed white teeth, then dropping the wooden car he'd been holding, he ran on chubby legs into the hall.

Samantha raced after him, marvelling at his speed. He'd only been walking for two months but in that time had become adept at a standing start. She caught him and scooped him up in her arms, making him gurgle in delight.

'Were you running away from Mummy, Oscar? Were you?' She tickled his stomach, making him squirm. 'You know what happens to little boys who scamper off. They get tickled by the tickle monster.' She ran her fingertips over the front of his T-shirt, making him chuckle louder until he shook his head from side to side.

'Enough? Want to go to the park now?'

He wriggled to get down and sat on the floor so she could put on his shoes. Samantha crouched down beside him and pushed on the small trainers she'd bought only the day before. Her boy was growing so quickly he'd soon be requiring new ones. She'd have to ask Daniel for some more money. He wouldn't be happy about it but tough. They'd agreed he'd support her and Oscar financially.

That was the trade-off. She'd give him the divorce he wanted only if he paid their rent and child support, along with some money for her. She wasn't greedy. She had her part-time job at the children's nursery to help make ends meet.

Daniel had seen reason in the end. She could have taken it to the lawyers and maybe even been granted half of his salary. Her friends had told her to throw him out and remain in the family home, then he'd be forced to pay the rent on it, but she didn't want to stay where there were memories. She wanted a fresh start. Besides, Daniel wasn't the only one seeing somebody else. She'd met someone too and the relationship was showing promise.

A knock at the door made her start. 'I wonder who that is,' she said in a singsong voice to her son. 'It might be Vicky.' That morning, she'd spoken to her best friend, who'd said she'd try and drop by before her work shift began. Oscar leant forward, picked up his other shoe and handed it to her. He liked Vicky a lot.

'Hang on a sec, Vicky,' she called. 'Won't be a minute.'

She dragged the shoe over Oscar's foot, leaving him to roll over and push himself to his feet, and headed to the door. She opened it, a smile on her face. 'You made it. Oscar's…' she said. The words froze on her lips. A small cry of terror replaced them and she shoved the door with the flat of both hands to shut it on the intruder on her doorstep. It was too late. It flew open, knocking her backwards into the wall. The door shut quietly and she scrabbled to regain balance, eyes widening at what was in front of her.

'Please. No. My little boy is here. Don't hurt us. Don't hurt him.' Oscar was now behind her legs, small fingers grabbing the back of her jeans. 'Please. Don't.' Her mind couldn't process what was happening. It defied logic. Her baby was behind her and she had to protect him. What could she do to save him? To save them both?

The blow came out of the blue. As she tumbled to the floor, all thoughts evaporated.

CHAPTER TWENTY

MONDAY, 5 MARCH – MORNING

Lucy twirled the pen between her fingers and waited for the manager of The Darkest Knights to arrive at the meeting point. Sasha Thorndike had been heading from London up to the Midlands when Lucy had rung her, and they'd arranged to meet at a small hotel at a halfway point, near Banbury, Oxfordshire.

The Walton Arms offered accommodation and food but also had meeting rooms available for hire and were happy for Lucy to talk to Sasha on their premises. The room Lucy had been given contained two tables pushed together and four chairs. A jug of water and four glasses were in the middle of the tables, along with notepaper and pens, each bearing the logo of the hotel. The windows overlooked the car park and she watched the comings and goings of the guests. It wasn't long before a black Maserati pulled into a space with a throaty roar, and a diminutive woman with a thin face and short bleached-blonde hair, dressed in a brown leather jacket, white blouse and jeans, emerged.

Within minutes, the same woman strode confidently into the room. She held out a hand, cool to the touch, and addressed Lucy. 'Sasha Thorndike.'

'Morning. DS Lucy Carmichael from Samford Police. Thank you for stopping off to meet me.'

Sasha dropped onto a chair and, resting an elbow on its arm, spoke first. 'You said you needed to talk to me about the band, and Jed in particular.'

'That's correct. As I explained on the phone, I'm part of a team investigating a murder that took place in Samford and I have a few questions concerning Jed and the band.'

'Okay.'

'I was checking the band's tour schedule and I saw no dates booked for this month.'

'They're not touring at the moment, that's why. They're writing new material and will be recording in the studio over the coming months.'

'So, they weren't performing any gigs last Friday?'

'No. They won't tour again until next year. We're in the process of booking venues.'

'Do you happen to know where Jed Malloney was last Friday?'

'Yes, I do. He was doing an interview for a radio show.' Her dark eyes remained fixed on Lucy.

'In London?'

'No. It was for one of the local radio shows. They were doing a special feature on drummers.'

'Which radio station was it?'

'BBC Radio Stoke.'

'What time did it air?'

'It wasn't broadcast that afternoon. It was a recorded interview set up for around four thirty or five, I think. He had to be at the studio for four. These things often don't go to schedule.'

'Do you happen to know what time he got back to London?'

'I can't help you there. I have no idea which train he caught.'

'He didn't have a return ticket booked?'

'Oh yes, he did, but he intended visiting his future in-laws while he was in the area and wasn't sure of his exact movements, so he had a flexible return ticket, allowing him to catch whichever train he wanted. I don't know which one he caught so I don't know when he returned.'

'But you made the travel arrangements?'

'The office did. That's one of our jobs, especially when it's to do with publicity.' Sasha pushed the sleeves of her jacket up her arms, revealing tattoos, before leaning across the table and pouring herself a glass of water.

'Do you know Jed's fiancée?' Lucy asked.

Sasha took a swig of the water. 'Phoebe. Sure. I'm friends with her, and with all the band members' partners. They sometimes accompany the band on tour or support them at gigs. Phoebe comes along when she's not flying. I try not to get too involved though. I have to maintain some distance to be professional. Primarily, I'm the band's manager and can't get too involved in the guys' personal lives. Apart from Seth, obviously.'

'How long have you been their manager?'

'Since they first started up in July 2016. I wasn't married to Seth then. We weren't even an item. We only got hitched a few months ago.'

'Congratulations. I expect you've come to learn a lot about the band members over that time.'

'What is it you really want to know, Sergeant?' Sasha's voice had become more cautious.

'Do you remember one of their early gigs in Stoke-on Trent the first week in December 2016?'

'What about it?'

'Two women managed to get backstage and spent time with the band until you broke it up.'

Sasha nodded. 'I vaguely remember that. The guys were on a real high after a great gig and were knocking back a few beers in their dressing room. A couple of groupies had sneaked past the security I'd set up and were with them. I'd started using security because the group were beginning to attract quite a following, and girls, women and even men would often throw themselves at them. I wasn't worried about what the guys got up to but I didn't want any toxic fallout from a drunken tryst, some kiss-and-tell story that might ruin the band's image or, worse still, cause a break-up, so I'd sometimes wade in and shoo the fans away myself. They'd pretty much scarper when I arrived on the scene.'

'Can you recall anything about the women that night?'

'It was ages ago. All I can remember is one scooted as soon as I told them to go but the other one hung around for a while.'

'Did you notice if she was with any one particular member of the band?'

'Like making a play for them?'

'Yes.'

Sasha shrugged.

'It would really help me if you could remember.' Lucy got the sense Sasha was protecting her clients and knew more than she'd so far offered. 'You must have some idea. It's your job to keep an eye on them. Come on, Sasha, help me out here.'

'She was all over Jed. That much I do recall. He was so high he'd no idea what was going on. All the guys were worse for wear, so I got us all back to the hotel. Once there, they went to bed, as far as I know.'

'You don't happen to know if that woman followed you to the hotel?'

'I have no idea at all.'

Lucy opened the file in front of her and pulled out a photograph of Charlotte taken from her Instagram account.

Sasha studied it. 'Yes. That looks very much like her although I can't be completely sure.' She pushed the photograph back across to Lucy and stared at her again. 'Okay, what's this really about? Is Jed in trouble? I have a right to know.'

'We're pursuing several leads and need to eliminate people from our investigation.'

'You think he's guilty of something? Will you be speaking to him about it?'

'We certainly shall. He's staying in Samford at the moment with Phoebe.'

'Is he? He didn't say anything to me about going away this weekend.'

'He didn't tell you it's Phoebe's sister, Charlotte, who's been murdered?'

Sasha's eyes opened wide. 'No. He's said nothing to me. How dreadful. Poor Phoebe. I didn't even know she had a sister. Neither of them mentioned that fact. I always thought Phoebe was an only child. I should ring her. Talk to her.'

'I wouldn't at the moment. Her parents are very upset, as you can imagine, and they have a lot to arrange.'

'I guess so. I'll wait until Phoebe and Jed get back to London.' She poured some more water and drank it quickly. 'Jed isn't a suspect, is he?'

'As I said, we have to eliminate everyone connected to Charlotte from our enquiries.'

Sasha nodded and glanced at her large, plain-faced watch. 'I don't want to be rude, but I have an appointment to get to. Is there anything else I can help you with?'

'That's all, thank you for meeting me. I appreciate your help.'

If Natalie thought the Crossways Estate looked grim, the Ashmore Estate was far worse, like a scene from a post-apocalyptic movie. Natalie and Ian pulled up beside a piece of charred land, once a playing field, now home to a burnt-out carcass of a car. Before them stood several grey blocks of flats, interlinked by paths, overgrown with weeds and broken up with time. In parts, it was little more than a fly-tip zone, and as Natalie's eyes lighted on a filthy, three-piece suite, surrounded by dirty nappies, takeaway boxes and empty beer cans, left on the grass verge outside the block where Hassan Ali lived, she winced at the thought of bringing up children in such a place. A large woman with several rings through her nose and wide eyes stared at them, whispering something to her companion, a twenty-something girl who kept her head lowered.

They walked on, mindful of a trio of teenage boys gathered outside the adjacent block, who watched their movements and spoke in loud voices, making big gestures like animals protecting their turf. Natalie turned quickly and approached them.

'We're looking for Hassan Ali and Finn Kennedy. Do you know them?'

One boy hawked up phlegm noisily and gobbed it onto the steps. 'Maybe.'

'Have you seen either of them around recently?'

The boy lifted slight shoulders and looked at his mates, who shook their heads and feigned indifference. 'Don't think so.'

'Any of you use Adam's, the boxing club?' She aimed her question at one youth, with a tattoo on his neck and wide shoulders, who looked like he worked out.

'What if we do?'

'You any idea why Adam threw Finn out of the club?'

'Finn got involved in a scrap. Adam wasn't happy about it. Finn gave him some lip back and Adam lost his temper, told Finn to get out.'

In Natalie's view, it was unlikely Adam would chuck a boy out because he'd been fighting. That was what he was learning to do. It had to be more serious than that. 'When you say scrap, you mean a fight, don't you? Did they use weapons?'

'Maybe. I dunno. I wasn't there. Why don't you ask Adam?'

Natalie wasn't going to waste any more time on these three. They either didn't know much or weren't going to be helpful. 'You haven't seen Finn then for a while?'

The boy with tattoos stared at her. 'No.'

'Either of you two seen him?'

She received the same blank stares. 'Okay, if you do, get in touch with Samford Police.' She knew her instruction was futile but it didn't hurt to say it. Occasionally somebody would turn informant. Dismissed, the youths sloped off into the dark bowels of the building.

'I have a feeling Hassan is not going to be home,' said Ian as they climbed their second staircase of the morning.

'He might be lying low. We'll try regardless.'

Natalie took the lead and knocked on the door and was surprised to find it answered by a petite woman. Natalie showed her ID card and explained the purpose of her visit. 'Could we talk to Hassan?'

'He's not in trouble, is he?'

'We want to ask him about one of his friends, Finn Kennedy.'

'You'd better come in, then.' She ushered them inside, peering out behind her to ensure no neighbours had witnessed the exchange. The flat was poky but clean, and the distinctive aroma of cinnamon and coriander suggested the woman was in the process of cooking.

'This way,' said the woman, leading them down a narrow corridor, past a galley kitchen and to a room that served as a family room. Furnished simply with wooden banquettes against walls and Moroccan leather pouffes placed around a gleaming round copper table that stood in the middle of the room, it appeared larger than its actual size. Ian studied the gilt-framed artwork on the wall. There was a sense of culture and pride in the place.

'I'll fetch Hassan.'

She was gone only a minute and reappeared with a spindly youth with dark eyes, jet-black hair and the beginnings of a moustache above his lip. His arms hung limply by his side.

'Hassan Ali?' Natalie asked.

He nodded dumbly. His mother stood protectively by his side.

'Where were you on Friday night?'

'Chilling,' he said. 'There's not much else to do here.' His voice was surprisingly deep.

'Who were you chilling with?'

'Mates.'

'I need names, Hassan.'

'There was a group of us. There's usually a group of us. Most of them live in Hounslow House. Why are you asking me this?'

'We're investigating the murder of Charlotte Brannon. I believe you know her husband, Adam?'

'I go to the boxing club sometimes. Got to be able to look after yourself around here.'

'Was Finn Kennedy with you on Friday?'

The quick flutter of his heavy lids was all the affirmation she needed. 'I don't think so.'

'Surely you'd remember if Finn was there. He's one of your mates, isn't he?'

'Not really.'

'That's not true, Hassan. His brother told us you're friends.'

'He's wrong.'

'Hassan, this is very important. A woman has been murdered. Finn has disappeared. Now, we're not saying Finn was involved but he might have seen somebody who was near the Brannons' house, and we must talk to him.' Natalie glanced at his mother in the hope she would help persuade her son. It worked. She said something in Arabic. Hassan replied, a volley of incomprehensible barks. He looked back at Natalie.

'I don't know where he is. He's not been round for a few days and he's not answering his phone.'

'Can you give me the names of the boys you were with on Friday night?' She knew it didn't mean much. Everyone they asked would say Hassan was with them. That was how it worked here. They stuck up for each other. She had no idea if he was the other youth they'd seen near the Brannons' house, but she noted he was about the same height and build as the second person in the photograph.

His mother said something else. He nodded. 'Abe, Leon and Mustafa. They live in Hounslow House. They go to the boxing club.'

Natalie suspected they were the same three youths they'd already spoken to. 'Thanks. Any idea why Finn was booted out of the boxing club?' she asked lightly.

Hassan shook his head. The eyelids gave it away again. He wasn't telling the truth. She ended the interview and she and Ian marched back towards the car.

'I think he's lying. He knows where Finn is and he might even have been there on Friday night. I might bring him in for questioning. Being off his home turf will make him less confident.' She slammed the car door as she got in.

'Inge's at college today. I checked with her mother before we left. She should be free in the next half hour. We'll meet her there.'

CHAPTER TWENTY-ONE

MONDAY, 5 MARCH – AFTERNOON

The college was a collection of buildings sprawling across a large industrial estate. Inge emerged from the glass doors of a brown building, books clutched in her arms, talking to another girl. She caught sight of Natalie waiting beside the car, excused herself and, leaving her companion, walked over to join the officers.

'My mum's majorly pissed with me and I haven't been able to talk to Adam.' Her tone was accusatory, filled with anger and upset.

'I'm sorry to hear that. We hoped you might be able to tell us about Finn Kennedy. You ought to have an independent adult with you though. I shouldn't question you alone.'

Inge frowned. 'I don't want an adult. I'm almost eighteen and I'll tell you whatever you need to know. What's Finn got to do with this?'

'You went out with him, didn't you?'

'And I dumped him.'

'When was the last time you saw Finn?'

'Ages ago.' The answer was quick, too quick, and she tightened her grip on her books, drawing them closer to her chest.

'Inge, when did you last see him?' Natalie persisted

'I don't remember.' Inge turned and was about to stalk off when Natalie spoke.

'We have reason to believe that Finn was at the Brannons' house on Friday night.'

Inge pivoted towards them, eyes blazing. 'He didn't do it. He didn't kill her.'

Natalie held the girl's defiant gaze. 'You're very quick to jump to his defence. This is somebody you broke up with yet you're standing up for him. I can only imagine there's one reason you'd do that. He's contacted you and you already knew he was there on Friday night, didn't you?'

'He didn't kill her!' she shouted, her face reddening.

'Inge, he was spotted holding steel piping and running down the street with an accomplice. If he didn't intend harming Charlotte, why else was he there? Was it to see you? Were you getting back together?'

'No! I love Adam.'

'It might be best if you come to the station with us to discuss this,' said Natalie calmly. 'I'll arrange for your mother or father to join us.'

'Mum will go mental. No. Don't make me go to the station. I'm in so much trouble already. Dad is furious and won't talk to me. I don't want them to be involved in this. My life is total shit. I just want to see Adam.' She dropped her head.

'Then help us, Inge. Did Finn contact you?'

She nodded miserably. 'When he found out Charlotte was dead he freaked out. Especially after what happened between him and Adam. He figured everyone would think he had something to do with her death. He came to ask me for money to get a pay-as-you-go phone so he could keep in touch with his mates and find out what was going on. He wanted to lie low until the murderer was caught.'

'What did he tell you?'

'He was going to smash up Adam's car. That's what he went to the house for. He'd found out about me and Adam sleeping together so he wanted to give him some payback, but before he did anything, he heard a scream from the house and legged it. He assumed Charlotte had spotted him from a window and would call the police. Then, the next day, he found out she was dead. He guessed you'd look for him.'

'We know he was with somebody that night. Do you know who that might have been?'

Inge shook her head. 'He didn't mention anyone else. I thought he was alone.'

'Do you have any idea where he's gone?'

'I honestly don't know but he'll keep in contact with his best mate. He might know.'

'That Hassan Ali?'

'Yeah.'

'We have learnt Finn got ejected from the boxing club. It was over fighting, wasn't it?'

'It was more than that. Finn and Hassan were in a serious fight with one of the other kids, pulled knives on him. Adam had already warned Finn about his temper and he lost it with him. Finn begged for another chance. Boxing was going to be his life. He had a sponsor and everything lined up but Adam wouldn't listen. He'd had enough of Finn. He was always picking on the other kids and starting fights. Adam said he was too volatile to be a professional boxer.'

'And Finn took it badly?'

'I suppose so. I'd stopped going out with him by then. He tried to talk me round but I was seeing Adam and didn't want to go back with him. He'd go off on one for no good reason although he was always okay with me.'

'How much money did you give him?'

'Fifty pounds. It was all I had. I had to take it out of my savings account. Dad will go spare if he finds out I gave it to him. Don't say anything to my parents. Please.'

'Why did you help him?'

'I felt sorry for him. He looked so scared. I've never seen him like that before. And because I believed him.'

Lucy had returned from Oxfordshire and was keen to follow up on what she'd found out about Jed. 'Murray, will you come with me to collect Jed Malloney? I want to bring him back here and interview him officially. He went to Stoke last Friday for a radio interview but didn't go straight back to London. He claimed he was going to spend time with the Hills. Doesn't sit right with me. They'd have said something about him if he'd turned up at their house, wouldn't they?'

Murray scraped back his chair. 'I'd have thought so.'

'You got anything?'

'Chased up that Lucia Perez case. I'd hoped there'd be more of a connection to this case, given she was also beaten to death and her child left alive, but can't establish any links other than the fact Adam was in Nottingham the day of the murder. Spoke to the DCI in charge and he still believes the husband was behind it even though there's no proof. Says the guy was a particularly nasty piece of work. Everything pointed to him. He thinks Lucia tried to scarper and Rodrigo found out about it and attacked her before she could get away. Doesn't appear to be connected to this case.'

'In a way, that's good. It doesn't cloud our investigation.'

They headed down the stairs and into the brightly lit entrance.

'You need bloody sunglasses down here. Every time the sun peeps out it's blinding with all the glass in the building,' Murray complained, squinting as he placed his pass on the control panel of the barrier and waited for it to automatically open.

Lucy was through before him and strode towards the car quickly. 'It's okay during the long winter months though. Better than the last place.' Both Lucy and Murray had transferred at the same time to the newly built Samford headquarters.

'You miss the old station?' he asked.

'Not at all. Great idea to put in a request for a transfer. I prefer it here.'

'Whose great idea was it?' he joked as they got into the vehicle.

'Yeah, yeah. Have another pat on the back.'

'Good to know though, isn't it?'

'What?'

'That your baby is going to have such terrific genes.'

'Shut up!' she said, smiling.

He eased out onto the road and accelerated away from the station. 'How's Bethany doing?'

'Good. She's seventeen weeks gone now. No cravings yet and she seems to be over the morning sickness.'

Murray pulled a face. 'Glad I'm a man.'

He concentrated on the route through town and out into the country, where the Hills lived, making no further reference to the baby. Lucy used the time to work out what she'd say to Jed.

There were four cars parked outside Walnut Cottage. Murray drew in behind a red Mercedes convertible. On the back seat was an Emirates flight attendant's hat.

'Phoebe's,' he said as they walked past it to the front porch. He rang the bell.

Phoebe answered. The smudges under her eyes indicated she'd been crying.

'We'd like to have a few words with your fiancé, please.'

'Whatever do you want with him?'

'It's okay, honey. I'll talk to them. You go back to your mom.' Jed, in tight jeans and a T-shirt bearing the name of his band, gave her a smile. 'Go on, scoot. I'll only be a minute.'

She didn't budge.

'It'll be standard police procedure, right, officers?' He looked at them, pale eyebrows lifted. He was saved by his future father-in-law, who appeared briefly and seemed agitated. Inside, a baby was crying, his wails increasing with each exhalation.

'Phoebe, love. Can you help your mum? She can't get Alfie to settle.'

Jed edged away from the door and whispered to her, 'Go on. This will be nothing important. They're just checking everyone who knew Charlotte and I haven't been interviewed yet.'

Phoebe threw him a look before departing.

As soon as she'd left, his eyes turned flinty and the smile vanished. 'So, what can I help you with, officers?' He continued to block the doorway, unwilling to allow them entry.

'We're clearing up a couple of facts,' Lucy said. 'You gave an interview on BBC Radio Stoke on Friday afternoon but didn't return to London until some time the next day. You told your manager you were going to visit your future in-laws, Kevin and Sheila.'

'That's right. I'd intended dropping in to wish them a happy anniversary but I finished the interview later than I expected, got chatting to the sound engineers at the radio station, you know how it is. Time went by and I changed my mind. I went into town and had a couple of drinks but I got the timings wrong, missed the nine forty-five train and caught the late train around eleven. That one stopped at Wolverhampton where I slept on a bench until the first train out at five in the morning. I got back to London at seven.'

'I see. Any reason you missed the nine forty-five train?'

'Bad timing on my part.'

'This wasn't your first trip to Stoke, was it?'

'I've been there before.'

'In December 2016.'

'If you say so.' He showed a set of perfect white teeth.

'You were playing in Stoke on Friday, December the second, 2016.'

'Again. If you say so.'

'It was also the night you met Charlotte Brannon.'

The teeth vanished. 'I don't know what you're suggesting but I'd better remind you there's a house of people in pain here. They're going through hell at the moment.'

'I'm aware of that, sir. Did you have an affair with Charlotte Brannon?'

'Hell no.'

'Did she go back to the hotel with you that night?'

Alfie's cries had strengthened. Jed pulled the door to block them out. 'I didn't know who she was, okay? I was completely out of my head that night. She was just some good-looking woman who had the hots for me. She must have followed our minibus to the hotel and gotten a room key off housekeeping. I was half-asleep when she climbed into bed with me. What was I supposed to do? It was one time. One time only.'

'You must have known who she was, Jed. Surely you'd met her before then, or at least seen photos of her? You were going out with Phoebe at the time. I can't believe you didn't know who Charlotte was.'

'That night is one big fucking fog. Honestly. I didn't recognise her. Maybe some part of my brain registered who she was, but it didn't stick. You have to believe me when I say I was as high as a kite. I really didn't remember what happened that night. By morning, when I came to, she'd gone.'

'I take it you've never discussed that night with Phoebe.'

'No. Can you imagine the fallout?' He rubbed a hand down his sideburns and over his chin.

'Have you any witnesses who can testify to your whereabouts last Friday?'

'I don't think so.'

'There might be footage of you at Stoke or Wolverhampton stations but it would help if you could remember which pubs you visited so we can talk to the bar staff for confirmation.' Lucy pressed on, 'Which pubs did you go into?'

'I haven't a freaking clue. I went into the first one I found, had a few drinks and moved on.'

'Charlotte was murdered around eleven that night, and unless we can find concrete proof of where you were, it's going to cast doubt on your claim.'

'I was in Stoke-on-Trent until just after eleven, when I caught the train that stopped at Wolverhampton. Look, it's over thirty miles to Charlotte's house. It would have taken me at least half an hour to get back to Stoke station from there. And I had no transport.'

'I'm sure there'd have been taxis available on a Friday night, sir,' said Murray.

'Find one that was stationed outside her house on Friday night and then come back here and accuse me.' His voice maintained its hushed tone even though he was clearly aggressed.

'Over thirty minutes,' said Lucy thoughtfully. 'How would you know that fact?'

He answered smoothly, 'I've been to their house. We visited them one time to take Alfie a christening gift because we missed the actual christening.'

'But how would you know how long it would take from Stoke to Samford, to Charlotte's house? You'd have no way of knowing that unless you'd checked it out.'

'I wasn't there on Friday night and that's it, got it?'

'I'm sorry but that's not good enough. I'm going to have to ask you to accompany us to the station.'

'You're kidding me.'

'No, sir. We need to establish your whereabouts.'

His face set. 'What if I refuse?'

'You can't refuse. We have the right to detain you for questioning if we believe you are connected to an indictable offence.'

'This is crazy.'

Phoebe pushed open the door and stared out, face ghostly pale. The baby's cries had ceased. 'What's going on? I thought this was only going to be a few general questions about Charlotte.'

'Nothing to worry about, honey.'

'We're taking him to the station for questioning,' said Lucy.

'What? I don't understand…' Phoebe looked from Lucy to Jed. 'What's going on?'

'I'll explain later. It's just some bullshit mix-up.'

'Jed?' Her voice was cagey.

'Honest. Go back inside and be with your folks and Alfie. They all need you right now. I'll be back later. Go on.' He steered her back inside, mumbled something at her that Lucy couldn't hear and reappeared. 'Come on, then. Let's get this over with.'

Natalie and Ian were back inside the Alis' flat. Hassan's mother, waving her hands in front of his face, was screaming at him. Natalie could only pick out the name Finn from the explosion of words that spurted from her lips. He held up his hands and placated her in his native tongue.

'*Wakha. Wakha.*'

She fell silent and stepped backward while he spoke to Natalie. 'I know where Finn is. I want to make a statement.'

'Does your mother want to come to the station with you?'

He shook his head. 'She's staying here. I'm eighteen. I don't need an adult with me.' He marched out of the flat without looking back at his mother. She didn't speak, only followed them to the door and shut it behind them.

Hassan strode ahead of them towards the stairs, his head high. Natalie was the first to notice the slight acceleration in his step, then, as he turned towards the stairs, she knew instinctively what was going to happen.

'Ian, he's going to bolt,' she said, spurting forward.

Ahead of them, Hassan bounded down the stairs, leaping over the rail and rolling away expertly before racing off down the dark corridor.

'Hassan!' she yelled. 'Stop right there.'

It was futile. She and Ian arrived at the bottom of the stairs, heads turning left and right in time to catch a movement from an emergency exit door. They careered towards it and outside into a no man's land of rubbish: bottles, junk, bin bags and weeds.

'Shit! Where's he gone?' Ahead of her lay two more flat blocks with alleyways and back entrances.

'I'll try that one,' Ian said and charged towards the door leading into Hounslow House.

Natalie worked out how far he could have run in such a short space of time and headed for the nearest point, an alleyway to the side of Hassan's building. It brought her out near the area of scrubland containing the burnt-out wreck of a car they'd pulled up next to, on their first visit to the block. Resting hands on knees and bending over to catch her breath, she decided she was getting too old to chase about. She was in her forties and – as fit as she was – unlikely to catch some eighteen-year-old. She hoped Ian had fared better, but as he burst from the front of Hounslow House, she could tell he was as frustrated as her.

'Lost him,' he yelled.

She moved towards him, cursing Hassan. 'We'll get his phone number from his mother and see if we can track him down. He's not going to get far.' Even as she said it, she knew there was every possibility they wouldn't be able to find him again. He too had probably gone to ground. They'd almost certainly just allowed the one person who could help them with the investigation slip through their fingers.

CHAPTER TWENTY-TWO

Dr: You seem more cheerful today.

Patient X: That's because I am. I feel lighter in my soul, more at ease and hopeful.

Dr: Would you like to share the reason you feel like this with me?

Patient X: I'm not sure. You might not believe me.

Dr: Why wouldn't I believe you? Try me.

Patient X: Earlier today, one of the angels of death visited me.

Dr: You saw an angel?

Patient X: An angel of death. I've met her before on a few occasions. At first, I thought she was my mother, but she isn't. Merely a facsimile of her, with the same hair and facial features, but with dark, empty sockets where her eyes should be. It was she who explained how I might find salvation and undo the wrongs my mother inflicted on me.

Dr: This is very new. You've never mentioned this angel before.

Patient X: That's because I came to you for a deeper understanding of my dreams not to discuss the angel who visits me.

Dr: Do you see her when you're asleep?

Patient X: She comes whenever the mood takes her – morning, night or during the day. Sometimes she manifests and says nothing to me, just waits as I go about my business. Today she assisted me greatly.

Dr: How did she help you?

Patient X: She guided me to the blood.

Dr: What do you mean by that?

Patient X: Just that. Blood.

Dr: Why blood? You're talking in riddles.

Patient X: Isn't that what you specialise in? Riddles or the confused nonsense that brews in people's minds?

Dr: I help people understand the significance of their dreams. They are not riddles. Dreams all have their roots within a person's mind. The angel is another example of that. She probably comes to you when you are emotionally charged.

Patient X: She comes whenever the mood takes her, although she almost always appears when she's tracked down fresh blood.

Dr: What blood are you referring to?

Patient X: You're the doctor. What do you think I mean by that?

Dr: Are you talking about blood of a victim?

Patient X: Bravo. The doctor understands.

Dr: Tell me more.

Patient X: Haha! No. I've messed with your head enough. See what a good mood I'm in? I'm really enjoying watching your reactions to my nonsense. You looked so earnest and shocked by my revelation. It's complete fabrication of course. I fancied winding you up a little today.

Dr: There is no angel?

Patient X: Maybe. Maybe not. Either way, I'd prefer to talk about my mother.

Dr: Are there any victims?

Patient X: It's funny to see that you completely believe me, but I really don't want to joke about any more. I want to talk to you about a troublesome dream about my mother that used to haunt me when I was a young child. For years it would play out night after night; then, for no reason, it stopped. Recently it's returned and I'd like your take on its significance and how I can bury it again. Let's discuss that, Doctor.

CHAPTER TWENTY-THREE

The desk sergeant greeted Natalie and informed her of the interview going on between Lucy and Jed Malloney. She headed for the adjacent room, linked by a one-way mirror, to watch and listen in. Jed was speaking.

'Okay,' he said, lifting both hands up in a submissive gesture. 'It's a holy mess, I grant you, but I'm not the person you're hunting for.'

'You have now admitted you *were* in Stoke-on-Trent on Friday evening and you went to Charlotte's home.' Lucy maintained eye contact with Jed, who wriggled in his seat before answering.

'Let me put it in perspective for you. Last Monday, I get a weird message on my answerphone from Charlotte saying she has to talk to me urgently and gives me a landline number to call. I figure it's her home number and it's to do with the family, or Phoebe, or something like that, so I ring it. She picks up and drops this fucking bombshell that Alfie is my son. Just like that. Not hello, how are you? No, she blurts out, "Alfie's your son." You can imagine how I react. I'm floored by the news and no sooner do I come up for air than she announces she's going to tell Phoebe the truth, that it isn't fair to keep something as important as this from her, and that her sister has a right to know about it before she marries me. I ask her to slow down and explain what the fuck is going on. She reminds me of the night, way back in December 2016, in Stoke when she slept with me. Now this strikes me as really crazy because she's never brought it up or said a darn word about it before.'

He shook his dirty-blond hair and continued in his lazy drawl. 'I tell her I don't believe her and demand a paternity test. I say I'll come visit her to talk it through, and advise her not to act hastily. She replies, saying that it's a bit late for talking. I insist. I tell her I'm going to be in Stoke-on-Trent on Friday for a radio interview at about four thirty, which will only take an hour tops, and can see her after it. She agrees to meet me outside Stoke railway station at seven. Adam usually goes out with one of his mates on a Friday night, so she's free to see me. I think it's all sorted. The interview at the BBC finishes at about five twenty. I hang around after it, have a couple of drinks to steady my nerves and then wait at the railway station, but she doesn't show. I wait half an hour. She still doesn't show. I ring the number she gave me and called *me* from but it's a phone box in Samford. Some random person answers my call and doesn't have a clue who I am. I don't have her freaking mobile number and I can't ask Phoebe or her parents for it without causing suspicion. I have no way of contacting her and can't work out why she isn't at the station as planned. I walk back into town, which, in case you didn't know, is a freaking long way, and work out what to do next. I need to clear this crap up. I don't know what game Charlotte's playing, but it's doing my head in. I grab another drink at a bar, and another, and then I make the decision. I order a ride from Uber and get the driver to drop me off down the road from her house. It's about ten fifteen, ten twenty, by the time we get there. I'm not sure I should even be doing this. It feels all wrong yet I need to know if Alfie really is my kid. What I'm actually worried about is Phoebe hearing about it first. If she has to find out, I want to be the one to tell her. I pace about, trying to get the courage to go to Charlotte's door. I'm worried I've come all this way and Adam's at home. I walk up the road. I see there's only one car parked on the drive, a BMW. There are no lights on in the house. I knock on the door and ring the bell. Nobody answers. And that is it. Nothing more. I leave. I walk back down the road and order another Uber, which takes less than ten minutes to arrive.'

He lifts both hands up. 'Gospel truth. The details will be on my phone. I reached the station in the nick of time to catch that eleven o'clock train and I didn't realise it was only going as far as Wolverhampton until I was on it. The rest is exactly as I told you. I caught the five o'clock in the morning train out of Wolverhampton and returned to London.'

'You were only at the house for a few minutes and didn't see Charlotte?'

'That's what I'm telling you. I didn't see her, speak to her or anything. I went no further than the front door. Surely your forensic guys would have been able to pick up something to prove if I'd actually been inside the house. I've got the call log showing the number for the phone box. There's also my Uber app, which will confirm I ordered cabs when I said I did. I'm not her killer.'

'Would you be willing to give a DNA sample?'

'Do I have to? I don't think I can handle knowing I'm Alfie's father now. I can barely look at the kid. He's over at the house with Phoebe and her parents, and I'm still pretending he belongs to Charlotte and Adam. I don't think I can go through with a test that proves *I'm* his father. What the hell can I offer him? And it's going to completely screw my relationship with Phoebe if the test proves positive. She isn't going to want to start bringing up her sister's kid with me. It's best if I don't know; if none of us know.'

Lucy insisted. 'It would be helpful to us.'

He leant in, fingertips pressed tightly together. 'Okay, here's the deal. I give you the sample so I can be eliminated from your enquiries or whatever, and if you use it to also determine Alfie's paternity, you don't tell me the result.'

'We *are* going to require a DNA sample. Now, could you hand over your mobile so we can confirm the times of your taxis, the phone call you received from Charlotte and the one you made to that call box number?' Lucy wasn't going to be drawn in, despite his pleading and earnest look. He let out a heavy sigh and pulled out his mobile, which he pushed across the table to her.

'I could refuse.'

'You could but that wouldn't be in your best interest. You were at the victim's house the night she was murdered. It would be advisable to cooperate.'

He lifted his chin and stared at the ceiling in silence. Eventually he spoke again. 'Okay, run the test or whatever you have to do. This is all a giant fuck-up. Promise me one thing. You won't tell Phoebe about Alfie.'

'I have no need to discuss the matter with her at the moment.'

His head bobbed up and down. 'Thanks.'

Back in the office, Natalie praised Lucy. 'You handled him well.'

'I felt a tiny bit sorry for him. It must have been confusing and a huge shock to be suddenly told he's Alfie's father. I bet he'll tell Phoebe, even if the test is negative, and then who knows what will happen to them?'

Murray muttered, 'We're not sodding marriage guidance counsellors. We dive in, rifle through evidence and get out again. It's tricky enough handling our own lives and relationships.'

'Speak for yourself. I'm managing mine just fine.' Lucy offered with a small shrug.

Natalie interrupted them. 'If Jed's whereabouts are confirmed and he seems confident they will be, we can strike him off our list, which will leave us with Hassan Ali, Finn Kennedy, Adam and Lee. Ian's trying to locate Hassan through his mobile although I fear he'll have dumped it and be using a burner phone. He's undoubtedly got a network of mates who'll squirrel him away for a while.'

'Inge was certain Finn had nothing to do with the murders,' said Murray.

'That may be, but she's emotionally involved with him, even though they're no longer an item, and she's possibly not the best judge of character,' Lucy replied.

'I reckon it's time to round up Adam and Lee. I'd hoped we'd get some more information first, possibly from those two youths, but I can't hang around on this any longer. We have to get to the bottom of where they really were the night Charlotte died. We'll talk to them both and that barman, Vitor, from the White Horse again.'

Natalie's mobile rang, a special ringtone that indicated her superior was on the line. A crease appeared between her eyebrows. 'You go ahead. I'll take this.'

Superintendent Aileen Melody, Natalie's boss, was as calm and collected as ever but her words chilled Natalie. 'I'm at a crime scene, Natalie. You need to get to Bose Street as quickly as possible. We believe your killer has struck once more.'

CHAPTER TWENTY-FOUR

MONDAY, 5 MARCH – EVENING

Natalie, standing in the doorway, could hardly tear her gaze from the small child dressed in trousers, sweater and trainers, his fist in his mouth and eyes wide in confusion. He was staring towards the house and tugging at the hand holding his, reluctant to accompany the gentle-faced policewoman and social worker who were attempting to coax him into the car.

It was the pullover that had done it: the blue patterned sweater with a red tractor that the child wore. Josh had owned an almost identical one when he was a toddler. This little boy was smaller than Josh had been at the same age. They'd identified him as Oscar Kirkdale, and he was thirteen months old. Natalie forced back the emotion. She was a professional but on this occasion the sweater had touched a part of her, the maternal part that she guarded purely for her personal life. She cleared her throat. She had a job to do. She cast about the hallway, noting the tiny blue slippers kicked to one side, the coats on pegs by the door: one an adult's black anorak, the other a child's duffel coat. A pale-blue handbag with a dog motif was upside down on the floor and a heart-shaped key ring bearing the name *Samantha* in large pink lettering was on the floor next to the staircase. A stuffed toy giraffe with a happy smile stood on the first step as if waiting to greet them.

'Oscar was found shut in the cupboard under the stairs. He appears to be unharmed but we don't know if he witnessed anything or not. His father, Daniel Kirkdale, has been notified and is coming to collect him. Apparently, he and Samantha have been separated a while.'

'Daniel Kirkdale,' she said, thoughtfully. Mike nodded. 'Where's Samantha?'

'Through here.' Mike walked ahead of her and turned right. Natalie brought up the rear and stared at the horror in front of her, eyes grazing the cereal box, the collection of coloured blocks on the table, the child's plastic cup with lid, the bib left hanging on the back of the high chair, and landing on the sight on the floor.

'From what I can make out, she was first attacked in the hallway. There are bloodstains on the wall directly behind the door and further droplets on the floor. There are also folds and rolls in her clothing which support the theory she was dragged in the direction of the kitchen, where she was butchered to death. They left behind the weapon,' said Mike. 'An eight-inch chef's knife.'

Natalie didn't respond. She was looking at the bloody smears left on the cupboards and preparation area, where Samantha had tried to get away from her attacker. Now she was face down, one arm outstretched as if still trying to escape the monster who'd stabbed her repeatedly. She was slight in stature, dressed in jeans and a loose-fitting cream blouse stained crimson. Strands of long auburn hair had come loose from an orange plastic hair clip and now trailed in sticky patches of blood.

Natalie's gaze travelled over the woman's body to the white fridge, where the killer had left a message in blood: '*who?*' The letters were sloped like those in the first message they'd found. This had been written by the same person. Without saying a word, she turned on her heel and left the room. Aileen Melody was still outside, talking to Pinkney, the pathologist. Natalie joined them.

'Looks to be the same perpetrator,' said Natalie. 'Mother's been brutally attacked, this time with a knife. We'll have to establish if it was one of Samantha's knives or if the killer brought it to the scene. Given it's been left behind, I'm assuming it'll be free of prints. The killer's a confident bastard.'

Pinkney hoisted his medical bag. 'I'd best go in.'

As they watched his retreating back, Natalie turned to her superior. 'Who found her?'

'One of her friends, Victoria Endon. She'd been trying to contact Samantha all afternoon without success so she called in on her way home from work. The door was unlocked. She heard Oscar crying and found him shut in the storage cupboard under the stairs. She called out for her friend, spotted the blood in the kitchen and dialled 999 immediately.'

'She still around?'

'I had an officer drive her home and wait with her. She was badly shaken. Lives near the community centre, Maple Drive.'

Natalie observed her officers, several doors down, who were currently canvassing the street. Ian was in conversation with a young mother, toddler by her side, pulling at her skirt for attention. Murray was at the door of the next house along, asking the same questions, hoping somebody had been at home at the time of the attack and spotted the assailant. Forensic staff in white suits, carrying metal cases containing testing equipment, walked down the path, one behind the other. They acknowledged the women as they passed by.

Aileen waited until they'd entered the house then spoke quietly. 'We have to track them down quickly, Natalie. We can't keep the lid on something this big. The press office is already under pressure to release more facts regarding Charlotte Brannon's murder, and now this changes everything.' Aileen didn't have to spell it out. It was going to be almost impossible to prevent panic once this news got out. 'I'll discuss it with the powers that be and see if we can figure a way to keep the enormity of this from the public.' She studied Natalie with glittering eyes. I'm relying on you and your team to nail this son of a bitch. Find me something, Natalie. And quickly.'

She strode towards her Volvo, leaving Natalie staring at the row of houses in front of her. It was a quiet street of terraced houses, whose occupants had probably been at work at the time of the murder. Murray had moved three houses further down and was knocking at another door.

Lucy materialised from the opposite direction. 'No one was at home at the time,' she said, indicating the houses she'd tried. 'Not one person.'

Natalie spoke quickly. 'We've got an important link. The victim is Samantha Kirkdale. Samantha is married to Daniel Kirkdale.'

'Isn't he one of Adam's boxing club sponsors?'

'Exactly. They've separated. Samantha lived here, not at the marital address, and she wasn't wearing a wedding ring. We need to talk to Victoria Endon. She found the victim's body. I'll let the others know.'

Victoria Endon gulped back tears and sipped the warm tea. Her eyes were almost swollen shut with crying. Her mother, who'd introduced herself as Heather, had an arm around her daughter's shoulder.

'I understand this is a terribly difficult situation for you, but we need to act urgently and we require your help, Victoria. How about you tell us when you last spoke to Samantha?'

'This morning. I told her I'd try to drop around and maybe go out with her and Oscar before I went to work. I was on an afternoon shift, twelve to six, but I was running late and didn't make it. As soon as I got to work, I sent a text to say sorry and I'd see her later. She didn't answer. At first I thought she was in a huff with me, but that wasn't like her. I sent another text asking if everything was okay but again I got no reply. I tried her on Snapchat but she wasn't online. I rang her during my break and still no answer, so I worried something had happened and maybe Oscar was sick. She's my best friend. We talk all the time. It wasn't like her to freeze me out, so I told work I was feeling ill and came away an hour earlier than normal to see what was happening. She didn't come to the door when I knocked, but for some reason I tried the handle and discovered it unlocked and then… I heard Oscar…'

She choked on sobs. Heather, brows knitted together, patted her hand. 'It's okay, Vicky.'

'Oh God! It was the worst thing ever,' said Victoria. 'He was in a terrible state, crying and crying. I called out for Samantha and all the time I sensed something terrible had happened. She would never shut Oscar away in a dark cupboard under the stairs. I held him so his face was against me and carried him along the hall. Her shoes had been kicked away and her bag was on the floor. There were red splashes of what looked like blood leading to the kitchen so I peeked through the door.' She took a gulping breath, words tumbling from trembling lips. 'There was blood *everywhere*. I raced outside and rang the police. I kept Oscar with me until everyone arrived. The paramedics took him from me. Where is he? Is he all right?'

'He's with an officer and waiting for his father to collect him.'

'Poor little love. He was distraught. He kept calling for his mummy. Oh, Lord. What he if saw the person who did this? What if he watched what happened to Samantha?' Tears fell fast now.

Natalie tried again. There was no time to waste. 'We understand Samantha was separated from her husband, Daniel.'

Victoria snuffled into a tissue. 'She left him two months ago. He'd been having an affair for over a year. She'd had enough of it and decided to move out.'

'She left because of the affair, not anything else? He didn't hurt her?'

Vicky shook her head. 'She'd had enough of being treated like a mug, and Daniel wanted a divorce to be with his new woman. She said it was time to move on.'

'Was Samantha dating anybody else?'

'Yes. That's one of the reasons she moved out. She wanted to start over again. It wasn't serious but I think she wanted it to be.'

'Do you know the name of the person she was seeing?'

'Lee Webster.'

Natalie could sense Lucy bristling at the name.

'Have you met Lee?'

'She went out with him for drinks a couple of times while I babysat Oscar, and I think she was keen on him but I haven't actually met him. I've seen photos of him though. She sent them to me on Snapchat. We were always swapping photos. She sent me a really nice one of the two of them at the pub...' Her words faded into a sob. Natalie was forced to wait for Victoria to regain her composure.

'Did she seem anxious at all when you last spoke?'

'Not at all. She was chatting about Oscar and how fast he was on his feet. She was quite okay about leaving Daniel. She had Oscar and her job, which she loved, and Lee. It was all getting so much better for her.'

'She didn't mention being followed or any strangers contacting her?'

'No.'

'And she got along okay with her husband?'

'Sort of. It wasn't easy once she knew about his affair. That's another reason she had to move. She couldn't pretend at playing happy families. Daniel promised to give up his girlfriend, Carla, and work at their marriage again, for Oscar's sake, but it didn't last. Within a couple of weeks, he was seeing Carla once more. That cow made sure everyone knew he'd gone back to her so it soon got back to Samantha, who was gutted. Then she picked herself up.

That was Samantha. She was a lot stronger than people imagined. She wasn't going to be walked over.'

'She told you all her secrets?'

'We were really close. We told each other everything. I'll never find another friend like her.'

'I'm very sorry indeed about Samantha. Truly sorry, but I'm going to ask you not to speak to anyone about what you saw in the house. It might hamper our enquiries if you do. I'd like a family liaison officer to drop by to chat to you. You can tell her everything and she'll give you advice and answer any questions you may have, but please don't discuss it with anyone else.'

She nodded.

'We really need to find whoever did this to your friend, and the less information that leaks out, the better that is for us.' Natalie stood up.

Heather squeezed her daughter's hand as she looked up at Natalie. 'She'll be fine. We'll look after her.'

CHAPTER TWENTY-FIVE

MONDAY, 5 MARCH – EVENING

'Lee Webster,' said Lucy. 'Who could possibly find that man charming?'

Natalie resisted the obvious answer. Lucy was in danger of letting her emotions hamper her judgement. Natalie preferred a more measured approach. 'I asked Murray to have both him and Adam brought back to the station for further questioning. There are too many coincidences here, they both lied about their whereabouts on Friday night and they're both connected to Samantha's husband, Daniel. Murray's fetching in that barman too. We'll drop off at Daniel's house first before we return and interview any of them. I gather he's been notified of his wife's death.'

They drove on. Natalie mulled over what they'd seen at the house then spoke again. 'What do you make of the messages the killer's been leaving behind?'

'They're telling us something but I can't work it out. Is it part of a poem or song lyrics?'

'None that I recognise. *Why? Who?* All I keep coming back to is that they're two of the five main questions asked in basic problem-solving. They're questions we as investigators always ask. Could they be directed at us?'

'Sure they could, but if that's the case, they're out of order. We usually ask who, what, when, where and then why. We don't start with why.'

Natalie let out an irritated sigh. 'It's fucking impossible to decipher the messages and I hate playing guessing games. We ought to concentrate on similarities between the two victims, or links: same interests, same hangouts – anything they both liked doing. The perpetrator might be after a certain type.'

'Both of them had long hair and brown eyes.'

'We'll examine their lives in more detail when we get back to the station. Social media ought to throw up something. As for the messages written in blood, we can only surmise. What we could really do with is a criminal profiler to help us work out what sort of crazed mind we're dealing with.'

A light drizzle was falling. The windscreen wipers flicked on and off automatically, dragging across the screen and leaving behind a smeary, grey rainbow. Daniel Kirkdale's street came into view, a different kind of street to where his wife lived, a cul-de-sac of bungalows with neat gardens and wide pavements. Natalie couldn't help but wonder if Samantha would be alive if she hadn't moved out of this neighbourhood.

Daniel answered the door, the top button on his shirt undone and a wild look in his eyes. Behind him was a woman with wide blue eyes, who moved away at the sound of Natalie's voice.

'Come in,' he said wearily. 'Carla's here. She's my... she's helping me through this.'

'I'm truly sorry for your loss. I appreciate you talking to us. How's your little boy?' Natalie asked, the image of the child in the sweater once more in her mind.

'Oscar's asleep. He crashed out as soon as he got here – shock and tiredness. We're keeping an eye on him. I don't know how I'm going to tell him his mum has gone forever. Thank goodness Carla's here to help. I couldn't cope on my own. You got any idea who killed Samantha? Adam's wife was killed too. Do you think this is connected in any way?'

'We're looking at every possible angle and not ruling out anything at this stage. We're doing our utmost to track down the perpetrator, and your information might help us.'

'You want to sit down?' He waved a hand at a couple of chairs. 'The liaison officer left a short while ago. She told me what to expect. You're leading the investigation?'

Lucy and Natalie took a seat each. Natalie answered. 'That's right. I'd like to start by asking when you last spoke to Samantha.'

'Spoke to her? Sunday. I went around to her place to take Oscar out. She let me have him twice a month. He came back here and played with Carla's kids. She's got two.'

'You all live here now?'

'Since Samantha moved out. I didn't force her to leave. It was her decision.' He raised sad eyes.

'How did she seem when you last saw her?'

'Fine. Things weren't fantastic between us but we managed to be civil to each other.'

'Do you know Lee Webster?' Natalie continued. Lucy remained silent.

'Lee? Yes. He helps out at Adam's place. Teaches boxing.'

'Are you friends with him?'

'Of a fashion. We're both involved in the club. I sponsor a couple of the kids. Hope they'll make it into professional boxing one day in the future.'

'And was one of the kids you sponsor Finn Kennedy?'

Daniel's eyes narrowed. 'It was, but Finn threw away the opportunity.'

'What exactly do you do as a sponsor?'

'I pay for a kid's training, promote tournaments, his kit, public-ity, travel and lodging when he's at an event, and support him when he fights by turning up.'

'How much does that cost?'

'Depends on the individual. If he's good, it can cost a fair amount to set him up and make sure he has everything he needs, around a grand per annum until they become bigger names.'

'Why did Adam throw Finn out? You must know. You were his sponsor.'

'He got completely out of hand. The more accomplished he became at boxing, the more his attitude became loutish. He began picking on some of the younger boys and there were a couple of incidents when he and another lad actually took knives into the club and used them. Adam has strict rules. That's what his club's about. It's to help those who haven't been given any opportunities in life to learn to stand up for themselves, develop pride and confidence; it isn't so they can become violent thugs. He thought Finn was too wayward. I agreed.'

'Do you happen to know who the other lad was?'

'Hassan Ali. He got thrown out too. He's a right troublemaker.'

Natalie heard Lucy shift forward in her chair at this news. She maintained the steady flow of questions. 'Did Samantha ever visit the boxing club?'

'She came with me a couple of times. Not to watch the fights or anything. She was with me when I stopped off to talk to Adam.'

'Did she know any of the boys?'

'Not really. She didn't chat to them. They might have recognised her but I don't think they ever spoke to her.'

'She didn't talk to Finn or Hassan?'

'Not that I know of.'

'Were you aware she was seeing Lee Webster?'

'Was she? I had no idea. Lee? He's not really her type.'

'What do you mean by that exactly?'

'He's a bit rough and ready. I wouldn't have thought Samantha would have been attracted to him. How did they get together? I wasn't aware she knew him that well. He was in the office once or twice, but going out together?' His face screwed up in puzzlement.

'What about Inge Redfern. Did you know her?'

'Name doesn't ring a bell.'

'Petite, brunette, used to go out with Finn.'

'He didn't mention her to me, not that we talked a lot about girls. I was his sponsor. I used to go to the club to find out how he was getting along with his training and check his progress. I didn't sit down and chat about his love life. Hang on, I think I remember him kissing somebody outside the club one time. That might have been her.'

'You didn't see her on your visits to the boxing club? Not in Adam's office, for example?'

He shook his head.

'Samantha didn't mention her?'

'Never.'

'Did Samantha mention any concerns – anybody suddenly taking an unwelcome interest in her, strange phone calls?'

'We didn't have much to say to each other at all after the split. We kept it civil for Oscar's sake. Conversations were limited and usually only about pick-up and drop-off times.'

'I have to ask you the following question. It's procedure. Where were you today?'

'Samford Electronics, where I work. There are plenty of people who can vouch for me. I didn't leave until the police came to tell me about Samantha.' He pressed fingers against his forehead. 'The officers wouldn't tell me how she died.'

'We can't release the exact details of her death, sir, however it appears she was stabbed. We're waiting for the pathologist's report to confirm that. As soon as we can release further information, we'll obviously let you know.'

He blinked away tears. 'Thanks. I want to know even though I don't want to think about what she went through, or what Oscar might have witnessed. I want him to get over this as best he can. Carla says kids bounce back quickly. I hope he does.'

'How long have you and Adam been friends?'

'Since he left prison. While he was inside, he became friendly with my brother, Jason, who was at the same prison serving a stint for dangerous driving. Jason mentioned I'd always been heavily into boxing. I used to box years ago although I didn't have the support, encouragement or money to make it into the sport big time. Adam looked me up as soon as he got out of prison, asked if I'd be interested in his project to help youngsters. That's how I became involved. I liked the idea of helping someone grab chances I never had. Those kids have it rough and I mean really rough in some cases. I don't need to tell you that. You'll have seen all sorts in your job. Like Adam, I wanted to give some of them a lucky break or opportunity to make something of themselves, and not be held back by family or circumstances. It was a shame Finn blew his chance, and Hassan. Total muppets, the pair of them.'

Natalie needed to wrap it up. She'd learnt something valuable: Hassan Ali had also been thrown out of the club and, according to Daniel, was a troublemaker. She wanted to act on it and locate the two teenagers, as well as speak to Lee, Adam and Vitor. She and Lucy left with assurances they would do everything they could to bring the killer to justice.

Back in the car Natalie thumped the steering wheel with the flat of her hand. 'Bloody hell, Lucy. Hassan Ali. We had him but the sneaky little bastard slipped away. He wasn't just covering for Finn, he was covering for himself.'

Ian and Murray had returned to the office ahead of Natalie and Lucy. Ian was tapping on the computer keyboard but looked up when Natalie spoke.

'Have you got a trace on Hassan Ali's mobile, Ian?'

'He dumped it. Left it behind at the flat. He must be using a pay-as-you-go.'

'Hassan and Finn are involved in this somehow. Can one of you speak to the IT department? Ask them to run the new facial recognition programme that connects to surveillance and CCTV cameras. We need to flush them out quickly.'

'Vitor's downstairs.' Murray waited for a response.

'He said anything?'

'Nothing yet but he looks like he might crumble.'

'Good. Where are Lee and Adam?'

'They should be on their way. I sent officers to detain them.'

'Right, we'll begin with Vitor. Murray, as soon as Adam and Lee get here, let us know. I want results tonight.'

She typed a quick text to David.

No idea when home. Don't wait up. X

The reply was instant

I thought we should talk again. I want to be sure you believe me.

She typed out a response.

Can't do this at the moment. We'll chat soon. X

She waited for a reaction, wondering if she ought to phone David and talk it through before realising she actually didn't want to speak to him. That's why she'd sent the text in the first place. It was simply easier than talking. She'd decided to believe him about the gambling. The bank account wasn't showing any withdrawals so although she was annoyed he'd even thought about betting or gaming again, she wasn't going to have another argument about it, and certainly not while she was conducting such an important investigation. If David was needing reassurance from her, he'd have to wait.

She replaced her phone and strode towards the door, calling out, 'Okay. Let's go.'

Vitor Lopes's knee bounced up and down in a nervous, irregular rhythm. Lucy had him on the ropes. Natalie watched her colleague, whose eyes were fully trained on the barman. The recording machine had been switched on and Vitor kept throwing it covert glances.

'We have a witness who can place Lee outside his house at ten thirty p.m. He can't possibly have been in the White Horse at the time you told us. So, Mr Lopes, would you like to tell us the truth?'

'Can we make a deal?'

'This isn't a television show. We don't make deals. You answer my question honestly, and if you don't, I charge you for perverting the course of justice and you get to spend time in the cells. Given you lied to us earlier about Adam being in the pub and were released with a caution, if we throw in this additional offence, you could get up to thirty-six months inside.'

'You don't understand—' Vitor began.

'I understand perfectly. You lied to give both Adam and Lee alibis. A woman was murdered. You could be protecting a murderer, and if that proves to be the case, you will be sent down for aiding and abetting, which will add even more time to your sentence. Your future is not looking too bright for you, so here's the *deal*. You tell us the truth and none of that will happen. Sound reasonable to you?' Lucy cocked her head for a response.

'But if Lee finds out, he'll do terrible things to me.'

'Oh come, come, Mr Lopes. You played that card last time. I'm sure prison will be a far worse option.'

His head swung from side to side like a wonky pendulum as he weighed up his choices. Eventually he agreed.

'Lee was on a job the night of the murder – a break-in. We have an agreement. I act as his alibi. Every time he's on one, I get paid a hundred pounds as a sweetener. If the cops, or anyone else, actually question me about his whereabouts, I get paid extra. He rang me in the early hours of Saturday morning and told me I had to vouch for Adam too because he was helping him. He promised to give me five hundred pounds if anyone showed up asking about either of them.'

'Where was this job – this break-in – supposed to be taking place?'

'I don't know for sure but he targets small businesses, warehouses, that sort of thing, and does them over. I honestly know no more than that. He pays me cash every time.'

'Why would Adam be involved in such a crime? He doesn't need the money.'

'Dunno. I did what Lee asked me. That's all.'

'Didn't it seem strange to you that Adam would be helping Lee with robbery when he apparently has sufficient wealth?'

'I didn't think anything. It was five hundred notes. I'd have sworn the pope was with Lee if it meant earning a few hundred quid.'

'Did Lee ever bring a woman into the pub with him?'

'Now and again. He wasn't a hermit.'

'Do you recognise this woman?'

Lucy pushed across Samantha Kirkdale's photograph.

'Yeah, he was with her a few nights ago. They had a couple of drinks.'

'How did they seem?'

'I wasn't paying attention.'

'Come on, Vitor. You see everything that goes on in that place. Don't play that game with me.'

'Like a couple: holding hands, occasional kisses, that sort of thing. He gave me a wink when they left.'

'You knew Charlotte Brannon, didn't you?' Lucy was taking a chance with her suggestion. He could easily deny it but he was defeated and willing to talk.

'Yes.'

'You ever see Lee with Charlotte Brannon?'

'Only the once. It was a while ago. I thought Adam was going to join them but he didn't. They had an argument and she walked out the pub. Lee asked me not to mention it to Adam, so I didn't.'

'When exactly did this happen?'

'Can't really remember. It was sometime in January.'

'Do you recognise either of these two individuals?'

She pushed across photographs of Hassan and Finn taken from social media.

He studied them carefully. 'I don't think so.'

'Does the name Finn Kennedy mean anything to you?'

'He shook his head.'

'Hassan Ali?'

'No. Is that them?'

'You haven't seen them in your pub maybe talking to Lee or Adam?'

'Never seen or heard of them.'

'Are you absolutely sure this time? I don't want to have to bring you back and charge you.'

'One hundred per cent sure.'

Lucy tidied the photographs away. 'Thank you for your assistance, Mr Lopes.'

'Is that it? I can leave?'

'Unless you want to tell us anything else?'

Vitor lifted his jacket from his lap and stood up. 'You put me in a difficult situation.'

'I think you'll find you put yourself in that position, sir,' Lucy said briskly.

CHAPTER TWENTY-SIX

MONDAY, 5 MARCH – NIGHT

No sooner had they wound up the interview with Vitor than they were given word of Adam's arrival.

'He's in room C with Murray,' said Ian.

'Did he request a lawyer this time?' Natalie asked.

'No.'

'What's he up to? Is he trying to convince us of his innocence by refusing a lawyer, or is he playing us?' Natalie shook her head. She couldn't fathom him out. She turned to Lucy. 'Head upstairs with Ian and see if there's any news on that white van Lee got into, or Hassan and Finn. I'll join Murray.'

Adam was chewing at a thumbnail. He cocked his head to one side when Natalie walked into the room and looked through half-closed lids.

'I hope you've nailed the fucker who killed my wife.'

Natalie ignored him. She spotted the manila folder Murray had brought with him and slid onto the seat next to him. He placed the folder on the table and she began.

'Mr Brannon, we're about to record this interview. I'm only going to ask you once if you want a lawyer to be present during it.'

Adam sat back in his chair and placed one meaty thigh over the other. 'Go ahead. Record it. I've nothing to hide. I don't need a lawyer.'

She signalled for Murray to set the recording device into action.

He spoke clearly. 'Interview with Adam Brannon begins Monday, fifth March, eight twenty p.m. Officers present DS Murray Anderson and DI Natalie Ward. For the record, Adam Brannon has refused to have a lawyer present during this interview.'

Natalie began the interview. 'Mr Brannon, you told us that on Friday the second of March, you dropped your wife, Charlotte, off at your house at around ten and then took the babysitter, Inge Redfern, home to her house in Brompton. You confessed that you had sexual relations with her, after which you left her house just before eleven and drove to the White Horse in Samford. There you met up with your friend, Lee Webster, and returned with him to his flat. After a drink, you left his place at eleven forty, arriving back home at approximately midnight, at which time you sat downstairs and watched *GLOW* on Netflix before going upstairs to calm your son, Alfie, who was crying, and discovering your wife's body.'

'That's what happened.'

'We have new information regarding Lee Webster that throws his alibi out and places him elsewhere at the time he claimed he was with you.' Natalie was bending the truth of what she'd learnt because all they knew was a witness had confirmed a sighting of Lee at 10.30 p.m. She had to follow her instinct again. If Lee had got into the van with the intention of committing burglary, there was no way he and Adam went back to his flat for drinks. 'We have a witness who saw Lee Webster get into a white van at ten thirty p.m.'

Adam's shoulders lifted and dropped. 'I don't know where he was beforehand but I met him at eleven by the pub like I told you and we went back to his place.'

'Yet we can't confirm that. Your car wasn't spotted in or around the area near his flat or the pub. It didn't pass any of the cameras stationed along the roads on the way to his flat or near the pub at or around that time. We have nothing other than your word you were together at that time.'

'Then you have to take our word, don't you? Unless you can prove otherwise. I met Lee by the pub at eleven. End of.'

Natalie nodded curtly and paused before saying, 'You also were unable to identify two suspects from a photograph we showed you. This picture.'

Murray spoke up. 'DI Ward is showing Adam Brannon photograph E101.'

'That's right. I can't tell from that photograph who that is.'

'If I showed you this enhanced picture, would you be able to identify the man on the left?'

'DI Ward is showing Adam Brannon photograph E102.'

Adam peered at it.

'Recognise the person on the left in it?'

'Not really. There's still not much to go on.'

'If I told you it was Finn Kennedy, would that surprise you?'

'Finn? What the fuck was he doing around my house that night? He didn't kill Charlotte, did he? That's mental.'

Natalie pushed the photograph to one side. 'You definitely had no idea he was in the vicinity that night?'

Adam shook his head. 'No idea at all. Who was he with?'

'We think it was Hassan Ali but we can't find either of them. Any clues as to where they might be?'

'Me? No. I did my best with them both but they had a different agenda. Finn could have been a good boxer if he'd got rid of his attitude but he used whatever I taught him out on the street. He took a delight in fighting anyone and everyone for the hell of it. I couldn't work with him. He wouldn't calm down. He has quite a few mates on the estate. Could be with any of them.'

'Okay. Let's move on to Daniel Kirkdale.'

Adam didn't flinch.

'You know Daniel.'

'Sure I do. He's one of my sponsors at the club. He funded that little shit Finn until I booted him out for bringing a knife into the club and threatening another kid with it.'

'I'm sorry to inform you Daniel's wife, Samantha, was murdered this morning.'

That provoked a physical response. Adam unfolded his arms and sat up straighter. 'Same killer?'

'We're looking into that possibility.'

'Finn?'

'We're considering a number of suspects. Where were you today?'

'At the club. I didn't feel like doing anything. I've shut the place for now. I stayed there.'

'All day?'

'Yes. I needed to be alone. There's been a lot to take in.'

'You didn't leave the club once? Not even to eat?'

'I've got enough to eat in the office. I can't return home to collect my gear and I don't know where else to go. I stayed at the club all day.'

'You didn't visit Alfie to see how he is, or speak to Charlotte's parents?'

'I can't do that yet. I'm still not ready to handle any of that. I'll go in my own good time.'

'Did you talk to anyone at all?'

'No. I haven't got a phone, remember? They're both here at the station with your forensic team. I worked out for a long session, had a shower and then worked out some more. I didn't feel like doing anything else. I lay on the bed for a while too. Tried to work out what I was going to do next, now Charlotte's gone. That's all.'

'Did you know Samantha Kirkdale?'

'I've seen her with Daniel. Didn't know her personally.'

'She ever come into the club?'

'With Daniel a couple of times, to drop off some publicity material. She hung around while we chatted.'

'When did you last have contact with Lee?'

'Not spoken to him since Saturday night. I haven't got a phone,' he repeated and stared hard at her.

'True but you could have visited him.'

'I didn't fancy it. Having trouble getting over losing my wife.' His eyes glowed darkly.

'Have you fallen out with Lee?'

'That's crap. Why would we fall out?'

'I don't know. Maybe you're annoyed about the weak alibi he arranged for you.'

He released a derisory snort.

'Did you know he was seeing Samantha Kirkdale?'

'What?'

'Surely he'd have told you that. You're his friend.'

'Straight up. I didn't know he was seeing anyone. He never once mentioned her.'

'Did you ever see her at the White Horse pub?'

'Can't say I have.'

'What do you know about Lee's *activities*?'

'What activities are you referring to?'

'The warehouse break-ins, the burglaries.'

'I haven't the foggiest idea what you're talking about.' His words were deliberate and slow.

Natalie didn't believe him. She decided to break off for the time being and tackle him again later. 'Okay, we'll leave it there for the moment but I'll be back to finish this conversation later.' She nodded at Murray, who turned off the machine.

'Interview terminated at eight forty p.m.'

'Do I have to stay here?'

'You got somewhere else you'd rather be?'

He let out another quiet snort. 'No.'

'Then we'd appreciate you helping us with our enquiries. You're free to go if you want. You haven't been charged.' She was taking a risk, giving him a chance to leave, but she banked on the fact he wanted to prove his innocence by appearing to be obliging. It was another hunch that paid off. He didn't move.

'Thank you. The sergeant will arrange a drink if you'd like one.'

Adam slumped back in his chair, eyes down on his nail again. 'Nah. I don't want anything; except for you to find Charlotte's killer.'

CHAPTER TWENTY-SEVEN

Dr: How have you been getting on?

Patient X: I finished the letter I've been working on all month and you were right. It was cathartic to put my thoughts and frustration into words and write to her, even though she'll never read the letter.

Dr: The main thing is that you've now fully opened yourself up. You've voiced what it is that's been troubling you all these months. The dreams might desist.

Patient X: I haven't had a bad dream this week.

Dr: I'm pleased to hear it. Maybe you're also coming to terms with the fact that your dreams, no matter how frightening or powerful they seem, are merely figments of your imagination. By letting your emotions escape through words, you are finding another outlet.

Patient X: Yes. I understand that now. I want to tell you something else. I hired a private investigator to track down my mother.

Dr: Don't have too high an expectation of that happening.

Patient X: Oh, he'll find her. He's very good.

Dr: What do you hope to achieve by locating her?

Patient X: I want to read her my letter.

Dr: That wasn't what we agreed. You were supposed to write the letter and then burn it, allowing the words, along with your anger and fears, to evaporate with the smoke. We worked on that image so you would experience the maximum release at the moment of setting fire to the paper.

Patient X: I did as you instructed but as pieces of charred paper curled and fell into the ashtray, I experienced a fresh episode – one far more powerful than all the others. I recognised the significance of the image.

Dr: What image are you referring to?

Patient X: Blood. It smelt so… wholesome.

Dr: Wholesome. That's an interesting choice of adjective. Tell me more about this episode.

Patient X: Blood poured from her wounds like a glorious crimson fountain. I wanted to lick it, taste it, bathe in it.

Dr: You mentioned blood before during our last session, when you told me about the angel of death.

Patient X: Oh, I wasn't being serious then. I was messing with you, testing your gullibility to see if you believed everything I tell you. This is different. It happened.

Dr: There's a possibility that the conversation we had about the blood actually caused you to dream about it.

Patient X: I disagree.

Dr: Was the woman in the vision your mother?

Patient X: No.

Dr: Describe her for me.

Patient X: A young woman in her twenties with long, chestnut-brown hair that shimmers in the light, and large brown eyes that stare at me in terror and wonder at the same time.

Dr: What happens in the dream?

Patient X: She's sitting on a settee next to her son. She spots me watching her and she tightens her hold on the young boy's hand. He has dark hair like his mother's, and gentle eyes. He needs to be freed. I can free him but first I must kill her. I approach her. My smile is friendly. She visibly relaxes. I am not threatening as she first thought. She is naturally suspicious of strangers. She has no chance to react. I lift the lamp and smash it against her face, shattering her cheek. I raise it once more and bring it down onto her again and again, until she stops moving, and then I look at the boy. His mouth is a perfect 'o'. I put a finger to my lips. 'It's okay,' I whisper. 'I'm going to free you.' Large wet tears roll down his face and he cowers in the corner of the settee, snivelling. He rolls into a ball. I am merciful. I lift him from the settee and carry him to the next room, where I leave him with the door shut, so he doesn't have to look at her any more. I return and I smell the blood. It's pure and spectacular. I want to touch it. I stretch my forefinger towards it but I regain consciousness and the last image I see is a pool of blood.

Dr: Would you like me to interpret it for you?

Patient X: Not really. I understand its significance. What are your thoughts about it, especially the blood?

Dr: Well, blood represents force, vitality and life energy, but dreams about it can't be easily interpreted. Much depends on the patient.

Patient X: I read if someone dreams of blood they might be going to meet a relative.

Dr: If what you are truly hoping for is to meet your mother, it would explain the pleasure at seeing so much blood in your dream, and the desire to touch it.

Patient X: I could read that explanation in any dream interpretation book and reach similar conclusions. You're not really telling me anything new and I'm doing all the work here, during these sessions, these expensive sessions. I tell you everything about my episodes.

Dr: I still believe we are making progress. You've already arrived at these conclusions alone, without my assistance. My objective is to help you reach a platform of self-awareness so these dreams no longer cause you fear or confusion and you can comprehend the reasons behind their manifestation. You worked out the significance of the blood in this latest episode without my input. That is a step forward. You think this dream has manifested itself from a deep desire to find your mother. I can give you many other explanations regarding the significance of dreaming about blood but that would only cloud the issue. There are religious connotations, of course, and a dreamer often dreams of blood when they are experiencing emotional stress.

Patient X: And you think I am merely suffering emotional stress, Doctor? I wanted to smell the blood, Doctor. I wanted to put my finger in it and paint with it. The urge to do so was overwhelming. I craved that feeling. Does that sound like emotional stress to you?

Dr: I think we're crossing a line here. We've been discussing dreams the last few months. Are you trying to tell me you want to act out the scenes in them?

Patient X: Dreams are dreams, aren't they? They're fantasies and desires made up in my head that explode to life only when I am not awake. I want you to explain why I would feel that way. Why I would want to touch, smell and taste the blood. Tell me, Doctor. Why?

CHAPTER TWENTY-EIGHT

A male cleaner, wearing khaki overalls and a pair of ear protectors, pushed an industrial cleaning machine down the corridor, its drone barely audible through the triple glazing of Natalie's office. She watched the man pass by before continuing with her questions.

'What else do we have on Samantha Kirkdale?'

Lucy read from her notes. 'She has a close network of friends, mostly other young mums. She's lived in the Samford area all her life. Her parents are divorced and both have been given the news of her death. Social media profiles reveal nothing untoward. Heavy emphasis was on her son, Oscar, and noting the progress he was making. There are lots of photos of him. She set her status on Facebook from married to single two months ago, about the time she moved into rented accommodation. There's no mention of a boyfriend.'

'And do we know if she and Charlotte were friends?'

'There's nothing to indicate they were. They're not friends online and Charlotte's number wasn't in her telephone contact list.'

'What about her relationship with Lee Webster?' Natalie directed her question at Ian, who'd just come back from the technical lab.

'The techies discovered several text messages between them that go back to January this year before she left her husband. I've printed them off. Nothing suspicious in them: arrangements to meet up, chats about what they're doing, watching on television – all normal stuff.'

'Nothing to suggest he was angry with her?'

'Quite the opposite. I think he was keen on her.'

'It might have been part of his plan: be Mr Nice Guy, then attack her,' suggested Lucy.

Ian gave a small nod of agreement. 'Except I can't think what motive he would have. He seems to like her.'

'We haven't yet explored the possibility Lee and Charlotte were having an affair. Charlotte has been described as wild and has had relations with other men. It wouldn't be out of the question to assume she and Lee had something going on. One of her friends claimed she liked bad boys. I think he might fit that description.' Natalie made a quick note on her file to ask him that very question before speaking again. 'And where are we on that white van our witness saw outside Lee's house?'

'Still working on that,' said Murray. 'I'll go back upstairs and assist in a minute. We've pulled all camera footage around the area and are going through it. We're gathering lists of all reported break-ins for that night too.'

'I don't need to stress how urgent that is. I can't leave him waiting too much longer or his lawyer will come up with some excuse to leave. We really don't have a lot of time. I don't want to release Adam yet either. I'm convinced he's holding back on us. We can't ignore the possibility Finn and Hassan might be behind or involved with both murders. Information on the pair has gone out to all units and the IT team are running a facial recognition programme, so if they pass any surveillance cameras, we'll be able to identify them and hopefully locate them. Ian, if we get a hit, let me know immediately.'

She put interlinked hands behind her neck and stretched into them before glancing at Lucy. 'Time to face Lee.'

*

Lee, in a sweatshirt and tracksuit bottoms, gave Lucy a smile when she entered the interview room with Natalie.

'We really should stop meeting like this,' he said.

'Don't think we've brought you in because we find you attractive,' Natalie replied, pulling back her chair with one free hand and nodding at the lawyer.

Lee grinned a reply.

Once the recording device was in action and she and Lucy were settled, she began by asking a question. 'Mr Webster, we'd like to know where you were this afternoon. I notice from your work schedule, you were not on duty today.'

'I was at home. Played on the Xbox.'

'You stayed at home all afternoon, playing a game?'

'Yeah.'

'Did you attempt to contact Samantha Kirkdale today?'

A flash of concern swept across his face. 'No.'

'You and Samantha have been involved in a relationship since January. Is that true?'

'What if we have? There's no law against it. We're two consenting adults and she's a free agent.'

'I'm sorry to inform you Samantha was murdered this afternoon at her home.'

'Fuck! Oh fuck, no!' His face crumpled up at the news and he looked away sharply.

'So, I'll ask you again, where were you this morning, and is there anybody who can corroborate your alibi?'

'At home. I was at home.' He shook his head and swiped at a rogue tear that had escaped. He turned to his lawyer. 'This is total bullshit. I didn't see Samantha today. I want that noted. I didn't go to her house or stay over last night. God, I wish had. This might not have happened if I had.'

'Did you also have a relationship with Charlotte Brannon?'

He turned to his lawyer. 'I don't have to answer this crap, do I?'

Natalie spoke directly to the lawyer. 'It might compromise your client if he doesn't answer the questions honestly.'

The man in the suit indicated Lee should continue. Lee's shoulders slumped and he nodded. 'She and I, we had a one-nighter, ages ago.'

'You were seen in the White Horse pub in January, arguing.'

'You've been talking to that wanker, Vitor, haven't you? Bastard! He's stitching me up here. It was something and nothing. Not like my relationship with Samantha.'

'Can you explain what happened between you and Charlotte on that occasion? Because at the moment you appear to know two women, both of whom have been brutally murdered.'

'Charlotte was in a devil-may-care mood. She got like that sometimes. She'd turn up at the club when Adam wasn't around and flirt with me. Then one afternoon when Adam was at a tournament, we had sex. That was the end of it. I told her it wasn't a good idea to do it again. That night in the pub, she was in the mood again to be adventurous and have some fun, but I was getting it on with Samantha. I told her I didn't want to and she got the hump. That was all.'

'You admit to sleeping with both women?'

'Only once with Charlotte. I shouldn't have. Samantha was a different matter. I liked her a lot. What happened to her?' He sniffed back tears.

'I can't give out details. You know that.'

'What's happened to Oscar? Is he alive?'

'He's with Daniel. He's okay.'

He flexed his fingers and pressed the point between his eyes. 'Fuck me, this is awful. Bloody terrible.'

'I'd like to go back to the night of Charlotte's murder. Where were you that night?'

'I already told you. I was at the White Horse, then I went back to my flat with Adam.'

'That's where we have a problem. It's come to light that you weren't at the pub.'

'If that Vitor told you otherwise, he's a lying bastard or you've deliberately leant on him.'

A light rapping on the door halted proceedings and Natalie excused herself. In the corridor, Murray held out a printout and a list of crime numbers, one of which was circled in red.

'Warehouse on Dunfold Street got done over sometime between eleven and twelve that night. Somebody got away with fifty grand's worth of kit. This van was captured on camera at two points en route from Lee's house and was picked up by a security camera attached to a building near the warehouse. This one clearly shows Lee at the wheel. The date and time stamps prove he was at the warehouse at eleven p.m. This other photograph captured on CCTV shows the van headed towards the Ashmore Estate.'

'Shit. That proves he couldn't have been at the Brannons' house at the time Charlotte was murdered.'

'It seems not.'

Natalie rubbed her temples. 'I thought we had him. I really thought we had him.' She righted her shoulders. 'Keep searching for Hassan and Finn. We have to hope they saw something or are involved in some way. I'm out of options.'

Murray disappeared down the corridor, leaving Natalie standing outside the interview room. Which way could she turn now? The only person without a solid alibi for the night in question, or for this morning, when Samantha was killed, was Adam and he was resolute he was innocent. She was going to have to try and crack him again.

'We've spoken to Lee and he's admitted to being elsewhere on Friday night. You can no longer claim you were with him. Looks like you're out of alibis and you know what that means.' Natalie folded her arms and stared at Adam coldly. He lifted his hands in a submissive gesture.

'Okay. I wasn't with him.'

'Care to elaborate or do I charge you now?'

'I went to the boxing club. I needed some time alone,' said Adam in his easy, lazy drawl.

'Why didn't you say that from the outset instead of all these bullshit lies?'

'Why do you think? To start with, I couldn't prove I was at the boxing club. It's not like there are any CCTV cameras there or anyone saw me. I went there straight after I left Inge's. After the meal with her folks, Charlotte and I had a pretty major row. She'd put away a fair amount of booze that night and she could be a right bitch when she was drunk – a complete nightmare, in fact – and I wasn't in the mood to take any more crap from her. I couldn't stay longer at Inge's cos her mum was due home so I figured I'd hang around the club for a bit, and by the time I got home, she'd have cleared off to bed and be asleep. I just messed about on my phone, playing games until I decided to return. Would you have believed me if I'd told you that from the off? Like hell you would. Lee's suggestion to say I was with him seemed the best option. You were dead keen to pin Charlotte's murder on me so I had to buy myself some time. I assumed you'd have found out who had killed her by now and I could come clean. Looks like I was way off with that.'

Natalie jumped up and leant right into his face until her nose was almost touching his. 'Have you any idea how many man-hours we've completely wasted on account of you and your mate, Lee? You've had us chasing our tails instead of actually getting somewhere and finding whoever murdered your wife. You could well have screwed it up completely for us. Ever think of that?' Natalie's nostrils flared in anger. Adam's attitude was getting under her skin.

'You…' She bit her tongue. Abusing the man wasn't going to help matters. She drew back and, turning from the table, directed her words to Lucy. 'Take him away. Get him out of my sight.'

CHAPTER TWENTY-NINE

With Lee charged for robbery and with nothing else to go on, Natalie had sent the team home before they all became too disillusioned. It was a tall order to regroup and go back to the beginning to search for their perpetrator. Adam was troubling her. She couldn't work out if he was telling the truth or was an accomplished liar. With no suspects to consider other than the teenagers who were in hiding, she was anxious the leads would dry up.

The taps were running next door in the en-suite. David was shaving. He used a brush and soap, a traditional method that she quite liked. It was nice to watch him scrape away the foam to leave perfectly smooth skin, but today she didn't want to slip into the bathroom to chat and watch him make his deft strokes. She couldn't face him at all. She didn't have the energy to go back over why he'd felt the need to stare at gambling websites. She dragged herself from the bed and headed for the family bathroom, where she sat on the side of the bath as it filled and thought back over the investigation. It wasn't moving along quickly enough for her liking. She'd followed protocol and got nowhere. What hadn't she done? Could she have handled it any differently?

She swirled pink gel that promised to cleanse gently and offered the soothing aromas of lotus flower and sage into the water. She hadn't a clue of how a lotus flower actually smelt but the scent was delicate and pleasant.

David tapped lightly on the door.

'Occupied,' she called, sending him on his way. Her heart felt solid in her chest.

What had she done wrong? Had she missed an important clue? She ought to have brought in a criminal profiler from the outset and ascertained what sort of sick individual they were dealing with. What was the significance of the messages? *Why? Who?* Surely these weren't left for the police. Or was the perpetrator taunting her and her team? On the other hand, they could be intended for either the victims or their husbands. What did it all mean? She sank into the water and stared up at the ceiling. It needed painting. A persistent rusty brown stain caused by an old damp patch had developed once more in the left-hand corner. As she studied it, images of the bloody messages floated through her mind. What was going on in the killer's head? They'd wasted time looking into Lee's and Adam's whereabouts, and meanwhile the real perpetrator could well strike again. She had to find them before a third message appeared on a wall.

'Did you get any sleep last night?' Bethany's voice was concerned.

Lucy was hunched over the laptop. 'Some.'

'It's getting to you, Luce. You won't be able to think straight if you don't rest up when you get the opportunity.'

Lucy looked up from the screen. 'Try telling that to my brain. It's like some sort of independent dynamo. It whirs and whirs but it isn't productive. I'm not getting anywhere.'

'What have you been looking at?'

'A victim's Facebook page – Samantha, the woman killed yesterday. Hoping for a clue.'

'I take it you haven't found any.'

Lucy shook her head.

'Don't lose heart. You're exhausted, you're feeling thwarted, but you work with a formidable team who don't know the meaning of the word failure. You'll find this killer.'

Natalie headed the morning briefing. She'd tried to leave the house before the children had surfaced, without breakfast or a chance for her and David to exchange too many words, but he'd insisted on dragging up the subject of gambling. The conversation had only served to rouse suspicion. In her opinion, it needn't have taken place. It was almost as if David was trying too hard to protest his innocence...

'I suppose you checked our bank account to see if I was telling the truth?' David says as soon as she appears in the kitchen.

'I told you I would.'

'And?'

'You were right. It hasn't been touched. You haven't been taking money out of the account and gambling it away. There's no need to go on about it.'

'I want you to believe me.'

'I believe you.'

'Good. So that's that?'

'Yes.'

'I didn't like being interrogated.'

'So you said, and I didn't like the thought of you staring at a gaming website while daydreaming about betting. I don't want to go back there, David. It almost ruined everything.'

'I'm not stupid. Don't treat me like I am.'

'I'm not. I'm just wary. Really wary. And when I see one of those sites flashing on your computer, I'm only going to think one thing, aren't I? That you've started betting, or playing poker, or gambling in some form.'

'Well I'm not.'

'What more do you want me to say?'

'Sorry?'

'For what? For being anxious?'

'For not having enough faith in me.'

'That's not true.'

'Yeah, okay. But at least I could prove I wasn't digging into our funds.'

'Can we actually drop this subject now? I really have nothing more to say on it.'

'I just wanted to make my point.'

'For crying out loud. You made it. All right? I have to go to work now.'

'Course. Josh has football practice tonight so I'll take Leigh out for a burger or something while we wait for him.'

'Sure. She'll enjoy that. I don't know—'

'What time you'll be back. I understand. See you when I see you.'

Lying in the bath, she'd come to some decisions about the investigation and a plan of action. She shoved away thoughts of the conversation with David and began the briefing.

'I understand your frustration. I'm as pissed off with Adam and Lee for lying about their alibis as you are. What we mustn't do is let it get in the way of any progress. We've squandered valuable time but we've eliminated a number of suspects and we still have our two youths who are hiding out. I highly suspect they either saw somebody or something significant, or are involved in some way. These are streetwise kids. They don't take off without very good reason. I suggest we monitor the phones and social media sites for Finn and Hassan's three closest friends who live in Hounslow House. That's Abe, Mustafa and Leon. Obviously, we require their surnames. If they have any contact with a pay-as-you-go phone, we'll take that as our cue to investigate and haul them in.'

'Why not bring them into the station, Natalie?' asked Ian.

'It won't be worthwhile. They won't speak to us. Best to keep an eye on their online activities and see if that yields anything. I'd also like us to follow up on Samantha's friends. See what we can learn. She might have had an argument or a run-in with somebody. See if she mentioned anything that gave rise to concern.

'Up until now, we've been trying to make connections between the victims and been searching for somebody who knew both Charlotte and Samantha. I want to think outside that scenario. My biggest fear is we have a killer targeting random women, women with children. I can't work out what sort of maniac we're actually dealing with: the writing in blood, the violence of the attacks. We need a professional angle and I'm calling in the services of a criminal profiler. Henrik Karlsson will be joining us later.' Henrik was one of the most renowned in the country and had written several bestsellers on the subject.

'I've found out something,' said Lucy. 'Samantha doesn't have auburn hair. She does now, but she's only recently begun to dye it. I looked through her Facebook photographs, and she's changed the colour before, but from what I can gather her natural hair colour is brown – a chestnut-brown.'

'Same colour as Charlotte's,' said Natalie. 'Might be relevant. We'll take note. I've received the pathology reports for Samantha Kirkdale. She died of multiple stab wounds to the chest and neck. There were twenty-two stab wounds in total.'

'She was twenty-two years old,' said Lucy.

'Maybe that's significant too. If so, it indicates the killer knew her age.

Mike, do you want to add your findings?'

Mike, who'd been sitting quietly at the far side of the room, spoke up. 'The knife we retrieved from the crime scene has been identified as the weapon used to kill Samantha. We were unable to lift any prints from it. We checked the kitchen drawers and discovered another eight-inch chef's knife. It's unlikely she'd own two similar knives so we can deduce the killer probably purchased this particular knife and took it with him to the scene of the crime. We've established it's an Acelink eight-inch professional chef kitchen knife with high carbon steel blade and ergonomic wooden handle, available online from a number of retailers.' Mike spread his hands to indicate he had finished speaking.

'If there are no questions, let's get on this.' Natalie left a gap for people to speak, and when no one did she dismissed them and marched outside with Mike.

'I don't know which way to turn,' she said in quiet voice. 'Have you anything to help us?'

'I wish I had.'

'No fibres, hair?'

'Plenty of both. In fact, too many. It'll take a long time to work out what they are and to whom they belong.'

'Any news on that paternity test request for Alfie?'

'I'll chase that up. We're swamped with work but we're giving you every priority, Natalie.'

'I appreciate that.'

His eyes rested on hers a second too long. She didn't break away. Part of her wanted to tell him about David but the last time she'd gone that route, they'd ended up in bed together.

'Everything okay?' Mike asked.

'It would be a whole lot better if I had some idea of who's responsible for these deaths.'

He waited in case there was more to follow, but she fell silent so he moved away. 'I'll see where we are with that DNA test.'

Natalie studied the pictures of the two victims once more – Charlotte with her glossy chestnut hair, large brown eyes under groomed eyebrows, and sad smile, and Samantha with shining auburn hair that hung past her shoulders, and wide lips. There didn't seem to be any other physical similarities between the two women. They didn't live near each other, frequent the same places, share any friends or interests but they were both connected to the boxing club in some way and each had a child.

Lucy put down the phone. It was the eighth call she'd made to Samantha's friends and found out nothing else useful. She pulled up the Facebook page again. For some reason she kept coming back to it. She scrolled through the messages from the last three months, searching for a name or something to give her the breakthrough she craved. Looking at the photographs of baby Oscar from birth to present day had been painful. She'd shared Samantha's experience of watching him grow from a helpless babe to a charming, happy toddler. Thirteen months. How quickly that time went by. One minute he was sleeping in his mother's arms, the next grinning at the camera and waving the remnants of a sausage roll in his chubby fist. It would be like this with Spud. He or she would grow in the blink of an eye. The idea frightened her. She had no way of knowing how she'd react after the baby was born. She scrolled through the pictures, pausing at one of them, a selfie, taken outside their new home, with the caption, 'New beginnings.' She stopped reading. There. She clicked onto the search engine and then double-checked with information on file.

'I've got something.'

Natalie materialised from nowhere. 'What?'

Lucy enlarged the photograph she'd been examining. Behind Samantha's head was an estate agent's letting board. 'Samantha rented her house in Bose Street from Cartwright and Butler estate agency in Samford. Rob Cooke, Charlotte Brannon's boyfriend, works for them.'

'Ring the agency.'

Lucy tried the number and was put straight through to Rob.

'Put him on speakerphone,' said Natalie.

'Mr Cooke, it's DS Carmichael from Samford Police head-quarters.'

'Hello, Sergeant. Do you have any news about Charlotte?'

'I'm afraid I'm not ringing about that. I wondered if you could tell me your whereabouts for yesterday afternoon.'

'Yesterday afternoon? Why?'

'I'd prefer you to answer my question, sir.'

'I was in Sheffield, at a departmental meeting.'

'Can anyone confirm that?'

'Ring Shelly Bradshaw, the company secretary. She arranged it.'

'Do you have a number for her?'

'One second.' There was a momentary silence and then he read it out. 'Why are you asking me these questions?'

'Do you know a Samantha Kirkdale?'

'Name rings a bell but I can't place her.'

'She rented one of your properties, a house in Bose Street, two months ago.'

'That's where I've seen the name. It was written on one of the contracts. She was my colleague Suzie Connolly's client, not mine.'

'But you remember her?'

'I might have seen her in the office when she came in to discuss arrangements with Suzie, but I don't recall her. I don't handle lettings and rentals, you see. I'm on sales. Shall I pass you over to Suzie?'

'That won't be necessary, thank you.'

She ended the call and faced Natalie. 'Fuck it! I'm going around in circles here.'

'Check his alibi.'

'But he didn't know her.'

'I know, but I'm also spinning around here, so it'd be best to check out his alibi and add him to the growing list of non-suspects I'll be able to hand over to Aileen when she asks for a progress report.'

Lucy dialled the number and spoke to Shelly, who confirmed Rob's presence at a departmental meeting that didn't end until 6 p.m. She flung her mobile onto the desk. 'That's that. Now what?'

'We keep digging. This is police work, Lucy. We keep going and going until we find whatever we're looking for.'

'Some days, I wonder if I'm cut out for this,' Lucy mumbled.

'Tell me about it. We all have days like that,' came the reply.

CHAPTER THIRTY

Patient X: I see you're surprised I've made our appointment. I bet you thought I wouldn't come back.

Dr: I admit to being surprised. You seemed to have finally understood the meaning of your dreams and why you were experiencing them. I thought you had no further need of me. So how do you feel today?

Patient X: Stronger. Much stronger.

Dr: That's good.

Patient X: I've found out how to exorcise the dreams and I came back to tell you that you were wrong. You were very wrong.

Dr: In what way was I wrong?

Patient X: You insisted they were figments of my mind: clouded memories mixed with emotions, coupled with fears from my childhood. But they aren't.

Dr: Have you come to ask for help with a dream?

Patient X: I've come to enlighten you, Doctor.

Dr: What do you mean?

Patient X: It's time I told you what's going on.

Dr: I don't understand what you're getting at.

Patient X: I don't need your help any more. We're done with all this dream nonsense. All this bullshit.

Dr: I'm afraid I'm going to have to ask you to leave.

Patient X: No. First I'm going to play along with your psychobabble nonsense. Here's a dream for you, Doctor. A woman steps out of her office. She's returning home after a long day to her flat and her cat, Loki, a beautiful breed, with long fur and sharp ears: Maine Coon, I believe it is. Oh my! How your eyes have grown in size, Doctor. Rings a bell, does it? Never mind. Let me continue with my episode or dream or whatever name you want to give it. The woman opens the door to her feline friend and is greeted not by her loving, mischievous companion she cleverly named after a Norse god, but by the devil himself.

Dr: Get out. Now.

Patient X: Don't you want to hear more about this episode? You've enjoyed listening to them up until now. You've hung on my every word, teasing every image from me and leaving in their place a gaping wound.

Dr: That wasn't my intention. You came to me to try and find a reason for them, to remove them from your life so you could feel at peace.

Patient X: And I do feel at peace, Doctor. Bravo. I've worked out the true significance of all of these episodes. I know why I dream about killing women. I understand why I experience such euphoria when I dip my finger in their blood. Are you clever enough to work it out yet?

Dr: Get out.

Patient X: Okay. Have it your way. I'll go. Until our next meeting, Doctor.

CHAPTER THIRTY-ONE

TUESDAY, 6 MARCH – AFTERNOON

Henrik Karlsson breathed onto the lenses of his red-framed glasses and wiped them methodically, holding them up to the light from the window to check for smears. 'I hate smudges,' he said. 'They're so distracting. I keep imagining there's somebody in my peripheral vision.' His tonal accent was slight but definitely of Scandinavian origin, elongating and softening the 's' sound. He fitted the spectacles onto his fleshy nose and sat down, placing one long leg over the other before studying Natalie with ice-blue eyes.

'The killer left two separate messages, both written in blood?'

'That's correct.' She handed him photographs of the messages left behind at the crime scenes.

His bottom lip protruded as he examined both pictures before placing them on the desk in front of him. 'The children. Ages?'

'The first, six months. The second, thirteen months.'

'Both boys.'

'That's right.'

He didn't move, his eyes focused on a spot some way in the distance. 'Both victims were women in their twenties, similar build and married. Can I look again at their photographs, please?' He put the pictures side by side and pointed at each in turn. 'They have brown eyes although not exactly the same shade of brown.

Their noses are slightly different, as are their lips, and their hair is of a different colour but a similar style – long and straight. The killer might be searching for women who remind him of one particular person. Ordinarily, if that were the case, the female victims would share more identifying features.' He ran long fingers over his blond beard.

'We discovered that Samantha dyed her hair. It is naturally chestnut-brown, the same colour as Charlotte's.' Natalie waited for him to continue.

'Then he might be targeting women with naturally long dark hair and brown eyes. Perhaps they remind him of someone.'

'Somebody he hates?' Natalie asked.

'Or loved or even still loves but feels that love isn't being recip-rocated. I understand he assaulted the first victim with a baseball bat found under the bed. That might have been opportune. He would have no way of knowing the bat was there unless he had entered the house on an earlier occasion. The second victim was killed with a knife you believe was purchased especially for that purpose. It would not surprise me to learn he took that knife to the first house to use as a weapon but was surprised by Charlotte and, instead, wrestled the bat from her to use against her. I think he intended to use the knife, and my reasoning is that, for him, it is important his victims bleed. He needs the blood so he can write his messages.' Yet again he tapped the photograph of the blood-written messages.

'That brings us to their significance. The first message he left was one word. "*Why?*" I believe this to be a question for either you, the police, or somebody who was close to him and who has caused him harm or upset – a lover, a sibling, a parent. I refer to the killer as male but they could be female. The majority of men committing murder opt for a gun, whereas far fewer women use a gun. Instead, they are more likely to use a knife, or indeed to strike their victim to death with a blunt object. Although I should point out that female knife attacks are generally against men, not other women, I would not discount the possibility the perpetrator of this crime is female.'

He nodded to drive home his point, and when he thought it was made, he continued. 'The second message, another question, "*Who?*" This one seems once more to be directed at those investigating the crime. He's asking the same question you yourselves are asking – who is responsible for this? If this is the case, he's challenging the authorities. He's bold and confident you won't establish his identity. There's another possibility: this question follows the first and is addressed to the same unknown – the lover, sibling or parent – as the first question, "*Why?*" If so, the meaning is obscure.'

'You can't hazard a guess?'

'I could come up with several but they'd only muddy the waters. He's asked two questions so far. As you know, there are five questions beginning with the letter W: *Who? What? When? Where? Why?* I fear he might ask all of them and there will be more victims. I also think the killer is in no hurry. He wants whoever these messages are addressed to to see what he's capable of.'

'Have I got this right? We're searching for someone who's on a mission to deliver a message to us, the police, or to somebody they know?' Natalie asked.

Henrik turned his gaze onto her. 'I believe so. He's full of anger but also controlled. I suspect the frenzied attack on each victim wasn't because the perpetrator hated them; it was to extract sufficient blood for the messages. Care has been taken with each stroke. See? The lines forming each letter slope and meet in the correct places. Look, here the W is perfectly formed. The lines, or upside-down V-shape attaching the uprights, have no gaps between them. The killer took time to compose each question and to make his writing neat. The messages are key to this.'

He paused to drink from a water bottle. No one spoke. When he was finished he carefully screwed the top back on before continuing.

'And the victims. Why not target men or even older women? He has chosen women in their twenties, both with young children. It is a deliberate choice. I'm unable to fathom the reasoning behind it, as there are many explanations as to why he has done so. The perpetrator might be a female in the same age group as these victims who has lost a child and feels an uncontrollable jealousy towards those who have not, a man who has lost a lover or spouse… You see what I mean? There are several options.

'Jealousy is a powerful emotion. There is one more thing. The murderer didn't stab or beat the children. The bodies of the female victims provided the blood for the messages.' He ran fingers and thumb down his beard once more, resting them on his chin before speaking. 'He doesn't want to hurt them, but it's important to the killer that his victims have children who are abandoned near the scene of the crime. That might be meaningful.'

Lucy picked up on his last sentence. 'The killer might have been abandoned?'

'Or felt he was. That's all I can give you for the moment. What you should mostly bear in mind is that the person you are hunting for is intelligent and careful – very careful. Chameleon-like. They're probably an expert in masking their reactions and feelings.'

With that, collecting his bottle from the table, he rose. 'I'll be upstairs for the next day or two. I'll search through the files, speak to Forensics and see if there's anything more I can offer you.' He took three strides to reach the door and disappeared into the corridor.

Natalie addressed her team. 'We have to return to the start with these victims and dig up some more information on both, talk to friends and families again. Go through witness statements. Bear in mind what you've heard.'

She returned to her desk and switched on her laptop. It was one thing having an idea of what the killer was doing – writing messages to an unknown other – but she was still no closer to establishing who that might be, and if the perpetrator was unconnected to the victims, it would be like hunting for a needle in a haystack.

The internal phone rang and Murray answered. 'Great.' He jumped to his feet. 'CCTV camera outside a Lidl store picked up Finn Kennedy two minutes ago.'

'I'll come with you,' said Lucy, leaping up and making for the door.

'Take vests,' shouted Natalie at their retreating backs. 'He could be armed.'

She pulled up a map of the area around Lidl on her screen. If Finn was getting provisions from the store, he must be hiding out nearby. She called Ian across to help work out where the youths were. Any traction on this case was a positive, and she was going to make sure locating Finn and Hassan paid off.

CHAPTER THIRTY-TWO

The Lidl store was situated in a recently built retail complex at the entrance to Samford. Most of the premises were not yet completed or occupied, and large posters bearing details of incoming retailers covered the fronts of them. Railings cordoned off what was to be a car park serving all the shops, leaving a rough area for parking in front of the supermarket.

It had taken Lucy and Murray only five minutes to reach the place, and after getting out of their unmarked car, Lucy headed straight into the store, leaving Murray outside to watch over the entrance.

The layout was typical of all supermarkets; once inside she was greeted with an aisle chock-full of fruit and veg produce. She slipped past it and, choosing the middle thoroughfare that would give her a chance to look up and down each aisle, she dashed towards the far side. Finn wouldn't be likely to be down a fruit and veg aisle, and given he'd already been here for eight minutes or so, he would have most likely made his selection and been on the way out or close to the checkouts.

Nevertheless, she turned her head this way and that, scouring each of the aisles. There was a couple clutching armfuls of bumper packets of toilet rolls, which according to the neon-green sign were on special offer. The sign over the next aisle indicated soft drinks and snacks. No sign of Finn. A woman in the supermarket uniform was stacking shelves with cans of soup, talking all the while to another assistant on her knees beside her. A mother pushing her child in a trolley, who was happily eating crisps, was to her left.

There were only three aisles left to check. In the chilled food aisle, an older woman was searching through yoghurts; near her, two young men. She paused. Neither of them was Finn. One glanced over and, clocking her, nudged his mate. She strode on, ignoring them. Ahead, to her right, was the alcohol section, and if she had to place a bet on where she'd find Finn, it would be here. She slowed her pace, trying to remain no more than a casual shopper. She flicked her eyes to the right. There was nobody but a woman in her late forties lifting a box of beer into a trolley. *Shit!* Finn must have already left. She spun to her left and glimpsed a young man about to pass through the checkout. It was him. She quickened her pace. Three people separated her from her target.

Finn reached into his pocket, pulled out a ten-pound note and handed it to the cashier, who sorted through change. The person behind him offloaded the contents of her trolley onto the conveyor belt, blocking the space between Lucy and her quarry. The checkout next to Finn's was unmanned, blocked by a metal barrier. Lucy sidestepped to push through it to catch him as he left the shop but he caught sight of her and, grabbing the pack of beer, sprinted away ahead of her.

'Police!' Lucy yelled, racing after him. 'Finn, stop!'

He drew to a halt outside the supermarket, spotted Murray, zigzagged away from him and belted towards the high barrier separating the car park from the supermarket. Murray was close on his heels, Lucy bringing up the rear. Finn was almost at the barrier when, without warning, he flung the beer cans behind him. They hit Murray full in the face, stopping him in his tracks. He dropped his head in his hands, blood pouring from his nose.

'Fuck!'

Lucy swerved past him and chased after Finn, who hurled himself up the railing like a monkey and clambered over speedily, dropping lightly the other side and sprinting again, this time towards the back of the unoccupied buildings.

Lucy hauled herself over the railings and dropped to the ground, landing heavily on one ankle. Ignoring the spurts of pain coming from it, she raced on. Finn had gained distance and was almost at an alley between what was to be a new DIY store and a shoe shop. She thundered down the dark passage, emerging into another passageway that led into the main pedestrian shopping centre. She followed it and reached the main street, looked left and right, then swore. Finn had disappeared.

Back at the car park, Murray was trying to stem the flow of blood. He'd attracted attention from a couple of shoppers, the couple who'd been purchasing toilet rolls, who offered assistance and gave Murray a roll of tissue paper.

'Shit, you're a mess,' she said, looking at his face.

'Fucking hurts too,' he replied.

'Best get you checked over.'

'I'll be fine. I've had a bloody nose before. I just need some ice.'

'I'll sort it. Supermarket will have some.'

'He escaped.'

'Yeah, bastard. We'll find him again. He can't stay hidden forever. I'll call Natalie.'

'What do you reckon, then?' Natalie asked Ian. They'd circled an area on a map within walking distance to the store.

'They're staying off the radar so they can't be far away if they can reach that store without being picked up by surveillance cameras. Finn didn't catch a bus or train into town or we'd have picked him up, and he obviously intends carrying his purchases, so he won't be staying far away.'

'My thoughts exactly. I think they're hiding somewhere within this area.'

'There are some garages there,' he said, pointing to them. 'And that's a disused small industrial estate. If they were hiding out in one of those, they wouldn't attract much attention from anybody. Otherwise, I can only think they're with friends.'

'No. I don't think Finn would risk going out shopping if that were the case. He'd have definitely sent a friend and remained hidden. He's savvy. He'll know he's taken a risk breaking cover. They're alone. I'm sure of it. Find out who owns the garages.'

She pulled up a Google Maps image of the disused industrial park to decide how best to flush out the pair. There were too many entrances and possible exits for her team. She'd need more officers if they were to storm it, and if she were to put in a request for those, she'd have to justify it to her superior. A hunch wasn't a good enough reason for Aileen Melody. Natalie might have to put somebody on it to stake it out first and look for any movement or sign of Finn and Hassan.

Lucy marched into the office. Murray followed her. Ian's eyebrows rose high on his forehead.

'Don't say a fucking word,' warned Murray, pointing a finger at him.

'I wasn't going to. It looks painful.'

'I'll live.'

'You'll probably have a nice shiner tomorrow. If it's broken, I mean.'

'Cheers for that. At least I'll still be good-looking. No fucking hope for you,' he snapped and turned towards Natalie. 'He caught me off guard. He was like a fucking gazelle. I was trying to gain on him. Forgot he had a potential weapon in his hand.'

Natalie fought back the disappointment. Shit happened and Murray looked sufficiently crestfallen at losing the suspect. 'As long as you're not too seriously injured.'

'Nurse Carmichael looked after me.'

Lucy looked across. She'd unlaced her boot and was checking her swollen ankle. 'Like hell I did. I don't do sympathy. He got a toilet roll and some ice and told to get back to the station, pronto. What's happening here?'

'We're looking at other possibilities. We reckon Finn and Hassan are holed up nearby. Either here on this old trading estate where there are ten small disused warehouses awaiting development, or here,' she said, indicating the row of garages. 'We're looking into who owns each of them.'

'I'll assist,' said Lucy.

'Might not need to,' Ian replied. 'This garage belongs to Adam Brannon.'

'What?'

'It's leased in his name.'

'We're going to check it out. All of us, this time.'

CHAPTER THIRTY-THREE

The plan of action was simple. They'd approach and open the garage. They couldn't be sure it wasn't locked from the inside so in the first instance they'd try the handle and failing that, use force. It was a question of her officers' safety that concerned Natalie most. She had no idea what weapons the youths were carrying or how aggressive they would be. To that end, she'd insisted on her team wearing bulletproof vests and had called in extra officers for backup.

With everyone in position, Natalie and Murray converged on the garage. It was the middle lock-up in a line of ten nondescript garages, each with a standard handle that twisted and turned, allowing the up-and-over door to open.

At Natalie's command, Murray yanked on the door handle while she issued instructions to the suspects inside.

'Finn Kennedy and Hassan Ali. You are surrounded. Do not attempt to run away.'

The door clattered open loudly and the youths, who'd been sitting on sleeping bags and playing cards, were caught unaware. They leapt to their feet, arms and feet scrabbling in urgency, scattering the cards, and kicking over tins of beans next to a portable gas stove, and as Murray advanced on them they shrank into the wall.

'Oh fuck,' said Finn.

'Hello, Finn. Remember me?' Murray said, head cocked to one side.

Lucy and Ian appeared behind him.

'Shit! You led them here, man,' said Hassan, turning on Finn. 'I told you to stay put. We were safe. You blew it.'

Finn shrugged an apology.

'You've quite a few questions to answer,' said Natalie as the boys were dragged from the wall. She indicated the cuffs Murray was clipping onto Finn's wrists, with a nod. 'Those are to prevent you from getting it into your heads to scarper again. You've already wasted too much of our time, so get a move on and get in the cars.'

As Murray and Lucy led the youths away, Natalie meandered across to several large cartons stacked against the wall and opened the top one. It was filled with unopened boxes containing power drills. She spoke to one of the officers. 'Check through these, will you? I think they might be stolen goods.'

Lucy stood in Adam's gym. Natalie had asked her to interview him about the boxes in the lock-up and bring him into the station for further questioning if she deemed it necessary. He raised his gloved fists, threw some hefty jabs against the weighty punch bag, speaking all the while.

'I used to store gym equipment in it when I was first getting this club up and running and when Charlotte and I lived in our first home near the Ashmore Estate. It was a terraced house and we didn't have a garage or spare room at the time. I took out a five-year lease on the lock-up, but once we moved to the house at Maddison Court, with its massive garage, of course I didn't need it any more. So, when Lee asked if he could borrow it, I gave him the keys. Told him to knock himself out.' He stopped hitting the bag and pulled off a glove, swiped at the sweat trickling down his brow.

Lucy could feel waves of warmth emanating from him. 'Were you aware of what he was storing in it?' she asked.

'Sure. It was for stuff he picked up from the recycling centre – old junk other people didn't want but was still in good condition. He'd take the best bits home and when he had enough of them he'd take them to a car boot sale and make some extra money. It wasn't illegal. The stuff had been chucked away.'

'You really believe that?' She noted the dark brows furrowing.

'It's what he told me and I believed him. You have an issue with that?'

'You never went to check it out? You must have trusted him.'

Adam looked at her steadily. 'I trusted him. Okay?'

'The goods we found in your lock-up were stolen.'

He let out a lengthy sigh. 'The stupid fucker. I had no idea he'd use it for that.'

'You deny knowing anything about what went on inside the lock-up?'

'I haven't visited it for over two years. I gave Lee the keys. I had no reason to check on him. You know I have nothing to do with any stolen goods. I don't even know what goods you're talking about. Are my prints on them? No. Do I need the fucking money from selling them on? No. I don't. Do I want to end up back inside? No, I sure as hell don't. I had my taste of prison and I didn't like it. Look around you at this place. I try to keep kids out of prison. I don't want them involved in petty crimes or worse. This is an outlet for their grievances and gives some of them a chance to escape the crap lives they lead. Now ask yourself why the fuck I'd get involved with some shit Lee's managed to entangle himself in. Then you check with Lee and find out what he was up to because I know nothing about it. I believed I was doing the motherfucker a favour, letting him use it. I helped him out in loads of ways – let him train here, even gave him money from time to time when he was hard up – and look how he fucking repays me. He mixes me up in stuff I know nothing about. Fucker!'

'If we find out you were involved in this, you know what will happen to you?'

'Yeah, I do but I *wasn't* involved. You talk to that piece of shit Lee about it.' He hunched his shoulders and continued throwing punches at speed until sweat flew from his brow and formed a wet pattern of drips on the floor. Then he stopped.

'I'm not involved in any of that lousy son of a bitch's business,' he said calmly. 'I'm not guilty of receiving stolen goods, or anything else for that matter. I've been keeping my nose clean ever since I got out of jail. I turned my fucking life around. Now I have to start again, without my wife. I've got a baby son who's lost his mother to bring up, and I definitely don't need any more fucking crap hurled at me. You interview him and you get the truth out of him and leave me alone. Now, shouldn't you be hunting down the bastard who's responsible for murdering two women?'

'We are, Mr Brannon. I can assure you we are. Thank you for your time.'

She drew away. Behind her she heard low grunts as he began his routine again.

Finn and Hassan had been placed in separate interview rooms and left to wait with an officer keeping an eye on each of them.

Natalie spread her hands on the desk and spoke to Murray. 'I don't want them to clam up. It's imperative they tell us what they heard or saw, so don't go in too hard. If they refuse to help us, we'll have to work out other ways to coax the information from them. Lucy just called in and Adam claims he knows nothing about what's been going on at the garage. I would surmise these kids either got the keys from Lee or stole them from him. You clear about everything?'

'Got it.'

'Okay. I'll take Finn and you speak to Hassan.'

A bruise had appeared under Murray's left eye, its colour deepening by the hour, and the angry gash across the bridge of his nose had crusted over. She studied him closely. 'You seen the medical officer like I told you?'

'Straight after we brought in that pair. She gave me the all-clear.'

Natalie wasn't convinced but if Murray said he was fit for duty, then that would be enough for her. She didn't want to be a man down. She picked up the necessary paperwork.

Ian stood up. 'Natalie, before you go, you should know that Phoebe Hill was taken off the Emirates flight from Doha. She was a last-minute substitute for a flight from Kuwait that landed in London at two thirty p.m. on Friday.'

'More sodding lies. How long would it take her to get from London to Samford?'

'By car? Three hours tops.'

'That'd give her ample time to reach Samford and be in Eastborough around the time Charlotte was murdered. Run her car registration. See if it passed any ANPR points on the motorway.'

'She could have used other transport – friend's car, taxi.'

'True, but what have we got to lose? We'll talk to her when we've finished with this pair.' She left Ian tapping at his computer and joined Murray.

'That's an interesting development,' he said.

'Looks like we're back on course,' she replied. 'I prefer it when we have something to work with. I was getting majorly hacked off with all the dead ends.' She separated from him outside the first interview room and, drawing a breath, steeled herself to do battle with a recalcitrant teenager.

Finn looked rough and smelt sour.

'You want a drink or something? I don't suppose you've had a lot to eat the last few days.'

His reaction was one of hostility. 'Why are you being so nice? Is this one of those cop routines where suddenly that ape who chased me earlier comes in and smacks me about?'

'Nothing like that. I thought you'd be hungry.'

'I'm fine,' he said.

'Please yourself. I'm going to record the interview.'

He hunched further into his seat. 'Whatever.'

Natalie set the machine into action, made the necessary introductions of who was present in the room, then opened her file and sat back in her chair, tips of her fingers together. 'I'll get straight to the point. You're in trouble.'

He barked a laugh. 'I know that.'

'Maybe you don't realise how much trouble. You assaulted one of my officers, hindered a murder investigation, broke into property and might even be charged with being an accessory to murder.'

A sneer wiped itself across his face. 'Yeah, right.'

'On Friday night, you were spotted in the vicinity of the Brannons' house, carrying a length of steel piping.' She waited but he said nothing, just observed her through pale-blue eyes. 'You make this as hard or as easy as you want. The easiest thing would be to tell me what you were doing there and what you saw or heard. The hardest thing would be to sit there saying nothing.'

The sneer was back. He picked some dirt from under a filthy nail and flicked it onto the floor.

She kept her voice gentle. 'A young woman, battered to death.' She deliberately neglected to tell him Charlotte had been hit with a bat and allowed this news to sink in. For a split second she thought he'd crack and tell her the truth, but he regained his composure and sat back, arms folded, head down.

'And you'd be happy for me to charge you rather than tell me what threw you into such a panic that you and Hassan fled? At the moment, you're my only suspects. You and Hassan ran away from a crime scene. The way I see it, I might have to charge you with murder.'

He dropped his guard for a moment, partly opened his mouth and shut it again.

'I tell you what. I'll come back in a short while. You sit here, have a Coke and a sandwich, and think about what I've said. Enjoy it because I hear prison food isn't very good.' She stood up slowly and left him. It wasn't progress but she hoped she'd sown sufficient doubt in his mind for him to speak to her on her return.

She slipped into the second room where Murray was interviewing Hassan. The youth was exhibiting the same belligerent attitude as Finn and was refusing to cooperate. Murray announced her arrival for the benefit of the recorder.

'Hello, Hassan,' she said. 'I've just been talking to your friend Finn about what happened on Friday night. He said you were frightened off by screaming coming from the Brannons' house.' It was a white lie. Finn had told Inge that's what had happened. She hoped he hadn't been lying to his ex-girlfriend or it would blow her ruse.

'He's been talking to you? He said he wouldn't. He promised me he wouldn't say anything.'

His face and words confirmed one suspicion. Hassan had been the other person seen running away from the house by the neighbour, Margaret Callaghan.

Natalie kept up her act. 'It might be advisable if you give us your version of events.'

'No. I don't believe you. You're playing us off against each other.'

'If you think that's the case, then you keep quiet. I don't have a problem with that,' answered Natalie smoothly. 'I'll leave you with DS Anderson. I have to ring your mother.'

'Why?'

'I ought to inform her where you are. She must be worried about you taking off like that. She'll need to be told about the charges so she can arrange a lawyer for you.'

'What charges?' Hassan's brow wrinkled in confusion.

'We'll discuss those once you've got a lawyer.'

She left them to it and waited in the corridor for Murray to appear. 'Did it work?' she asked.

'Yes. He wants to talk but only if I can stop you from ringing his mother.'

'Good. I thought we'd sailed too close to the wind with that one. I couldn't help but notice his interaction with his mother back at their flat. He obviously respects and listens to her and that gave me the idea. You extract what information you can. I'll see how Finn is enjoying his sandwich.'

CHAPTER THIRTY-FOUR

TUESDAY, 6 MARCH – EARLY EVENING

Lucy found Ian alone in the office. He was keen to get her up to speed.

'Murray and Natalie are with the pair we brought in. Found out Phoebe Hill wasn't on the Emirates flight from Doha due in Saturday morning. She swapped shifts and was on a different flight that landed in London at two thirty on Friday afternoon.'

'Wow! I've been wondering about her, especially since Henrik said the perpetrator could be a woman. What's happening about her?'

'Natalie said we'd talk to her after she's finished with Finn and Hassan.'

'I wouldn't mind being part of that interview.' Lucy flopped onto her seat. Tiredness and her sore ankle were taking their toll. She could do with a rest or a pick-me-up. 'Don't suppose you would be my lackey and fetch a coffee and chocolate bar. I twisted my ankle chasing after that little punk earlier and it could do with some time out.'

'Lackey?'

'It's an old-fashioned word meaning servant.'

'Never heard of it.'

'You obviously haven't watched some of the period dramas I've been subjected to,' she joked. 'Essential Sunday night viewing for pregnant women, apparently.' She caught the look that flickered across his features. 'Oh shit, I forgot, you know all about that. You've got your own little bubba. How is she?'

'Fine… growing… thanks. Any preference for chocolate?' He stood up in an instant.

'The largest you can find. Thanks, Ian.' As she handed over some coins for the machine, she took in the strained smile. She'd obviously put her foot in it but she didn't know how. 'Make sure you get something for yourself.'

He beetled off. Lucy untied the lace on her boot and glanced at her ankle, which was ballooning in size. She needed to ice it and raise it. For now it was best to keep her boot done up tightly and carry on.

The internal phone rang. She hobbled across to it and lifted the receiver. It was the officer manning reception.

'I've got a call from a woman who thinks her life is in danger. I can't patch it through to anyone else. Can I put her on to you?'

'Yes, sure, but we're up to our eyeballs.'

'I know but you could talk to her, she's in a dreadful state.'

'Okay. Put her through.'

It was only a few seconds before she heard a voice. 'My name is Fabia Hamilton. I think someone's going to try and kill me.'

'Where are you, Fabia?'

'I'm at my private clinic in Samford but I can't stay here.'

Ian came in, put a coffee on Lucy's desk and tossed over the chocolate bar, which she caught with her free hand. She mouthed her thanks.

'Tell me more, Fabia. Why do you think somebody's going to kill you?'

'I've been treating a patient over the last few months with serious issues towards women. I realise I shouldn't break patient confidentiality but I'm scared. I'm really scared. I think I've been treating a killer. I'm going to stay with a friend. I have to get away.

Hang on. There's somebody outside.' Her voice had dropped to a whisper.

'Don't hang up. Tell us where you are.'

The line went dead.

'Shit!' She rang the front desk. 'You got the number that rang in just now?'

'It was a withheld number.'

'Didn't you ask her for it before you put her through to me?'

The young officer on the desk sounded flustered. 'No, Sergeant, I didn't, I was busy…'

'Spare me the excuses. This woman could be in real danger and I don't know how the fuck to reach her.' She slammed down the receiver and moved back to her desk, typed the name Fabia Hamilton into the search engine and scrolled through the results. Fabia was a psychologist specialising in dreams and dreaming, who'd made several appearances on television and radio discussing dream analysis. She worked out of a clinic she owned in Samford in Hartford Street, a smart street of Victorian houses, now housing several medical and holistic practices.

'When Natalie returns, tell her I've gone to Hartford Street to check on this woman who thinks she's been treating a murderer.' She shoved the paper with Fabia's name written on it at Ian.

'Is there a connection to our investigation?'

'Don't know but I'm concerned about her. She thought some-body was outside her house and dropped the call, and I haven't heard from her since.'

'You want backup?'

'I'll call in if I need any.' Lucy was out of the door in a flash, tiredness now banished.

Murray shook his head as he spoke to Natalie outside the interview room. 'Little shit's clammed up on me.'

'Damn, I thought we were getting somewhere with Hassan at least. We'll leave them to cool their heels for a while. We can keep them here on grounds we fear they'll abscond if we release them, and they're assisting us with our enquiries. If they start bleating about being held, begin the questioning process again. Take Ian in with you. I'm going to talk to Phoebe Hill.'

She stepped out to her car, noting it was almost six. It was another long day in which they'd achieved very little. The case was proving to be a huge frustration.

Phoebe Hill, eyes red-rimmed, opened the door to Walnut Cottage. She clung to the oak door frame with both hands, displaying perfectly painted fingernails, before saying, 'I've been expecting you. You'd better come in.'

Natalie found herself in the same room with the horse sculpture she'd been in four days earlier. She sat opposite Phoebe, who curled up into a large, round chair.

'Are your parents in?'

'They've gone to visit Grandma with Alfie. Jed's left.' She raised damp eyes. 'I'm sorry I didn't tell the truth.'

'It would certainly have been more helpful if you had.'

'I realise that but it was… complicated.'

'Then enlighten me now.'

'Charlotte messaged me. Told me she and Jed were having an affair; that sometimes when I was away, he'd spend time with her. Said he was going to visit her on Friday. I didn't believe her at first so I asked Jed what his plans were for Friday and he told me had a radio interview in Stoke. There was something about his manner that made me suspect he was lying. I suggested he drop by my parents and wish them a happy anniversary while he was up here, but he couldn't because he'd already made arrangements to meet some guy in the same industry as him for a couple of beers, and then was catching a late train home.

'Jed's not good at lying. He can't make eye contact. I knew straight away he was making it up. He was going to meet Charlotte like she'd told me. I intended catching them at it. I asked my supervisor if I could swap flights so I could be with my parents at their big wedding anniversary celebrations, making out it was an important occasion with all the family attending. She was accommodating and found a colleague willing to swap with me at the last minute. I flew out on the Kuwait flight on Thursday and got back at two thirty p.m. on the Friday, although Jed believed I was going to Doha on Thursday and returning on the red-eye flight, due back into London early Saturday morning as usual. After we landed, I collected a hire car at the airport. My car is far too obvious. Charlotte and Jed would have recognised it in an instant if they'd seen it.

'I arrived at Charlotte's house just before five p.m., parked down the road and kept watch for any sign of Jed arriving after his interview, or of Charlotte going out to meet him. Charlotte was at home. I could see her through the windows. She was with Alfie. After an hour and a half, Adam came home, and sometime later they headed out to meet my parents. Jed had been telling me the truth after all. He'd gone from the interview to see a musician friend, not to meet up with Charlotte.'

'What did you do after Charlotte and Adam left?'

'I drove straight home. I stopped at a service station, had a coffee and sat there for ages. I got in some time after ten p.m. I expected Jed to return soon after I did and I was prepared to tell him I'd done a last-minute swap, but he didn't show up until the following morning. He came in just before I got the call about Charlotte. He told me he'd crashed at his musician friend's place. Now I know the truth. He and I had a heart-to-heart after he went to the station with you. Seems I was right to be suspicious. He had intended seeing her. And Alfie! He's Jed's son. The bitch. She ruined everything yet again.' Hot tears welled in her eyes.

Natalie understood Phoebe's anger. Her own sister had been equally cruel.

'How could she do that? How could she deliberately chase after him, have *his* baby and not tell him until now? How could she wait until now, when we're engaged, before blowing the lid on it all and ruining our relationship? I thought she was heartless, but I'd no idea she was prepared to go to such lengths to destroy other people's happiness, to wreck my happiness.'

'I'm truly sorry these circumstances have come to light; however, I still have to corroborate your alibi. You see, you have a strong motive for wishing your sister dead.'

'I knew nothing about Alfie until Jed told me today.'

'Nevertheless, we must eliminate you as a suspect. Do you have the paperwork for the hire car, or anything to support what you've told me?'

'I paid for my coffee and sandwich with my credit card. I didn't have any cash on me. There'll be a time on the transaction slip, won't there? And there'll be CCTV or surveillance camera of some description at the service station too.' Her words tumbled more quickly. 'I don't have the hire car details here, but I have a loyalty card with them and a phone number. If you ring the company, they ought to be able to confirm everything.'

She fumbled in a large Chanel handbag, drew out a purse and handed Natalie a receipt and a plastic loyalty card.

Natalie examined both. 'These should help us establish your exact whereabouts when your sister was murdered.'

'I wouldn't have killed her, even if she and Jed had been having a full-blown affair or if I'd found out the truth about Alfie. I hated her but she was still my sister and part of me loved her. I couldn't have put my parents through all of this living hell.'

Her eyes were trained on a large photograph of two girls, arms around each other, laughing for the camera. 'I don't understand why she was so vindictive. She took everything that was mine away from me, even Jed.' The tears were back.

Natalie stood. 'I'm not in the habit of doling out advice, but it is my experience that if you want something badly enough, you go after it. She hasn't taken Jed. If you still want him, you can change that.'

As she left the house, she thought about Phoebe's words – that she'd hated her sister but loved her at the same time. Natalie felt the same way about her own sister, Frances. Was it also how the killer felt? Did he love and hate somebody close to him, the same way Phoebe and Natalie did?

CHAPTER THIRTY-FIVE

TUESDAY, 6 MARCH – EVENING

Fabia's clinic was actually the front room of her semi-detached Victorian residence, a grey stone building shrouded by tall hedging. Lucy drew into the small parking area to the front and, standing inside the arched porch, hammered on the blue door. A bronze plaque to the side of it attested to the fact this was Fabia's clinic, with her name and list of abbreviations after it, revealing her to be a highly qualified psychologist.

The blinds at the downstairs three-bay window were drawn and there was no sign of activity. Lucy walked to the side of the house and peered through a frosted-glass window into what appeared to be a small utility room with a toilet. The gate to the rear was locked.

Returning to the front of the house, she rang the bell and stood back to look at the window above, another white-framed bay window that appeared to have curtains rather than blinds. A slight movement caught her eye so she rang once more, opened the letterbox and shouted, 'Dr Hamilton, it's DS Lucy Carmichael. We spoke earlier. Can you open up, please?'

There was no reply. Lucy tried again. 'Dr Hamilton. It's the police. Open the door.'

'She's not in.'

Lucy spun around. An elderly man with rheumy eyes and pale, downy hair stood behind her.

'She rang me earlier. I'm DS Carmichael from Samford Police.' She pulled out her ID. 'Have you any idea where she is?'

He shook his head. 'She said she had an emergency and had to go away for a few days. Asked me to look after Loki for her. Her cat,' he added.

'Are you related to her?'

'Me? No. I'm a neighbour. I live in the flat above the wellness clinic next door. I've got a key. Was on my way around to check on Loki.'

'Would you mind letting me come inside with you?'

'Has something happened to Fabia?'

'I don't know, but I'd appreciate it if I could take a quick look around to make sure everything is okay inside.'

He gave her another look. 'Who did you say you were?'

'Detective Sergeant Lucy Carmichael. Would you like to ring the station to check?' She handed him her ID card, which he examined carefully before stating, 'You can't be too careful these days. You could be a hustler. You're not in uniform and that isn't a police car.'

'It's an unmarked car, sir, and I don't have to wear a uniform. I wear plain clothes.'

He chewed at his lips before deciding to return Lucy's card. 'All right. I'll let you in. I hope Fabia's okay.'

'Thank you, Mr...?'

'Milligan, Pete Milligan.'

He unlocked the door and stood aside for Lucy to go ahead. The door to her right opened into what had once been a front room, now a consulting room complete with desk, chairs and a sofa. Certificates hung above the ornate fireplace with its tiled surround.

She stole back out into the tiled hallway and into the kitchen at the rear of the property. It was empty. Passing the gentleman who waited by the door, she took the stairs slowly, turning right and right again into a small but stylish sitting room. There was no sign of a struggle. The room was neat and tidy, with a chair and settee facing another fireplace, filled with a dried floral arrangement and decorated with fairy lights. Above it, a flat-screen television. Lucy made a 180-degree turn and took in the large black-and-white portrait photographs on the wall of a woman with dark hair and a wide smile, arms wrapped around a small child, a toddler with eyes, nose and smile that matched his mother's. Fabia had a son.

A sound, a thump, from an adjacent room caused her to tread carefully. She eased the door a crack, ready to force her way in and confront any intruder. She had no need. No sooner was the door ajar than a cat, one of the largest she had seen, appeared, pushing its furry face out and surveying her with pale-green eyes.

She checked the other two rooms. They were empty. She called downstairs, 'It's okay, Mr Milligan. You can come up.'

The man appeared and was greeted by Loki, who wound himself around the man's legs. He bent to stroke it and gave a smile. 'Big bugger, isn't he?'

'Not seen one that size before.'

'It's the breed. Maine Coon. They come from the States. He weighs about twenty pounds. Come on, fella. Time for your dinner.' He made his way down the stairs, clinging to the handrail. The cat bounded on ahead.

'Mr Milligan, have you got a contact number for Fabia?'

'Got her mobile number.'

'Could I have it, please?'

'Hang on.' He rummaged in the pocket of his trousers and extracted a flip phone. Squinting at it, he pulled up Fabia's details and passed the phone to Lucy, who added them to her phone and returned it with thanks.

'When did you last speak to her?'

'She rang me at lunchtime.'

'How did she seem?'

'Hassled, bit out of breath, in a hurry. I didn't think that was abnormal behaviour. She'd had an emergency and had to get to it. I asked if Philippe was okay and she said he was fine. She was collecting him from the after-school club and taking him with her.'

'Philippe? That's her son?'

'Yes.'

'Have you known her long?'

'Pretty much since she moved in and set up her practice here. That'd be about four years now.'

'Has she seemed different the last few days?'

'Not that I noticed, but I don't see her all the time. I look after Loki when she goes away. She comes around and checks to see if I'm okay when the wellness clinic is shut for any period of time – you know, neighbourly stuff. We sometimes speak over the garden fence at the back.'

'There's no boyfriend or husband?'

He gave an awkward laugh. 'That wouldn't be my business. I don't spy on her. She lives with the boy, that's all I know.'

'You haven't seen any men coming and going?'

'There's almost always somebody going in or out. She runs her clinic from here. I see people all the time.'

'I meant out of hours.'

His mouth turned down as he pondered the question. 'She works late. I wouldn't know if the callers were patients or friends, sorry.'

'You have no idea of her whereabouts?'

'Again, I'm sorry but no.'

'When she goes away, does she leave a contact number?'

'I have her mobile. That's enough.' The cat miaowed. 'I'd best feed him.'

Lucy gave him a grateful smile. 'Of course, and thanks for your help.'

'I hope she's not in any bother.'

'I'm sure she's fine. If she phones you, would you tell her I was here and let me know too, please?' She handed over a business card.

He pocketed it then shuffled down the hallway, making clicking noises at the cat, who weaved between his legs. Lucy let herself out and tried the number Pete had given her but it rang out. She called the station.

'Ian, can you run a search including social media on Dr Fabia Hamilton? She's not answering her mobile.'

'Will do.'

'Thanks. I owe you. I'm going to knock on a few doors and then come back to the station.'

'Bring some chips with you, will you? Looks like we're in for the duration. Natalie's returned and she's determined to squeeze information out of these two downstairs.'

Lucy grinned to herself. 'Roger that.'

'I need a search warrant,' said Natalie.

Aileen raised an eyebrow. 'For?'

'Hassan Ali's flat.'

'And the reason for this is?' Aileen asked.

'I want to search for stolen goods. The boys were found hiding out in a lock-up that Lee Webster uses to store stolen goods. The fact they know about it and have got the key to the place makes me wonder if they are helping him and handling stolen goods. I'm hoping to pin something else on them to get them to speak about what happened at the Brannons' house. They aren't saying a word. And because they aren't talking, in spite of my threats, it leads me to believe they are withholding vital evidence. The more leverage against them I have, the better.'

'I'll arrange that for you and I won't ask the obvious question.'

'Am I getting closer to finding this perpetrator? Let's just say, I'm pinning my hopes on finding something I can use at Hassan's flat.'

'I'm going to call a press conference for tomorrow morning. I can't keep a lid on it any longer, and we should ask the public for assistance.'

'Can you make it late morning?'

'I'll see what I can do.'

Natalie had decided to change tack so each boy was being individually interviewed by both Murray and her. Finn looked slightly less assured when Murray, whose bruise was now deep blue, tossed his file onto the table and sat in silence opposite him.

Natalie spoke first. 'If you don't want to be charged with being an accessory to murder or even of murder, we suggest you speak up now.'

'Murder? You're joking.'

'Let's get something clear: I don't joke. First Charlotte Brannon, Adam's wife, was murdered; and then, when you were off the radar and with no alibi, Daniel Kirkdale's wife, Samantha, was killed. And who would have reason to attack them? How about somebody who was thrown out of a boxing club, lost a sponsor and a future career in boxing? Somebody who hated both men.'

'That's total bollocks and you know it.'

Natalie sighed. 'Finn, if a jury heard that you were seen fleeing from a murder scene, wielding a long steel pipe, and then disappeared for three days, during which time another woman – your ex-sponsor's wife – was murdered, and that you ran from police officers, assaulted one in an attempt to escape and refused to cooperate with police when questioned, how do you think they'd vote? You're not stupid. You know how the system works. Keeping quiet doesn't get you off. You will be charged and those charges will stick.' She gave him a moment to digest her words. She and Murray were about to try a risky tactic, one they had just discussed, but one she was confident would work.

'And then there's the matter of forensic evidence.'

There was a slight twitch in his left shoulder.

'During an investigation like this, forensic teams go to extraordinary lengths to examine every piece of evidence, every fibre, every hair, every microscopic spot of dried sweat or blood and the DNA that it contains. Eventually we can identify everyone who entered the Brannons' house.'

Finn's eyes flicked left and right and his tongue shot out over his lips. Natalie had been right to check Hassan's flat. It had yielded one piece of evidence – a small pottery sculpture made by the same artist who'd produced the angel figurines she'd seen in the Brannons' house. Its absence hadn't been noticed.

'And that would be damning evidence, especially for a jury.'

She gave him a smile that didn't reach her eyes and held her peace. Murray crossed his legs and sat back in his chair, a casual pose. Finn looked away.

'Final chance, Finn. Speak now or we call in a lawyer and charge you. The judge will probably give you a life sentence minus a few years. I wouldn't hold out a lot of hope of spending much time this side of the bars.'

She held her steady, cool gaze. Finn was about to crack.

'We never had anything to do with Daniel's wife. I swear. I didn't know she was dead until you said. We *were* at Adam's house the night Charlotte was killed, but we had nothing to do with it.'

Natalie didn't want to appear keen. She maintained a steady pitch, careful not to make any sudden movements that might force Finn to retreat into silence. He had to be handled with care, coaxed to tell the truth. She'd got him to confess but she needed more.

'When were you at his house?'

'Elevenish. The door was open.' Finn blinked a few times, trying to dispel the recollection. 'It was open and we went inside.'

'Why were you there?'

'That fucker Adam. I wanted to pay him back for dumping me. He told me I was going to be a top boxer and got me a sponsor and all, and then he blew me off. Suddenly I had no boxing career and no fucking sponsor. And then, the bastard took my girlfriend Inge. We went to smash up his motor. Man, he loved those fucking wheels. Thought we'd whack it up: headlights, windscreen, a few dents. It was to teach him a lesson, that's all. Nothing serious.

'We got to the house. The lights were all out and the fuck-off Bentley wasn't on the drive but his BMW was. With him out it was going to be even easier than we expected. Just as we reached it, Hassan noticed the front door was slightly open. It was an opportunity, wasn't it? Silly fucker had left his house door open, so I crept in and left Hassan outside as a lookout. They had this massive lounge with all sorts of shit in it. There was nobody about, so I thought I'd take a couple of items. There had to be something valuable, right? I found some fairy figures, figured I'd get a few quid for them, shoved one in my pocket, and then I heard a kind of muffled scream. Then there was a thump and crying and shouts and then there was a really horrible scream and I was fucking frozen to the spot. The door upstairs opened and Adam came out and I legged it. I hurtled out of that house, grabbed Hassan, and we both ran for our lives. I'm certain he saw me before I ran. I'm fucking sure he did.

'When we found out the following day Charlotte was dead, we knew we had to get into hiding. Hassan thought he'd be safe with his mum, cos Adam didn't see him, but when you turned up at his mum's flat he got shit scared, ran off and found me. That's why we hid out. I knew Lee had the garage. I help him out sometimes – move boxes and stuff. I have a second key to the place.'

Natalie wasn't interested in his involvement with stolen goods for the moment. 'You thought Adam was in the house?'

'For sure it was him. Why do you think we've been hiding? He'll fucking murder us both if he finds us.'

'Did you see him that night?'

'No, but I heard Charlotte shout at him.'

'What exactly did she shout?'

'Adam. No.'

'Those were her very words?'

Finn nodded.

'How did she say they them?'

'I don't fucking know. She shouted, "Adam," then, "No."'

Natalie glanced at Murray. 'Would you like to take Finn's statement?'

'Is that it?' Finn looked at her miserably.

'No, it isn't. You'll have to stay here for a while longer. There'll be charges against you. DS Anderson will explain the procedure.'

'Oh fuck, man. I told you what I saw. We never left the lock-up either. We didn't kill Daniel's missus. Come on. Let me go. I haven't done anything serious.'

Natalie stood up and, ignoring any further protests, handed him over to Murray.

CHAPTER THIRTY-SIX

The strip light hummed above them as Adam sat in the same interview room Finn had occupied earlier. His elbows were splayed on the desk and he leant as far across it as possible, staring at Natalie as intently as he could.

'That's total and utter bullshit. I did *not* attack Charlotte. This witness is a lying son of a bitch.'

'They signed a statement testifying to this claim. They heard Charlotte shout your name and scream, "No!" They're positive that's what they heard.'

He spoke slowly through gritted teeth. 'I don't know what happened. I don't know what was shouted or said and that's because I… wasn't… there. If she actually shouted my name, she could've been calling me for help. You think about that? She could have been screaming *for* me…' His voice trailed and he swallowed. 'You any idea how hard all of this is for me?'

'I understand and you must also appreciate our position. A witness—'

'Screw this witness,' he said, his fist hitting the table as he drew himself upright. 'This witness is wrong.'

'Calm down, Mr Brannon. It won't help anyone if you lose your temper.'

'I'm not losing my temper but I sure as hell am frustrated. All you do is keep hounding me and dragging me back here to the station for more questioning when I'm the one who needs support. I ought to be getting help to get through this. I'm a mess. I feel responsible because I wasn't there to protect her. I can't visit or speak to my in-laws or even go see my little boy because of guilt I feel that I wasn't there that night. I certainly can't face Inge. I'm sitting in a vacuum, waiting for you to unearth the bastard who killed her, and then, and only then, will I be able to pick up the shattered pieces of my life and work out how to move forward. I've repeatedly told you I did not kill Charlotte and you know where I was. I wasn't at home when she was attacked. I've wished a million times I could have changed the events that night: that I hadn't been so pissed off with her I'd gone home with Inge and then hung out at the club. I messed up with the whole alibi business but I've always told the truth about Charlotte. I didn't kill her.'

Natalie couldn't refute his logic. Charlotte might have been yelling for him rather than at him, a fact she'd already considered, but to not interview Adam at this stage would have been foolish. Finn and Hassan were convinced he'd been in the house, and she had to check out that claim. Besides, she had no one else in the frame. It was a tough call to make. She couldn't keep him here without more concrete proof. She couldn't pin this on him merely because she wanted to be able to tell Aileen Melody she'd cracked the case. Adam had never requested a lawyer. He'd come to the station voluntarily every time she'd asked him to. He hadn't absconded. Although he'd lied about his whereabouts to protect Inge and then Lee, he'd done nothing else to make her suspect he was anything other than cooperative and wanted to prove his innocence, yet her investigation kept leading her back to him, to this man with a prison record and a history of violence. She drew a breath. She had to make the call.

'Fair enough, Mr Brannon. I accept your point. It isn't clear why your wife shouted your name. You're free to leave.'

He stood slowly. 'Thank you.'

'Don't thank me. It isn't over yet.'

Murray waited until Adam had been escorted from the room. 'Now what?'

Natalie stood up, aware her bones ached, and ran a hand over her head. 'Fucked if I know. Probably have to wait for the press conference and hope a member of the public can come up with something.'

Lucy placed rolled newspaper on Ian's desk. 'Got you some cod too.'

'Brilliant! Thanks. I'm starving. You want any?'

'Ate mine in the car. The smell of vinegar and warm chips was driving me mental so I couldn't wait.'

He unwrapped them, releasing the warmth that carried the familiar chip shop smell, and shoved a couple of fat, yellow chips into his mouth. 'Mm. Heaven,' he murmured.

'You find any contacts for Fabia?'

He nodded enthusiastically. 'Got a list of them here but this woman appears to be her closest friend.' He wiped his fingers clean on his trousers and brought up the Facebook page for Louise Roberts. 'They went to the same university. Louise is also a psychologist, working for the NHS, and lives in Derby. She's got a profile on LinkedIn and her phone number is on the site.'

'Great,' said Lucy, taking note of it. 'Enjoy those chips. You've earned them.'

Punching out the number as she went, she headed outside on the roof to leave Ian to eat in peace. It was chilly on the roof terrace, and as she inhaled, cold air rushed into her lungs. The phone call was picked up and a soft voice answered.

'Louise Roberts? This is DS Lucy Carmichael from Samford Police headquarters. I'm calling with regards to your friend, Fabia Hamilton. She rang me earlier and I wondered if you had any idea where she might be. I'm trying to trace her and her son. She isn't at her home.'

'Who did you say you were?' The voice was hesitant.

'Lucy Carmichael. Detective Sergeant Carmichael.'

'I'll phone you back immediately.'

'No. Don't hang up.'

Too late. The line went dead. She tried the number again but got an engaged tone. She swore then dragged out a cigarette from her pocket. 'Sorry, Spud. I promise to try harder,' she said, staring at it before she lit it and inhaled deeply, letting the smoke spread its tendrils inside her chest. She ought to give up the fags. For Spud's sake. She stared at the cigarette, took one more quick puff then stubbed it out. Her phone rang. It was Louise.

'I'm sorry I put the phone down on you. I had to make certain you were who you said you were. I checked with Fabia first to see if she had called you. She turned up here a short while ago, with Philippe. She was in a bit of a state.'

'Can you put her on so I can speak to her?'

'Wait a sec.' Lucy could make out a muffled exchange. She tilted her head back. The sky was clear and pinpricks of light were puncturing the night sky. She shivered as cool air wafted around her shoulders. A different voice spoke to her, one Lucy recognised from earlier. It was the woman who'd rung the station.

'Sergeant, I'm sorry I didn't ring back. I thought I saw somebody outside the back door and panicked. I drove straight to Louise's house, then I calmed down and decided I'd been overreacting and shouldn't have involved the police. Louise and I have talked it through and maybe I'm making too much out of it.'

'You told me you were scared. You sounded frightened and you must have been really worried to have raced off to your friend's house.'

'It seems silly now. I was being melodramatic. I'd had a shock.'

'Earlier you told me about a patient who you believe to be a killer. Tell me some more about him.'

'I've been treating him at my clinic for a few months. He's been having recurring bad dreams that were troubling him. At first we discussed these dreams and we established they were linked to or came out of troubled childhood memories. He had abandonment issues. His mother walked out on her marriage when he was very young, leaving him to live in squalor in a caravan park, in the care of his father, a violent and difficult man. His dreams were all linked to this but then things began to take a turn. He introduced details and scenarios that I started to think weren't fantasies or dreams. He claimed to have what we named *episodes*, periods when he was unconscious and unable to control his dream self. In these episodes, he would murder women in horrible ways, usually in front of their children. I tried to help him get rid of the aggression, which I felt was directed towards his mother. I employed various techniques to alleviate the episodes but the last time he came to visit me, he was different. The unconscious self was morphing into the conscious self and I suspected the dreams weren't dreams any longer; they'd turned into realities.'

'You believe this man to have murdered women?'

'That's right. At least, that's what I began to think.'

'What made you decide this?'

'The grotesque detail of the murders. Initially, I thought he had a vivid imagination, but recently he began to describe the smell of blood as he cut or beat the women he murdered, and how he wanted to dip his finger into it and write.'

Icy fingers ran up Lucy's spine. This man couldn't have known about the messages on the wall. They'd not released any such details.

Fabia continued, 'There were children in the dreams too. He didn't kill them. To his mind, he was setting the children free, much as he wished he'd been set free from the abuse and torture he suffered as a child. It was the women he wanted to punish because they reminded him of his mother.'

'Did he describe them?'

'Only to say they had long hair and dark eyes.'

Lucy's pulse quickened. 'Do the questions "why?" and "who?" in isolation mean anything to you?'

There was a heavy pause before she replied. 'They were used in the first paragraph of a letter he wrote one session to his mother. He composed a list of questions as the opening to it. He couldn't understand why his mother had left him behind and moved on without him. I recall it started with, "Why? Who? Where? What? How?" He expanded on each of the questions, asking his mother first why she'd left them, who she'd left them for, where she'd gone, what she'd done after she'd left and how she'd felt, knowing she'd deserted her son.

'He was supposed to complete the rest of the letter alone, put down everything he wanted to say to his mother, and then he was to burn it, thus allowing all the frustration and aggression he'd poured into it to disappear in flames. It was supposed to liberate him, and at that stage, I believed once that happened, the dreams would end too.' Her voice became shaky. 'He is a killer, isn't he? He wasn't describing dreams. He was recounting details of murders he'd committed.'

'Fabia, I want you to remain where you are with your friend. Don't open the door to anyone. Police officers will be with you shortly.'

'Okay.'

'And, Fabia, I know it breaks patient confidentiality, but this is a truly serious situation. What is this patient's name?'

'Robert Cooke.'

CHAPTER THIRTY-SEVEN

TUESDAY, 6 MARCH – NIGHT

It was almost 9 p.m. when Natalie turned off the light and accompanied Murray to the end of the corridor. 'Go home and put some ice on that eye.'

He touched the bruise and winced.

A voice called from upstairs. It was Ian. 'Natalie!'

She turned at the sound. 'Yes?'

'I've uncovered a link between the murder victims.'

Both she and Murray raced to the office, all thoughts of clocking off forgotten.

Ian brushed aside the chip wrapper, still containing cold chips, and twisted his screen around so Natalie could see it.

'I did as you suggested and went back to the beginning. I was looking through the Brannons' files and examining details of who purchased the property, trying to fathom out why her parents would buy a house and not let Adam be party to that knowledge, when it struck me. The house is in Eastborough, the posh side of Samford, and there are only a handful of estate agents in Samford who'd handle an upmarket property like that. Scarlett and I were looking for a place of our own and I've looked in a few windows over the last few months. Most estate agencies deal with the more affordable end of the market, not luxury properties, so I got onto Zoopla and found out Cartwright and Butler sold the property.'

'The same estate agency that rented a flat to Samantha Kirkdale,' said Murray. 'Rob Cooke.'

Natalie's face screwed in concentration. 'He had a cast-iron alibi for his whereabouts. We rang the event organiser, who confirmed she checked him in and handed him a name badge – what was her name?'

'Serena Holloway. I wanted to double-check it was definitely Rob she'd spoken to, not somebody using his name. I couldn't find the card he gave us, so I rang the Fairfield Hotel where the conference supposedly took place, to get Serena's number and spoke to the receptionist, Aarav. He'd never heard of Serena Holloway or was aware of any estate agent conference having taken place at the hotel. He went through the hotel event records and found nothing about it. That rang alarm bells so I followed up immediately on Rob's second claim he was at a departmental meeting. The only Shelly Bradshaws I could find on the general database live in completely different areas to this one, and aren't secretaries, so I rang Mr Cartwright of Cartwright and Butler estate agency and learnt the company secretary is called Kelly Fielding. He'd never heard of a Shelly Bradshaw, and to his knowledge, there's never been a departmental meeting of any kind.'

She pressed her fingers to her forehead and released a slow groan. 'The sneaky bastard! He handed me an authentic business card for the hotel. We rang the number on it. He arranged it all perfectly so we'd be completely foiled.'

Murray continued, 'He's either duped someone into covering for him, has an accomplice or used a fake alibi agency.'

Natalie knew about the fake alibi agencies who ostensibly provided alibis for people cheating on their spouses or who wanted a day off work. The police had cracked down on such websites ever since Ace Alibi had come to light in the media, but they popped up now and again.

'We'll definitely follow up on all those possibilities. For the moment, focus on Rob,' said Natalie, snapping into action. 'Everything you can on him. Now!'

As Natalie dropped onto her seat, Lucy clattered into the office, phone in hand; she waved it at them. 'Rob Cooke. He's our man.'

'Mother's maiden name was Anne Oatridge before she became Anne Cooke. Father, Donald Cooke,' Ian said loudly. 'Born in Blackpool, 1984. Father unemployed. Mother catering assistant. Nothing on mother after 1988. She disappeared: no employment history, no driving licence, no passport, and not registered on the national registry of voters. I suppose if Rob couldn't find her, she was completely under the radar – change of name perhaps?'

Murray, typing next to him, asked, 'What about his father, alive or dead?'

The atmosphere was tense, each sentence clipped and functional as they laboured as a team. Ian's fingers flew across the keyboard faster than anyone else's.

'He's in a nursing home in Blackpool: Sea View.'

'Lucy, how do you feel about an early-morning trip to the seaside to interview him?' Natalie looked up from the phone conversation she was having.

'I'll pack my bucket and spade,' came the reply.

Natalie lowered her head and continued speaking to the officers who'd been called to Louise Roberts' house.

'I've got an address for him,' Murray called out.

Lucy suddenly piped up, 'Hey, Murray, I've got his employment record here, and before he moved to the office at Samford, he was at a branch in Nottingham. That's where Lucia Perez was murdered, isn't it?'

Murray's brows lifted as he digested Lucy's words. 'That's a mighty coincidence.'

'He was certainly in Nottingham at the time it happened. I bet if we checked back, we'd find he knew Lucia; maybe the Perez family bought or rented from the agency.' Lucy shrugged. 'Worth looking into.'

'I'll check that out,' said Murray.

Natalie addressed the room. 'Officers have arrived outside Louise Roberts' house in Derby and will remain stationed there on the off-chance Rob decides to track down Fabia.'

'He had plenty of opportunities to murder her when he was alone with her having therapy. Do you think she's in real danger?' Murray asked.

'I'm taking no chances. The officers will keep the house under surveillance and challenge anyone who comes close to it. Louise has been advised to keep doors and windows shut and locked. Tomorrow we'll interview Fabia, and if we don't find Rob tonight, we'll consider moving her out to a safe house. Who's got his address?'

'Here.' Murray lifted the piece of paper.

'Fingers crossed he's asleep and no trouble. Let's go get him. I'm bringing in support officers too to assist. There's no way I want him escaping. Collect your gear.'

Stapleton Avenue was one of several streets curling and curving around a recently constructed housing estate. It was an unexceptional street of modern, characterless houses, on an equally anonymous estate, the sort inhabited by business people who'd relocated to the area so they could easily make the daily commute to Birmingham or Manchester, and who'd taken out hefty mortgages on their properties so they were in the correct catchment area for their children to attend the local school with a good Ofsted report. Each property looked to be a carbon copy of the other. It was obvious why Rob lived here. He could exist without attracting attention or anyone noticing his comings and goings.

The police cars drew into the street. Silently, dark figures left vehicles and, in a coordinated sequence, hastened to the side and front of number 22. Natalie looked up at the darkened windows. It was almost eleven and nobody was about. A cat scurried past, quickening its pace as it scooted past Murray, who was dressed in a police-issue flak vest and ready to break open the door with the battering ram he carried.

'Be in, you bastard,' Natalie said under her breath, lifting her hand to give the order.

Lucy and Ian were to the rear of the property and other officers were strategically positioned in front and to the sides, to prevent any escape. Murray raised the ram, a manually wielded heavy metal unit known as the enforcer, and struck the front door. It took only a minute before it gave way, wooden shards splintering from the door frame and hanging in situ like hardened cotton strands.

The team slipped inside, storming downstairs and upstairs simultaneously. Natalie led the team to the upper floor and flung open the first door into a bedroom. It was empty. She thundered to the second, and the bathroom, and found the same. They searched the rooms, under beds, in cupboards, behind the shower curtain. They checked windows and even the attic but Rob wasn't at home.

Having searched under beds and in wardrobes, Natalie kicked out at the bedroom door with her boot and swore.

'He must have found out we were coming,' said Lucy.

'How the fuck did he know we were after him?' Murray asked.

Natalie shook her head. 'There was no way he could have known. He's either done a runner or got lucky and happened to be out. I don't think he's aware we've worked out his involvement. Henrik thinks he's intelligent and confident. I think he's too cocky to suspect anything. Fabia told Lucy he started his letter to his mother with five questions. He's only written two of those on walls beside victims. He hasn't finished whatever this is, yet. He'll be back. Get everyone out immediately, replace the door and we'll leave a team in position in case he returns. Don't disturb anything. Murray and I are heading to Derby to talk to Fabia. You two go home. Lucy, call in tomorrow as soon as you've spoken to Rob's father.'

'Roger that.'

The adrenalin that had kept her going the last few hours drained from her in an instant, leaving her limbs leaden. She clambered into her Audi to wait for Murray to join her and stared at the house. Rob had escaped, and in spite of her words to her team inside the house, she couldn't really be sure he'd return there. All she knew was she had to find him before he killed another young woman and left another child motherless.

Louise's detached house was on a leafy no through road in Mickleover, a suburb of Derby. An orange light glowed over the porch, illuminating the plain grey door.

Natalie acknowledged the officers sitting in the car outside number 15, Louise's house, and showed them her ID. Nobody had been near the place. The other houses nearby appeared to be in darkness with curtains or blinds drawn, and there was no activity.

She and Murray tapped on the door. Following a phone call made on the way to Derby, Louise had been expecting them. She showed them into the sitting room, dropped onto a plump beanbag and lifted a mug to her lips.

Fabia, taller than Natalie, stood by a mantelpiece, a shawl wrapped around her shoulders. In the dimmed lighting of the living room, her dark eyes shone like jet. She moved towards Natalie and Murray with the grace of a dancer. 'Thank you for coming out. I hope I'm not wasting your time.' She didn't sit. Instead, she pulled at the shawl and looked first at Natalie then Murray.

'We take such matters seriously and we believe you might be able to assist us,' Natalie said.

'You think Rob *has* killed women?'

'We're certainly looking into your accusations. Were you aware there've been two murders recently in Samford?'

'I'm sorry. I had no idea. I don't get a paper and I rarely watch the news. If the television is on, it's invariably tuned to kids' programmes. I have a son, Philippe,' she added.

'Have you ever met Charlotte Brannon or Samantha Kirkdale?'

She shook her head. 'Were they the victims?'

'Yes. Did Rob mention them?'

'No.'

'What can you tell us about Rob?'

'I'd be breaching patient confidentiality if I went into it in great detail. If he's absolutely innocent and I tell you what we spoke about, I could be in serious trouble.'

'Then explain what it was that made you ring the station in a panic.' Natalie's tone reflected the fact she was irked at the response. She'd hoped for more cooperation. Now she was no longer as frightened for her life, the woman was retreating behind the professional mask.

Her question had the desired effect, though. Fabia drew the shawl ever tighter and began. 'He'd been having dreams about murdering women, and the way he described them in such detail gave me cause for concern. It was completely plausible he had a vivid imagination, and maybe he was spurred on by reading about the deaths of the women you mentioned. However, in our last session he threatened me.'

'In what way?' Murray asked.

Fabia turned her eyes on him. 'It was an indirect threat: a suggestion of what he might do.'

'Can you be more specific?' Natalie asked.

'He said something along the lines of, "The woman opens the door to her feline friend and is greeted not by her loving mischievous companion, she cleverly named after a Norse god, but by the devil himself." I knew he was referring to me. I have a cat called Loki, named after a Norse god. I think he was calling himself the devil.'

Natalie spoke again. 'Did he say anything else that made you anxious?'

'Only that he knew why he dreamt about dipping his fingers in dead women's blood, and had I worked it out yet? I'm paraphrasing that bit. I don't remember exactly what he said. By then he'd scared me. It isn't much, is it? I got it into my head he was going to attack me and bolted and now I feel such an idiot. I've gone over it all again and maybe I read too much into it. He was angry with me because I couldn't help him find the underlying cause of his dreams or help him. I've had patients become angry before. I don't know why I had such a knee-jerk reaction this time.'

Louise spoke up. 'You did the right thing. You were frightened. You had reason to be scared. The guy could have gone for you in your office.'

Natalie had wondered why Rob hadn't attacked Fabia on one of the many occasions he'd visited her. If he'd wanted to harm her, he would surely have already done so. She'd concluded he'd needed Fabia's help. Maybe the dreams were a reality with which he struggled. His words to her could be taken as a threat and also interpreted as anger born from frustration.

'Was he referred to you?' Natalie asked.

'No. He was a private patient. He found me online and chose me because of my qualifications. When he booked the first appointment with me, he said he'd chosen me because he firmly believed I'd be able to fix him.'

'Fix him?'

'He felt he was broken. He couldn't sleep properly because of the dreams and they were ruining his life.'

There wasn't a lot more Natalie could learn by staying here. Rob was either on the loose or would return home. Either way, they'd catch him. 'We'll need to talk to you again and for you to make a statement, but for tonight, stay here. The officers will remain outside the door in case Rob turns up.'

'You think he could have found out about Louise? I've never mentioned her to him.'

'Only if he really is trying to locate you. It seems his threat was veiled but we'll take it as serious. You told DS Carmichael you thought somebody was outside your house when you rang her?'

'Yes, I had a freak. There was nobody. I was just jittery. Sorry. I should have stayed on the line and finished the conversation with her.'

'That would have been the better option.' Natalie glanced at Murray. He had no further questions. 'Is your son here?'

'He's upstairs asleep.'

'Okay. Keep the door locked and we'll talk again tomorrow.'

CHAPTER THIRTY-EIGHT

WEDNESDAY, 7 MARCH – EARLY MORNING

'You okay?' David asked.

'No. Had a shit night and my suspect got away.'

'I guessed as much,' he said.

For some reason his supposition needled her. 'How could you possibly guess that? You're not involved in the investigation. You've no idea what happened.'

He held up his hands. 'Whoa! I only meant I thought the case was going badly. Naturally, I don't know the specifics. Mind-reading isn't one of my superpowers,' he added, aiming for levity and a smile. He didn't receive one. 'You've been coming in at all hours of the night since it began, and last night you were calling out in your sleep.'

She backed down, annoyed with herself for jumping down his throat. The real reason for her hostility was the elephant in the room. She was still irked he'd even considered gambling again, even if he hadn't done so. 'What was I calling out?'

'Never mind.'

'No, come on, what was it?' she persisted.

He gave her a serious look. 'Frances. You shouted for Frances.'

'Oh.'

'So, that's why I thought things were going badly.'

'Yeah, sorry. They are.' She hunched over the mug of tea and stared at it.

'You want to talk about it?'

'Do you mind if I don't?'

'Sure. You know I'm here if you need me.'

She drained the cup. 'Thanks.' She sloped off to get dressed. She was being bitchy. It wasn't like her. She needed to find the equilibrium that allowed her to function as a police officer, a wife and a mother.

Lucy had risen at 6 a.m. and tiptoed downstairs so as not to wake Bethany. It was a two-hour drive to Blackpool, a direct route up the M6 motorway, and if she left before the heaviest traffic was on the road, she'd be there for breakfast time.

Losing Rob had been a wrench. They'd been so close to capturing him. Her sole consolation was that at least they knew who they were hunting for – a man deserted by his mother and left under the care of a man who they'd discovered had a violent history, been in prison and had never held down a steady job. Lucy wondered if this was why he'd targeted Adam's wife. On paper, Adam sounded exactly the same sort of man as his own father, yet how wrong Rob was. And Daniel. There'd been nothing to indicate he'd been anything other than a loving father to Oscar. She shook her head. She was sleep-deprived and her thoughts had got jumbled. Rob had his own agenda and she couldn't work out the link between his own childhood and the revenge he was exacting on his victims. One thing was sure: Adam was unlike Rob's father. He would never have harmed Alfie, a son he hadn't fathered but loved.

Sea View nursing home was not overlooking the sea. In reality, it was closer to the airport than the waves, but given it was only a five-minute drive from the coast, Lucy decided they hadn't taken too much liberty with their name.

It had once been a privately owned home, a bungalow, that had been extensively extended and transformed into a care home with all bedrooms having access to a private garden. On this bright March morning it seemed quite tranquil, with its immaculate gardens and a true hint of spring in the fresh air. Donald Cooke had ended up in a far nicer establishment than the one in which he'd brought up Rob.

The matron told Lucy that Donald's son had not visited for many years but had turned up a month ago to see his father and left after a blazing row that had shaken the man. She gave permission for her to meet Donald in the orangery, where all visitors were permitted to spend quiet time with their relatives when they came.

'Be gentle with him. Seeing Rob upset him greatly,' she said before departing to seek out her charge.

A radio played quietly in the background, and a tabby cat woke, stretched then repositioned itself on one of the sun loungers and dozed off again. Lucy took up position by a table of well-thumbed magazines and waited for Donald. She didn't have to wait long.

Donald, seated in a wheelchair, head drooping to one side, was pushed through the open doors into the bright room.

'There you are, Donald. I told you you had a visitor.' The nurse spoke in an overly cheerful voice as she slipped the brake on.

Lucy took in the sunken grey cheeks and the mask that covered Donald's face, attached by a tube to an oxygen pump, and knew in an instant that he wasn't much longer for this world. She introduced herself and sat on a seat close to him. He regarded her with yellow eyes.

'Thank you for seeing me, Mr Cooke. I wanted to ask you about your son, Rob. About the last time he came to see you. Do you remember it?'

Donald pulled the mask away and spoke in a raspy voice. 'It was… the first time… for years.' He replaced the mask and inhaled quickly.

'What did he talk about? He must have come for a reason?'

Donald nodded. With a shaking hand, he pulled the mask away once more. 'His mother.'

'What about her?'

'He found her.'

'Was he planning on seeing her?'

'No… he was so angry… so very angry. She was living with another man – an Italian doctor – and had a new family: two daughters and two grandsons, one by each daughter. He was furious about it and especially about her using this man's surname. I told him it didn't matter that she wasn't Anne Cooke any more. What was done was done. He wouldn't listen. Started shouting, saying I'd allowed it to happen and she should pay for what she did to us. I tried… but he stormed off. He was always a difficult boy.' He replaced the oxygen and flapped a hand to show he was weakened from the effort.

Lucy's thoughts flashed to Rob's mother. Would he try to kill her?

'I really appreciate you telling me this. Do you know the name of the man she's with?'

Chin down, he shook his head slowly, as if the weight of it was too great to move. The mask was dragged away to free his lips. 'No but I know they live in Samford. I explained to Rob she'd done nothing wrong, but he isn't right in the head. My flesh and blood and he isn't right. Said she deserved to be punished.'

'Your ex-wife still lives in Samford?'

He nodded. 'I think so.'

'Was there anything else he spoke about?'

The man's eyes became dewy. 'How much he hated me. It's okay. I don't much like him either. He and I had our moments and he gave as good as he got, although he seems to have conveniently forgotten that side of it. Is he in trouble?'

'I'm sorry to tell you this. We think he's responsible for two murders.'

'Who? I deserve to know. Tell me the truth.'

'Two young women – Charlotte Brannon and Samantha Kirkdale.'

'He always had a vicious streak in him. I realised the second I set eyes on him in this orangery, it had developed into something more serious. His manner was so hostile and frightening at the same time. The way he spoke, the way he looked at me.' He paused, head down again, digesting what he'd been told. When he spoke again, it was with genuine sorrow. 'I'm sorry. I'm truly sorry for those poor women. They didn't deserve to die. He's really not normal, you know? I had so much trouble with him when he was growing up. Yet I never once thought he'd turn into a murderer. The shame of it. If you need anything, you ask. If I can help, I shall. Anne left him to me to bring up. He was such a difficult child and Anne couldn't cope with him. She gave up on us both. He's *my* responsibility. You understand what I'm saying here?'

Lucy said she did. Donald felt accountable for his son's actions, that much was evident not only from his words but from his demeanour: the shaking hands that twisted endlessly in his lap, the heartbroken sorrow visible in his dull eyes and the intense regard he gave her as she stood. She thanked him and, leaving him in the orangery, returned to the matron. 'Who pays for his fees to live here?' she asked. 'We were under the impression he was long-term unemployed.'

'No, he worked for a long time, at Blackpool Pleasure Beach. He was a theme park attendant. He pays his own bills. He inherited a substantial sum from his partner, who was herself a wealthy widow. He told us he had no one he wished to leave his money to, so he uses it to see out what little time he has left, with us here at Sea View.'

'He hasn't got long, has he?'

'Stage four lung cancer. It's only a matter of time now. We'll make him as comfortable as possible.'

Lucy leant on the roof of her car, wind striking her face and stinging her cheeks, as she spoke to Natalie. 'Rob found his mother. She lives in Samford. She has two daughters, two grandsons, and is living with an Italian doctor. I don't think they're married but she's adopted his surname. Rob's dad didn't know it, but we must be able to locate the man.'

'We'll handle it. You get back here as soon as you can.'

Natalie ended the call and faced Murray and Ian, both at their desks. 'Anne Cooke, Rob's mother, is living in Samford, except she isn't using Cooke or even her maiden name, Oatridge. She's living with an Italian doctor and taken his name. We need his surname.'

Using the general database that housed names of all professionals in the area, Ian scrolled through a list of general practitioners working at the three medical centres scattered around Samford.

'Any idea what sort of doctor he is? Surgeon?'

'Got no information other than he's a doctor.'

'There are quite a few,' said Ian. 'How do you want to do this? Hunt through for names that sound vaguely Italian?'

'It's as good a way to start as any. Run background checks on all of them to determine nationality.' Natalie stood behind him and scoured the list with him. 'Murray, will you take the private practitioners?'

She checked the time. It was coming up 9 a.m. Rob hadn't returned to his house and the press conference was arranged for later that day. Aileen would be in her office by now. She had to update her superior before swinging by and interviewing Fabia. 'I'm going to check in with Aileen. Back in a minute.'

She took the stairs to the top floor and padded along the carpeted landing to Aileen's office, where she rapped on the door, all the while choosing her words for the meeting.

'Have a seat,' said Aileen.

Natalie dragged one of the ergonomic-designed conference chairs away from the desk and dropped into it lightly. 'We have a suspect by the name of Rob Cooke. We're sure it's him who's responsible for killing Charlotte and Samantha. He's been using fake alibis for his whereabouts on the dates in question. We also received information from a psychologist treating him for recurring nightmares. She contacted the station because she was frightened by him and thought he was threatening her. She hasn't told us the exact details of what they discussed during therapy but she voiced concerns that the dreams he described, in which he killed women, weren't dreams at all. She's in hiding at a friend's house for the moment and we have officers outside it. We're currently hunting for Rob Cooke. However, his phone isn't emitting a signal so we think he's dumped it. I've put a call out to all units to watch out for him, and the tech team are checking surveillance cameras for signs of him or his vehicle.'

'You any idea where he might be heading?'

'He's recently located his mother, who abandoned him as a child, and we suspect she could be one of his intended victims. The team are on it. Once we identify her, we can send officers out and place her under protection. We're unsure of his movements. If he's following the same MO, he's on the search for at least two more victims.'

'What makes you think that?'

'The questions written in blood. We believe he has five questions which correspond to the five questions he wrote in a letter to his mother, and so far, we only have two victims and two messages. That potentially leaves us with three more victims. Maybe Anne, his mother, will be the last victim, although we are also looking at the possibility that he killed another woman, Lucia Perez, in Manchester in 2016, and she was his first victim.'

'And Adam Brannon? Where does he fit into all of this?'

'Doesn't appear to be involved.'

'The conference is scheduled for four p.m.' Aileen's face said more than her words. She wanted Rob located and caught before she spoke to the media.

Natalie nodded a response and rose, replacing the chair. 'I'll keep you informed.'

Ian and Murray were working as one. 'We're through this list,' said Ian, switching his screen from that of general practitioners to private ones. He groaned. 'There are so many foreign-sounding names.'

'One at a time,' cautioned Natalie. 'Don't let this faze you. Here, let me assist.'

'Askari, is that Italian?' He clicked on the name and sighed.

'You take surnames beginning A to I; Murray, you take J to R; and I'll take the remainder.'

It was surprising how many doctors existed in Samford, each a specialist in his or her own field. As her eyes grazed over the names and she checked each, she wondered for a fleeting moment if there was one able to help with gambling addictions.

Time passed in silence. 'I'm done,' said Ian, interlinking his fingers and stretching them backwards before placing them on his head. He glanced at Murray. 'What letter are you up to?'

'P.'

'I'll take R. Quicken thing up.'

'Cheers. There were loads of surnames beginning with M.'

There was nothing but the sound of keys being struck then an exclamation. 'Rossini!' said Ian. 'Gianni Rossini. I've found him. He's married to Anne. Wait a minute…' There was more typing and then Ian continued. 'He has two daughters. One's called Chiara, a pharmacist, and the other's a psychologist called Fabia.'

'Oh, holy fuck. It has to be Fabia Hamilton. Her maiden name is Rossini.'

Ian hunched further over the keyboard and after a minute said, 'You're right.' Natalie pinched the bridge of her nose to relieve the pressure suddenly building there. 'So Anne and Gianni's daughter and her son, Philippe, is one of the grandsons Lucy mentioned. Rob deliberately chose her. He didn't need a psychologist. He wasn't suffering nightmares or episodes at all. He was playing her all along. It isn't only Anne he's going to harm, it's her daughters. They're Rob's half-sisters. He wants to kill them.'

'Chiara Rossini is currently living in Florence,' said Murray, who'd also been searching for information on them.

Natalie shook her head in disbelief. A picture was beginning to build in her head of Rob's intentions. 'Five questions and five victims: Charlotte, Samantha, Fabia, Chiara and possibly Anne herself.'

'Why did he kill Charlotte and Samantha though? It makes little sense. They're not related to him,' Ian asked.

'He described their deaths in detail to Fabia. Maybe it was part of his plan all along. He wanted her to work out he was a murderer,' said Murray.

Natalie agreed. 'I think that's a reasonable deduction. He probably got a kick out of telling Fabia about their deaths and waiting to see if she realised or understood she was going to become one of his victims. Alert the units stationed outside her friend's house. We must get them out of there. And get someone round to Gianni and Anne Rossini's house too.'

She stood up and crossed the room, thoughts on how to trap Rob. Outside, the morning traffic passed by unaware of the turmoil in her head. She had to locate Rob before he acted again. Would he target Fabia next or go for Anne? Had she made the right call or was he going to target strangers, women with young boys?

Murray called her name softly. 'Natalie. Bad news. She's gone. Officers went inside to fetch her but she and the boy have disappeared. Her friend is unhurt and doesn't know what happened.'

'How did Rob slip past the officers? They were supposed to be watching out for any suspicious activity.'

'They're looking into it.'

'Oh, for—' Natalie bit her tongue. She wouldn't lose her cool in front of her officers. Henrik had said the perpetrator was intelligent and he'd outwitted them once more. Rob had planned this meticulously. He'd been one step ahead of them all along. 'Fuck! No. This is not happening. He is *not* going to kill her.'

Natalie strode to the window. *Think, Natalie. Think.* The problem was, she didn't know what to do next.

CHAPTER THIRTY-NINE

WEDNESDAY, 7 MARCH – MORNING

Lucy entered the office and drew to a halt. 'Okay, something's gone wrong. I can tell,' she said, looking at Murray. 'Eew, can you see through those?'

Both of Murray's eyes had swollen during the night thanks to the blow to the nose.

'Just about. Rob's kidnapped Fabia and Philippe. Fabia's his half-sister.'

'Jeez, no. Where's Natalie?'

'With Aileen.'

'How did Rob get to her?'

'Crafty little shit was hiding out at the house next door to Louise's the entire time Natalie and I were there. The house owners are on holiday and he broke in, then bided his time. When we went to talk to Fabia, he was already in position. Probably sat back and watched the show – must have made him chuckle seeing us come and go – and then, in the early hours, he sneaked over the fence that separates the two houses and broke in through Louise's back door. The officers there think he used a lock pick set because he even managed to open the deadbolts, and there's no sign of a forced entry. Which probably explains how he broke into Charlotte's house too. There's also no sign of a struggle, so we suspect Fabia probably left with him because he was threatening her or Philippe with a weapon.'

'For Pete's sake! He's a cunning bastard. Got any idea where he might have taken them?'

'Natalie's asked that criminal profiler, Henrik, to give it some thought. Talking of which, here they come now.'

Lucy turned to see the pair approach, Henrik towering over Natalie, who in spite of the lack of sleep and setbacks still maintained a businesslike air, walking sprightly and gesticulating as she talked.

The door opened. 'Henrik has a theory,' said Natalie. 'One I believe we should act upon.'

Henrik took centre stage. 'This appears to have been about Rob's relationship with his mother. He is carrying an abundance of hate for her and has never got over the abandonment he experienced as a child. The questions he wrote in blood were lifted from a letter he wrote to her, expressing his true emotions. I'm of the opinion he wants to hurt her emotionally, probably in the same way he felt hurt, so he intends doing that by taking her daughters and grandchildren from her. All the women he's killed so far are of a similar build, have long, chestnut-brown hair and brown eyes like his mother, Anne. As for leaving the children alive and behind at the scene of the crime, I imagine he sees something of himself in them. Consequently he doesn't kill them.

'This desire for revenge and the build-up to kidnapping Fabia and her son stems from his childhood. He clearly harbours painful memories and feelings of rejection which began at the moment his mother walked out on him. Given he's been recounting dream-like situations to Fabia and has clearly been preparing for this kidnapping for a long time, I have a suspicion he'll take her and her son back to that point where all this misery began.'

Murray spoke up. 'You mean, if we can find out where he lived when his mother deserted him, he'll be holed up somewhere in that area?'

'Yes, he might try and return to that very place.'

Natalie issued instructions. 'Find out where he and his father were living when Anne walked out on them, and we might yet find them.'

'He was brought up in a caravan park,' said Lucy. 'I'll talk to the matron at the nursing home and see if Donald can help with that.' She moved away to make the call.

Ian spoke up. 'His mother must have left them in 1988. I couldn't find anything on her after that year.'

'How many residential caravan parks are there in Blackpool?'

Ian typed the keywords into a search engine, and when the results came back, he replied, 'Nowadays, three. Might have been more in the 1980s.'

Lucy ended her call. 'She's going to ask Donald. We'll have to wait.'

'If you don't need me…' Henrik moved towards the door. 'I'll get off. I have to be in Edinburgh tonight.'

Natalie held up a finger. 'I have one last question for you. What if Rob was also responsible for Lucia Perez's death? Should we consider her to be one of his five victims?'

'If Rob killed her, he left no message and that is an important part of his MO. From that fact alone, I'd deduce she wasn't part of his grand plan. There's a chance, however, he was preparing himself and killed her and maybe even others in readiness for this. He has been planning it for some considerable time.'

It was the answer she'd expected. 'Thank you for your help.' Natalie extended a hand that was swallowed in his own.

'Good luck,' was the response.

Natalie spun back to face her team. 'We have no time to waste on this. I agree with Henrik and don't think Rob is still in the area. I'm going to act on the premise he's retuned to where he was left as a child. As a result of that, we're heading to Blackpool. If we don't get an exact address for the caravan park, we'll try all of the parks there. It'll be the same arrangement as last night for the cars: Lucy with me, Murray with Ian, and we'll stay in contact using the communication units. Okay. Let's go nail this bastard.'

They were some way along the M6 motorway when the phone rang, only fifteen minutes away from Blackpool. Lucy connected the call on the hands-free.

'Sergeant Carmichael?' It was the matron from the care home. 'Yes.'

'I'm sorry it's taken so long to get back to you. Donald got quite agitated and it required a lot of effort for him to talk.'

'Did he remember where they lived?'

'Sunshine Caravan Park in Great Marton. It used to be a run-down residential site but it's since had something of a revival and now it's a static caravan holiday park.'

'Thank you once again for your help.'

Natalie got immediately onto the police headquarters at Blackpool and requested assistance. Lucy, using the comms unit, told Murray exactly where they were heading.

A sign welcomed them to Sunshine Caravan Park and informed them they needed to check in 100 metres on the left. Green railings with the gold lettering 'SCP' confirmed they were at the right place. One side of the gate was closed, the other half a height-restriction barrier that both cars slipped under.

They arrived in a courtyard, complete with small roundabout stocked with spring flowers. To their left was an office and opposite it a car park. Lucy called in the registrations of all the vehicles. Pointing to a silver Nissan Qashqai with a sticker in the rear window, she said, 'Hire car. Could be his. I'll get further details from the hire company.'

Natalie motioned for Ian and Murray to remain in their vehicle, and leaving Lucy to find out the information about the hire car, she marched to the office. The counter was unmanned so she called out.

A pleasant-faced woman, wiping her hands on a tea towel, responded. 'Sorry, I was out the back.'

Natalie explained who she was and, pushing a photograph of Rob towards the woman, asked if she had seen him.

'I haven't checked him in or seen him. My husband might have. He's been dealing with all the arrivals this week.'

'Is he here?'

'Sorry, you missed him. He'll be back this evening.'

'Have you got a phone number for him?'

She gave an apologetic smile. 'He's switched off his mobile. He's gone fishing. He always turns it off when he goes fishing.'

Lucy burst through the door and interrupted the exchange. 'It belongs to him. Hire car firm confirmed he rented it in his own name.'

Natalie turned back to the woman. 'How many people are renting units at the minute?'

'Off the top of my head, about ten. It's the quiet season. Doesn't pick up until after Easter. We'll have the details in the back office. Come through.'

The woman took them into another room filled with box files and a table cluttered with paperwork and fired up the computer.

'How many caravans are there in total?' Natalie asked.

'Only thirty. We're the smallest of the sites in the area and we don't have all the facilities some of the others offer, but we do have excellent accommodation and peace and quiet.' The computer slowly whirred into life. She clicked onto a document. 'Yes, it was updated yesterday. These are the people renting at the moment and these are the vans they're in.'

She pointed at the list of names on the screen. Natalie recognised none of the names. If Rob had hired a van, he was using an alias. A sudden thought struck her.

'Which occupied vans are the most private?'

'Apple and Strawberry. We name all the vans after fruits,' the woman replied, noticing Lucy's furrowed eyebrows. 'Apple is one of our prestigious vans, accommodating between two and six people, and offers central heating and a decking area so it can be used all year round. If I remember correctly, two couples are currently renting it. Strawberry is the more basic of the two, a standard caravan, comfortable with two bedrooms and a lounge, but no extras, no luxuries.'

Natalie chewed it over. There was every chance Rob would have requested a caravan some distance from all the others in a more private spot. He wouldn't want anyone to notice anything suspicious, or risk hearing Fabia call out. He had to be in Strawberry. She was going out on a limb but there was no time to spare. They couldn't surround all the vans, draw attention to themselves and risk Fabia's life. 'I'd like you to shut and lock the office. Shortly there'll be police officers throughout the site, and we will keep the place secure, so there's no cause for alarm. The man we are after has taken hostages and we have to get them out. I think there's every chance he's holding them captive in that van – Strawberry. We'll need a map of this site.'

In the caravan park office Murray, Lucy and Natalie discussed their limited options.

'If we get vision on Strawberry, establish Fabia and her son are there and alive, we could bring in a trained police negotiator along with armed units.'

Murray's suggestion was sensible but Natalie didn't think Rob was prepared to negotiate. Natalie firmly believed he would die first rather than give up Fabia and Philippe.

Natalie shook her head. 'We haven't got that amount of time to play with. He could kill Fabia at any moment. Show me the interior layout of the van.'

Lucy pulled up the image of the van on the computer.

Natalie scrutinised the picture and spoke again. 'It has only one entrance, reached by front steps. There's a large window in the sitting room, at the left end of the caravan. There's a bedroom window the same side as the front entrance, to the right of the door, and another window in the bedroom at the rear of the caravan. He'll spot us if we approach from any of those directions. That only leaves us the blind side – the right-hand end of the caravan which faces a wood and is separated from it by a high-wire fence. If we got through or over the fence, we could climb under the van. There's enough space under the van for a person. Two of us could shuffle underneath it and that would give us the opportunity to work out if Fabia and Philippe are inside the van and alive, and maybe even locate their actual whereabouts. Then, we cause a diversion to distract Rob, separating him from Fabia, and storm the van. It's risky but we can manage it and we have one advantage: Rob might not know we're here at the caravan park.'

'I have an idea how we can distract him,' said Lucy. She explained it to Natalie, who agreed it was a good ploy.

While Lucy made the arrangements for the distraction, Murray asked Natalie, 'How can we be certain they're not dead already?'

'His car's still parked here. He'd have left if they were dead. Ian and other officers are in unmarked cars, waiting to block him should he return to the car, and nobody has raised any alarms yet. He's here all right. He wants to take his time and relish this moment. This is what he's been building up to and he's not going to rush it. Henrik told me he thinks Rob wants Fabia to suffer, so he'll undoubtedly prolong her ordeal to maximise his own pleasure. It's this or we wait for a negotiator, by which time it could be too late.'

Lucy shoved her phone in her back pocket. 'All sorted. Let's do it. I can't see what other viable options we have, given the time restraint. It'll be a miracle if he hasn't already killed her.'

'You both happy with my decision?' Natalie asked.

They nodded. As they left the office, Natalie fought back the nausea that had risen. It was a product of self-doubt and anxiety and she had no time to deal with such issues. She had to save Fabia and Philippe.

CHAPTER FORTY

They'd scouted the area and established it was possible to reach the van without being spotted by Rob. Pushing through the undergrowth on the other side of the fence, they could observe the caravan called Strawberry, secluded at the far end of the pitches, a cream building with a pitched roof, a set of steps leading to a front door and overhang porch; in brief, it was a house on a raised platform, and it was that platform the team were looking at.

Murray had spied movement inside the van and was certain he'd glimpsed Fabia. He ran through their plan one more time.

'Lucy and I will make a dash for it and squeeze under the van, see if we can establish where they all are inside,' said Murray. 'Once the diversion is in place, it will give us time to separate them and take appropriate action.'

Ian gave him a look, 'With all due respect, mate, you can barely see through those peepers of yours. You were having trouble when we were driving here. You might not be able to pick up on any peripheral movement and could be in danger. I'll go.'

'You trying to brown nose again?' asked Murray, bristling.

Ian shook his head seriously. 'No, I'm trying to save you from getting hurt or worse.'

Murray looked him up and down through swollen lids and tipped him a grateful nod. 'Fair enough. You're a skinny runt. You'll slide under the van more easily than me anyway. Natalie?'

Natalie agreed. 'You can be part of the diversion, Murray. It makes more sense.'

Lucy's phone vibrated in her pocket. She answered it. 'Ten minutes,' she said to the others.

Natalie's face was serious. 'Okay... go!'

Lucy shot up the fence like a professional climber, fingers and toes finding spaces in the wire with ease. She landed effortlessly on the other side, raced towards the van and threw herself underneath it, crawling to the far side where they knew the sitting room to be. She rolled onto her back, chest rising and falling quickly, straining for sounds above her. Ian, more ungainly but equally quick, pursued her and launched himself onto the ground, rolled over three times and reached the near side of the van, where he remained transfixed, head facing her.

'Anything?' she mouthed.

He gave the thumbs down.

There were footsteps above her and then a voice, a man's voice. It was Rob, his words surprisingly clear.

'I didn't burn it because I wanted you to hear it all, be the recipient of what I've been harbouring all the time you've been happily growing up and enjoying family life. This is what I have had to live with. You wanted to know what was in the letter, so here it is. I hope you're sitting comfortably. Please try not to interrupt or analyse me. It would be very much the wrong thing to do.'

Ian hissed Lucy's name quietly and pointed above him to the bedroom. 'Philippe – crying.'

Lucy whispered into the comms unit, 'Child, bedroom one. Vic and perp, lounge.'

'Copy.'

In the sitting room, Rob was monologuing. 'Why did you leave me, Mother? Why couldn't you love me enough to take me with you? Do you have any idea of the emotions that tore me apart daily as a consequence of your actions? Why?

'Who convinced you to desert me? Who whispered in your ear that it was right to desert your son? Who, Mother, who?

'Where did you go? Was it better than our home? Of course it was. You hated the claustrophobic hell-hole as much as I did, yet you allowed me to continue suffering and found somewhere far more agreeable for yourself. Where did you hide, Mother?

'What did I do so wrong you had to leave me behind? Was I so awful you had to leave me with a man who didn't care whether I lived or died, who either ignored me or beat me, who hated the very sight of me, because every time he looked at me, it reminded him that you had abandoned us both? What did I do wrong, Mother?

'I love you. I hate you. Love you. Hate you. The constant seesaw of emotions is exhausting. One day I crave to see you. The next, I wish you were a rotting carcass. Bitch!

'I have never lived. My life has been nothing but a desire to seek you out and to ask you these questions. It has been a life filled with bewilderment, desperate hope and pain, and one that has had no meaning. I have not been able to form any relationships with others, because who can I trust? If my own flesh and blood deserted me, then what might a stranger do to me? Besides, I have nothing left to give. Every ounce of love was for you.

'When I was little I used to dream you would return, carry me away with you and hold me to your heart. As I grew into a teenager, I loathed you and that anger turned inwards and twisted and deformed my development. How could I grow and mature when my need for you held me back? As an adult, I found the solution: Look for you. Find you. Take back what was lost.

'Which brings me onto this letter. I found you, Mother. After many fruitless years, I hired an excellent private detective who tracked you down and told me the horrible truth. You had left my father and me for another man, turned your back on us both and walked away without a word of explanation so you could start afresh, have a new family, a sparkling, happy new family.

'Were they better than me, Mother? Was it easier to bring up two girls than your little boy, who you couldn't bear to touch or hold? Did you have endless joy playing with them and holding their hands as you walked home from school with them? Did you pour all your love into them and mould them and pray for them and have hopes for them?

'You can't shake off the past, Mother. It comes back to haunt you. My hatred has been brewing for many years and the nightmares that haunted me gave me the idea to murder not only you but those you love. It's taken skilful planning and endless time to hone my skill, unfortunate women who reminded me of you – the same hair, the same eyes and the same beautiful expression when they look at their children – have been sacrificed in preparation for this task.

'Now I am ready. By the time you learn of this letter and its contents, you will know what it feels like to lose that part of you that is joined to your own being, the very essence of you that makes you human. Your children will be dust, and you too will be desperate to experience ever-lasting oblivion.

'So, Mother, I do this out of love and out of hate for you.

'Your son. The one you left behind.

'Rob.'

Lucy winced. The man was deranged. Her comms unit crackled softly, and she heard the whispered command: 'Decoy. Prepare.' Lucy glanced across at Ian and nodded then watched the wheels of the wheelchair being pushed in the direction of the sitting room window and recognised the boots of the supposed orderly behind the handlebars. She strained to hear what was happening above her. Timing was crucial.

Rob was talking again. 'What do you think, Doctor? Reckon she'll shed as many tears as I have over the years? Of course, she won't actually be able to read the letter – or rather, like you, listen to it – until I've got rid of you and your sister. It'll take a while before I reach the endgame, but I'm a patient man, and by the time I read it out loud again, I'll have turned my attention to her and she'll be eager for death. What the fuck? What's *he* doing here?'

Footsteps rang above Lucy's head and she turned onto her belly, ready to take action. Ian copied her movements. The front door swung open and Rob exited, standing on the top step. 'What the hell are you doing here? Haven't you died yet?'

He stepped down, his Gucci loafers and white socks now visible. One more step and she'd be able to act. He descended another step and another swiftly, all the while volleying abuse at his father. Lucy's hands shot forward and, grabbing him by the ankles, she tugged with all her might, felling him. Ian bounded from his cover and hurled himself at Rob. Murray thundered across from his position behind the wheelchair and a scuffle ensued. Lucy held on tightly. Events unfolded at speed: a flash of steel, a yell, Murray's boot in Rob's face, and more flashing as the blade swung left and right towards Murray, Ian launching himself in front of Murray, a scream of pain, another boot, and Murray on top of Rob, yanking the man's arms behind him and cuffing him in one swift movement. Rob didn't move. His feet went limp. Ian slumped to the ground. Blood turned the grass crimson.

'Bloody hell! You okay, mate?' Murray's voice was pure concern.

Lucy scrambled out from under the van and raced to Ian's side. Natalie hurtled towards them alongside a couple of officers. Lucy examined the wound and pressed hard on it with the flat of her hand. 'Ambulance!' she yelled.

Natalie barked instructions to the officers and halted at the foot of the stairs, taking in the scene.

'I've got this,' said Lucy, pushing her hand hard against Ian's shoulder to stem the flow. 'Go check on them.'

Natalie's chin dipped once and she tore up the stairs into the caravan. Fabia was tied to a chair with duct tape, her face blank with shock. Natalie pulled away the piece covering her mouth.

'Are you all right?' Natalie asked.

'Yes. Philippe?'

The boy's terrified cries were loud.

Natalie followed them and rattled the bedroom door. It was secured but the key was in the lock and she turned it. The toddler stood directly behind the door, tears streaming down his face.

'Hush, hush. Everything's okay, now. Your mummy's here. Let's go see her.' Natalie scooped him into her arms and carried him through, speaking softly to him all the while. 'You stand here next to your mummy. We have to unstick her from the chair. You look after her.' The boy laid his head in his mother's lap, thumb in mouth, shoulders shaking as he sobbed silently, while Natalie searched for some scissors and released Fabia from her bounds.

Once her wrists were cut free, Fabia leant over her boy, stroking his head. 'He's crazy. He was going to kill us both.'

'It's over. You're safe now. You're safe,' Natalie repeated. She glanced through the door at the manic scene outside. Rob's head was lowered in defeat, his hands cuffed, two officers either side of him, as Murray read him his rights. An emergency medical kit was open on the grass and paramedics busied around Ian, attaching a plasma bag and attending to the knife wound.

'I have to go outside. Someone will be with you in a minute. Stay here.'

'I'm not going anywhere,' said Fabia.

Natalie bounded back down the stairs. Ian's appearance shocked her. He'd lost a lot of blood and was fading fast, his eyelids fluttering. 'How bad is it?'

The older of the two paramedics spoke as they worked quickly to stem the blood flow. 'Bad. We'll stabilise him and get him to hospital immediately.'

She placed a hand on Ian's good arm and smiled at him. His eyelids fluttered open briefly. 'You did great. I'll be sure to commend you,' she said. His lips stretched into a smile momentarily before he fell unconscious.

Lucy watched them lift Ian onto a stretcher and waited until they were out of sight before walking across to Donald, now being looked after by a nurse.

'I appreciate you helping us. It can't have been easy.'

He pulled the mask away and spoke. 'Easier than I imagined. Throw the book at him. He's rotten to the core.'

'Is it okay if we return to the home now?' asked the nurse.

Lucy nodded. 'Thank you, again.' She placed her hand on the man's and received a nod in return.

CHAPTER FORTY-ONE

The man who sat opposite her was completely different to the man who'd professed to be Charlotte's lover. Rob, no longer well-groomed and gentle, stared at Natalie with open hostility.

'Rob Cooke, you have been charged with the murders of Charlotte Brannon and Samantha Kirkdale. We have the letter you wrote to your mother, Anne Rossini, and statements from your half-sister, Fabia Hamilton. I understand from your lawyer that you wish to make a full confession.' She nodded at the man sitting next to him.

'No point in denying anything, is there? As you say, you have evidence. My lawyer thinks it's best I come clean.'

'When we first spoke, you claimed you were romantically involved with Charlotte Brannon. Was that true?'

He snorted in an ungentlemanly fashion. 'No. I only said that to clear myself from any investigation. I wasn't sure if your forensic team had found anything to incriminate me, so it was best to bluff you.'

'What about the phone call you made to her on Thursday morning at ten a.m.? You told us you'd rung her and wished her a nice time with her parents.'

'Oh yes. That was all part of my plan too. I fancied being part of the investigation from an early stage. I thought I'd play the grieving boyfriend and then you'd lose interest in me. As you did for a while. I actually did meet Charlotte in a coffee shop. The first time was about three weeks ago. I sat behind her and had a loud, fictitious conversation with a fashion magazine editor that she couldn't help but overhear. When I ended the call, she asked what I did for a living and I told her I was a photographer for a fashion magazine. It didn't take long before she was talking about her love of fashion and showing me her Instagram photos. I suggested she might like to come to a photo shoot at the magazine and maybe even be photographed. Naturally she was keen and we swapped contact details. I made the call so you would find me. I rang her on the Thursday morning but the conversation was quite different to the one I told you. I started off by telling her I had some rather exciting news but she was to keep quiet about it for the moment and asked if she was alone, to which she replied "no". Then I asked her to keep what I was about to tell her to herself and lastly that I'd be in touch the following day to invite her to a big fashion shoot for Vogue. It didn't matter what she said, I'd have made up something to account for her responses. The objective was for you to track me down.'

'How did you know she went out with her parents on Friday evening?'

'Oh, she told me that at the coffee house the second time I saw her. She'd been shopping and brought a wrapped gift in with her. I asked what it was and she mentioned their wedding anniversary and that she was seeing them for a meal. I thought that was going to scupper my plans, but when she told me they'd only be out for a short while because she didn't want to leave the baby for long, I knew it would still be okay to go ahead and kill her.'

'What about her husband, Adam? How could you be sure he'd go out afterwards?'

'Because I'd been watching their house for quite some time and Adam *always* goes out on a Friday evening.' He folded his arms and sat back with a satisfied smile on his face.

'You also told us at the time Charlotte was killed, you were away at a conference in the Isle of Wight. This proved not to be the case and your alibi was false.'

He gave a smirk. 'Clever of me, wasn't it? You were fooled, admit it. I had you running around, didn't I?'

With the interview being recorded and all eyes from the other side of the one-way mirror on them, she was not going to be drawn, even though she wanted to wipe the sneer off his face. Murray, who was sitting beside her, also said nothing and continued to stare at Rob through swollen lids.

She continued without answering his taunts. 'We established it was a lie and you had no alibi for that day.'

'Aren't you going to ask me how I arranged it?' Rob, like murderers she'd met before, was keen to show off, and now he'd been caught, he was more than happy to tell them exactly how he'd executed his plan.

'If you want to.' Natalie sat back in her seat, arms folded to encourage him to talk, and he did.

'I used Reasonable Explanation, a website that provides fake alibis for people having affairs. They provide, funnily enough, reasonable explanations as to why you might not be at work or home, and cover for you if you take a day off or want to pull the wool over your other half's eyes. I contacted them, said I was having an affair and needed somebody to confirm I was elsewhere on certain days, and that my spouse was a police officer. See, I thought it through. I didn't indicate if my partner was male or female so I covered myself. Should an officer call about me, they'd assume it was my partner not an official enquiry.' He looked at Natalie for approval or acknowledgement, a smug expression on his face. She made a slight gesture, which seemed sufficient for him to continue.

'For a fee, Reasonable Explanation provide fake business cards with phone numbers on them that go back to the central call centre. If anyone phones the number and asks for me, for example, the switchboard operator checks my name on their system and then swears I was where I said I was.'

'Ingenious,' said Natalie. She'd decided the more she flattered him, the more he'd tell her.

He licked his lips and looked at her with hard eyes. 'You're not taking the piss, are you?'

'No. You had us running around in circles.'

'Ha! I knew it.' He seemed pleased at the thought. Natalie capitalised on the moment to ask more questions.

His lawyer made notes and did not interrupt although he threw wary looks from time to time.

'Why did you kill Charlotte Brannon and Samantha Kirkdale?'

'Isn't it obvious?'

'Not to me.'

'Go on, hazard a guess.'

If she wanted answers, she'd have to pander to him. 'They resembled your mother and both had children but neither intended leaving their sons, so that's flummoxed me.'

'Flummoxed? Good. I like that. You're right about their looks. That's what attracted me to them. As you rightly say, they reminded me of my own mother: long, brown hair, brown eyes and about the same height. That made it all the sweeter. They weren't going to leave their children but to find women who intend running out on both their husbands and children isn't that simple. I was one of the lucky ones, eh? My mum managed it.' His lips stretched into a thin line. For a moment Natalie thought he'd stop talking, but he recovered quickly. 'I wanted to learn how to kill properly. I didn't want to swing out at my mother and half-sisters in rage and for it to end too quickly. They had to suffer, truly suffer, like I did. I experimented on my first victims. I tested out the most effective methods of killing them. I considered strangling but then I might not have been able to enjoy looking into their eyes as they died and it would have been too quick a death. I settled on stabbing them, but Charlotte was prepared and tried to attack me with a bat, which I took from her and used as a weapon instead. Charlotte certainly took a long time to die. I had to hit her quite a few times before she gave in. I was right to choose stabbing though. Samantha took even longer. She survived almost an hour.'

Natalie swallowed the bile in her mouth. 'You decided to knife Fabia to death?'

'Yes. I found Fabia some time ago and spent a long time hatching my plan. Her being a psychologist was perfect. It allowed me to pretend to be a patient, one who was having nightmares about killing women. I wanted to mess with her head first before I killed her, and then, when I was ready, I was going to make her death long and drawn out.' His lawyer advised him to say nothing more but Rob raised his hand, palm outwards to stop him. 'No, she wants to know and I want to tell her.'

'How did you plan on killing Chiara? She lives in Florence. It would have been harder to locate and kill her,' Natalie prompted.

'She'd have had to return to the UK for Fabia's funeral. I know where Anne lives. I'm acquainted with all the roads near her house and I'm positive I could have passed myself off as a grieving patient, one who was very fond of Fabia, and isolated Chiara long enough to have snatched her and her son. If not, I had time on my side. I'd have been quite prepared to have travelled to Florence and visited the pharmacy where she works. That's the beauty of it: I had time. No one would have worked out what was happening until it was too late. I had such plans for Anne – a cut here, a cut there, until she was so weak she begged for mercy.'

'That's enough,' said the lawyer. 'My client doesn't wish to say anything further.'

'But I do. I want to tell them about another woman – the very first one – Lucia Perez…'

*

Superintendent Aileen Melody commended the bravery and hard work of her team. 'Without their dedication and resolve, we might have had a very different outcome. I would like to thank DI Natalie Ward and her colleagues who worked this investigation.'

'Superintendent Melody, can you give us a name?' The journalist who'd asked the question looked earnestly at her.

She shook her head. 'You know we can't tell you that at the moment. Suffice to say we have arrested and charged a man in connection with the murders of Charlotte Brannon and Samantha Kirkdale. We shall be releasing further details in due course and that is all, ladies and gentlemen of the press. Thank you.'

Aileen took leave of the stage that had been prepared for the conference and met Natalie outside the room. Together they walked towards her office. 'How's Ian?'

'Latest prognosis is positive although it was touch and go for a while. If that knife had struck a few centimetres to the left, it would have been a different story.'

'Thank goodness that wasn't the case.'

They turned into Aileen's office. She shut the door behind them. 'Nottinghamshire police are grateful for your assistance in solving the Lucia Perez case.'

'Murray Anderson is to thank for that. He uncovered the fact the Perez family had rented their home from the estate agency where Rob was working at the time. A call to the agency confirmed his suspicions. Rob showed Lucia and her husband around the premises and completed the rental agreement with them. I understand they found DNA which is a match for his and placed him at the scene of the crime. Lucia was his first victim. Her murder wasn't intentional although it became the trigger for the others. Rob had been harbouring a desire for revenge for some time but not worked out a plan; then one day, in a café, he'd overheard Lucia telling a friend she was going to leave her son and her violent husband as soon as she plucked up the courage to do so. This revelation sparked off the memory of his own mother, and recognising Lucia as one of his clients, he'd bided his time until she was alone in her house and attacked her. Her murder set him on the path to vengeance. Coincidentally, Lucia looked a little like his mother, so when it came to choosing victims to "practise" on, he chose other women who reminded him of his mother.'

'Has he confessed to the other murders?'

'Fully. There was no point in holding back. We had the letter he wrote. He dropped it in the struggle, so once we showed it to him, he admitted to all the murders. We also found evidence on his computer: searches for Fabia, dream psychology websites, and purchases made, including an eight-inch chef's knife that matched the description of the one used to kill Samantha.'

'And what about the website that offers fake alibis? I thought we'd done away with them.'

'One or two periodically turn up. The website in question, Reasonable Explanation, reportedly offered alibis for people wishing to cheat on spouses or lie to their bosses. The technical team is handling that and I understand the site will not only face prosecution but also be shut down.'

'That leaves me with only one thing to say – thank you. You were all outstanding.'

Natalie bowed her head, unable to respond. It hadn't been an easy case, and as always in any of her investigations, she still felt she'd let some people down. Adam, for one, had deserved better treatment. The only crumb of comfort she'd been able to offer him was that his wife hadn't been cheating on him.

Back in the office, the mood wasn't one of jubilation. Murray picked at some paperclips. 'It's my fault. I shouldn't have let him replace me.'

Lucy glowered at Murray. 'Oh, for crying out loud, will you stop beating yourself up about it? You weren't in a fit state and he was right: with your limited vision, you wouldn't have seen that movement Rob made when he pulled the knife. If it had been you in Ian's position, you'd have been stabbed right through the heart. He probably saved your life.'

'Yeah, the fuckwit. Now I'll have to be nice to him when he comes back.' He gave a sheepish grin.

'I can't wait to see that.'

Natalie came in, tidied a strand of hair from her face. 'Aileen is very proud of you all. As am I. Thanks for pulling together and getting a good result. Just for information, Fabia and Philippe are staying with her parents for a while. They wanted to extend their thanks too. Right. I could do with a drink – a really fucking strong drink. Who wants to join me?'

Murray tossed the paperclips onto the desk. 'Defo. I think I'd like to get completely shitfaced.'

Natalie hesitated. The house was in darkness and she ought to go straight upstairs to bed, put the day, the investigation and everything that was bothering her behind her, but she'd had too much alcohol and it had emboldened her. This entire gambling business had been niggling her. There was something about the way David had been a little too righteous that had bothered her. That wasn't normal behaviour for him, and if she remembered rightly, the last time he'd behaved in a similar fashion had been after the discovery he'd spent most of their savings. If he'd continued being his usual self, she might not have suspected anything, but as it was, her intuition was telling her David was keeping something from her. Had he been on the gambling websites again or had he discovered another outlet for his frustration?

Creeping in to David's office, she pushed the door to, using the desk light to illuminate the room. She didn't dare switch on the computer. She cast about the desk, lifting and replacing pages of law articles David was in the process of translating. There was nothing here to confirm her suspicions. The last time he'd been gambling, he'd cleaned out their joint account, and in the pub, she'd checked it yet again. It hadn't been touched. Yet still, she was convinced he'd begun gambling again. If he was, he'd need money. Where would the money come from? They only had Natalie's salary and anything he made each month. Both went directly into the account.

She wavered. Tiredness was washing over her, and still she had to find out. She slumped onto his chair, a wide leather seat they'd purchased when he'd declared he'd be working as a translator, a comfy chair for all the hours he'd spend at his desk.

She swivelled with it, studying the room. He'd covered the walls with photographs of the family. Each one a happy moment captured forever: Leigh after she'd won a school gymnastics event; Josh at ten, looking serious, holding up a certificate for swimming. She recalled how pleased he'd been to receive it – their little Josh who'd been afraid of water and had conquered that fear. Next to it was a picture of David and her in a gondola in Venice, her in a white and blue dress, and him in light-beige trousers and black shirt. The swell of her stomach under their entwined fingers gave away the fact she was expecting their first child. She couldn't throw all this away. It was best if she ignored the stupid, prickly feeling that had been bothering her and got on with married life. Sometimes, it was best not to pry and not to know.

She swung back a little too quickly, dislodging papers onto the floor with her elbow. As she dropped to her knees to replace them, one sheet caught her eye. It was from a loan company. David had borrowed £5,000.

She sat back on her heels, staring at the words in front of her, and then angry tears began to fall.

A LETTER FROM CAROL

Hello, dear reader,

Firstly, thank you for buying and reading *The Last Lullaby*. Once again, I hope you enjoyed spending time with DI Natalie Ward and her team.

For the first time in my writing career, I locked myself away to write, far away from any interruptions. I headed to an extremely peaceful area in France where, thanks to incessant rain, I spent my entire time writing with absolutely no distractions or interruptions and got to really know my characters. It is, therefore, one of my favourite novels and one I thoroughly relished writing.

I have always been fascinated by people, especially those who wear a mask to hide their true emotions and feelings. People are sometimes not who they seem to be; sometimes they live a lie. That is the premise of this book, and I drew much of my content from real-life situations.

If you enjoyed reading *The Last Lullaby*, please would you take a few minutes to write a review, no matter how short it is? I would really be most grateful. Your recommendations are most important.

If you'd like to keep up to date with all my latest releases, just sign up at the following link. Your email address will never be shared and you can unsubscribe at any time.

www.bookouture.com/carol-wyer

I hope you'll join me for the next book in the DI Natalie Ward series, which will be out in early 2019.

Thank you,
Carol

AuthorCarolEWyer

carolewyer

www.carolwyer.co.uk

ACKNOWLEDGEMENTS

My name may be on the cover of this book but it certainly couldn't have been published without the support of many others who deserve a mention.

As always, I am indebted to my truly wonderful editor, Lydia Vassar-Smith, who once again guided me through this novel with helpful suggestions and oodles of encouragement.

I must also thank the entire team behind the publication of *The Last Lullaby* – and there are many of them who have helped get the book prepared for my readers.

I would like to offer special thanks to Serge Chaloupy, who not only let me write this book in his picturesque *pigeonnier* in South-West France but prevented me from starving by leaving bowls of salad or strawberries outside my front door for when I finally emerged from my writing odyssey.

Hugest of thanks to all my fellow Bookouture authors, who cheered me on as I battled to write the first draft of the book in record time. They are not only all exceptionally talented writers but downright hilarious people who I love to bits.

Finally, my sincerest thanks to our ace Bookouture PR team – Kim Nash and Noelle Holton. I can't thank these ladies enough for the humongous support they offer. I am convinced neither of them ever sleeps!

Lightning Source UK Ltd.
Milton Keynes UK
UKHW021811130119
335510UK00013B/446/P